MW00613890

TOWN LAWE

TOWN LAWE

Bruno Pirecki

Publisher's Note
This is a work of fiction. Names, characters, places, and incidents either are the product of the author's imagination or are used fictitiously, and any resemblance to actual persons living or dead, business establishments, events, or locales is entirely coincidental.

Library of Congress Control Number: 2020951268

Published by Redfern Ink, Franklin, Tennessee

ISBN 978-0-9994690-8-8 (Paperback)
ISBN 978-0-9994690-4-0 (e-book)

Cover painting "Autumn Moon" and all illustrations
by Bruno Pirecki
Cover design Dan Harding of Blue Mile Design
Developmental editor Scott Norton
Copyeditor Elissa Rabellino
Interior layout Andrea Reider
Proofreader Sunah Cherwin

1 3 5 7 9 10 8 6 4 2

First edition

For Opal Lee Stansberry,
who chose life on May 24, 1961.
Your selfless courage and depth of spirit was my gain.

For Roberta K. Barry: One is rarely blessed
with two mothers, and I count myself among such.
Thank you, Berta.

CONTENTS

BOOK ONE

POLE PASS

BOOK TWO

THE EMBRACE OF CHANGE

BOOK THREE

THE ARCHIVE

BOOK FOUR

REVELATION

-TOWN LAWE-

My birth, that is, the occasion of the descent of my immortal soul into this embarrassingly corruptible vessel, was—like all human births—a moment of ineffable catastrophe and won't bear discussion.

—Plotinus, c. 204–270

BOOK ONE

POLE PASS

1

A GREATER KNOWLEDGE

It was mid-October when I awoke to the golden drape of an autumn moon across my bed. A glance at the clock confirmed what my circadian rhythm told me every morning at four, and I emerged from the warm cocoon of blankets, quickly exchanging my pajamas for jeans and a thermal. With more ritual than routine, I crept downstairs and started the coffee maker on my way out the door to collect our Idaho daily for Dad's breakfast reading. The undisputed morning person of the house, I enjoyed the anonymity of this predawn hour, accompanied only by the crunch of gravel beneath my feet and, in this case, the brilliant moon that lit my way. The quiet trek down our third-of-a-mile driveway each morning served as a meditation, and many times I would find myself standing at the front gate without remembering the journey.

On rare occasions I'd arrive before the *Pole Pass Gazette*'s night editor tossed the paper out on his way home from work. Eddie Night Raven would say he was handing me the morning and to take good care of it. But today the fresh newsprint already lay inside the driveway gate and I smiled, acknowledging that it took a combination of luck and skill to thread the needle between the vertical bars from his moving vehicle.

I grabbed the tightly rolled paper and started home, taking a longer side trail that bordered the aspen grove along the river. The yellow moonlight reflected a layer of mist covering the water, which gave an eerie, cauldron-like glow that appeared to bubble with the underlying current. Wanting a closer look, I picked my way through the trees and scrub oak until I caught a game trail that led to the riverbank. Seconds later the snap of a twig told me I was no longer alone.

Confident in my ability to identify sounds in the woods, I determined this wasn't one I wanted to hear on my morning jaunt. As I cautiously moved ahead three steps at a time, it now matched my pace, but slightly behind, like an echo. Then I stepped only once, and it took two. I froze in my tracks. I desperately wanted to deny my senses and press on unabated, but the gravity of my situation took hold, and a tingle up my spine only gave credence to my suspicion.

Growing up in these mountains of the Pacific Northwest, we were taught young about predators. I knew that mountain lions patiently stalked their prey until within striking distance, then ferociously attacked the neck from behind. There were two defense strategies: maintain eye contact and slowly move away while making myself look as large as possible, or quickly locate anything that might be used as a weapon to fight off the attacker. As a ten-year-old boy weighing no more than eighty pounds and armed only with a newspaper, I had little chance against a hungry cat that could easily be twice my size.

The house was an impossible half-mile away from where I stood petrified in my quandary. *Seventy-five yards through the trees is the sauna on the riverbank*, I thought, *and if I can get there in one piece, it will be my shelter until Dad or Carol comes looking for me.*

I was jarred out of my rumination by the rustle again, this time only about forty yards to my right but still hidden in the shadow of the trees. Though I couldn't see anything, my senses shifted into overdrive when I felt the cat's eyes boring through me, assessing its potential meal. Survival instincts overtook fear, and I finally coaxed my feet to move again.

Facing the direction of the sound, I exaggerated my posture with arms raised high to appear larger and slowly backed my way toward the river. Five steps later I paused; hearing nothing, I felt a sense of relief wash over me, but this was premature. On my sixth, it boldly moved from the shadows into the full moonlight, and I felt a cold stab shoot through my body. Its charge, like my terror, was immediate—but this was not a cat!

My heart in my throat, I screamed and put one foot in front of the other as fast as I could, deeper and deeper into the aspen grove. Weaving through the trees, I realized that I was cut off from getting back to the house; a mossy, single-logged river crossing was my only chance of escape. When I was thirty yards from safety, his guttural sounds signaled that he was quickly closing the distance; *just a little farther*, I told myself, as the gap between us narrowed to only a few scant trees and underbrush. I reached the riverbank as he caught hold of my trailing right wrist . . . and from that point on, everything happened in nightmarish slow motion.

Squirming violently, I strained to yell at the top of my lungs, but no sound came out. I stretched my body away from him, leaning out over the water, desperately struggling to break free, but he was too strong and began dragging me back toward the woods. I bit into his hand, and he stopped for a second, only to slap me hard across the face, busting my lip—and that's when it happened.

In my haze, I heard a deep train-like roar come from the river as the mist flashed up the embankment and lunged between us, severing my attacker's arm at the elbow joint. I heard his throaty scream. I saw the dark spray against the moonlight, and I smelled the unforgettable odor of what I now know was blood. The last thing I recall was a floating sensation as the sudden release of my adversary's hold sent me flailing backward off the eight-foot riverbank into the mist-covered water below.

A loud clap of thunder opened my eyes to the glow of the river sauna's wood stove. My clothes hung on a towel peg, and a patch of fresh moss pillowed my head. Lying on the bench, I looked up through a small window to see daylight breaking across the sky and storm clouds rolling in. It took a minute to get my mind around what had happened. Was I dream-walking again?

I sat up in the warm room and felt the throb of my lip and the sting of several scratches as sweat rolled down my body, but the burning of my right wrist demanded the most attention. In the dim light of the stove, I saw the torn skin and finger-shaped bruises covering my lower arm. That was when my bewilderment gave way to fear.

~

Until last night, I had not dreamed about that predawn episode in almost three years, and I was glad I hadn't. Other than smeared footprints from our struggle at the riverbank and some traces of blood that the rain hadn't washed away, no evidence of my assailant was ever found. After an exhaustive search, investigators concluded that he must have met his demise falling into the quick-moving river, and their reasoning was understandable. The rocky one-hundred-foot drop of Eagle Falls is just over a mile downstream; at its base the water flows into a tributary of the Snake, on its way toward the rugged terrain of Hell's Canyon.

"He's fish food. We'll alert the hydroelectric authorities in Lewiston to be on the lookout for what's left of him" were the parting words of the Pass County Sheriff, Sam Waterson, as he and the deputies left our house that evening.

We had our own sheriff on tribal lands, but with the implications of an attempted kidnapping or worse, Sheriff Max Running Bear welcomed any resources the Pass County Sheriff's Department could offer. The official Pass County report claimed that I escaped my attacker by jumping into the river at the eddy so as not to get washed downstream, then climbed out and made it into the sauna to get warm. That sounded good on paper, but it wasn't accurate. I knew the event had happened exactly as I said, and I was confident that at least my dad, my sister, and our tribal sheriff believed me.

Native lands are full of mysteries that don't translate well to a mainstream culture that tends to label them as impossible or supernatural at best. However, in First Nations communities throughout North America, we know such things to be in keeping with the natural law of a living and conscious Earth. I'm not sure one ever gets used to these occurrences, but I've found that it makes life much less complicated when you accept them as they are presented.

Perhaps the catalyst for last night's dream was anticipation of my impending Weyekin, scheduled to begin in a few days. As a tribal youth now of age for this Native rite of passage, I had just been given the blessing of the medicine man to make the journey, and perhaps the prospect of seven or more nights alone in the ancestral forest had brought this up. Regardless of the impetus, I hoped last night's retelling was not going to become a thing of habit.

~

Pulling myself into the present moment, I stared through the hypnotic aquamarine swirls of our pool and continued folding towels for my sister's guests. Suddenly, any remnant of post-nocturnal angst was replaced by her familiar voice ringing out like a siren: "And run, don't walk!" Carol commanded, sending me across the deck into the pool house for a pitcher of iced tea. I slowly filled the container while looking out the window at the five bikini-clad girlfriends sunning themselves like royalty on our poolside chaises. As their only staff member, I knew that Carol would enjoy giving me the business on this, the official first pool day of summer vacation 1973.

The predicament was entirely of my own making. I had agreed to pay Carol in servitude for letting me drive her car up our road when we returned from the grocery store the day before. This was an oral contract as far as she was concerned, and it included a clause regarding dress code. Not only did she require that I wear a uniform of white jeans and an overly patterned Qiana shirt, but also she insisted that I sport an old Halloween moustache that looked like a caterpillar with mange.

"Ahhhhh, boy," she crooned again.

I thought to myself, *Don't push it, Carol*, but I would soon discover that this day of self-inflicted drudgery was a doorway leading to much more than I could have imagined. Snapping to attention, I was back on the pool deck tout de suite—sans the ridiculous moustache—and carrying a large tray with the brightly colored tumblers. As an awkwardly bookish thirteen-year-old, I was just beginning to appreciate the long legs and fine balance of the sixteen-year-old female physique, as modeled by Carol's friends.

A new girl named Virginia Tecoi was definitely worth appreciating. Her lean athletic pedestal supported the mane of dark blond hair falling effortlessly over smooth olive skin. The evenly set sea-green eyes were so deep and clear, looking into them was like diving into a bottomless pool . . . and I quickly determined that she was the most beautiful creature I had ever seen.

This was her first summer in the mountain town of Pole Pass, as well as her first visit to our house. Today also marked the only time I stood speechless—stunned, actually—by the sight of a female. I guess I was on the verge of gawking when Carol said, “Hey! Are you going to give her the tea or what?”

I reached toward Virginia’s outstretched hand with the lime-hued glass. Her voice, soft and permeating: “Thank you, Town . . . may I call you Town? Or do you prefer James?”

Other than the sounds of Karen Carpenter singing “Close to You” over the static-filled AM radio and my own heart beating in my head, I was absolutely blank, bereft of my faculties. And then, in those few long seconds, I felt something about myself change. The girls laughed at my outward appearance of dismay, but internally this momentary liberation from subjugated servanthood transformed me from a mere boy to one suddenly crushed under the weight of a greater knowledge. In an instant, I was transported out of the proverbial garden, wrapped only in a cloak of shame, but at the same time comforted by the revelation.

For teenage girls playing heiresses, they were friendly enough, and even moderately considerate, as they took up residency in our pool area those summers. In seasons past, my friends would also be coerced into the service ranks as their fee for entry to the pool deck. Like jet-setters on the French Riviera, the troupe entertained our presence for a time, but when they began any serious dialogue, we were given our leave. It was a no-boyfriend zone, a sorority that had always been gender exclusive, except for their private staff of eunuchs. A perfectly symbiotic arrangement as far as I was concerned, one to which I remain indebted for assisting in my navigation through social adolescence.

Today, the troupe's hot topic was a creepy secondhand tale that one of the girls had heard from another who lived down mountain in East Valley. The story was of an East Valley High School junior and her boyfriend who had found a secluded make-out spot just off the mile-long gravel road that dead-ended at the gate of the old Title Mine. The abandoned mining camp had been shuttered in the 1870s and sat like a tomb on the northern outskirts of Pole Pass ever since.

Our town cemetery bore proof of its hazards with too many monuments dedicated to adventurous children from each generation who perished exploring the old shafts, and after much public outcry, the mine was fenced off at its property line. Most locals heeded the warnings and stayed clear of the area, making it an ideal spot for a young couple in a nosy small town to find a little privacy.

Over the past month, these lovebirds parked their car under the branches of a large cedar tree on a hillside above the mine's gate, spreading out their blanket under the stars. The previous week, during a full moon, the couple had heard several cars drive up the road without their lights on. Watching from their hidden perch, they witnessed the driver of the first car get out and unlock the gate before waving the others through; then he secured the gate and followed the other vehicles up to the site of the old mining camp. It was now eleven thirty, and the girl had to get home or risk reprisals for breaking curfew, so the couple packed up and put the car in neutral, coasting all the way down to the highway without headlights or starting the engine.

"Wait a minute! That's it? No murder? No guy with a hook for a hand, or a chainsaw?" I said, clearly disappointed with the lack of a macabre punch line.

Virginia spewed iced tea down her front with a sudden laugh at my disdain. The girl relaying the story added, "Oh, the gatekeeper was wearing a black hooded robe."

"Well, why didn't you say so?" I replied, handing Virginia a towel from the stack I was carrying across the deck.

Carol addressed me by my full name, James Townsend Lawe, and told me to cool it, or she would find some less enjoyable chores for me in the remainder of my shift.

In spite of Carol's proclivity to control, we enjoyed an unrivaled sibling relationship. Three years my senior, she took naturally to the role of a doting big sister, especially in our mother's absence from the time I was five. Although she possessed an extended patience for me, it didn't stop her from ordering me around if she felt I needed to be straightened out. A statement like "Let me try this on you" or "Come at me like you have a knife" usually preceded such instances, often resulting in my being put in some sort of lock while flat on my back or stomach, sometimes in tears. Nevertheless, I always knew that she was there for me, whether I needed a study partner, a confidential adviser, or just my big sister, who understood me better than anyone else.

At sixteen, she was a 4.0 student, attractive, and a fine athlete. With varsity letters and team accolades, she was driven, and she either excelled at what she pursued or didn't waste her time with it. I learned many of my study patterns from Carol's remarkable ability to focus on the task at hand under pressure; of equal importance, I recognized the intrinsic value of time itself. Putting such lessons into practice relegated me to a somewhat solitary childhood, but in the grander scheme, they helped me immeasurably throughout my academic journey.

My remaining hours of poolside service that day were split between catering to the girls' whims and daydreaming about what was going on up at the mine. I was a sucker for a good mystery, and that evening I marked the calendar with the date of our next full moon and made a plan to satisfy my curiosity. I also could not escape the electric sensation I felt around Virginia, and as I drifted off to sleep, I hoped she would become a regular sight at our pool that summer.

2

MINE YOUR OWN BUSINESS

Offspring lean toward one parent's genetic code over the other, and though I had my dad's blond hair and build, there was little doubt that I was indeed my mother's son. Carol, on the other hand, aside from her chestnut hair and feminine features, demonstrated a preponderance of our father's traits. While I vacillated between interests in archaeology and biology until my sophomore year in high school, Carol had always been resolute in her vocation. She would follow in the footsteps of our father and become the seventh family member in as many generations to practice law. With this in mind, I had a pretty good idea of her answer before I posed the question.

"Are you crazy? I am not driving you up there to conduct a stakeout."

"C'mon, I'll be your pool servant again, and I promise I'll mind my own business—I'll even wear that moustache!" I practically begged her to reconsider.

"Town, you can plead your case with those blue eyes all you want, but your desperation is really unattractive, and for the last time, *no!* That story is probably just bullshit anyway, plus Dad would take my car keys away if he found out that I went near that mine, much less brought you with me!"

"Yeah, I guess so . . ." I saw her logic, but in true Carol fashion, she helped me without compromising her position.

"Look here, if you're that curious about it, why don't you grab the binoculars and climb out of your window onto the roof. I bet it's a straight shot to that hill. Just promise me you won't fall off, OK?"

Carol was right. It was a distance of about twenty miles as the crow flies, and certainly better than nothing.

Three weeks later, the night of the full moon arrived, and just after eleven p.m. I quietly eased out my bedroom window and onto the pitch of the roof. I scaled up to the dormer and steadied myself by straddling the peak. Finding the northernmost end of Main Street was easy, as the lights faded quickly on the way out of town. Despite the challenge of holding the binoculars steady, at eleven thirty I caught the brief smear of lights in the darkness along the rural stretch of highway heading out toward the mine. That was good enough for me.

Over breakfast, I enthusiastically relayed what I had witnessed. Carol told me that I was talking too loud when our dad came into the kitchen from his study, where he had been enjoying his morning coffee and newspaper. Having exceptional hearing, he asked, "What's this about the mine?"

Carol gave me a look that I understood well. I told him everything, with the exception of her counsel, figuring there was no need to involve her in the forthcoming lecture.

"Don't you go anywhere near that mine. Those shafts are unstable and full of gases; the ground above them can give way at any time, and it's a toxic wasteland from decades of mine discharge. So you stay away from it, and keep off the roof too—we don't need any leaks, or broken necks. Have I made myself absolutely clear on this, Town?"

"Yes, sir. Perfectly. But what do you think is going on up there?"

"Oh, I don't know . . . maybe a witches' coven? Devil worshippers?" Dad said with a laugh before picking up his briefcase and keys on the way out the door. "You two have a great day. I love you, and I'll see you tonight. Remember what I said about the mine. That goes for you too, Carol."

"Yes, sir. Love you, Dad," we both replied as he closed the door behind him.

Since my mother's departure, saying "I love you" became a deliberate part of our farewells. It added a comforting layer, knowing that we always parted with one last word of affection.

Now, it's not like either of us had never been to the mine before. The Title Mine was a major part of Pole Pass history, and prior to being fenced off, it had been on the meager list of local school field trip destinations. The original clapboard buildings had long since weathered to a pewter gray, with their tin roofs, now oxide-hued blankets, resting atop the sagging structures. Abandoned tools and machinery littered the landscape where they had fallen, as if left mid-shift, never to be wielded against the earth again. The mining camp was a Western ghost town, complete with a half-burned sawmill and the other buildings that made up the settlement; I could certainly see the attraction for those who wanted to explore the area with their metal detectors, hoping to find treasure that others had missed. I always felt uneasy when on that property during those school field trips, but though I would never disobey my dad's directive, my curiosity remained.

"Town, remember you have your monthly meeting today at the Center, with Aunt Myra," Carol reminded me.

"Thanks, I didn't forget."

"OK, just be ready to go at twelve; otherwise, you're going to have a long bike ride."

"Don't worry about it, I'll be ready!"

Aunt Myra Three Moons was one of my mother's two closest friends, the other being our godmother, Chilok. The three oversaw design, construction, and operations of the Northwest American Indian Cultural Center in the heart of Pole Pass. As tribal elders, Myra and Chilok accepted the responsibility for my tribal education, while another elder, Peter Lone Elk, taught me the skills necessary to coexist with nature and survive the wilderness in preparation for my Weyekin. Myra was a young graduate student majoring in Native American studies when she was hired, with an initial responsibility of recording and organizing tribal customs and legends that stretched beyond a millennium. The resulting volumes will always be considered a masterwork among many tribes and scholars. Whether she was reading a story to a group of elementary school children or lecturing on a modern Native sculpture, she loved to pass along knowledge of First Nations lore and our way of life to those interested.

Much had transpired over the past month, and I looked forward to sharing the experiences of my Weyekin with her. This would also be a great opportunity to ask some questions about the old mine, as it had certainly played its role in our tribal history. I rushed through my chores and caught a ride with Carol into Pole Pass on her way down mountain to East Valley. When we pulled up to the Cultural Center, she handed off a checklist of legal books for me to bring home from our dad's law office after my meeting with Aunt Myra.

"Your toll for the ride." We said our goodbyes as I grinned, and I stuffed the paper into my pocket before climbing the steps of the four-acre complex.

When I entered Aunt Myra's office, she was already seated at the usual round table anticipating my arrival. "Come in, Town, sit! How was your time in the forest?" she asked, her dark brown eyes escorting me to the chair.

"I learned a lot about myself, that's for sure," I answered, taking my seat.

"I remember being a little frightened of the dark until the third night or so. Were you?" she asked, smiling.

"Not of the night. I found that when you match frequencies with the forest, there is a symphony that plays. It's soothing, and takes your mind off any scary stuff."

"That's very astute, Town—it sounds like Peter Lone Elk prepared you well for the journey."

"Yes, he's very wise. I was actually more afraid of seeing a Sasquatch than the forest at night, but that passed."

"Did you see one?" Myra asked, unable to stop her grin from forming.

"No, ma'am, but I did see some Shadow Warriors."

With that, her eyes widened. "You did? Tell me what happened," she said, reaching for the pen resting on the spiral-bound notebook in front of her.

"Yes, ma'am, on my oath, I did. It was my tenth day at dusk. I was seated high on a large rock deep in the forest. It was farther than I had ever been, but it seemed familiar to me all the same. Out of nowhere, I counted five of them passing through the trees below me. They were huge, maybe ten feet tall, walking west toward the mountains, and then they were gone."

"You know, a sighting is very rare."

"That's what Peter Lone Elk said too."

"Your mother encountered them as well. Did anyone ever tell you this?"

"No, Auntie." I leaned forward, resting my arms on the table, to absorb the account.

"It wasn't long after we found the glyph. She began to spend a lot of time on the ancestral side of the river and told me about her encounter, very similar to yours. She said that she had a theory and wanted to be certain it was correct before telling Chilok and me. It was less than a month later that she left us."

Following the story about my mother, I saw sadness come over Myra's countenance, and I decided to change the subject. I repeated the tale that I had heard about the mine and what I witnessed from the rooftop. She didn't hide her concern as she echoed the message of rebuke that my dad delivered, but she topped it with another reason.

"You should stay away from there. Whatever may or may not be going on is something you want nothing to do with, and you should put it out of your mind. That land is bad medicine. Understand?"

"Yes, Auntie."

"Good. Now, I hear that Chilok is in the office this afternoon, and I know she won't forgive me if I let you leave without seeing her."

We walked downstairs through the atrium and into a spacious office directly below Myra's. Chilok was in her mid-eighties, and though becoming frail in body, she kept her mind razor sharp by planning the Center's youth activities and teaching Native art techniques on Saturdays. Myra rapped on the frame of the open door.

"Not so loud—I'm not deaf yet!" came a reply from the back of a recliner that was set to view the exterior courtyard of the complex.

"My apologies, godmother," I said, just able to see her crown of silver hair over the recliner as I gave Aunt Myra a wink.

"Town Lawe! My dear young man has come to see me! Please come around here, and sit with me."

Myra accompanied me to the front of the recliner, greeting Chilok as mother, out of respect. "Mother, the clay will be here in time for Saturday's class on hand building."

"Oh, thank you, dear—I was hoping that it would be back in stock."

"I'm glad to deliver the news. You two enjoy your time together. Town, I'll see you next month, and remember what we discussed."

"Yes, Auntie, I promise I will, and thank you," I said, as she left the office.

Chilok reached over and took my hand, holding it as we sat side by side looking through the expanse of curved glass onto the large, manicured courtyard with its small lake and walking path.

"Now, please indulge me with a thorough account of your Weyekin."

Without interrupting, Chilok nodded intermittently as I recalled my experiences during those eleven days in the forest. When I finished, she smiled and said, "Very good. Eleven days is a long journey for a young man of thirteen. Most at your age only stay a week, and a Shadow Warriors sighting too! What insight did Lone Elk give you?"

"He told me that I was on my way to a much deeper path, and I must continue practicing the meditation and grounding rituals. As I did, the path would reveal itself. But I'm not sure what some of it means."

Chilok said softly, "That's to be expected. To us, this life is a paradox. What I mean is that our path is straight, yet it is made up of corners. It was designed this way, so the splendor unfolds only in glimpses. This is for our own benefit and for the preservation of all. It is one reason that we are only given what we are ready to receive each day. This lesson is about patience, you see . . . patience develops virtue. The reward is found in digesting the fullness of each glimpse before moving on to the next. Do you remember when I used to teach you youngsters to chew every bite of food twenty times before swallowing it? That was in preparation for this lesson. What you have experienced is very powerful, and you must be careful—remember to chew what you have in your mouth so you don't choke, OK?"

"Yes, I understand. Thank you."

"Good. Now, I need you to listen carefully to me. This is the time that you know certain things. I can sense the abandonment that lurks inside of you. This will hinder your journey unless we address it. You may find this difficult at thirteen, but you must accept that your mother did not want to leave you. She had no choice in the matter. It was her obligation, you see. You and Carol were her only babies; your father, her only husband. This is all I can say to you, and I know it seems unfair, perhaps even cruel. But you have to trust my words, young Tumlok—there is much more coming."

Chilok's intuition was known far beyond the local Native community. She had gained a reputation as a revered healer in her youth and was still recognized for her abilities by many chief and elder councils; I wasn't taken aback by what she shared with me. With all I had experienced to date, it didn't surprise me in the least that she knew of my tormentor, this specter that periodically crept into my thoughts, pushing its script of unworthiness and blame. My tribal language skills were decent, but I didn't recall the word *Tumlok*, thinking in the moment that it might be a term of endearment, but she dismissed me before I could ask its meaning.

"OK, Town, that's enough for today—you have plenty to work on. Besides, I'm in need of a nap," she smiled.

"Thank you, Godmother, I love you," I said, hugging her neck and kissing her soft weathered cheek before making my way toward the door.

"One other thing, Godson. You listen to Three Moons and stay away from that mine. There is something darker on that land than the lust and greed of those who ravaged Mother Earth in search of temporary riches."

That zinger caught me off guard, and I assured her that I would respect the warning. Chilok's uncanny ability to reach into the ether and retrieve this type of information could be disconcerting to some. There were people who thought she was a witch and stayed away from her. Most of these folks had left the traditional ways behind, to become part of the *civilized* ranks of society. These tribal descendants no longer participated in the Weyekin, nor did they possess any desire to learn the legends or stories of their own ancestry. Instead, this group held the position that the time-honored ways of coexisting with nature were ignorant, superstitious, and even dangerous, not only to our progress as a species but also to one's immortal soul.

With almost an hour to spare before meeting Dad at his office for my ride home, I walked a ceremonial lap around the small lake in the courtyard that Chilok and I had just been viewing from her window. I never gave much thought to the fact that my family had lived on this piece of land for over a century: seven generations of Lawes on this very site, with me being the first who hadn't called it home. Still, it always felt familiar. The donation of the four-acre property that gave birth to the Cultural Center was initially met with stiff resistance by Pole Pass civic leaders who were in the founding-family lineage. The Listers in particular had schemed to retrieve this parcel since it was lost by their patriarch in a card game back in 1852. So when my parents signed the property over to the tribe, they encountered significant blowback from the City Council, and ultimately it was my dad's expertise in federal land trusts and government funding that persuaded the shortsighted local leadership to support the project without a protracted battle. This cooperation would give the area access to federal and state funds, as well as the positive notoriety and recognition that the founding heirs craved.

According to my parents' vision, downtown Pole Pass would become a tourist destination, resulting in consumer dollars, tax revenues, and social currency that could be spent in numerous ways. The founding families might even receive a few federally recognized historical markers to stroke their egos if they put their differences aside long enough to see the benefits of the deal. They eventually did, and the Center was built. In return, the tribe honored our family with stewardship of the four-hundred-plus-acre parcel on which we now lived. We were also recognized as full tribal members, even though my dad was only one-quarter Native by blood.

The Northwest American Indian Cultural Center delivered all that was projected in the way of legitimizing the region of Pole Pass beyond its modern legacy as an agricultural breadbasket. It was fast becoming a destination for Native studies, known for housing one of the most respectable collections of First Nations artifacts west of the Mississippi River.

3

THE OLD SCHOOL BOOK AND ITS COVER

After leaving the Cultural Center, I walked the few blocks up Main Street toward my dad's law office, passing the barbershop along the way.

"Good summer so far, Town?" Barber Jimmy asked as he enjoyed a smoke and a *Life* magazine from the bench in front of his shop.

"Yes, sir, thank you, and you?"

"Beautiful afternoon in the mountains, can't ask for much better . . . and tell your dad he's due for a haircut—it's on the house!"

"Yes, sir, I'm going to see him right now."

"Yeah, I figured," Barber Jimmy retorted.

It reminded me of a story he had told me during a haircut just over a year before. Until that one afternoon in May, I thought I knew pretty much everything there was to know about my father. I knew he had not always been a small-town officer of the court but was a man of pedigree, born and raised in the family home that stood on the site of the Cultural Center. He had enlisted in the United States Army and departed for boot camp the morning following his high school graduation. After his tour in Army intelligence, he went to Harvard Law School and joined a notable Wall Street firm after graduation. By the time he met my mother at age thirty-four, he was litigating some of the largest corporate cases in his office.

The father we knew at home rarely displayed the ardor of a trial lawyer; instead he was rather quiet in his demeanor, both contemplative and relaxed. I have no memory of him ever flying off the handle or even raising his voice around us. With my mother's influence, he became a daily yoga practitioner, and I believe this contributed to his calm, centered Zen-like state. Weighing about two hundred pounds and standing six-foot-one with a posture that made him appear taller, my ruggedly handsome father cleaned up very well, and it was apparent that the women in town still thought as much. As a small child, one of the things I enjoyed was sitting in the bathroom and watching him shave. I recall being fascinated as he worked the shaving soap into lather with the brush. He would paint his face with the dense foam, only to take it off with each passing stroke of his double-edged razor, reminiscent of the plow clearing the road after a fresh snowfall. On one occasion, he nicked himself, getting a little blood on his T-shirt, and when he took it off, I remember studying his defined physique in the mirror and thinking to myself in childlike innocence, *My dad is really Superman.*

In general, he was measured, even when you knew he had to be angry about something, so I found it strange that there appeared to be an unspoken language in play among some longtime locals who gave him a wide berth. I just interpreted this as common courtesy and good manners. But it was during that haircut on my twelfth birthday that my eyes were opened much wider.

Barber Jimmy Peets ran his shop like a men's club. A small black-and-white television set perpetually ran *Wide World of Sports* or *The American Sportsman.* Camel butts dominated amber-colored glass ashtrays, girlie magazines were mixed among other periodicals of the day, and within those walls my haircut cost four bits instead of fifty cents. The shop had a masculine atmosphere that was palpable when you walked past the rotating barbershop pole and through that heavy wooden door, with its thick blue-green plate glass. There was no reception area, so you were thrust into the middle of the action upon entry, like being pushed out onto a stage with the expectation of ad-libbing some pithy remarks while you found a seat to wait your turn in the chair.

Barber Jimmy was a battle-hardened World War II naval vet, complete with blurry tattoos of dancing hula girls and palm trees that adorned his permanently tanned forearms. His silver flattop, and the faint scent of bay rum that followed him wherever he went, provided a heady mixture that matched his character perfectly, and whenever I sat in his chair, I had vivid images of those far-off tropical adventures he must have experienced while fighting global tyranny. Like all great local barbers, Jimmy was a fully stocked dispensary of town history, politics, gossip, and life lessons. When I hopped up on the leather and chrome chair that afternoon and the soft, rhythmic squeak of his scissors commenced, he asked how my dad and Carol were doing, if I was studying hard—just the typical barber-to-client opening conversation. He then began speaking with the three older gentlemen now waiting for their turns, when the topic of the Frontier Room becoming a fancy restaurant was mentioned. Jimmy was recounting a few choice memories about the famed 110-year-old local watering hole when his reminiscence was interrupted by the screams of a teenage girl out on Main Street.

"I hate your fucking guts!" were the shrill words that suddenly penetrated the massive plate glass barbershop window.

"Carla, wait just a goddamned minute, will you!" said the man trailing several paces behind, the quickening click-clack of his fancy cowboy boots indicating that he was speeding up.

Jimmy instantly stopped his expert scissors-over-comb work and said, looking toward the glass, "Jesus H. Christ! What in the hell is going on out there?"

"Looks like the Listers are having some sort of family meeting," said one of the men with a chuckle.

"Yeah, that's Marty the tractor dealer down in West Valley, and his daughter Carla. Man alive, they are really having it out," added another.

"I recall a pretty bad divorce a while back, a real doozy," Jimmy said.

As the men commented about the street scene unfolding before us, I felt a helpless despair when I saw the petite girl dressed in black on the opposite side of the glass. I caught only a flash of her face as she stormed past the shop window, her eyes ablaze with anger, hurt, and a haunting warmth that stuck with me.

"That whole Lister clan is a pain in Pass County's neck!" said the first man.

"You won't find any argument from me—I hear a lot of B.S. standing behind this chair."

"You know, they are to blame for the Frontier Room shutting down like it did," added the third man.

"Yep, right after they bought the building, they jacked up the rent. I'm going to miss that place. After a hundred-plus years, it's the end of an era."

Directing the conversation toward me, Jimmy said, "You all know this is Dan Lawe's son, right?" I watched through the reflection in the mirror as he pointed to my head with the comb and the three nodded.

"So, Town, your dad ever mention the Frontier Room?" Jimmy asked, in a leading manner.

The others began to chuckle, with one reporting that he had worked in the mayor's office at the time, and he witnessed the aftermath firsthand, loud and clear. I responded with a quizzical look indicating that I had no idea what they were talking about. Barber Jimmy smiled and said, "Well, let us tell you a little story, but you didn't hear it from me." Enlisting the three patrons to assist with some choreography, Jimmy set his tools down on the barber tray before giving me a history lesson, complete with reenactment.

"It was Christmastime, and your dad's first visit home in two years after leaving for the service. He was enjoying a cocktail over at the Frontier Room when three founding-family boys—Stanley Lister, Reginald Harrison III, and

Barley Adams—didn't like the attention he was getting from their dates. Well, they decided to throw him an unwelcome-home party out in the parking lot when he left. I had just closed the shop and was walking up the street for a glass of holiday cheer myself when I saw the commotion begin and . . . end. Stanley Lister threw the first punch while Harrison and Adams had your father's attention. I swear I never saw anything like it, I tell you! Your dad wheeled around and smashed Lister in the face with his elbow, knocking his two front teeth down his throat, and while he was choking on them, your dad kneed Lister smack in the nuts!

"Next, he caught Harrison's arm in some kind of lock and broke it like it was a Popsicle stick—I heard it snap from the other side of the street! Then he busted Harrison's nose and knocked him out cold. Adams tried to rush in and got three fractured ribs and a punctured lung for it. That all happened before I could make it over to help out, but when I did, the only mark on your dad was a black eye from the sucker punch that Lister threw. The whole scene raised blue hell in the Founder community. Eunice Lister, the mayor, the chief of police, and a few City Council members were up in arms, with talk of lawsuits and even jail time over the ordeal."

Then the customer who had worked in the mayor's office at the time piped up: "Woo boy, it really heated up when a state senator sent his Army-captain son, who was also home on leave, up from Boise. He arrived at the mayor's office and began tearing them all a new one! He came in yelling at the top of his lungs: 'Who here is responsible for damaging the property of the United States of America War Department?' I remember their faces when he hollered, 'You can get federal effing prison time for that!' Only he didn't say 'effing,' and he kept on yelling without even a pause: 'Don't you shitbirds know that we are at war? What in the hell are you, anyway? Fascists? Commies? Or just your garden-variety type of retards?' The mayor made a feeble attempt at a defense, saying, 'But, but, but, one of these young men might now be sterile from this incident.' The captain's response left no room for misinterpretation: 'Now you listen up, shitbird. It doesn't sound to me like these United States of America or the blessed state of Idaho needs any more inbreeding, and if you freedom-mooching layabouts are too dense to get ahold of that, then maybe I go back to the Pentagon and suggest we build a training base and a goddamned bombing range up here!!' He screamed it like a drill sergeant while jabbing his finger into the mayor's chest, of all things! Well, that was that. Any notion of charges left town along with that captain."

Between the waves of laughter and the thigh slaps, Jimmy admonished me to close my mouth, which I guess was hanging so wide open that I was in danger of inhaling some of the cuttings as he finished up my haircut with the buzzer. He concluded the tale: "Town, your dad is a fine man. I've known a few, and he's a rare breed, don't you ever forget that." After whisking some Vitalis through my hair, he wished me a happy birthday, saying that today's haircut was on the house, and on my way out the door he reminded me, "You didn't hear that story from me—I need what few teeth I have left!" as everyone laughed.

"Yes, sir," I replied, still trying to absorb what I had just heard. At twelve years old, I was aware that Pole Pass had its own caste system. I had witnessed the behavior first-hand since kindergarten, but I never imagined that my own father might have been bullied by it. Even though I had always respected my dad, I was proud to hear that story from Barber Jimmy and those men.

4

KINCAID ESTRANGED

I walked into Dad's law office and greeted his clerk, Bernice, who sat at her typewriter intently pounding out a letter.

"Hi Town, Sam is in with your dad, they've been in there a while, should be wrapping up soon," she said, barely looking up.

"OK, thanks, Bernice, I think I'll wait." She nodded with a laugh, knowing full well that Dad was my ride home.

I took a seat outside of his closed door, where I heard a rumble of deep conversation on the other side. Bernice had anything but a light touch when it came to typing technique. It didn't matter that it was a new IBM Selectric; her banging away made it impossible to hear what was being said behind the door. She finally hit the last keystroke, zipped the letter out of the machine, and asked me to mind the store while she walked across the town square to the post office.

"I'd be happy to, Bernice."

"Thank you. Would you like a malt from the drugstore? I'll bring one back for you."

"Nah—thanks, though, but feel free to treat yourself to one."

Bernice headed out onto Main Street, and I leaned in closer to the office door.

"The Order?" I heard Sheriff Sam Waterson say. I could tell that Dad wanted to keep this quiet because everything afterward was much harder to make out, even without Bernice on her typewriter, and soon my ear was flush against the door.

"Sam, we both know it's the Listers up there."

"Sure it is, but you remember what happened last time the Pass County Sheriff's Department got involved in their bullshit."

"Reassigned—yeah, I remember."

"You know that Eunice has her hooks in all the right places, and I swear to God I don't need the grief. You know damn well she still holds a grudge against you for kicking her son's ass, and that's twenty-some-odd years ago!"

"Trust me, I'm well aware of that."

"Look, we have to produce more than a hunch that they were involved in that incident out at your place. If we had something solid, you know I'd put my badge on the line to nail Lister ass to the wall."

"Yeah, I know. Thanks for that, Sam. I'm not looking to bust up their little club. I just want you to keep an eye out. Maybe park a unit up there during the next full moon. Just to let them know someone is aware of their hangout."

"Oh I see . . . more of a deterrent."

"Exactly. Maybe they'll find a new clubhouse."

"I can do that, but you realize I'm going to get a phone call about it."

"Yes, yes . . . it's like poking a hornet's nest, but I know you are just as curious as I am."

"Well, you got me there. I'll keep you posted."

I pushed back from the door just as Bernice came in off the street. Thinking quickly, I reached for a book from the adjacent bookcase while producing Carol's list from my pocket.

"Oh, I could have sworn this was on the list," I said to conceal my eavesdropping.

"More books for Carol?" Bernice said as she took her mouth from the straw.

"Yes, ma'am. Do you recognize any of these?" I asked, handing Bernice the paper.

"These all appear to be case law books. They would be in the barrister cases in your dad's office, if he has them."

"What did you get this time?"

"Vanilla and banana, my new favorite."

"Yum, that sounds good."

With that, the door opened and the two men stepped into the hallway of the outer office. "Howdy, Town," the sheriff greeted me.

"Howdy, Sheriff, nice to see you," I replied, as he made his farewells and exited onto Main Street.

"Hi son—I forgot today was your meeting with Myra. How was your time with her?"

"It was fine. I saw Chilok too."

"Well, that's a nice surprise. You can tell me about it on the way home."

"Yes, sir, I will. Oh, I have a list of books for Carol—may I grab them?"

"Sure, you do that while I pack up."

I gathered the books for Carol while Dad finished clearing his desk and tidied up his office.

"All set. You got those?" he asked, curious about the five books stacked to my chin.

"Yes, no problem here," I replied, teetering down the short hallway.

We said goodbye to Bernice and were walking out the door when the phone rang. Dad paused, tipping his head back toward Bernice's desk.

"Yes, Sam . . . no, no . . . he's right here." She passed the phone over her desk.

"Hi, Sam, what's up? OK . . . OK . . . OK, what do you think happened? Well, let's hope not. Yes, hold on a second. Town, have you seen or heard from Kincaid?"

"No, not since the last day of school. Why?" I rested the stack of books on the corner of Bernice's desk.

He held up his hand and continued the phone conversation. "No, Sam, he hasn't seen him in a week. OK, will do. Keep us posted, and I'll coordinate the tribal lands."

Dad hung up the phone, and the concern that had been evident in his voice during the call was on his face. Looking at Bernice and me, he gave us the news.

"Kincaid LeToure's mother showed up at the sheriff's office, reporting him missing. He hasn't been seen since yesterday at around six o'clock, when he stormed out of the house after an argument. She's called everyone, including the hospital, and nothing. Town, do you have any idea where he might have gone?"

"I'm not sure . . . We haven't been all that close over the past couple of years."

"Well, think about anywhere he may hide out or anything else, no matter how trivial it might seem, OK?"

"Yes, of course."

During the twenty-five-minute drive home, I thought a lot about Kincaid. He and I had been best friends. We met in the spring of 1970 in the fourth grade when his family relocated from East Valley up to Pole Pass. I clearly remember his first day in Mrs. Morgan's class. Physically he was on the smaller side, a bit wiry, and a little shy, but he seemed friendly enough. My initial take was that he was more or less a regular kid just trying to assimilate into his new environment. He did, however, have one glaring problem that was no fault of his own. Even though he had moved up a thousand feet from the valley below, he had just done so. This made him a "flatlander" by Pole Pass standards, causing a bit of an integration issue during his first week at school. He was subjected to the typical new-kid welcome: taunts that lead to a shove, then escalate into a minor brawl at recess or after school.

I didn't like Reginald Harrison IV much from our first meeting, four years earlier in kindergarten. The kid ate paste like it was frosting on a cupcake and would steal anything not screwed down. To make matters worse, he blamed classmates for his thievery, and by fourth grade he was growing into a big gloating bully, a real son of a bitch for a kid. A member of one of Pole Pass's founding families, Reggie constantly reminded everyone of his importance.

One of his favorite quips was, "I could make trouble for you and your w-h-o-l-e damn family if I wanted to," like he was some big shot in a mobster movie. Even as fourth graders we knew this behavior trickled down from home. His father, Reginald III, was a crooked-nosed ass of a man who would show up at school events with so much pomp and circumstance that you would think President Nixon himself was arriving. He served one term as the mayor of Pole Pass and then lost his primary bid for a congressional seat in a mudslinger. These days he ran the family business as president and CEO of Northern Passage Land & Title Company and never hesitated to introduce himself as such, handing out his business cards like candy on Halloween.

This particular schoolyard brawl started like most others, and even though Kincaid was quite a bit smaller, I could plainly see that he wasn't afraid of Reggie. So when Reggie shoved him and started cussing at him, Kincaid just tried to stay away from his fists, but that didn't last long, and inevitably when Reggie connected, Kincaid hit the ground. This generally ended these things. Today, it didn't satisfy Reggie, and he kept pushing him around with his foot, telling him to "get up and take his beating like a highlander or he was going to get stomped on like a flatlander." Several girls yelled at him to leave Kin alone, but he just stood straddling his victim, mocking and telling everyone to shut up or they would get theirs too.

I was about to intervene when the kicking began . . . and I don't mean Reggie kicking Kincaid. It happened with two decisive blows so quick and accurate that I still slow it down in my mind to enjoy it. First, Kin grabbed Reggie's lower right leg and pinned it to the ground while planting his own right foot squarely in Reggie's balls.

As Reggie crumpled down, Kin switched feet and kicked him in the middle of his tailbone with the point of his cowboy boot, making the sound of a stick hitting a hollow log. Ten seconds of silence followed the thud of Reggie's face hitting the hardened playing field dirt until his body finally summoned enough air to release a cry so bloodcurdling that up to that point I had never heard any human or animal make that sound.

We all stood there slack-jawed, taking in what we had witnessed, as Reggie required a full minute to make it to his knees from the fetal position. By that time, his wail, and the ring of fifteen or so kids, had drawn the attention of the playground teacher, Mrs. Scott. She marched across the playing field and pushed her way through the crowd, shrieking, "What happened here?" Reggie stood up, brushed himself off, and, wiping tears across his dusty face with his arm, said, "I tripped chasing that damned kickball," pointing to nowhere in particular. She looked at us suspiciously until interrupted by the bell, releasing all from further scrutiny. As we ran back to class, I still remember laughing when Mrs. Scott yelled out, "Where's the kickball?" and Kincaid, disguising his voice, responded, "Ask Reggie—he has *two* of them!"

Our classroom at Pole Pass Elementary School agreed that Reginald Harrison IV had gotten what he deserved that spring day, and in his moment of ultimate humiliation, Reggie knew it too. I later asked Kin why he let Reggie hit him at all, when it was obvious that he could have bested him from the start. He told me he was expecting there might be some trouble, but he really wanted to make friends up here and would take a punch or two for it. That was just the kind of boy Kin was back then. The following year, when his parents separated, Kin began to change. He and Reggie eventually became good friends, and I saw much less of him apart from school. We never fell out, just had different interests.

"He took his bike, right?" I asked my dad as we crossed onto Native land.

"Yes, according to his mother."

"At least we know he's probably traveling on the road and not in woods. That should make finding him easier."

"That's a great point; let's hope so. I can't imagine what his parents must be going through right now," Dad said as we pulled through the gate and started up the driveway.

An unwritten code of mountain living is that everyone assists in search and rescue. The parties were already being organized, and sector responsibilities had been determined by the time we made it back to the house. We were just playing the original message from Mrs. LeToure when the sheriff called. Kin had been found! He was spotted wandering through the canyon on the way down to West Valley after apparently sliding off the road on his bike. Dirty and confused, with a broken arm and a few insect stings, he had no memory of where he had been and was having difficulty recalling his own name. He was now on the way to Pass County Hospital in an ambulance.

"Thank God he's OK," Dad said as he hung up.

"Yes, should I go see him at the hospital?"

"Why don't you give it a day and then call his folks. I'm sure they'd love to hear that his friends are concerned."

5

GROWING PAIN

One day in early September, Carol suggested we go for an after-school hike along the river for a chat and to take in the changing colors. As the two of us ventured down the trail heading south toward Eagle Falls, we casually talked strategies for our college acceptance. Carol had her coursework all set up and was prodding me once again to make a declaration regarding what I wanted to study. We arrived at the falls and continued our discussion as we sat watching the water cascade onto the rocks and fallen timbers below.

Then she said with more intensity, "Town, you have got to take this step seriously."

"What do you mean? Of course I'm taking this seriously—I just haven't decided yet, that's all."

I was shocked when she voiced her concern over my infatuation with Virginia, something she had taken note of over the summer. "What you are experiencing is completely natural, but now is not the time to get engrossed in a romantic fantasy. Virginia has just as much to lose by this diversion, so get your mind back onto your educational goals. There's plenty of time for entanglements down the road."

She was very gentle about it—for Carol—but nonetheless, I felt exposed, then mad, and then devastated. I couldn't hear any more. I got up and said, "Race you back to the house," and took off like a rocket. Her plea of "Wait!" fell behind me as I ran faster than I had in my entire life. I crossed to the other side of the river and ran another quarter-mile into the ancestral forest, where I finally dropped onto a bed of moss surrounded by giant ferns. I cried for what seemed to be thirty minutes, until a soft hand on my shoulder let me know that Carol had finally caught up with me. But when I looked up, my only companion was a bat that circled a few times before darting back toward the river.

I made my way to the crossing point to find Carol waiting on the other side, like a sentinel. She gave me a big hug and, with tears in her eyes, led me over to the chairs on the porch of the river sauna.

"Town, I'm sorry. That was really insensitive of me. Sometimes I don't think about how my bottom-line approach affects others."

"Thanks, it's OK, I know I get distracted."

"It's a perfectly natural distraction, and just so you know, Virginia never said a thing about your admiration to me."

Carol took the importance of prioritizing my educational goals during this last year of middle school personally, and this conversation was her way of keeping me on track to attend the college of my dreams.

Darkness had fallen by the time we made it back to the house. Pausing for a second before opening the kitchen door, Carol put her hand on my shoulder, smiled, and said, "Virginia's a science geek too—she's going to become a doctor, and that requires a lot of study. Smart girls like smart guys, Town." Painful as this afternoon was, the sobering reality of it had to be addressed, and I always knew that Carol had my best interests at heart.

The summer yielded a cornucopia of new experiences. Most present was the awareness of emotions so raw and powerful that they consumed me before I realized it. I was thankful that Carol cared enough to guide me back onto the path, while knowing the churning it brought in the process. I regained my focus and managed to tame the unbridled emotions I felt when Virginia came around. With my principal interest returned to academics, the time flew by. It was as if I went to bed an eighth-grade student of Pole Pass Middle School and woke up a freshman at Pole Pass High.

The high school integration was seamless, thanks to the troupe of girls who spent the bulk of their summers on our pool deck. Now highly regarded seniors, they insisted that I be allowed into their study hall and extended circles. Much of that time was spent helping Carol prep for her first year at Yale, and for the other girls, I was a flash card partner, which broadened my general knowledge in the process. Virginia sequestered herself much of that year, cramming natural sciences as she readied for the accelerated pre-med track in northern Idaho. When the school year ended, the troupe resumed their historic pool routine, and I felt like the days would continue on forever. Then, as if without warning, summer was over . . . and the girls scattered like birds leaving the nest within days of each other. I also heard from a classmate that the LeToures had sold their house and moved all the way to Boise. I knew that Kincaid and I had drifted apart, but I didn't recognize how far until then.

I fell into a funk when I realized that a large part of my own youth had departed along with the girls, and I failed to savor the passing of the chapter. During the next weeks, I spent a lot of time in the forest contemplating my own existence, sometimes lost in thought, listening attentively to the beauty that surrounded me, and other times asking questions aloud like a yodeler awaiting the responding echoes. The questions in my head went unanswered, but my heart filled with peace when the bat appeared to escort me back to the river crossing at dusk.

After Carol went off to Yale, her absence in the house was readily apparent, and I missed her. She was the next best thing to having my mother around, and it was easy to tell that Dad experienced the void right along with me. He now had nobody to throw legal jargon back and forth with, although out of habit he did attempt that with me. I responded with a salvo of biology terms for him to define and he would laugh, but it wasn't the same satisfying exchange they enjoyed. I knew Dad always worked to balance his affections between Carol and me, but the ease of his common ground with her afforded him an opportunity to avoid similarities that I shared with my mother. I guess those reminders were too painful for him to embrace at the time. Now fifteen, I began to ask questions about her. She had been gone for over two-thirds of my life at this point, and I had just experienced the "death" of another season, sharpened by the departure of the summer troupe.

Myra and Chilok had always been the primary sources for stories about my mother. The three women experienced much in their eight years together. Dad held things close, and he rarely shared those cherished memories with Carol and me. Over the ensuing months, I would ask a question or two while we were splitting logs or grading the driveway, but he gave me only one-word answers. The superficial replies reminded me of what Chilok had told me a couple of years earlier about the pitfalls of not addressing things, no matter how painful.

So one day, I just flat-out asked him, "Respectfully, sir, are you ever going to tell me about her, or just keep tap dancing?" I could tell he was surprised that I had put him on the spot.

"All right, what do you want to know exactly?"

"Well, I have always found it best to start at the beginning, and we can take it from there."

6

DR. LOUISA GENVIER-LAWE

My mother was as formidable in her fields of archaeology and humanities as my father was in the courtroom. Her unyielding quest for knowledge and refusal to be marginalized to a lesser role as a female were unparalleled for the time. Apart from serving at Cambridge University as an adjunct professor, she directed both privately and governmentally funded excavations and procurements in the UK and beyond. Educated, accomplished, and notoriously minimalistic, when probed about her origins she became somewhat elusive, often answering with a quote from the Alexandrian philosopher Plotinus when he was asked the same:

"My birth, that is, the occasion of the descent of my immortal soul into this embarrassingly corruptible vessel, was—like all human births—a moment of ineffable catastrophe and won't bear discussion." Her delivery was enchantingly warm rather than curt.

She was masterful at gaining the information needed from interactions without leaving her own footprints behind, not unlike her vocation, which mandates the least impact on its study. In her appearance, she resembled the quintessential archetype of the 1950s-era professional woman as portrayed by Hollywood. She wore her hair cropped, her clothes tailored; and looking more like an Italian fashionista than an academic, she had an exotic air about her that turned heads wherever she went. That's exactly how I remember her.

The serendipitous meeting of my parents occurred in the fall of 1955 at a museum fundraiser in Chicago. She was a guest speaker invited over from Europe to discuss the importance of private funding and ethics in antiquities procurement. My father's appearance was a last-minute decision after a grueling week of corporate litigation in Manhattan. Earlier that year, Dad had successfully defended the museum in federal court against the Smithsonian Institution, and upon receiving the invitation with my mother's photo and bio, he knew. Rushing to the airport, he barely made the five p.m. flight out of New York. From the moment they met in an encounter he later described as an event of "instant attraction" when they were introduced at the VIP cocktail soiree, their eyes never wandered far from one another.

They spent the balance of the weekend together in the city, and from then on they were inseparable. Within months they were married, and she became a global consultant for humanities and antiquities. Dad segued from the lifeless grind of Wall Street to Washington, DC, where he worked as an adviser to several federal agencies, one of which included legal oversight of US conservation and land trusts. The change offered each the opportunity to work remotely in a pre-internet age, and when my mother became pregnant with Carol in 1956, they broke from the Eastern skyline, selecting Seattle, Portland, and San Francisco as the top contenders.

It was while making the exploratory trip out West that they stopped in Pole Pass to visit my ailing grandfather and essentially never left. During the visit, he made a casual reference to a proposed Native cultural center that was to be built on a parcel of tribal land several miles outside of town. Perhaps my mother's nesting instincts were enhanced by the pregnancy, but remarkably, mention of the Center was all it took to change her mind about their relocation. My father, however, was more reluctant about a return to his launching pad to raise a family of his own. Pole Pass was certainly a nice mountain town with much in the way of potential. The educational and other social systems had been recently updated, crime in the region was the lowest in the state as measured by population percentages, and the beauty of the area was indisputable. His primary concern was convenience; prior to construction of the West Valley airport terminal, travel options were limited and cumbersome.

My mother didn't disagree, but in the end, he knew that they were going to be living in Pole Pass. Her closing point was that my grandfather should have a baby—or two—around, and it might bring him some joy and happiness during his last years. Dad officially conceded. At my grandfather's urging, they moved into the family home on Main Street "at least until Louisa recovers," he said. They had barely settled into life in the Pass when my mother, now eight months pregnant with Carol, charged ahead, requesting a meeting with the tribal leaders. It would be two weeks before they could gather at the tribal offices, and she spent that time pulling together as much local history as possible.

Not one to mince words, she offered her expertise to the project immediately, following formal introductions and the review of her credentials. Slightly dismissive, they explained that the undertaking was in its infancy, and the tribal committee had yet to conduct the examinations necessary for the motion to be carried before the tribe. However, with her résumé and the fact that she was married to a respected local of tribal bloodline, they agreed to review her proposal if she put one forth. This excited her—so much that she experienced her first contraction.

The men in the room helped her to a sofa, where Chilok, the tribal historian, kept her calm while they arranged for medical transport from tribal lands to Pass County Hospital. Chilok, an experienced midwife, was taking her pulse while gently rubbing her belly when contraction number two arrived, followed by her water breaking.

Chilok leaned in: "It's going to be OK, this baby girl is coming. She wants out, Louisa, and we are going to see that you both have a wonderful birth."

"I'm having a girl?"

"Oops, dammit, I did it again," Chilok muttered, realizing what she had done.

"The ambulance is on its way, Miss Chilok!" shouted a young man running into the room.

"Thank you, now call her husband and get him here, *now!*" she ordered.

"Yes ma'am."

"John!" Chilok yelled, calling Chief Red Horse by his first name. "Call the clinic and tell them we are having a baby in this office! That doctor needs to get his butt over here pronto and bring whatever and whoever he needs with him, because he's going to be delivering this one!"

"I'm having a girl?"

"Yes, honey, you are. But try to relax and don't push just yet."

A minute later, contraction number three came.

"We are in labor, people! Where's that sorry doctor?"

"I'm here, Auntie!" came a voice from behind, as Chilok's nephew, Dr. Dale Winter Fox, and his nurse rushed into the room, trailed by two men rolling a gurney full of equipment, blankets, and towels. Minutes later, Mom was in a gown, had an IV drip, and was connected to a portable monitor.

"Nice job, nephew!" Chilok said, pinching his cheeks with both hands. "Oh, by the way, she's having a girl."

"So she says—I guess that means you did it again, huh? Geez, Auntie, you get so excited."

"I know—I can't help myself."

"OK, folks, we are getting ready to have this baby," Dr. Dale announced. "Louisa, I'm going to give you something for the pain—"

"No thank you, Doctor. I want this experience. Chilok, will you please hold my hand?"

"Of course, my dear."

"I can feel her moving around inside me."

"OK, then, let's breathe together, you and I."

"All right."

"Very good, Louisa, how do you feel?"

"I-I-I think it's time."

"Then you push and you breathe, and you push and you breathe, and you push and you breathe, slow and steady, until she comes to us."

In three pushes, out she came, a healthy baby girl, soon to be named Carol Venus Lawe. Dad arrived minutes later, sliding sideways into the gravel parking lot, leaving the car running and the door open as he burst into the office, out of breath and elated. Mom's vitals were normal, and true to her nature, she thought she might get up and walk around with her baby girl.

"Oh no you don't, Louisa. You are going to the hospital with the nurse and the nice paramedics that just pulled up in their brand-new ambulance," ordered my dad.

The paramedics and nurse spoke with Dr. Dale and then checked Mom's signs again before transferring her onto the gurney. The prenatal nurse who accompanied the paramedics gave Carol a quick once over and commended everyone on a great job delivering the baby, joking that perhaps they should take obstetric team shifts at the hospital.

The aftermath of Carol's birth was the first time my dad witnessed my mother not working on one task or another. Giving birth seemed to have a mesmerizing effect, and she was consumed with getting the early stages of motherhood right. Her intuition had been correct about my grandfather. He was beside himself with the new family member, reenergized by the whole affair. As he cooked the meals, went shopping, and did the laundry, his ailments took a back seat to the new family member's presence at home.

He was the first to the crib if she cried out early in the morning, absconding with her to his oak rocker in front of the large stone fireplace, where he whispered softly and rocked her back to sleep. That was the spot where Mom found them early one winter's morning, both fast asleep in the warmth of the fire, but on this occasion only one would awaken.

The loss of my grandfather was difficult, as the juxtaposition of life and death were played out so acutely and yet inevitably. Feelings that had long been dormant were aroused, bringing with them a layer of sadness necessary to release the pain hidden away for years. In my mother, it evoked emotions cataloged away since the passing of her own parents, while my father had to contend with words that had been left unsaid and would now always be, at least on this plane.

My parents found a degree of solace in the last months with him, and Dad was forever grateful to Mom for sensing his father's unspoken need to have a baby around during his last season. That was a true gift.

7

DIRTY DEEDS

Following the funeral, Mom refocused on the Cultural Center. Her work on the project returned life to the house, helping them shift into the new phase. Contacting several museum curator friends and private collectors of Pacific Northwest tribal artifacts, she painted a grand picture of the Cultural Center and confidently made her requests for exhibit loans and donations. When the tribal leaders saw her productivity and reviewed the operational drafts she had developed, they presented her with a financial offer, which she respectfully declined. Instead, she asked if the funds might be directed toward the hire of two tribal members with whom she had been discreetly meeting over the past month. The Tribal Council was happy to accept these terms, and the first hire was our godmother Chilok. She possessed more historical tribal knowledge than anyone else, and Myra Three Moons joined soon afterward.

As point person for the architectural spirit of the design, my mother knew that further clarity was required regarding the westward expansion of pioneers and the "seizing" of these Native lands by the US government. This was of course an unpleasant part of the story, but in her vision, it should be reflected in some way within the structure itself.

The first step was to review the finer details of the treaty signed between the tribe and the federal government. She reviewed the tribal copy but now wanted the federal file, so Dad asked his clerk in Washington, DC, to send a copy. The treaty was a four-page compact ratified on August 15, 1848, ceding all rights, within the determined area of 175,000 acres, to the US government. In exchange for the cooperative and peaceful transfer, the tribe was given proper deed to 400,000 acres of reserved land. Tribal members were also permitted access to the public facilities, doctors, medicine, and protection under the law as afforded to all citizens. Curiously, this document was ratified by Congress and signed by President Polk within the year of draft; typically the process took twice that. After reviewing the paper, my mother tossed it on the table, disgusted. A quick-trigger activist lurked behind her usual tempered analytical demeanor, and once her injustice button was pushed, she transformed into a charging bull protecting its pasture.

"You know these people had their land stolen from them," she pronounced.

"Yes, of course they did, Louisa; fundamentally, they were all victimized by an insatiable appetite for land and resources in the guise of progress. But this . . . this is oddly much better than other treaties I have reviewed. At least the land in exchange was fertile, and we have inarguably reaped the rewards from it. Before you fly off the handle too far, you may want to examine the atrocious treaties regarding the Cherokee nation, or review the Hellgate and other so-called confederated tribal treaties of the 1850s."

Dad then noticed his clerk's handwriting at the bottom of the last page and turned the document over as he read aloud: "Deed amended and a notation of public to private land transfer dated Monday, August 21, 1848, giving clear title to a 12,000-acre parcel of land, to the Northern Passage Land & Title Company. Sale price $7500. *FYI—Dan, I really had to dig for this one, it was buried between map drafts of the formation of the Oregon Territory, probably hasn't seen daylight since originally filed sometime in 1848–49.*"

"Well, they obviously knew about the gold and copper . . . then struck a deal with the politicians to fleece the indigenous population, and turned this place into a mining town," Mom continued on her diatribe.

"Yeah, I mean yes, but wait a second; this is interesting," said my father.

It was common knowledge to those who grew up in Pole Pass, or met Reginald Harrison III, that the original credited town Founders were the original partners in Northern Passage Land & Title. They consisted of Zeke Adams, Caleb Butterfield, Reginald Harrison, and Stein Lister.

Their signatures were present on the document along with those of a few federal officials. But there was another that occupied a witness line, and this signature belonged to my great-great-great-grandfather Townsend Jacob Lawe.

8

TOWN FOUNDATIONS

Jake, as he was called after moving West, was an enigmatic figure. Little was known other than what had been handed down through the family. My relationship to him was unique, in that we shared a name and a birthday. He was born in London on May 24, 1791, his father a barrister, his mother an only child who died of an infection after giving birth. When Jake was ten years old, his father made arrangements for him to immigrate to the New World and live with relatives in the state of Virginia for his rearing and further education. After graduation from William and Mary, Jake worked for the family attorney in Philadelphia. In October 1821, Jake arrived at Fort George in Oregon Country, where he took a job with the Hudson Bay Company and eventually set out on a series of treks accompanying trapper brigades throughout the region. He later settled in what would eventually become Pole Pass and established his legal practice as the Title Mine was discovered.

Jake married a Native woman, which a few people of both cultures didn't appreciate. The most outspoken of them was one of the town Founders, Stein Lister. The story went that the level-headed sheriff of the town intervened in what was about to be a duel. The lawman suggested that the two men play a hand of blackjack rather than killing someone over a difference of opinion. The stakes were Lister's newly constructed homestead on the outskirts of town and his future silence on the issue, versus Jake and his family departing Pole Pass for good. Each player was dealt his two cards, one up and one down. Lister flipped his down card over and stuck with his king and queen, brandishing a smug look that the Listers are still known for. Jake coolly revealed his pair of sevens and took a hit. The shock of seeing three sevens spread across the table wiped the smug off of Stein and the rest of the Listers' faces. Stein flipped the card table over and went for his gun, but the sheriff jammed the barrel of his peacekeeper in Lister's ear, prompting him to reconsider reneging on a fair game of chance. During the commotion, however, one of the Listers' trigger-happy lackeys drew and was shot dead by a deputy, but not before his errant shot grazed Jake across the back. As per the terms of the wager, Lister had to keep his mouth shut and build another house.

When Dad saw the signature on that land transfer, it made him question our family involvement in the history of the Pass. How could someone who married a Native woman and was willing to fight to the death for her be party to a deal like this? In his eyes, it crossed a moral boundary, but without further information, it left my parents guessing. Since this was a post-treaty document, it was doubtful that the tribe knew our family name was involved in a manipulation that divested them of certain wealth. In the end, my parents felt that helping the Cultural Center become a reality was an opportunity to set some of this right, and they tabled the discussion seventeen years ago.

"All water under the bridge now," Dad said as he wrapped up the tale, but I knew him well enough—this still gnawed at him.

I was grateful that he had finally opened up about my mother in more detail, and he seemed to enjoy recounting the stories as well. Over the next few months, as we marked off the days on the calendar until Carol's return home for Christmas vacation, I learned to accept the building of a legal vocabulary while Dad agreed to broaden his understanding of biology. Occasionally we would land on a subject of common interest, like history. With the earlier questions about Jake Lawe looming in the background, we discussed another local puzzle.

The first recorded visits to the Pass were in the 1520s. A French duo consisting of famed explorer Jean Baptiste Renault and his Northern Territory fur-trapper guide, Jacques Dubois, conducted trade at the Pass for two consecutive summers. Renault portrayed these particular natives in his journal as non-hostile, exhibiting vibrant artwork, textiles, and patterns, distinctive from other tribes in the vicinity or any they had encountered in his travels. The tribe called this land Skagit, interpreted as "hidden from enemies." Even today, it is apparent why. The manner in which the two main peaks offset each other makes the Pass almost invisible if one is traveling east to west.

Looking west from East Valley (left)
and east from West Valley, c. 1840.

The duo returned in 1526 for a third summer of trade, only to discover "*le nid vide*" ("the empty nest"). The tribe had abandoned the area, leaving no trace of their previous habitation or clue as to a future destination. The team traded for a remnant piece of artwork with a local medicine man, who had received it from this tribe. That was Renault's final mention of the elusive group in his journal, except that the neighboring tribes refused to discuss the former inhabitants.

9

A HISTORY OF MYSTERY

The Cultural Center possessed the only known artifact in existence from the mysterious tribe encountered by Renault and Dubois. The piece was displayed only on high-traffic weekends or for special celebrations, and Carol once told me that our mother had something to do with its procurement. When I asked Dad to tell me more, he recommended that I bring it up to Chilok and Myra during my meeting the following week; they had been present when it was received, and according to him, there was much more to the story than he could tell.

I stood in the quiet chill of a Saturday morning on Main Street, waiting for Chilok and Myra to arrive. The first snow of the season had fallen the night before, adding a quaint flair to the shops decorated in their fall motifs. There in the cold, it crossed my mind that due to the weather, Chilok might not make it in that morning, but then Myra pulled up with her in a 4x4 that had definitely seen better days. I greeted the two women and helped Chilok from the vehicle. "Oh, please don't fuss over me, Town," she said, as I held her arm while we walked up the snow-covered steps to the Center. Myra let out a laugh and advised, "She says that, Town, but you stop fussing over her and see what happens."

"Your Aunt Myra knows me well," Chilok snickered.

Myra unlocked the front door, and the three of us entered the warmth of the Cultural Center, making our way toward Chilok's office, where we were greeted by the smell of freshly brewed coffee, as Myra had thoughtfully set up the automatic coffeemaker the night before. I was not normally a coffee drinker, but it smelled so good that I accepted the offer to join them for a cup. We had just sat down in Chilok's office when Myra began telling the story of the mysterious artifact.

"On the day the shipment arrived, your mother used a socket wrench to unscrew the bolts securing the lid of the wooden shipping crate. The larger crate contained three smaller versions, sized for their own contents. These new arrivals came all the way from the rural English countryside, courtesy of a friend of hers, whose family had been avid collectors of 'New World' indigenous artifacts. I cataloged each piece as she unpacked it, listing the tribal information necessary to contact the rightful nation for repatriation after a brief showing at the Center. The first item was a beautiful Blackfoot war bonnet perfectly preserved. The next was a finely crafted Tlingit ceremonial rattle of a raven and kingfisher. Finally, there was a very old Kwakiutl mask depicting a wild woman.

"Your mother glanced down into the crate and looked over at me with a curious expression. She scanned the manifest again and then swept both hands through the straw until she found a smaller container secured in the corner. I remember her excitement like it was yesterday. The object was identified in the manifest as acquired from the Renault-Dubois team. This had to be the piece mentioned in the journal, we hoped. She removed the vessel from its small crate and placed it on the table. We didn't know what to make of it. Your mother was the first to voice her concern over its provenance. Her initial thought was that perhaps the donor might have inadvertently pulled the item from the wrong collection.

"In spite of our confusion, the craftsmanship and material used in the piece were far different than anything either of us had seen before from North American First Nations people. Your mother said that she had encountered this technique used once before on similar material, but not in this hemisphere and much older. She went straight to the phone and called the donor. Years earlier, the man's great-grandmother told him that the item in question had come from America and that it was acquired directly from Renault the explorer in 1524. He referred to the meticulous records that his family kept and read to her directly from the ledger. The piece had been received in a tribal trade from a medicine man, on Niimíipuu land, but from an unknown tribe. The date was August 1523, and the item was described as a medium vessel, with marked bottom.

"The donor explained that it was common for Renault to hock items from time to time for financing purposes, and this particular piece originally had a note of credit attached. Renault never returned for the collateral. He died suddenly and left no heirs. The item had remained in the family collection ever since. Now, as the sole heir of the collection, the donor had come to a place of conscience, one that insisted he return these items to their rightful communities. We were even more baffled after your mother hung up the phone. We both knew that if anyone could confirm that this piece was part of a local tribe, it would be Chilok."

Chilok said, "They found me in the library here at the Center, where I was reviewing student artwork as part of a big contest. Your mother handed me the vessel, and I put on my magnifiers to carefully study it. I told them it definitely wasn't anything I had ever seen from us or other tribes. Then Louisa asked me to review the symbol on the bottom. When I turned it over and saw the image, I was shocked. I stared at it intently, almost becoming catatonic. I gathered myself and said I had seen a similar marking when I was a little girl. The memory was blurry, and maybe I was blending events together, but I would try hard to remember. They didn't want to push me, so they just asked that I think about it over the next week or so, you know . . . to see if any memories returned.

"When your mother and Myra arrived at work early the next morning, I was already here and greeted them with a big grin and a fresh pot of coffee. You should have seen their faces light up when I told them that I had dreamed about the mark and its location. I knew it was out in the country and saw it while picking berries with my grandparents. It was a long time ago, but I believed we could still find the spot. Our coffee wasn't even finished before we hopped into Myra's new truck and headed out onto the tribal lands."

Myra said, "I followed Chilok's driving instruction, or instructions as it were, and after several false starts, dead ends, and turnarounds, we arrived at a cutoff from one gravel road to a washboard dirt version. This was deep into our lands, but Chilok was absolutely sure that it was the way. 'Go right! Go right!' she insisted. So I turned onto a road that was barely that. It clearly hadn't been used often, if at all, over the past several decades. Potholes that could swallow a Volkswagen bug, islands of tall grass, and five-foot-tall tree-shoots growing randomly through the trail created a slalom course, making for a slow, nauseating ride. After traveling about a half-mile, we came to another dead end. Louisa and I resigned ourselves to failure, and I was about to shift into reverse and begin a three-point turn, when Chilok said, 'This is it! Go here!' pointing uphill toward an overgrown 30-degree pitch through the trees. 'What, with the truck?' I replied. 'Yes, yes, you can make it! Go, go!' she urged me. I shifted into 4Lo, and we began a slow climb through the trees. The overhead cedar bows reached across the trail toward each other, occasionally sweeping up the windshield like brushes at a car wash. About a third of a mile up, the thick canopy suddenly broke open to a rolling alpine meadow.

"On our right was a gentle uphill slope leading to the base of a lengthy ridgeline about a half-mile in the distance. To the left, a meadow fell away sharply to the thick forest that cordoned the meadow. We headed up toward the mountains and soon came in sight of a stand of cascading thimbleberry bushes spanning the entire length of the base. 'I knew it! This is the place!' Chilok said triumphantly, as she started out of the vehicle before I had a chance to stop. It hadn't changed much in sixty years, according to her, and now more determined than ever, she marched ahead with us trailing.

"We searched for almost three hours scrutinizing anything that looked remotely out of place on the rocks. I remember that my eyes were getting so fatigued that they began to cross, when I noticed that Chilok wasn't with us. Then we heard her yell from around a small outcropping: 'Hey! I found it! I found it! Right here! Hurry up, you two!' We carefully made our way over the rocky terrain as she peeled back a sagebrush plant from the granite rock face, and there it was. Faded, but Chilok had found it. 'I knew my dream was true!' she said."

Chilok interjected, "I told them that my grandparents and I were picking berries down below and I got bored. I started climbing up the rocks, playing a game pretending that I was a lone scout. My grandparents were mad because I had ventured off without letting them know. They hollered for me, and I didn't hear them, and when I did show up, they beat my butt, rightly so. I had been gone for two hours and it was getting late. I didn't even tell my grandparents what I had seen; it was like I had forgotten all about it until I saw that mark on the bottom of that vessel. Sorry to interrupt you, Myra, please continue."

"Not at all . . . then Louisa poured some water from her canteen onto the surface of the image, clarifying it as the water ran through the design. It was worn from years of exposure but still legible, remarkably complex for a petroglyph that was supposedly hand-tooled into granite. It appeared to be a match to the image on the vessel, more than likely produced by the same people group."

"Was there anything else?" I asked. "Like other signs?"

"Not that we found, and believe me, we looked," Myra replied.

"Could you tell how old it was?"

"It was protected by a small ledge that had eroded over time, a clue that the glyph, with its degree of wear, was much older than something exposed directly to the elements, and definitely far older than the Renault and Dubois expeditions into the area."

"Did you ever figure it out?"

"Louisa didn't say it at the moment but told us later that, considering the wear to the image in a sheltered location, she suspected it could easily be more than ten thousand years old."

"Whoa."

"We took photographs and made a relief etching, but the afternoon was fading, and to avoid driving out in the dark, we started back to the truck. Chilok was also beginning to tire as the adrenaline wore off, and it wouldn't be good if something went awry and we had to camp with her overnight. The sun was halfway behind the western range, leaving the meadow awash in an orange glow as we arrived at the truck. There was just enough light to see our tracks in the meadow grass as we drove toward the tree line. Without any warning, Chilok suddenly grabbed hold of my shoulder from the passenger seat, scaring the hell right out of me. She yelled, 'I remember something else my grandparents told me after my punishment for running off! They said that this place is not for us after sundown! This is the valley of the Ancients! It's the realm of the spirits! We can't be here, Myra, we have to go now!' 'We are going now!' I told her. 'Well, go faster then!'

"The sun was just a sliver peeking out behind the western ridgeline with maybe a minute before it disappeared behind the curtain of mountains. Then Louisa grabbed me from the back seat, scaring me again! 'Myra, where is the exit, where's the gap in the trees? I can't see it anymore!' 'I don't know!' I said, 'it was right in front of us a second ago!' Suddenly I saw what I thought were our inbound tire tracks and yelled for your mother and Chilok to hang on as I punched the gas and drove through what now appeared to be a solid wall of brush at the edge of the meadow. The tree branches made an awful sound when they scraped along the sides of my truck as we careened down the steep grade in complete darkness. I downshifted and braked, but it was too late. *Bam!* We bounced off a big fir tree with the driver's side door, leaving the mirror swinging against the side, and the impact bucked us over to the right of the tree line. We clipped the passenger-side rear quarter panel, and I stopped just before we slammed head-on into a massive cedar tree. 'Shit! Shit! Shit!' I yelled.

"Thankfully, with the exception of my truck, we were OK, and slowly made our way down the mountain. The three of us agreed that the journey and our discovery should not be disclosed until we had a chance to conduct more research for ourselves. The last thing we wanted was for the so-called authorities or any treasure hunters traipsing around Native lands to contaminate the site. So we made a pact to keep it within the Tribal Council."

As she finished up the story, Myra walked over to a large totem carved of natural cedar standing in the far corner of the office. It was perhaps nine feet tall and must have weighed several hundred pounds, judging by its girth. She easily slid it forward a foot or so, revealing a safe concealed in the floor of Chilok's office. After opening it, she produced a small crate, along with a large envelope, and brought them over to us. Chilok handed out white gloves, and Myra removed the vessel from its enclosure, placing it atop a felted carousel that was on the table. I had seen what was left of the artifact on a field trip back in elementary school; I remembered that it amounted to a small handful of shards from what was once a cylindrical cup made of dark limestone with a scribed pattern. The exhibit also included an artistic rendering of what it supposedly looked like intact. The object now sitting in front of us was not what I saw that day.

"I don't understand."

"Town, what the public sees on display is obviously not what we uncrated that day," Myra explained. "They see a prop, an unfortunate but necessary precaution."

"But why?"

"We were advised by your parents to protect this, and the location of the glyph, from the Smithsonian, as well as other interests that are less than benevolent. We created the myth of an accident here in the museum, where the piece was pulverized, and then we substituted fragments from another non-cataloged piece that dates from around the same time period as Renault."

Still perplexed, I began to examine the object in front of me. Six inches tall and three inches across, it was crafted out of a single piece of black rock, the same as the basalt I would find in our own river. This was cylindrical, in the shape of a simple cup, but the execution of its tolerances was so exacting, down to what appeared to be the micron. I couldn't work out how someone four hundred or more years earlier could have created it without a lathe and a bit hard enough to fabricate this stone with such precision.

When I turned it over, I saw the symbol that started the quest for Chilok's glyph. It was an advanced geometrical design so intricate that it appeared to have been cut into the rock with a laser. It was also in relief, making its craftsmanship even more boggling. I questioned whether it would be possible to re-create the piece today. Myra opened the envelope and produced a series of eight-by-ten photographs that were taken at the glyph site the day the trio had been there. I studied each of them closely. The mark on the bottom of the cup and the glyph were a match, but something else caught my attention. A small mark above the glyph itself . . . it could have been a chip, or a shadow, but it appeared to be a perfect half-circle. In two of the photos, a tape measure was across the image, recording its height and width, and I asked Chilok for a ruler, to measure the image on the cup. The proportions were the same, but the glyph was an exact double in size.

Chilok and Myra sat silently for a moment, waiting for the gears of my mind to stop turning.

Then Myra said, "Town, we understand that this comes as a surprise, but it was in the best interests of the tribe and the tribal lands to keep this quiet. Shortly after the discovery, a tribal member carelessly mentioned the glyph while in town. We began getting phone calls from locals and then every agency imaginable requesting access to tribal lands to review the site. It didn't take long until the trespassing started, and Sheriff Running Bear had his hands full. Tribal members were putting up 'Trespassers will be shot on sight' signs all over their property and the surrounding lands. We had to put a stop to it before someone got killed. Our official story was that there had been a mistake, and someone simply mistook natural erosion as something else, that was all. Just like seeing a face in the clouds or a savior in a sandwich. It was only pareidolia and nothing more. Fortunately, we never revealed the location of the glyph, not even to Red Horse, but that first week we weren't as discreet about its existence within the tribe, and you know people love to talk, especially Tribal Council members."

"Why are you telling me all of this now?" I asked, gingerly setting the artifact back on the carousel.

"You wanted to know the story," Myra replied, "so we believe that it is your time. After all, it's just as much yours as it is ours."

I picked up the vessel once more, this time paying closer attention to the small bevel that went around the rim and the base. I took the ruler and stood it vertically against the side of the cup on the table and used the straight edge of one of the photographs perpendicularly to eyeball the angle.

"Do you have a protractor?" I asked Myra. She returned shortly with the tool, and the pot to refill our coffees. After applying the protractor, I concluded, "Both bevel angles are just slight of 52 degrees; it would be cool if it were 51.8."

"Is that significant?" Myra asked.

"To this piece, I don't know. It is the same slope angle used to build the Great Pyramid."

"In Egypt?"

"Yes. There's a lot of fascination with pyramid power at the moment. I think it's interesting, that's all. Probably just an artistic decision, but with something this unique, we should pay attention to every detail, right? I'll have to do some research and report back."

"You really sound more like your mom every day, Town," Myra said, while Chilok just smiled.

When I returned home that morning, I made a crude sketch of what I had seen, adding my initial thoughts. Several things occurred to me, but a few things intrigued me beyond its mystifying construction. The geometry contained a puzzle, or a message. The relief-style carving reminded me of the rubber ink stamps we made in school, or a metal signet that would be pushed into cooling wax to leave one's mark. Of course my morbid self entertained the idea that it could be a cup that was filled with sacrificial blood and consumed, or dipped and stamped on the participants' bodies in some murderous ritual, but that was a little much even for me.

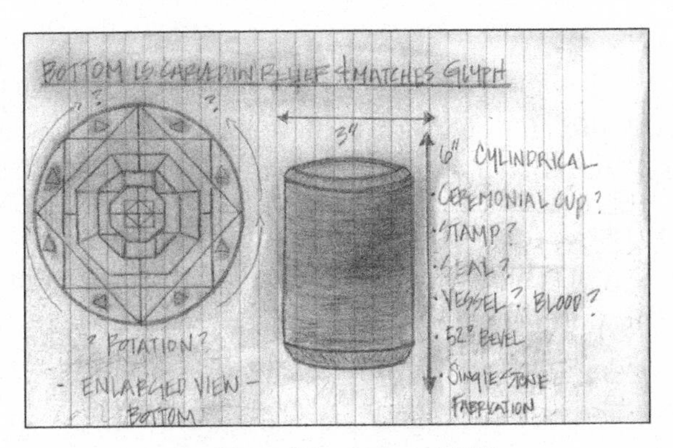

Artifact, November 1975.

10

DECIDED DECISIONS

I showed Dad the sketch, and he said he thought it was a decent rendition of what he remembered, which wasn't much.

"I let many of those memories fade away with the passing of your mother. It was necessary to get through the pain that flooded the vacuum of her absence."

"Does seeing this bother you now?"

"Not really. Time has a way of moving us down the river of life. It's a balance of embracing and releasing, like the ebb and flow of the tide. All part of our survival mechanism."

"Do you still miss her? I mean, feel the pain of her not being around?"

"Town, some of the unpleasant things in this life will remain with us as long as we walk around in these bodies. They teach us, they remind us, about what it is to be human. We can't run away from those experiences forever.

This was something that your mother taught me when your grandfather passed away."

"Oh, I see."

"I never considered I would be using that exact lesson to handle the despair I felt when she left us so suddenly. In retrospect, I believe she was preparing me for her own transition."

"I don't remember much about her passing," I said, leaving an opening.

"I'm confident that you will when it's time." Dad left the conversation at that point, putting an end to our discussion.

Carol's first Christmas home after leaving for Yale was highly anticipated. Though her departure had been only a little over four months earlier, it felt like she had been gone twice that. When Carol arrived, I noticed something different—she looked more grown up, and I swear a bit taller. Dad was excited to have his protégée home for a two-week stint, and he didn't waste a second getting every detail of her first semester. I also realized something else that first night: Carol brought home her feminine energy, another aspect that Dad and I didn't realize was lacking until she refilled the house with it.

The initial evenings of her homecoming were occupied with our playing Scrabble long after Dad went to bed. We talked a lot about what she was experiencing at college and how it differed from primary education.

"Everyone, I mean everyone that I have met so far, is driven. No coasting. It's very competitive, but in a good way. You won't have to worry, Dad has prepared us well, and you'll be fine if you keep your studies up. Have you decided on your major?" Her question held a different tone than when she used to ask. It was much more nonthreatening than the voice of the strident academic taskmaster I remembered her being around this topic.

"Not yet; I'm still split between archaeology and molecular biology."

"Both are great fields of study. I'm sure you'll figure it out when the time comes. Whichever you choose will be the right decision."

I thought to myself, *Who is this girl?* Certainly, not the one I had lived with for fifteen plus years. Then suddenly it clicked! This was what awaited me at college: independence. Such freedom came with the responsibility to live out my choices, to enjoy or to endure the consequences of my decisions. The feeling was similar to when I was five-and-a-half years old and she took her hands off the back of my bicycle for the first time. She clearly saw the light go on and gave me a wink before laying down the winning Scrabble tiles. That brief exchange prompted me to finally resolve my double-mindedness around the issue.

Virginia made the drive down from Coeur d'Alene to spend a few days with her mother, Eve, and to stay with us that Christmas night. During our evening Scrabble tournament under the twinkle of Christmas lights, I deduced the fact that her rigorous class schedule left zero time for social engagements, and when Carol and Dad teased me openly about my pronounced interest in her activities, both received kicks under the table, but not before I felt the redness cover my face.

"Is it warm in here?"

"I think you're right, Carol, Town's face is red."

"Yeah, Dad, I think I see some sweat too. Virginia, you're in pre-med—what do you make of it?" Carol asked, going for my jugular.

Without missing a beat, Virginia took my hand and said, "According to my training, I believe that Town is exhibiting all the signs of a perfectly healthy, and might I add very handsome, young man."

Her diagnosis and accompanying smile unintentionally drove my blood pressure through the roof, but the cool, dry touch of her hand and caring wit were worth it. When the girls announced that they were turning in for the evening, Dad motioned for me to linger as he stepped out of the room. I flopped down on the sofa across from the Christmas tree, curious as to what was on his mind. He returned seconds later from his study with a small neatly wrapped present and handed it to me. He sat silently as I carefully unwrapped the gift, finding it to be an old leather book about the size of an average paperback novel, with a simple clasp. Its cover was well worn and stained; it had yellowed pages of heavy stock that felt thick to the touch.

"She wanted you to have this at the right time. It's full of her writings and observations, some which never made sense to me, but she once told me they would to you." It was my mother's archaeology notebook.

"I thought as you approach deciding how you want to continue your education, it might be helpful to have the notes of an actual archaeologist to refer to."

"Yes, sir. I don't quite know what to say . . ."

"I can see that you are happy—that's better than words."

"Thank you, Dad, and Merry Christmas."

"On behalf of your mother, you are welcome, son, and Merry Christmas to you. She loved you dearly, you know, as do I."

Dad quickly left the room, saying goodnight, and headed for bed. I knew that he was as choked up as I was about the presentation.

~

Over the next year and a half, I paged through Mom's handwritten notes. The journal was densely packed with information: specific digs, sketches, cryptic writings in foreign languages—she spoke seven—and it soon became clear that this was a long-term puzzle to decode, not a Reader's Digest guide to archaeology. Despite my periodic wrestling matches with the book, and my love for the mysteries of human origins and lost civilizations, I finally made the decision to declare myself as a molecular biology major. The choice surprised some who knew of my penchant for exploration, but the study of our biological origins fascinated me just as much, and I didn't feel that I was betraying my mother's memory in taking this route. I also saw a more lucrative career path and opportunity for resources in the rapidly advancing science.

11

IT COMES IN THREES

When I pulled up to the house after school one day in April 1977, I was surprised to find Dad already there. I could tell by the look on his face and the way he greeted me that what he was about to say wasn't good news. I had a sick feeling in my gut, and knowing me well, he preempted my concern.

"Carol is fine, but I do have other tragic news."

"Yes, sir?"

"Sheriff Sam received a courtesy call from the Boise Sheriff's office today. Kincaid LeToure . . . son, I'm so sorry . . . Kincaid is dead."

It was as if my brain had shut off; I couldn't process what I was hearing. I hadn't thought much about Kincaid since he and his folks left Pole Pass for Boise.

"When? What on earth happened?"

"Today. His father found him; it appears that he hung himself."

The tears came as I began to assimilate what I had just heard, my mind and body frozen in space and time.

"The sheriff said that his parents are inconsolable. They thought he was a little depressed, but he seemed to be doing OK in Boise."

"I'd like to go to the funeral."

"Yes, of course. I'll make sure we are in the loop about the arrangements."

I changed from my school clothes and walked the path down to the swimming pool. As I sat in silence reminiscing about the times we had at this very spot, the unshakable chill of death permeated the heavy Yale sweats that Carol had given me for Christmas. Kin was part of our servant cadre for two great summers and relished attending to the troupe of girls who regally roamed this deck with implied authority. Still in a haze of disbelief, I went numb as it began to soak in. In my mind's eye, I watched us both frolicking in the water, as we did back in the fourth and fifth grades. Cannonballs, can openers, preachers' seats—you name it, we did it; 'the higher the splash, the better' was our mantra. My heart broke for Kin and his parents, and amid the pain, I pledged that I would not forget him.

A week later, Dad and I, accompanied by several kids from the Pass, made the three-hour pilgrimage to a quaint Anglican church that his parents had been attending for the past several months. The feeling was surreal as I sat in the peace of that sanctuary honoring a friend who had been so desperately in need of both. There were many parishioners in attendance but hardly any kids our age, leading me to conclude that Kin had not made many friends since moving here two years before.

The sight of his parents as shells filled by the grief of losing their only son was something I would not soon forget. Losing him to suicide must have added a depth of hell to their suffering that I couldn't fathom. In the receiving line, as I offered my condolences to Kin's folks, his mother pulled me in tight, squeezing me as she sobbed. It was as if I were a surrogate son for a mother needing to hug her child just one last time. I wrapped my arms around her, returning the embrace, and remained there until she let me go. I tearfully told her and Kin's dad that I would never forget Kincaid and that he was a really good kid who would be missed.

After the burial, Dad asked if he could treat the carload to dinner on the way back to the Pass; uncharacteristically for teenagers, we all declined. From the silence during our three-hour return trip, I knew that everyone in the car just wanted to get home to their families and process Kin's sudden departure in their own way. Sleep evaded me that night, when a loop of his parents began to play as soon as my head hit the pillow. I couldn't help but think about what they were going through this evening. I journeyed through the emotions of anger at Kin for taking his life and causing so much pain to others, and then guilt about my thoughts and for not being there for him when he was in need. The poor kid . . . how could he have arrived in a place this dark at sixteen?

I thought about the lack of his Boise classmates in attendance indicating his isolation—self-imposed or otherwise, I couldn't know. Then it crossed my mind that I had not seen many people from Pole Pass there either. I was surprised that Reggie Harrison didn't attend. He and Kin had been good friends from sixth grade until he moved. I just assumed that they had remained in touch. I guess it was possible that Reggie was too torn up to go; regardless, I found it sad for Kin's parents, who clearly needed the support and reassurance that their son was loved and well thought of.

When I told Carol about Kin's death, I heard the silence of shock on the other end of the line before her faltering voice spoke again. She sent the LeToures a heartfelt note sharing her fond memories of Kincaid at our pool and the seasons he spent around our house. As tough as she could be, Carol was always among the most tender-hearted people I knew.

The weeks passed, and those immediate thoughts of Kin fell behind the academic commitments I had made to myself, but the irony that our relationship was in death as it had been in life didn't elude me.

Six weeks of school remained in my junior year, which meant that I was in the final push to complete my college applications. I needed to center myself during these last days to maintain my GPA while gathering the required letters of recommendation for my candidate packet. Carol would not be home to mentor me this summer, as she was staying on the East Coast to work at a YMCA summer camp in Vermont with some school friends. Her mothering nature prevailed, and she did manage to call home once a week to check in on Dad and my application progress. One of those phone calls from Carol brought us more sad news. Virginia's mother had succumbed to a battle with cancer. Eve had been hospitalized in Spokane, just across the border from where Virginia was hunkered down in her pre-med grind. At least she was able to spend the final months with her mother—a blessing, according to Carol.

I asked if I should drive up for the funeral, but Carol said Eve's final wishes had already been carried out. She also shared that Virginia was working through some things and needed privacy as she balanced her grief with pushing through an exhausting schedule of finishing a four-year degree in three. I chose an arrangement of birds of paradise and anthuriums to send with a card expressing our condolences and to make it clear that if she ever needed to come home, she always had one with us. We missed her thank-you call, but I saved the voicemail and played it from time to time to hear her voice.

A few days later on a rare sweltering August day, Dad and I were hanging out at the pool when Sheriff Sam walked through the creaky arbor gate and onto the deck.

"Howdy, men! I saw the cars out front, so when you didn't answer, I figured y'all might be out here trying to stay cool in this heat wave."

"I'll get you a suit and beer, Sam—you can join us."

"Thank you, I really wish I could, but I have a ton a paperwork to finish today. I sure wouldn't mind the distraction, though."

"Sorry to hear that. What's up?"

"I got a wake-up call around three this morning. Someone reported a fire down in the west canyon. You know, it's been so dang dry that I thought some fool threw a cigarette out the window or it was heat lightning, but when I arrived on scene and hiked up to the fire crew, a mangled vehicle was the cause."

"Oh no."

"It plowed through the guardrail at the hairpin and flipped end over end to the bottom of the ravine. Single-occupant fatality is one hell of a way to start off a Saturday morning."

"God, that's awful. Make the ID yet?"

"Yeah, it was the tractor dealership guy in West Valley."

"Marty Nelson-Lister?" Dad asked in disbelief.

"Yep, the guy in the commercials. I've already done the worst part: notifying his daughter, Carla. Poor kid is my own girl's age, for Christ's sake. There are times when I really hate this job, ya know?"

I recalled that incident on the street during my haircut years earlier. The girl's face came back to me as clear as day, making the news feel more personal. "What will happen to his daughter now?" I asked.

"Well, she just turned eighteen, so she'll have to make her own way. The rest of the Listers will watch out for her; they tend to take care of their own," said the sheriff.

Just then, his walkie-talkie shrieked with a nauseating squeal followed by deputy Shug's voice: "Sheriff, we have a 10-103f at the morgue—it's the Listers. Can you get down here right away?"

"10-4, on my way, Shug, and try not to let them destroy anything before I get down there, will ya?"

He turned to Dad and me. "Good Lord, now they're fighting at the morgue of all places! Sorry, guys, I've got to run. Rain check on the pool and beer, though! I'll swing by your office on Monday for a chat; it's regarding the Order."

"OK, I'll see you Monday, Sam. Thanks for coming all the way out here."

"Don't mention it—I needed a nice drive in the country to clear my head. Wish I could stay, but duty calls. Keep cool," he said with a grin and lifted his hat briefly to let some heat escape before heading back to town.

As Sam departed, Dad got up and dove into the pool without a word. Five laps later, he climbed out and gathered his stuff. "All right, I have some work to do. Need anything before I go inside?"

"No, but thanks anyway."

I remained on the pool deck a few more hours, dozing off thinking about Carla and how our one encounter told me she was different than your average Lister. I ventured that even founding families had their black sheep.

Roused by the smell of burgers, I made my way toward the house. The sheriff's mention of the Order reminded me of that conversation in Dad's office four years earlier.

"What is the Order exactly?"

"I like to put the burger on the bottom bun and then dress the top," he chuckled while handing me a plate.

"No, Dad, it's a group or something . . . what you and Sam were just talking about on the deck."

"Oh, that Order. Well, the Order is an abbreviation for a club that the Founders have. They'd like to believe that it's a secret, but it's really not. They have disguised the Order for decades within the shell of another organization called The Fraternal Order of Farmers, aka FOF. You've seen their hall down in West Valley. Many agricultural families in the region, including some tribal members, belong to that organization, and they do a lot of good work through fundraisers for children in need, among other philanthropic endeavors. The man who died in the wreck this morning was the lodge master, or whatever they call it, of FOF. But the Order is a direct-Founder-lineage-only group, known by the insiders as TOM. It's an acronym for 'the Order of the Mine,' and they are pretty cagey about it."

"You mean, the Title Mine?"

"Yes, and then some. You see, the Founders formed the group after the Title Mine pinched in the early 1870s. They believed that old legend of more gold elsewhere in the Pass, and their goal was to harvest it. The activity of the group appears to rise and fall depending on the current generation's interest."

"So, they are pretty much just a club of treasure hunters, then?"

"Yes, but unfortunately ones who feel entitled to trespass onto our tribal lands and federal holdings in their searches. They have defaced and desecrated a lot of sites in their hunt, but so far they have never been caught in the act."

"Do you think they might be active again? Meeting up at the old mine?"

Dad was onto my probing, and his tone got serious: "Look here, Town, if they are, it's on private property, and I really don't want you distracted by this now. Founder nonsense like this has gone on as long as I can remember. I expect you to focus on your upcoming senior year academics. If you promise to do that, I'll keep you in the loop if I hear something. Fair?"

"Yes, sir. More than."

I knew Dad was right, and I intended to hold up my end of the bargain.

Only a few weeks remained of summer vacation, and I had plenty to do before school started. Top of my list was a hike deep into the ancestral forest for a couple of days. I had not visited the spot of my Weyekin since the ceremony, and I knew that a return would be a helpful precursor to my last year at Pole Pass High.

12

THE ANCESTRAL FOREST

My chores were finished by ten o'clock, and I took a ritual dunk in the river to set my intention for the pilgrimage. I recalled the words that Chief John Red Horse told my parents when they received the stewardship of this land: "Beyond this riverbank is an ancient ancestral site. The forest is a very sacred place for all tribal members and one of initiation for elders, chiefs, and medicine men. It is the land of mist, and ancient spirits watch over this place. Daniel and Louisa, this is very important: you must train yourselves and your children to approach them in peace and humility, paying them due respect as you steward this land. In time, they will come to know and accept you as we have."

As I walked into the forest, my scholastic stress and expectations fell farther behind with each step of the three-hour journey. I wasn't in a hurry, and as long as I arrived by two o'clock, I would have plenty of daylight to set up camp. My mind drifted to the stacks of esoteric books I had devoured throughout my youth. By the age of thirteen, I had exhausted the local libraries of their inventory containing alchemy, aliens, astral projection, and anything with a keyword of paranormal. I had also consumed a steady diet of tribal lore over the years, which definitely helped broaden my view of the world. But during my Weyekin, I encountered things in this forest that altered me . . . experiences that blurred my own freehanded lines of reality.

Those eleven days stretched out my consciousness, yielding much more than a rendezvous with my spirit animal that now accompanies me each time I cross the river. The conscious state of being truly grounded in nature opened my eyes to the existence of another world that is all around us—one that each of us can experience if we choose to align ourselves with the proper frequencies.

I made it to the site a little after two and set up camp before gathering the deadfall and other tinder that would kindle my evening fire. Then I set out on a short hike to further clear my mind and open my heart. Sitting next to a small stream, I listened contently to its voice channeled by the water rolling softly over the stone-strewn bed. It was a greeting . . . an invitation to once again coexist with our true nature. The bluebirds came close for a visit, as did a doe and her fawn, also enjoying the tranquility as they drank from the brook only a few yards upstream from where I sat in harmony. Dusk arrives much sooner under the canopy of the forest, and as the light began to fade, I made my return to camp.

Within a circular border of rocks, I added dried grass, sage, leaves, and twigs, making a nucleus of tinder to catch the spark. Thankful for each component as I lay them onto the young flame, I patiently nursed the small fire before incorporating the larger pieces of deadfall, until I was cradled in a sphere of amber light. I unrolled my sleeping bag and sat in silent meditation taking in the pitch of the moonless forest from my cocoon. After adding a bundle of fresh evergreen boughs and white sage to the blaze, I watched the thick fragrant smoke rise toward the heavens, finding its path through an opening in the tree canopy.

Suddenly, a great flash appeared within the column of heavy smoke as the flame inside it took shape. My gaze was transfixed on the figure as it began to communicate with me. Whatever this being was, spirit of the ancients or a dimensional traveler, I don't know. But I held no fear in its presence. When I awoke from this trancelike state, my eyes followed a wisp of smoke skyward to the familiar small bat circling above, as if bidding me farewell by carrying the night to meet the new day. I must have been locked in that position the entire night, and my body felt it. Slowly rising to my feet, I stretched out while trying to remember what had happened after encountering the being. Though frustrated by the lack of recall, I knew I had little choice but to trust that it was for good, I hoped.

After a quick breakfast, I grabbed my compass, charted a southwest course, and set out. As the sun rose, I took in the isolating quality of the dense forest, a place where one could see only fifteen to twenty yards in places, and after an hour of walking at a rhythmic pace, I tied a white T-shirt strip on a western-pointing tree branch and headed in that direction. An hour and a half later, I passed the big rock where I had encountered the Shadow Warriors during my Weyekin.

After following their route through a ravine, I walked for another hour and began gaining elevation as I was joined by a stream, which led to the small pool that was its source.

Climbing what appeared to be natural steps, I found myself standing on a plateau about ten feet above the pool, pausing to look eastward at the terrain I had just scaled. When I turned west, I could see a rocky ridge peeking through the ponderosa pines that were plentiful at this elevation and decided to stop here for a snack before pressing westward toward the ridge. A large trunk of a fallen cedar at the periphery of the plateau made a great backrest as I absorbed the solitude and rich smell of the forest. Watching several chipmunks as they playfully gave chase around the natural obstacles, I soon nodded off deeply enough for a crazy dream. A girl and I were playing tag in the forest, and when I got close, she would turn away so I couldn't see her clearly. I almost caught her, and then I heard Mom whispering in my ear: "Wake up, Town—it's time to wake up, honey," gently stirring me from the nap.

It had been so long that I had almost forgotten the sound of her voice. There was a period between the ages of eight and ten that she would regularly visit me in my room, always sitting on my bed in a warm relucence that was soothing, not alarming, and usually during the last minutes of sleep, in those semiconscious moments. At one point, I told Dad and Carol about these visits, relaying a message from her: "I miss you, your sister, and your father, who is the most lovely man I've ever known." Carol's reaction was to cry and leave the breakfast table; Dad looked over at me and tenderly suggested that it might be best not to mention those dreams in front of Carol for a while.

He came around to my side of the table, put his hands on my shoulders, and kissed the top of my head. As he walked down the hall to check on Carol, I saw him wipe his eyes. I felt so bad that I stopped talking about her appearances. Eventually the encounters with my mother gave way to boyhood dreams of adventure and every season of changing interest that my imagination would conjure. It was comforting to hear her again.

Checking my watch, I saw that I had been sleeping for only about thirty minutes, but it felt like hours. The chipmunks had moved their playground elsewhere, and the forest was now utterly silent. I remained sitting against the cedar, taking in my surroundings while trying to retain the imprint of my mother's voice, when I noticed what I thought was just a couple of moss-covered rocks in front of me; and then more came into focus. I climbed on top of the large tree trunk and surveyed the area. There was a lot of underbrush and small felled trees crisscrossing the plateau, but I detected a design of some sort beneath the debris. I began the process of removing enough deadfall and brush on the periphery to reveal the circumference of a circle. By the time I finished, the afternoon was slipping away, and I had to decide between sleeping here and starting the four-plus-hour return trek to camp. If I didn't leave in a few minutes, I would be trying to find my way back in the darkness of this forest, a feat that I would attempt only in an emergency and under the light of a full moon.

I had barely arrived at my campsite as the blanket of night fell, and I built a fire from the deadfall I had collected the day before. After dinner, I recorded the day's activities in my notebook. Although I had stopped short of my destination, I felt the plateau site was even more important, and knew I'd return there soon.

Sleeping soundly through the night, I found myself back in the dream of chasing the girl through the forest. This time I could hear her giggling as she maintained enough distance to keep her anonymity, and sure enough, when I got close, my mother's voice roused me. "Wake up, Town—it's time to wake up, honey." This time I was a little irritated and said so, but received no reply. Packing my supplies and restoring the site to its natural state, I departed for home, muttering about the dream along the way.

I visited the plateau twice more before school started and cleared the remaining debris from the interior of the twenty-foot-diameter circle. When I finished, I stood up on the tree trunk to review my handiwork and was met with an undulating emerald carpet of moss that reminded me of the velvet drapes in our high school auditorium. With the space cleared, I could make out a definite pattern beneath the surface and also confirm something else: the circle had a gradual slope toward its center. My initial thought was that this might be what some call a medicine wheel; it did have the look of a ceremonial circle of some kind just covered by thick moss. Dreams of the girl returned each night I stayed in the forest, and as before, so did my mother's wake-up calls.

When my senior year began, I didn't expect the pressure that landed on my shoulders. If there was one thing I had never encountered in terms of academic performance, it was a lack of confidence. That is, until now. It must have been the sudden realization that I was playing for all the marbles—my collegiate experience and the life thereafter.

Carol's indication of the consequence of my independence became a fixation. By the end of September, I was worn down from questioning myself at every turn and retreated into daydreaming about the girl in the forest, to find relief.

Without Carol to turn to, I needed to tell Dad that I was struggling and ask him for help, something that I really didn't want to do. Not because he wouldn't be supportive, but because I held a foolish notion that I wanted him to be proud of my ingenuity and fortitude. Dad took my call for help as strength, and his guidance of *doing my best in the moment* dissipated the self-defeating chatter. I thought much less about venturing out into the forest to chase the girl in my dreams and was relieved to return to my academic self in a few weeks' time.

~

After Christmas break, I began driving through the heart of town on my way home from school to collect the mail at the post office. Dad and Bernice understood that I was looking for a certain letter that included a coat of arms in its sender address header. Finally, on January 17, 1978, it arrived. I had a lump in my throat the size of Montana as I hurried across the street to Dad's office. Bernice was banging away on the typewriter and looked up just long enough to read the expression on my face.

"It's here, isn't it? Dan, the eagle has landed!" she announced before I could confirm her suspicion.

Dad rushed to his door, looking out into the main office at Bernice and me. "Well?"

"I'm a little afraid to open it," I choked out, as Bernice handed me a letter opener. My hands trembled a bit as I carefully slid the blade of the opener through the envelope, but I managed; removing its contents, I opened the crisply folded letter and read the results out loud. I was invited to attend Princeton University and join the graduating Class of 1982.

13

SUMMER 1978

A huge sigh of relief accompanied the letter of my acceptance into Princeton. Apart from the educational standards and resources, the insular qualities of the campus and small-town feel best complemented my learning style. Princeton also held a mysterious allure, and somehow I knew I belonged there. The following week, I received the enrollment packet and the terms of my education, but something else arrived: the awareness of my achievement.

I came to appreciate the uniqueness of my invitation to attend the university. Princeton had enchanted me from the time Dad brought home packets of each Ivy League school for Carol and me to dream about, and I worked very hard to get to this point. Yes, I enjoyed the benefit of having influencers in my life who instilled a code of conduct and pointed me in the right direction. I was also identified as an Ivy legacy student. But there was no hiding the fact that I alone made the sacrifices necessary to earn this opportunity. The fruits of my labor had been recognized and rewarded, and thus a goal that had traveled with me since third grade was now accomplished. "Admission," however, meant only that. A long road remained, and I would not take it for granted.

Carol's first words after "Congratulations, Town, I never doubted you!" were "Now, please, just enjoy your last semester of high school, will ya?"

She said it with a laugh, but I knew she was serious. Carol's one regret was that she had shifted into college mode immediately upon her acceptance to Yale and all but lost her last semester at home in the process. I followed the advice and took a scholastic hiatus from anything other than maintaining my high school grades. I spent more time at the Cultural Center assisting Chilok and Myra and did extra work around the land at home. Freeing myself from the myopic academic self-scrutiny allowed a deeper dive into material like my mother's writings, and I'm sure this was a factor in the return of her communication with me.

The visitations now seemed more urgent and regularly crossed over into daylight hours. They were like heat lightning: thunderless flashes of intense radiance as if some invisible curtain parted and closed in a nanosecond, immediately followed by an invasion of thoughts blending into my own, like two radio stations competing for your attention. Priding myself on being a lucid thinker, I was initially annoyed by these intermittent manifestations until I learned how to distinguish them from my own meanderings. Whenever this occurred, I would retreat to our pool if at all possible. Enclosed by twenty-foot-tall hedges of mountain laurel, the deck was a cloister, sequestering me from the overbearing beauty of the surrounding landscape.

This was a place I could drift away in privacy and allow my mind to wander through layers of open thought, recording them as they presented themselves.

On a Thursday morning in mid-May, I felt her words gathering once again, like a subsonic rumble leaking into my consciousness. Deciding to cut my last two elective classes, I headed home at noon to the seclusion of the pool deck.

Changing into shorts, I grabbed a soda, a towel, and my notebook before walking out the kitchen door and heading along the stone path that led to the pool. I was deep in thought, already writing in my mind, as I looked down at each deliberate step taken. Walking past the relaxing scents of honeysuckle and pine, I made a right turn through the rose-covered arbor into the pool area.

As the gate creaked open, I looked up for the first time since leaving the house, only to discover a half-bikini-clad Virginia Tecoi in full stretch, basking in the sun like a lioness on the savannah. We hadn't seen each other in almost a year, but I knew she had aced her pre-med track and scored high on the MCAT. She was also accepted to the University of Washington School of Medicine. Peering over the top of her sunglasses, she casually said, "Oh, Town . . . sorry if I startled you . . . when Carol dropped me off, she told me you wouldn't be home until about three thirty or so," quickly slipping back into her bikini top.

In keeping with the humor of the moment, I responded nonchalantly, "Oh, hi Virginia, no trouble at all, please carry on as if I weren't here." Somehow I managed it without a stammer, but not lacking a grin.

"Well, you really *are* growing up," she chuckled, shaking her head at my conciliatory gesture.

I was now grateful for the grueling workouts I had endured after joining the wrestling team my senior year. The muscle it added to my six-foot frame didn't go unnoticed, or at least that was what I told myself in the moment.

"Been in the water yet?" I asked, heading toward the pool house to fire up the electric sauna.

"Already turned it on, and no way, not until that sauna heats up."

With my original motivation dashed, I pitched the notebook onto the deck and angled a chair toward her chaise as we began to catch up on local happenings and small-town gossip.

Taking notice of the dog-eared copy of *Grey's Anatomy* peeking out of her satchel-style bag, I asked, "So, have you dissected a human yet?"

"Yes, in AP. It was really fascinating; I bet you'd love it."

"Yeah, I think I would. What did you enjoy most about it?"

"Oh, that's easy—it was the screaming."

With her answer, the soda I had just taken a gulp of shot out my nose, as I began coughing and laughing at the same time.

"Just a little cadaver lab humor—you OK there?"

"Yeah, I'll make it. Good one, though!" I coughed out, trying to regain my composure with watering eyes. "Decided which area of medicine you are going to pursue?" I finally got out as my coughing subsided.

"I'm definitely moving toward pediatrics."

As she began to elaborate, I tried to focus on the content of her words, but the brief glimpse of her bare breasts with their soft pink nipples reentered my mind, and soon the words began to float away on the silken thread of her voice before they could quite reach me.

My eyes slowly wandered from her white teeth and full pink lips to the notch of her clavicle and down the delicate centerline between her breasts. I paused for a second to give a casual "Uh-huh" to whatever she was saying and continued along the road of her well-toned abdomen to the top string line of her fuchsia and orange bikini bottom. I would be eighteen next week, and although intellectually mature for my age, I was no match for the testosterone now surging its high-voltage current through my body. This nuisance had the capacity to divert every ounce of blood to a particular appendage at the most inopportune times, a malady that haunts every guy in high school. I sat there fully aware of my maleness, now entranced by the colorful reflection that the conservative triangle of fabric painted against the inside of her thighs. Just as I was thinking it resembled the wings of a butterfly, I detected a faint voice in the distance drawing closer with each repetition of the sentence "What do you think?"

"A butterfly!" I blurted out before I knew what I was saying.

"What?"

Thinking quickly, I recovered with a half-truth: "Sorry, I completely spaced out there. I skipped breakfast this morning, I think just need some lunch."

"Yeah, that's what I've been saying! So, what do you feel like?"

"What about the Triple?" I asked.

The Triple was a local drive-in, famous for three things in Pole Pass: giant burgers, fresh-cut fries, and onion rings. Their root beer floats and fresh fruit shakes were delicious too, but the Triple had a better ring to it than the Quintuple.

"Sounds great—I've been craving it for about a month. I'll buy, you drive!" she insisted.

I panicked. In my current condition, there was no way I could stand up, let alone walk with her back to the house. I took the only escape route available and quickly crossed one leg over the other, spinning counterclockwise into the water. Now, at five thousand feet above sea level, our pool was never actually warm until late August. However, at this time of year, the top two inches were deceptively tolerable. Beyond that depth lurked a temperature about forty degrees colder than the 98.6 my body was accustomed to. Suffice it to say that the ensuing shock yielded the intended results.

Virginia howled while I scrambled out of the pool, unable to speak and trying to catch my breath as I belly-crawled across the deck toward the sauna to melt the ice cube that now encased me. I heard a splash, and seconds later Virginia ran into the heated cedar room with me. Our teeth were chattering, and every muscle tensed as I threw about half a bucket of water onto the hot stones. The whoosh of steam enveloped us like a warm wet blanket, unwinding each muscle instantly. We sat there laughing about it for a couple of minutes, and then she prompted "round two," and off we went, jumping into the icy depths and back into the refuge of the hotbox. More water on the rocks, and with the steam blast we both reclined on the top bench forming a perfect 90 degree angle feet to feet. Five minutes later, our stomachs were both talking. After a quick shower and change, she jumped into my Ford Bronco wearing UW Track and Field sweatpants and companion T-shirt, while I wore my favorite cutoffs and a faded Pole Pass Varsity Wrestling hoodie.

"I think you may need a wardrobe upgrade if you are going to be seen around here with me this summer," she said.

"What?"

"Yeah, I'm staying with you guys until orientation week so I can be ready for the UW course load this fall, no distractions!"

The surprise of her declaration must have registered on my face.

"Didn't anyone tell you?" she asked. "It's OK, right?"

"Of course it is! Mi casa, su casa," I shot back almost defensively.

"Carol said that you might even help me study, since you're the real brains in the house, and I remember you helped her get ready for the first year at Yale. That is, if you have any spare time. I know you probably have a lot of your own things to do as you prepare for Princeton."

Without hesitation I answered, "OK, I know how this can work."

"Yes?"

"This is a quid pro quo arrangement. You have to help me with my studies as well."

"It's a deal, then!" she said, as we ceremoniously shook on it.

Striking an academic bargain with Virginia abated much of the tension that would have been distracting or, in my case, debilitating. I embraced the challenge by immediately putting aside my schoolboy crush and establishing a five-day-a-week study schedule. I was so impressed with her discipline and focus that it created a degree of competition between us. I would coach her Monday and Wednesday, and she would coach me Tuesday and Thursday. Fridays were our quiz days.

The complementary nature of our pursuits and stimulating challenge of preparing and then presenting new material made it clear that we thrived on learning from each other. This cerebral infatuation became such a bonding experience that our relationship evolved from Virginia being my sister's best friend to her becoming mine as well.

Carol was embroiled in her own studies that summer in preparation for the first year at Yale Law. Thanks to Dad, she was completely immersed as he inventively wove her undergrads of Native American History and Political Science into a complementary and practical legal framework. She participated in mock trials litigating everything imaginable to the point of indignation. Dad presided as judge, while Carol alternated between prosecutorial and defense positions for benchmark cases. Virginia and I sat as jury members and produced the verdicts based on the legal instructions from the judge. Many evenings were just the four of us bantering across the dinner table about local history, law, medical sciences, or whatever organically developed.

This particular evening, Dad expressed his consternation over the use of plenary power that was placed like an anvil on the throat of First Nation cultures. The reason for such disgust became evident as he detailed the systematic genocide brought to bear through US government policies like the Major Crimes Act of 1885 and the Dawes Act of 1887. We all sat quietly as he voiced his analysis of the impact.

"When the Supreme Court sustained the federal government's authority over all Indian Nation activity," he began, "it opened the door to much greater carnage. The premise of the Dawes Act insisted that American Indians were incapable of caring for themselves, that they were in fact 'wards of the state,' and therefore it was the all-seeing, all-knowing, and all-powerful federal government's solemn duty to act as their guardians. This degrading philosophy had the support of the Supreme Court of the United States, and in hindsight, it widely contributed to the disastrous results we see today across tribal cultures."

Carol interjected, "Yep, we were taught that the Dawes Act was one of the most insidious policies ever implemented. It's the legal mechanism that was used to dispossess tribes of almost one hundred million acres of formerly treatied Native lands while dismantling the tribal structure. This was all sold under the name of progress and assimilation into the new Euro-American dream."

"That's exactly right, Carol!" Dad exclaimed. "It was the first of several misguided, or planned, social engineering experiments by the federal government. It continued until the privately funded Meriam Report of 1928 investigated and verified the suspicions of concerned anthropologists."

"That's what Herbert Hoover used to seek additional funding to initiate emergency actions outlined by the report."

"Correct again," said Dad. "The three main points were food, health, and education. This was also used as a cornerstone for the Wheeler-Howard Act, signed by Franklin Roosevelt in 1934. They called it the Indian New Deal—for extra credit, it was also known as the Indian Reorganization Act."

"I remember now; it helped remedy the cause of damages inflicted upon the tribes by the earlier nanny-state policies, but with the catastrophe now generationally entrenched, it was impossible to satisfy all tribal factions. My takeaway was that, tragically, no act or agency could reverse the demise of an entire civilization."

"Impressive, Carol," said Dad.

We were all ears when Dad spoke passionately about things, as he tended to shed new light in a fashion that always stuck with us, but I had to admire Carol for keeping up with him step for step on this issue.

"The Dawes Act, as damaging as it was to the American Indian Nation, did not overtly affect our tribe. We held clear title to our lands, and because of our agricultural contributions to the Union, we were viewed as effectively integrating the policy of economy-based farming. Our history of self-sustaining practices insulated us from the common overreach of the federal government and minimized the suffering within our community. You know, Red Horse, as a teacher of tribal advocacy law, has a notable opinion regarding the demise of tribal culture. He holds that the United States government did in fact commit genocide of the Indian Nation. He further believes that this action exemplifies the human condition—that of man's basest nature of conquest and control. He also believes, unpopular as it is within tribal communities, that the Indian Nation collectively was naively complicit, contributing to our own destruction. This was demonstrated by readily adopting the 'deficient' mantle that the federal government had assigned to us."

"It's hard to comprehend how those fiercely independent people who tamed life on this land for millennia accepted the words from a handful of federal government bureaucrats that they were incapable of functioning autonomously," Carol said. "It's a good lesson."

"Your mother always said that 'it wasn't the invasion, the slaughter, or even the dispossession of ancestral lands that ultimately conquered Native culture. It was the seizing of their individualism, their very liberty, that finally broke their spirit.' In my opinion, it's a prime example of what happens when citizens blindly yield any governing body plenary powers over them. The results are consistent throughout history, and the propensity for abuse far outweighs any possible benefit. The inescapable fact here is that it took only forty-seven years of federal government policy to render several thousand years of indigenous culture extinct. This is the stuff that got your mother really worked up."

"Yeah, and it's getting to me as well," Carol fumed.

"It should. Unilateral power is never a good thing in a governing body. No human construct can bear up under the weight of possessing ultimate authority. Sadly, the old cliché is true: history repeats itself, and I'm sure we'll see this pattern repeated in the future, but on a grander scale."

As the discussion waned, Carol and Virginia excused themselves with a goodnight, both hugging Dad before heading off to their respective rooms. I remained behind to help him clean up and load the dishwasher. After we were finished, he asked if I wanted to have a shot of bourbon with him. I could tell he was in a talkative mood and readily obliged. This was the first time I was invited to have a real drink with my dad, and it felt like I was passing some milestone in accepting his overture. We went to his study, and he directed me to the pair of perfectly aged leather club chairs that had been there since I could remember.

The room was decorated in rich masculine appointments of dark wood and embossed leather that exuded accomplishment and exclusivity. I felt like I should be wearing a suit or at least slacks and a collared shirt but smiled as I took my seat in my jeans and plain white T. He produced a bottle from his cabinet and poured the tobacco-colored liquor into heavy crystal glasses, asking if I had ever tasted good bourbon.

"No, sir, only the cheap stuff—tasted like aftershave."

"Oh, so you've been drinking aftershave? Reminds me of a guy I knew in the army," he chuckled while motioning to the substantial coffee table that separated the facing chairs. "Go ahead, kick back and relax—put your feet up if you want."

Handing me a glass, he offered the toast "Vida" and then sat opposite me. It was a turning point in our relationship. His smile was bright, as were his eyes. I knew he was enjoying the moment but from a different perspective.

"I'm probably not the best at conveying my feelings as often as I should, Town, but I want you to know that I'm so proud of you."

"Thank you, Dad. The Princeton acceptance was something I feel good about too."

"Well, your academic achievements are great, son, but they are only a small part of my admiration. On a much wider view, I respect you as the man I've watched you growing into."

I let his words sink in. Dad always taught Carol and me the importance of self-respect and individuation. His recognition of me in such a way was an honor, as it was one of the highest standards in his syllabus of life.

"You know, you remind me of your mother in so many ways, and I couldn't be more pleased to be your father."

I didn't know what to say other than to thank him for the encouraging words, as we enjoyed the moment together sipping our bourbon.

The talk of my mother reminded him of a story, and he dove right in. "I never met her parents. She told me they had perished during an excavation in northern Syria when she was thirteen. At the time, it was common for explorers in the field to board their children to receive an education, and that was true with her upbringing, although on occasion they would bring her along, and that's how she got bitten by the archaeology bug—that's how she remembered it, anyway.

"The fateful trip was a last-minute request from the British Museum of Antiquities to assess a dig site and offer opinions of value versus resources in conducting a full-scale excavation. Time in those days was critical. Claims had to be established quickly, and the site had to be guarded, often with deadly force. There were Arab factions still at odds from World War I, tomb robbers, and other competitors with no hesitation of murdering whoever was in their way and then employing the same workers to continue the dig. Your mother was at school when the news arrived. Ushered into the office of the headmistress, she was met by an attaché that she knew well. This gentleman, with his proper British accent, broke the news and her heart as tenderly as he could. That was your great-uncle, Sir Langley Carlton. A kind man and confirmed bachelor of vision and adventure, he stepped in as more than just her guardian; he cared for your mother as if she were his own daughter. Sir Langley drove her to excellence, and is the person she credited for keeping her flame lit in the darkest hours of her life. It was his influence, and her aptitude, that procured the first of many expeditions with her in a lead role."

"Did you ever meet him?"

"No, unfortunately I never had the pleasure. He passed away the year that I met your mother."

"Any pictures?"

"Yes, but they are packed away in the attic. I'll get up there and go through those boxes before you head off for school."

"Wow, that would be great, but only if you're up to it."

That after-hours meeting became our ritual, and when the girls retired for the evening, we migrated into the study for a nightcap and our chat. I didn't realize it at the time, but I now know that Dad was savoring each moment of the last weeks before the house would fall silent. One evening he surprised me with the photograph of Sir Langley, and I knew he had been into the attic boxes. The black-and-white image was similar to what I imagined. Sir Langley appeared to be in his late sixties at the time, strong jawed, with kind eyes, wearing a traditional three-piece suit. There was a presence about him that was evident even in the decades-old photograph. He stood beside his charge, a girl close to my own age, with his hand resting on her shoulder.

"Wow, that's Mom, isn't it?"

"Yes, it is. I think she was about sixteen years old at the time. It was just before she entered university. This reminds me of a story from when she worked among the British elite as a young archaeologist."

"I'd love to hear it if you feel like telling me," I replied.

Dad paused for a sip of bourbon and then began. "Your mother was passionately independent and accomplished much in her short career. She was known for plowing through the patriarchal barricades of the male-dominated field. In doing so, she had developed some strong opinions regarding a very polarizing issue. Sir Langley voiced concern that she might become ostracized after authoring one such opinion in the foremost archaeological publication of the day. The fallout was as he predicted, and the piece put her at odds with the top brass in the British government. The article in question was a plea regarding the preservation, restoration, and return of cultural pieces to former colonies from which they were originally 'acquired'—she used the inflammatory but accurate term 'pillaged'—under the banner of the Empire.

"She knew these artifacts should be repatriated to the former colonies that had demonstrated stability in their period of autonomy from the Crown. Further, for the former colonies in turmoil, the artifacts should at the very least be recataloged and displayed as 'on loan to the British Museum' from said country. Her reasoning was sound, and as a nation-building gesture, the opinion was infallible. The government of the day didn't see it that way and censured her for making an unauthorized statement by a government representative. However, word of her intercession on behalf of these nations traveled beyond the UK, and she began to receive lucrative employment contracts to lead important digs for other countries. Many of these she didn't accept, but one of the later expeditions intrigued her enough to sign on as the lead archaeologist. It was the site where her parents had been lost."

"In Syria?"

"Yes."

"While on the dig, she had an experience that changed her view of life, and the afterlife. It started with a dream, which led to a site just beyond the ruin that she was currently excavating at the ancient city of Edrei. I'm sure that you'll find a record of the event somewhere in her journal. And something else—from what I recall, a portion of the funding for that Edrei excavation came out of Princeton."

"Really?"

"That's what I remember. It was also the last dig that she participated in. After that, she became much more hermetic in her approach to her beliefs."

"Princeton, huh?" The coincidence of her involvement, if only tangentially, caught me.

"The lesson of this story is that when you have the courage to make a stand for truth, adversity is always close behind. It may cost you something initially, but ultimately, that investment will pay off."

"Thanks, Dad, I won't forget."

A few days later on an early August afternoon, Virginia and I took a break from prepping for the final exams we had crafted for each other after our summer as study partners and opted for a trail run, followed by a river sauna. This trail run, river sauna break had become part of our routine over the past month, and we both enjoyed the semi-competition that went along with the exercise. After a warm-up jog down to the sauna, I started a fire in the stove, and we took off on our four-mile jog through the woods. Once we settled into our pace, Virginia's track and field experience often prevailed. She chatted casually out in front of me while I maintained the pace behind her gazelle-like stride. I didn't mind the view, but I was competitive enough to battle for the front position whenever the trail widened. We jostled back and forth in those spots along the way as we probed various theories of medicine and biology while attempting to trick one another into revealing what we might have included in our respective exams. We were nearing the final stretch and sprinting all-out for the last chance of the lead before the trail narrowed, when her shoe struck the side of a root, turning her ankle, and down she went. The tumble was followed by a cry of pain, a few choice words, and a brief flow of tears.

"You OK?" I asked as I jogged back the few paces to her. "You went down really hard."

"I think so—I didn't hear anything pop, did you?"

"No, thankfully!"

She briefly protested my picking her up, as she wanted to see if she could bear weight on the ankle.

"Look, you're covered in trail dust; I want to be able to see that ankle before you stand on it. So don't give me any trouble, OK?"

She smiled at me and put her arms up, indicating her surrender as she placed them around my neck. I scooped her up and carried her the remaining hundred yards to the river, letting her legs cross the finish line first.

"Well, you were a step in the lead when you went down."

"You're such a gentleman, Town Lawe."

Wading into waist-deep water, I set her on a large, flat rock, where the cold mountain current massaged her ankle for a few minutes.

"Better?"

"Yeah, I think it's just a mild sprain," she said with a smile.

"I suggest the R-I-C-E protocol to reduce the swelling. I would also alternate cold and hot because theoretically, the constriction and dilation should speed recovery."

"OK, let's try it."

After dunking ourselves in the deep part of the eddy to wash off the trail dust, I carried the now-compliant Virginia up to the top of the riverbank.

"All right, now see if you can put some weight on it."

"Feels pretty good so far; let me walk on it a little."

She navigated the few steps up to the covered porch of the sauna. "Yeah, it's sore, but just a mild sprain," she confirmed before stepping inside to change in privacy, while I did the same outside.

Wrapped only in our towels, I positioned Virginia on the top bench so that her injured left ankle was extended out onto the "L" section of the bench and elevated it with a rolled towel. As her right leg dangled freely, I asked her how I had done.

"Textbook. Are you sure you don't want to practice medicine?" she said, patting the spot next to her on the bench, indicating that I should sit closer to her than I normally did. Something was different about this. It was intimate, more than just the best friends that we had become over this summer together.

"Do you feel ready for Princeton?" she asked.

"Yes, thanks to you." I smiled. "What about you, and the UW?"

"Yes, thanks to you." We both laughed as she mimicked my reply.

"Listen, I really enjoyed this summer," I said. "I would rate it as one of my top two."

"Really? Are you just saying that?" Virginia asked.

"No, I swear, it's the honest truth."

"What's the other one?"

"That's easy. It was the summer that I met you."

"Town, that's such a sweet thing to say. I remember it well," she replied, and placed her hand on mine.

There was an odd silence as we both noticed the palpable electricity coursing around the room. Virginia brushed me with her lean calf, asking if it was just she, or if I felt it as well. I certainly did, and we lifted our joined hands into a stream of light from the window, where we could see the hairs on both of our arms standing up. I also was aware that it radiated throughout my body.

"What do you make of it?"

"Not sure, but I don't mind," she said, keeping her leg and hand in contact with mine.

The charge in the room, her accepting words, and the touch of her smooth skin against mine set off a chain reaction of desires more sensual and erotic than I thought possible. When these washed through me, they carried away any remaining inhibitions that I held. The freedom induced a state of arousal so heightened that I became like a steel rod lifting the towel that covered me. I had never experienced an erection so intense that I actually felt my heart pounding through it with a slow, steady thump. Instinctively, I leaned back against the wall in a brief moment of self-admiration.

Virginia looked over at me and asked softly, "Umm . . . is that for me?" I was almost in a hypnotic state as she removed my towel, dropping her own as our mouths met. When I reached to pull her close, she grasped me firmly with a little sigh as we kissed deeply and with such passion that I felt I was floating away with no regard for time.

Sliding my hand from her ribcage, I began exploring her body by first massaging her breasts, then taking her nipples delicately between my fingers and thumb. She sighed in approval when they became erect, rocking herself back and forth while gently pumping the hand that held my heartbeat. Virginia only stopped kissing me to make her way to the lower bench and kneel on the towel that I had rolled for her ankle. Looking up at me with her eyes full of desire, she took me into her mouth, slowly rolling her tongue around, sucking and licking me into another state of consciousness. I was so intoxicated with pleasure that I don't know how much time had passed when I flipped her up and on top of me. As I buried my face and mouth into her, she giggled and moaned, our now-sweat-covered bodies gliding frictionless against one another.

Rising up, she led me down to the cedar floor, where we devoured each other almost like animals, as if trying to blend ourselves together into a single form. When I ran my fingers across her lower abdomen, she parted her knees, inviting me to touch her for the first time. Her body quivered and quaked while delighting in every little pattern that I traced with my fingertips. Wrapping her smooth-muscled thighs around me, she began pulling my hips toward her. I tried to resist as I gradually but firmly rubbed the tip of myself into the spot that made her jump uncontrollably.

She pulled me hard, digging her fingertips into my lower back, drawing me steadily onward with urgency. When our bodies collided, they instantly found the perfect rhythm, trading time signatures between a slow and deliberate beat and a powerful up-tempo groove that seemed to tie us directly into harmony with the universe. I throbbed with each effortless pass, as I slid in and out of her while cloaked in the slippery sweetness that she was.

Her body began involuntarily twitching and heaving amid the cries of her passion. Again and again, locking me tightly between her thighs, she gyrated while throwing her pelvis up and down as we consumed each other. I felt the volcano within me about to erupt, and withdrew while rubbing her with the tip. She shuddered, just before grabbing me firmly as I released a torrent of passion with every cycle of her hand until I had nothing left but the aura of our afterglow.

Totally consumed, we collapsed into each other and lay there speechless, our hearts pounding chest to chest. I rolled her on top of me and gently caressed her body. She kissed me tenderly and stroked my face as we listened to the tranquil sound of intermittent pops and crackles from the sauna stove.

Virginia was the first to speak. "I love you, James Town Lawe. I'm sure that I always have."

I felt the same and wanted her to know that without reservation. "I'm glad you do, because if you didn't, I'm not sure that anyone on earth could ever send the tremors through me that you do. I knew that I loved you from the first time we met, wherever that was," I said, realizing now that she was the girl I had been chasing through the forest in my dreams.

The union had undeniably joined us in a way that made it impossible to conceal. The first evidence was when we sat down to dinner that evening. Carol took one look at us and said, "Well, it's about time, you two—the tension around here was killing us."

In a week's time, we would be departing for schools on opposite coasts and separated by an entire new world of experiences that awaited us. What that would bring, neither of us could know. One thing we were certain of was that she and I shared a space that no one else could. The final few nights, we rendezvoused in the small orchard, making love in the cool mountain air, talking for hours underneath a canopy of stars before dozing off in each other's arms.

That last week, we flooded Dad with attention, and like a good litigator he put up a convincing front, but we knew he was going to miss having his family around. There was nothing we could do about it, except post our homecoming visits on the calendar in the kitchen for his reference.

"I'll be fine," he assured us. "I have several projects that need my attention through the fall, and now that I'm an empty nester, I might make a few trips of my own. Maybe out to Connecticut, New Jersey, or over the hill to Seattle," he proposed.

"Dad, you know that you are welcome anytime!" Carol announced as Virginia and I echoed the open invitation.

The girls departed two days before me, which was probably for the better, as Dad wasn't instantly faced with a silent house. The summer was one I cherished, and I knew that no matter what, my home was here on this land and with these people. Dad and I spent my final evening at home together. He grilled two excellent steaks, and after dinner we retired to the study and those leather chairs much earlier than usual for our bourbon ritual. He wasn't somber; rather, he was excited for me and the journey ahead.

"Your mother and I have done our best to get you here—the rest is up to you," he said with a smile.

"Yes, I suppose it is," I replied, noting that he included my mother in the present tense.

"I had the same conversation with Carol when she first left for school."

"I'm sure you did." I smiled, sipping the spirit and catching a glimpse of something he held in his hand, which was draped over the arm of his chair.

"With one exception," he said, as he refilled my glass and handed me a five-by-seven black-and-white photograph.

This one featured both of my parents; it was taken the evening that they first met in Chicago. I noticed an inscription written in Latin across the back in the elegant flowing hand of my mother, and read it aloud: "In aeternum te amabo." Translation: I will love you for all eternity. "Wow, that's really beautiful."

The story that accompanied this photo kept me awake all night. Not because I wasn't ready to hear it, but because I knew it was time.

During the second year of my mother's absence, the loss began taking its toll on my Dad. He could no longer bury himself in work projects for distraction and continue living under the pretense that she was only away on a long trip. He was successful in shielding his pain from Carol and me; however, Chilok, Myra, and Red Horse knew he was losing himself not only in the grief, but to a deep anger building up inside. After consulting the medicine man, they persuaded Dad to undergo a sacred cleansing ritual.

He was ushered deep into the ancestral forest, where the site was consecrated and a small sweat lodge quickly erected. The ceremony started with him seated at the fire inside the structure, where he was given a tea to drink by the medicine man. As he drank the tea, the healer started to chant while slowly hitting a drum. The four elders who were posted at compass points outside followed in unison, and his passage to the spirit world began. He awoke standing inside what appeared to be a vast subterranean chamber at one end of a long wooden bridge spanning a wide chasm over what he called a dimensional river. He could still hear the drumming and chants, but he was alone in the space. When he stepped onto the bridge, four very large Shadow Warriors surrounded him in a diamond formation, and they started across the divide at a steady pace. With every step, the drums and disembodied chants began to recede into a low-pitched harmonic tone that rose from the river beneath. At the halfway point, he noticed airborne wisps of yellow-eyed creatures with spindly fingers watching from the periphery. An eerie garble swirled around them as they attempted to approach the party, only to be dispatched by the guard using their huge clubs.

Upon arriving at the other side, they were met by a traditional longhouse resting on a small knoll. After ascending the gentle slope, the warriors took up positions around the rectangular building, and my father entered through a central door hewn through the base of a massive totem pole. Inside the structure, he found the space empty except for a dying fire in the center of the dirt floor. He glanced around the dimly lit room and saw colorfully painted symbols and mythic creatures adorning the cedar plank walls. Eyes drifting up toward the roofline, he discovered that it wasn't of pole and plank construction like the rest of the structure; instead, it was a limitless indigo vault of stars, planets, and vividly colored nebulae. With the return of his gaze downward into the room, he saw three masked figures standing shoulder to shoulder, dressed in simple buckskin attire. Of the two flanking attendants, the one on the left wore a mask adorned with the image of the frog, which represents cleansing and renewal. The attendant on the right wore a butterfly mask, symbolizing a chrysalis and the acceptance of its natural evolution.

The prominent central figure wore a transformation mask. These sophisticated two-part masks feature an exterior carving of one creature that opens to a different interior subject when a cord on the mask is pulled, personifying the transformation. The exterior image of this mask was so intricately carved and brilliantly painted that my father took note of each detail. The face was made up of various-sized angles that were patiently and meticulously rendered by a master's chisel as they subtracted only the necessary amount of material needed to release the bat suspended within the cedar block from which it originated.

Bats are known throughout Native culture as guardians of the night. They are reborn at dusk, emerging from the womb that is Mother Earth, only to retire at dawn in a powerful allegory of death and rebirth. The two attendants disappeared into the shadows as the central figure stretched out its palms, indicating that Dad should approach. The mask opened, affirming the transformation. It was my mother. His knees buckled, and he dropped into a weeping mass on the floor of the longhouse. As his tears soaked into the earth, the dwindling fire began to rekindle itself, burning much brighter, being fueled by the release of what he thought was his grief. "Not grief, Daniel, but Love—Love gives life to the fire," she conveyed without words, as he felt the shock wave of her throughout his being.

Kneeling beside him in silence, she placed her hands on his low back, gently pressing the tears and cries upward, until there were no more. When he had gained the strength to raise his head and sit up, she handed him a cup of tea, and with her eyes she bade him to drink. Consuming the tea induced a profuse sweat, and though unable to speak, he was calm. With her hand she directed him to look into her eyes. What he witnessed was an explosion of human history: civilizations, cataclysms, monarchies, empires from ancient to present, some puzzlingly unfamiliar, others more obvious. Sumerian, Egyptian, Babylonian,

Persian, Phoenician, Vedic, Hellenic, Asian, First Nations, Pre-Columbian, European—all were presented as powerful flashing images through the screen of her eyes. During the montage, he noticed a common participant who drifted between the scenes, mostly female, but sometimes male; it didn't matter. They were all my mother.

As they sat across from each other, their souls met in the blue smoke above the fire that now burned bright between them. They were unified in a realm that he referred to as "the everlasting." To say this encounter was personal would be incomplete. It was a cohabitation of souls, the joining of their very essences. A human word has yet to be revealed that properly illustrates the entirety of this wholeness.

This is the sacred language of a Glider.

14

THREE YEARS GONE

The story of Dad's cleansing ritual encounter gave clarity to the ongoing devotion he held for my mother. Somewhere I recalled hearing of a Glider, but I couldn't put my finger on it or know if in fact I wasn't imagining it. Maybe this was the being that had appeared to me through the column of smoke in the ancestral forest years before; it was something I occasionally considered when not consumed by my studies at Princeton.

Though Virginia and I were physically separated by three thousand miles most of the school year, we were completely connected on a spiritual level, and that made it far easier to devote ourselves entirely to our educations. When we saw one another every Christmas and summer break, we were inseparable. As I stepped off the plane at West Valley airport in this June of 1981, I remembered Carol joking the previous summer that she would turn the hose on us if we weren't more discreet in our displays of affection around the property. I smiled and couldn't wait to put her to the test.

When Aunt Myra was waiting for me at the gate, I knew there was trouble before she spoke.

"Town, we have to go see Chilok—she's . . ." Myra Three Moons couldn't finish the sentence before she broke down in my arms. "I'm sorry, I'm not ready to say goodbye to her . . . she's been asking for you," Myra barely managed, between her tears.

The thought of Chilok not being with us presented itself as a sickening chill throughout my body. I had heard she was dealing with a few health nuisances, and though she was in her nineties, I was shocked that death was imminent. It was hard to imagine life in the Pass without her. I choked back my emotions as Myra updated me on the way to Chilok's home, where Dr. Dale was overseeing her care. When we arrived, she was situated in her bedroom, resting peacefully in a hospital bed. She greeted me with her mischievous smile and dismissed Dale and Myra from the room by waving her hands as if shooing them away, indicating that she expected a word with me in private.

"I knew you were on the way," she said softly, grabbing my hand.

"I'm so sorry, I would have come earlier if I had known."

"No matter, you're here with me now. I wanted to tell you in person that you have always been a son to me. I leave this life content, knowing that you are who I always believed you to be. Louisa is so proud that she gave a piece of herself to you, you will see soon, my Tumlok."

Words failed me as the tears filled my eyes and then spilled over my bottom lids like Eagle Falls.

"Oh, don't you start that just yet," she smiled.

"I can't help it. I'm going to miss you," I mustered.

"My work here is finished, but I'll always be close."

After that, Chilok's gaze focused on the entrance into the room behind me, and she said, "Of course . . . why didn't I see this before? She's W—." Chilok looked back at me and smiled a last time before transitioning from this life.

When I turned around, Virginia stood silently in the doorway, her eyes sparkling with tears as she had watched us spend those last precious moments together. I leaned down and kissed Chilok's forehead, stroking her face as I told her that I loved her and would always do my best to honor everything that she had taught me. The shock of her departure brought with it a level of grief that I hadn't experienced before, with latent emotions that threatened to pull me under like a riptide.

We walked outside, and Virginia held me as I sobbed for a couple of minutes.

"I'm so sorry, Town, I came straight here," she said, wiping away her tears with her fingertips.

"I figured. It's great to see you. You must be exhausted from driving all night."

"No, I'm used to not sleeping. I'm just sad," Virginia said, as we walked to the car after Chilok's body was taken away.

We rolled down all the windows and let the mountain air wash through the car as Virginia drove us the few miles to Dad's house. We didn't say much along the way, but the reality of Chilok's passing crushed me, and my face didn't leave my hands until we pulled up to the house and the car stopped. Virginia sat silently as I took a long wipe across my face with my sleeve like a five-year-old boy who had skinned his knee.

"Well, at least I was able to have a few words with her before she passed on; I'll write them in my notebook," I said.

Virginia looked at me curiously as she rubbed my back comfortingly.

"What is it?" I asked, wiping my eyes with the other sleeve.

"Town, Chilok passed away fifteen minutes before you arrived at the house. Dr. Dale told me that when I got there. I saw the death certificate myself."

"He must have been mistaken, or you misheard him." I was adamant. "Look, when Myra and I arrived, Chilok sent her and Dale from the room so we could talk. She grabbed my hand; we spoke to each other. You heard us talking, right?"

"Honey, I was in that doorway ten minutes as you stood over her. Chilok didn't speak and she didn't move."

"No way. She looked over to where you were standing and said, "Of course . . . why didn't I see this before? She's W—," and she was going to say something else; then she looked at me, smiled, and just expired before she could finish."

"Wait a minute, she said what?" Virginia gripped the steering wheel and pushed herself deeper into the driver's seat as she stared out the front windshield, clearly dazed.

"She looked in your direction and said that of course you were 'W—,' I swear."

"Yeah, that's what I thought you said. Can you give me a minute?" Virginia said.

I was numb as I kissed her cheek and headed to the house with our bags. Virginia walked toward the river in search of the space she needed.

Night was approaching when Carol became insistent that I go find Virginia and bring her back to the house for dinner, or she was going to. I found her sitting on the porch of the river sauna, where she looked out over the water as it swirled through the eddy below.

"Hey, you OK?"

"Yeah, I guess . . . I had these dreams when I was younger, before Mom and I moved up to Pole Pass. I can't rationalize it . . . not sure I want to try."

"Talk about it?"

"Yeah, for sure, but I really want to organize it first."

"OK, whenever—now I'm even more curious. Feel like heading back to the house for some dinner? Carol's been asking about you."

The house was quiet when we arrived. Carol and Dad were grieving Chilok in their own contemplative way, and after dinner I went upstairs to search for photos of Chilok for her service. I found a few that my mom had taken during the construction of the Cultural Center, along with a packet containing some miscellaneous pictures, including a few shots of Kincaid from the days at our swimming pool. One, in particular, I thought perfectly captured the excitement of a ten-year-old, as Kin tucked into a cannonball position after leaving the diving board. I had just put the pictures and negatives aside with the thought of sending copies to his parents when Virginia joined me.

"I'm better now—can I help you with anything?"

"Thanks, yeah, you're just in time to help me choose the best photos for her service."

After making the selections, we lay on the bed, Virginia resting her head on my chest.

"Do you believe me about Chilok?"

"Town, I have seen several people die in the hospital, and when they died, that was it, but one time I swear the light in the room pulsed with the flatline. Two other docs were there, and neither reacted; if it was a power surge, I'm sure they would have commented, especially those two jerks. A critical care nurse said she often experienced the same thing when some folks passed. So yes, I do believe that something unseen happened in Chilok's room."

"I think she was about to say that you have a wolf spirit."

Virginia brought herself up into a cross-legged sitting position and turned to meet my eyes. "When I was a young girl, I had crazy dreams. Dreams that I was roaming in the forest, sometimes frolicking, other times chasing. I knew I belonged there."

"Do you think it may have been you in the woods that morning I was attacked?"

"I don't know, Town. I don't remember anything like that, only a freedom of being in nature and at peace. Maybe the dreams were just an escape hatch because of what I was going through at home. But when you told me what you heard, I immediately thought wolf. "

"All I can add is that the only time I ever dreamed about the attack was the night before we met on the pool deck."

"Yeah, that's quite a coincidence."

"You want to talk about this with Myra? She might be able to help, at least provide an explanation . . . if there is one."

"I think I probably need to—come with me?"

"Sure, we'll set it up after Chilok's service."

"Thanks, that makes me feel better, I think."

Three days later, Chilok's life service jammed the heart of downtown Pole Pass, as two thousand bereaved made their way to the Cultural Center to pay their last respects to someone who had touched their lives through her Native wisdom. Attendees included representatives from throughout the Columbia River Basin, all the way to the Oregon and Washington coastal tribes, giving credence to the many stories of Chilok's reputation among First Nations people. Following the service, Chilok's body was privately interred across the river where medicine men and women have been laid to rest over the centuries. I was honored to be among the contingent that carried her deep into the ancestral forest to the resting place. Our party spent the night burning sweetgrass braids, sage, and other herbs, while singing our farewells to this amazing healer.

A few days after Chilok's service, Virginia and I drove down to Boise State for a lecture on pediatric pharmacology that she wanted to attend. I brought along the photos of Kin with the idea of personally delivering them to his parents while I killed time waiting for Virginia. After dropping her off, I telephoned Kin's house to make the arrangements and discovered that the LeToures had divorced a couple of years earlier. Kin's mother was now living in a newly constructed adults-only apartment community on the outskirts of Boise. She told me over the phone that she was heading out for a day on the lake but would be home for another hour if I wanted to stop by.

When Barbara LeToure opened the door to her apartment, I was slightly taken aback by the two-piece swimsuit and its thin, flowing gauzelike cover-up that she wore.

"I'm starting over, Town. I had to, for my own sanity," she said, and asked if I wanted something to drink. It was hard not to do a double-take as the tan, slender forty-five-ish divorcée strode into the kitchen for my glass of water. Without question, she had as many options in this complex as she wanted to make a fresh start.

"Well, I'm glad that you're moving ahead with your life," I said. "I don't mean to cause you further upset."

"Oh, no, I'm sure it's healthy to revisit. If I didn't believe that life extended beyond this place, then I might feel differently, I guess."

"I'll just leave these pictures with you and get out of your hair."

"Oh, please have a seat and finish your water—I have time," she said.

When I handed her the photos, I could see that the images of Kin in those happier days moved her. She sat down on the sofa across from me.

"You know, Town, it's nice to see him smile again, even if it's just in a photo. We rarely witnessed that after the accident. His dad and I hoped that us getting back together and the move to Boise would help, but he was never again the same boy that's in these pictures. We sent him to a neurologist here, and after the scans and battery of tests, they found no abnormalities or neurological causes for his amnesia."

"I'm sure that was disheartening."

"Yeah, I know the discouragement played a part in his bouts of depression, but he seemed to be pulling out of it. Then the flashbacks started, and I think it overwhelmed him."

"Flashbacks? Did he say what he was remembering?"

"He didn't want to talk about it, and he threw a fit when I suggested he see a psychiatrist."

"I see."

"There is something that still bothers me about the amnesia thing, though," she said.

"What's that?"

"When they ruled out any neurological and physiological causes, the neurologist told me it was his opinion that only three explanations remained. One, Kin was fabricating the amnesia. He didn't think that was the case. Two, the psychological trauma of the event was too much for him to cope with for recall. He felt it was unlikely after a bike wreck like that. And the third, Kin's amnesia was drug induced. He didn't have to say anything. I knew he believed that to be the case. I feel like we didn't do enough to get to the bottom of it. That we may have failed him in that way."

"No, you can't take that on yourself," I insisted.

"My mind tells me that, but my heart . . . well, I can't help but think we missed something. I still have a copy of the medical report from his stay at Pass County Hospital, and the neurologist didn't seem to think it contained any clues."

"I could always ask Virginia to look at it if you like. The lecture she's attending will be over soon, and we are driving back this direction on the way home. I mean, if it would help you at all."

"Sure, why not? If I'm not back, just leave the folder under the doormat. You remember the gate code, 1121#?"

"Yes, I've got it. I'll leave a note along with the folder."

"That will be fine, and Town, thanks for the photos—they really captured Kin at his best. You feel free to come visit me anytime. We have a great pool here, and I have an extra room and a nicely stocked bar if you or your Dad find yourselves in Boise and need a pad to crash." She smiled.

"Thanks, Mrs. LeToure, I certainly will."

"Oh please, Town, call me Barbara."

Virginia examined Kin's medical report on the ride from the university back toward Barbara LeToure's complex. "Seven insect stings on his torso, arms, and buttocks, all presumed to be from yellow jackets that were known to inhabit the canyons in abundance. No known allergies, treated with common antihistamines. Moderate dehydration treated with IV fluids. Contusions and abrasions to both knees and elbows, cleaned and dressed. Moderate concussion with associated amnesia-type symptoms specifically: name recall, location, and event. Transverse fracture of right ulna and right radius set and cast. Fractured right clavicle eight-point sling." Dr. Ray Lautermilk had been Kin's physician in the ER and remained his caregiver through his weeklong stay in the hospital. Eleanor Higgins was the attending nurse when Kin was admitted into the ER. Virginia remembered Nurse Higgins. The nurse had transferred from Pole Pass to Sacred Heart Hospital in Spokane and was on the same floor that her mother occupied during the last months of life, and they had spoken several times over the course of Virginia's visits. The next morning, she decided to call Sacred Heart Hospital for Eleanor and ask if she remembered anything of the case. After they exchanged pleasantries, Eleanor said she was uncomfortable talking about it on the phone, but she was going to be down in Lewiston tomorrow and would meet Virginia and me in person for coffee at a place called the Pioneer Restaurant.

After the ninety-minute drive, we pulled into the restaurant's parking lot as the nurse was exiting her vehicle.

"You know all of this is off the record," Eleanor prefaced the conversation as our waitress departed with the coffee pot.

"Absolutely, you have our word," Virginia said as I nodded in confirmation.

Eleanor gave us a contemplative look and began. "That episode happened about four months before I moved to Spokane. When the child was first admitted, I told the attending—Dr. Lautermilk—that I thought the boy was on drugs. He exhibited the same behaviors that we see in post-op recovery after patients have been under the influence of benzodiazepines. Lautermilk feigned interest but ultimately said I was mistaken. He didn't even order a toxicology workup to rule it out. In those days, we nurses didn't argue with you docs, or we were out of a job or ostracized."

"Well, you know there is still some of that today between female docs and the old guard. Trust me, I believe that nurses are the backbone of practical medicine," Virginia affirmed.

Eleanor sipped her coffee as if putting off delivering her most disturbing speculation. "The other thing that always troubled me was that the boy had rectal trauma, and that never made the chart. I became aware of it during a sheet change. Lautermilk said he didn't notice it during intake and dismissed the injury as a result of the impact from the bike seat when he crashed into the canyon. I found that lacking, and still believe to this day that he had been drugged and sexually assaulted."

"That's a volatile assessment."

"You asked," Eleanor replied almost sarcastically.

"I did; thanks for your candor. I meant no offense," Virginia said. "You mentioned drugs. Did you note any possible injection sites?"

"In my opinion, those weren't all insect stings."

"Is there anything else that might prove helpful to us or to Kin's mother in closing this chapter?" Virginia asked her.

"Not that I can think of. When the boy was discharged, that was that, other than my getting ousted."

"Thank you for the help, Eleanor. If I can do anything for you, let me know, OK?"

"Just keep my name out of this. Dr. Lautermilk derided me at the hospital after I spoke up. I started getting bad shifts and the cold shoulder from some of the doctors. The whole business ultimately forced me to move away from the Pass. I like Spokane just fine, and I don't want to move again."

Virginia and I were nauseated by the theory that Eleanor Higgins had put forth.

"What can we do?" I said as we walked out to the car.

"There's nothing we can do on the medical side of things."

"I really want to tell the sheriff about this."

"Ok, so there is no proof," she said, "and there is no way we can drag Eleanor into this, at least now. I say that we talk to your Dad and let him ponder any next steps."

"Yeah, of course."

We discussed it over dinner with Dad and Carol. After the initial shock wore off, Dad didn't couch his concern about the story.

"My advice is that you three don't talk about this to anyone else, OK? Let me dig around, and I'll let you know if I find anything. But in all seriousness, keep this between yourselves for now."

That night, Virginia came up to my room, and we lay in bed talking about Dad's response.

"Did you catch his bristle over that?" I whispered.

"Totally. Like someone walked over a grave."

"Yes."

"He suspects something," Virginia said confidently.

"Just too many ifs, if you know what I mean," I said, shaking my head.

"The truth will eventually come out."

"I'm not so sure, but I like your optimism."

15

REBIRTH

The next day, Virginia and I sat with Myra Three Moons and told her of Chilok's parting words and our conclusions. Unfortunately, Myra didn't have the answers to Virginia's questions. She did, however, confirm that Chilok's body was dead when we arrived at her house from the airport that day, and my communication was with her essence, which obviously hung around to see me.

"Virginia, do you have Native blood in your family?" Myra asked.

"I don't know; my mom was of French Canadian descent. She did have an olive complexion, which she passed on to me."

"Your father?"

"I honestly don't know. I never met him or heard anything from my mother about him," Virginia replied, unable to hide the shame with her answer.

"Honey, that is not your fault," Aunt Myra said, patting her shoulder.

"Poltergeist? I've read that those energies can be activated by young females," I clumsily said.

"Maybe. I don't know, I guess they could kill . . . oh, sorry, Virginia," Myra said, catching herself too late.

"So, did I murder a man or not?" Virginia finally burst out, confessing what had been so troubling for her since our interpretation of Chilok's last words.

"Oh, Virginia, no!" Myra said emphatically. "I understand the upset, but whatever happened was in the defense of a child. You must believe that if Chilok saw you as a wolf on her deathbed, and if you were sent there to act, it was to do so decisively. You have to accept that."

"Sent there by whom?" she asked.

"Well, I have very limited knowledge of these spirit activities. We should meet with White Feather—he has a much broader experience of these matters."

White Feather was the medicine man whom Chilok held in the highest regard. She always said, "He has Great Spirit medicine." His tribal affiliation was unknown, and he circulated freely among several First Nations communities, assisting all while providing medicine training where needed. He was the medicine man whom Chilok entrusted to appoint my Weyekin time and who conducted the sacred cleansing ritual of my father. He had always been a somewhat elusive figure who would routinely disappear into the forest for weeks at a time, then return for a period before departing to destinations like Mexico, South America, or as far away as the Himalayas. At the moment, he was on one of those excursions, having left immediately after presiding over Chilok's interment ritual in the forest.

"I know it's not what you want to hear, Virginia, but maybe he'll be back in the next couple of weeks. I promise I'll let you know if I hear anything at all," Myra said.

Virginia was a bit deflated after the meeting. I knew she needed answers and at least a distraction until the meeting with White Feather. The best place I knew was deep in the ancestral forest, and on our drive back to the house I made the overture.

"Hey, do you want to see something really cool?"

"Like what?"

"Never mind. It's a bit of a hike plus an overnight or two in the forest. We'd have to build our own shelter, pack in some food. You might not be up for it."

"Really? Yes, I want to go!" she declared.

~

The next morning, we jumped in the river for a quick ceremonial washing before heading into the ancestral forest.

"Slow down, will you?" I called out to Virginia as she took off ahead of me.

"Sorry, I can't help it! Why haven't you taken me across the river before?"

"Well, I wasn't supposed to, I mean, that's before we knew . . . If you aren't supposed to be here, we'll know soon enough."

"What the hell's that mean?"

"Don't worry—by your tempo and sense of direction, I don't believe you are a stranger to this place or to the Ancestors. I think Myra believes that too."

We hiked past my Weyekin campsite, and I began teaching Virginia Native techniques used for navigating the deep forest. We reached the moss-covered plateau at about four o'clock and pushed on a little farther, to where the pine forest thinned, at the base of the ridge.

"Almost there—about twenty feet up is a big ledge and a small cave for shelter if it rains."

"Great, I'm about done for the day."

"Yeah, it's a long hike in for sure."

We dropped the gear on the ledge, and I climbed back down for some firewood as Virginia unpacked our stuff. Outside of the canopy, we had daylight for a little longer but not much, as the western ridge at our backs created an early but lasting dusk.

Over dinner I whispered, "You hear that?"

"No, I don't hear anything."

"That's perfect, Virginia."

"But wh—"

"Shhh," I said softly as I touched my finger to her lips. "In this place we learn to hear without listening. City living steals from us; it dulls our natural senses. Our mind becomes disconnected from our body and our spirit; then we fill in all sorts of detail, prejudging based upon the grid of personal experience or doctrines that we have been programmed to accept. It's unhealthy to walk that path for long periods. The forest is made up of different laws. If you want to commune with her, you will first learn to hear her voice. It takes practice, but I'll teach you."

"Is she speaking now?" Virginia whispered as she smiled.

"Yes, she welcomes us and extends an invitation to responsibly use her resources while we are her guests."

We continued to talk until our small fire was reduced to an orange glow, and the night surrounded us on three sides, leaving a magnificent window to the clear heavens above. With rain unlikely, I pulled our sleeping gear out of the cave and after zipping our bags together, we lay on the ledge searching the Milky Way and tracking an occasional satellite as our conversation gradually diminished. I dozed off thinking of those few summer evenings we had spent in the apple orchard before leaving for school and how time just seemed to stand still for us.

There was something unmatched about sleeping in the open air of the mountains, and upon awaking the next morning, I felt like I'd slept for two days. I wasn't alarmed that Virginia had slipped out of the bag undetected, thinking that perhaps she had gotten up to relieve herself or to enjoy the morning solitude. I restarted the fire so that we could have coffee and something to eat, and then went looking. Not spotting her in the general vicinity, I backtracked a short way down to the site of the plateau, and that was where I found her. She was sitting in the small pool below, enjoying the spring water as it flowed around her before spilling down the hill as the brook that ran alongside the trail.

I smiled and said, "Hey, what's up? You backtracked on me," as I stepped down to the site.

"Good morning! Come on in, the water's fine."

I readily stripped down and joined her.

The water temperature was warmer than I remembered. "Did you pee in here?"

"James Town Lawe! Don't be gross," she said as she splashed me.

"Now you sound like Carol."

"Isn't this great?" she said, ignoring the comparison.

"This is definitely the way to start the day," I replied.

"I followed them here."

"What did you follow here?" I asked, expecting her to answer that it was a herd of deer, bunnies, mountain goats . . . anything but what she was about to say.

"Shadows."

"Whoa, OK, back up. Shadow Warriors? What happened, exactly?"

"Just before dawn they walked by us. I followed them here, and they were gone. I wasn't afraid, though."

"OK, one more time. You are telling me that you actually saw Shadow Warriors, not in a dream but with your own eyes, and you followed them here to this spot?"

"Well, not here to this pool, but above us where the moss is. Yes, that's what I'm saying."

"They passed by our camp?"

"Yes, right across the ledge where we were sleeping. It was five o'clock, I'm sure, because when I woke up, I looked at my watch to decide if I would try to go back to sleep or get up. I just lay there watching the sky when suddenly they went by."

"How many?"

"A bunch, ten maybe? I got up and followed them here, where they just dissolved—it's the only way I can describe it."

"Did you see where they came from? At least the direction?"

"It had to be from the west."

"I know Myra will love to hear this story. You should feel pretty special."

"So you believe me?"

"You have to ask me that? Yes, I believe you."

"Good, because it didn't take long for me to doubt it myself."

"I understand. These things are usually best kept within the community."

"I'm not breathing a word of it, trust me."

"That's probably for the better. I planned for us to do some exploring around this area today. I thought it might be special if we did it together. But now I'm not sure; maybe we should head back?"

"No, please, Town, let's stay another night. Maybe we will see them again. I really want to hang out here with you."

"OK, but there are some rituals to perform. Just traditional peace offerings—we can gather the items while walking today. I'll show you how."

"Whatever you say."

By the time we returned to our campsite from a day of hiking, it was half past five and we needed food. After heating some water, I regretfully rehydrated a freeze-dried dinner of beef Stroganoff. "Sorry, I never eat this stuff; I just thought I'd ease you into the whole great-outdoors experience."

"Believe it or not, I've had worse in hospital cafeterias," Virginia laughed.

"Hopefully dessert will make up for it," I said as I handed her the bowl of thimbleberries we'd collected on the way back to camp."

"Yum, definitely worth the Stroganoff."

"You know, I was thinking a soak might be in order before bed tonight."

"Great idea—my legs and feet could sure use it."

"Perfect, but first let's make an offering to the forest and the memory of all those who stewarded this land before us."

"How do we make it?" Virginia asked.

"Just like when we harvested the items, we approach it from a posture of humility and gratitude, thanking the plant, then the forest, and then Mother Earth for giving of herself. Now we set the intention of our offering. What do you think it should be?"

"I'm not sure I understand the parameters."

"There is only one: it must come from your open heart."

"Can you do it this time so I have an idea?"

"Sure, but if I don't represent you truthfully, you have to say. Otherwise it's an offense and we wouldn't want that. You understand?"

"Yep."

The ritual began with laying items on the fire, recalling the moment we harvested each one. Then I spoke of our gratitude and honor for every creature in creation, seen and unseen. I thanked the Great Spirit for Truth that holds all of existence in balance; and lastly I asked for the continued blessing of our presence here in this sacred place. When the ceremony was finished, we reverently made our way down to the pool, slipping in as darkness approached. Aside from an occasional chirp and the sound of water spilling softly from the pool, all was quiet as the forest transformed from day to night.

"I'm overwhelmed and can't explain how I feel at the moment, like I never want to leave," Virginia said quietly.

"I know exactly what you mean. This place can be intoxicating."

"Yes, but it's also being here with you, now."

Something about the way she said it struck me enough to look up from the fading reflection of the trees and full moon on the water's surface. I felt a chill as I realized that this wasn't Virginia across from me. I mean, it was, but it wasn't . . .

She exited the pool in one fluid movement and motioned silently for me to follow her. It was as if I didn't have a choice in the matter. As our bare feet sank into the moss of the plateau, she pulled me to the ground, where she ravished me. I don't remember how we got back to camp, but suddenly it was daylight.

I slowly wriggled my way out of the double bag and onto the ledge, trying not to wake her.

"Thank you for last night," Virginia giggled. "How'd you sleep?"

"Pretty good, I guess. Not that I remember."

Virginia smiled, saying nothing as she got up and stood naked before me, completely uninhibited and one with the forest.

"How do you look so radiant in the morning?"

She put her finger to my lips and took my hand as we climbed down and walked naked to the spring. We remained silent, taking in the peaceful morning sounds and early sunlight as it filtered through the trees, surrounding us with prismatic shafts.

"Thanks for bringing me here, Town. I really needed this."

"You're welcome, I did too."

"You know, I was thinking," she said.

"What about?"

"Really just that there is so much that we don't know. I grew up here and never thought about those who lived in this area a thousand years ago and beyond . . . Who were they? How did they live? What were their dreams? That type of thing."

"It's nice to release all the pressure of school life and consider something other than the grindstone we put our noses to. This forest has always grounded me; sounds like you've found some answers in here too?"

"Yeah, and more questions as well."

"Anything you want to share?"

"How high is up?" She smiled.

"I'm not so sure that it's relegated to up. I think it's all around us, as if we are in the middle of a sphere. I remember a sketch in my mother's notebook with a notation prompting that idea. It was of a circle with a thin line from the center to the edge. The line represented physical life on Earth. The remaining space was the ether, or the collective consciousness of humanity. Legends say that we are always connected to it but have limited access when earthbound."

"I'd really love to stay here longer; we could talk more about all of this?" she said.

"We'll come back, I promise, but for now, Dad wouldn't be happy if he had to come looking for us."

After breakfast, we restored the site and departed for the six-hour journey home. Virginia navigated the forest almost flawlessly all the way back to the river crossing. The time away nurtured her in a manner that made her

OK with things she couldn't readily answer through her conditioned scientific viewfinder. I totally got it. We all have areas of our mind that need to be pushed past the self-imposed importance of our ignorance and pride. I certainly did. It was a privilege to witness Virginia's awakening to something deeper. I knew she had encountered her truth, and once discovered, its magnetism was virtually impossible to outrun.

A few days after our return, Virginia and I met with Myra at the Cultural Center to report her Shadow Warrior sighting.

"Well, apart from Louisa, you are the only supposed non-Native person I have known to have seen them. I always doubted Louisa didn't have some Native lineage, and I'm having the same feeling about you, Virginia. You were obviously welcome in the forest, or else we'd know it. Like Chilok used to say, 'This sounds like *us* to me.'"

Over dinner, Dad said he spoke to Sam about Nurse Higgins's Kincaid theory, assuring us that he hadn't mentioned her name or vocation in the process. The sheriff didn't dismiss the idea of an assault, but he said that without an eyewitness or an actual plaintiff, they had nothing.

"What about Dr. Lautermilk? Can't someone sweat him?"

"Town, this isn't Perry Mason. Besides, Dr. Lautermilk moved to the Oregon coast two years ago to be closer to his grandkids," Dad said, as Carol and Virginia looked at me from across the table as if I had lost my mind.

"OK, so I'm reaching, but don't you forget that Kin was your friend too, and we owe it to him and his folks if there is something more here!"

"Of course we do, Town. I'm sorry, I didn't mean to minimize this, but at this point we don't have even circumstantial evidence."

"I know you're right, but I just have a gut feeling about this and it's gnawing at me."

The following day, Carol, who had been preoccupied with overpreparing for her last year at Yale Law, finally broke away and hung out with Virginia and me for the last week of summer break.

Those remaining days served as a great reminder of how close we three were, and also that time was evaporating before our eyes. We would be graduating the coming spring and couldn't help but acknowledge the evolution that accompanied that milestone. Carol had already received employment offers in Washington, DC, Alaska, and Seattle, and there would be more on the horizon for sure. Virginia had to choose where to conduct her residency. I faced down the pivotal decision of whether to commit to an expedited master's program that would place me in the PhD ranks at Princeton the following year. These choices would be made by the time our trio reunited in May at our graduations. In the space between, each of us would experience the fullness of Chilok's lesson regarding the paradox of life, discovering for ourselves that even the straightest of paths are made up of corners.

BOOK TWO

THE EMBRACE OF CHANGE

16

EMANCIPATION

When Carla Nelson graduated from West Valley High School in 1977, she was a talented artist with dreams of one day opening her own gallery. After her sophomore year at West Valley Community College, she determined that a love of creating art was not enough to sustain her interest in pursuing a degree in the discipline. Two years had passed since the death of her father, and she needed distance from the ever-encroaching Lister family. Carla's odyssey took flight one early spring morning in 1979 when she loaded up her Datsun pickup truck and without fanfare headed west over the mountains in search of new inspiration and another life.

During her second week in Seattle, she met Mary Burke at the Surrogate on 15th Avenue East. The Surrogate was a favored local eatery, where Carla began taking her breakfast upon renting a studio apartment in the Fredonia building just around the corner. After witnessing five straight mornings of the bright-eyed girl poring through various help-wanted sections, Mary slid into the booth across from her with two cups of fresh coffee and some remaining quiche. She introduced herself and asked Carla where she was from and what she hoped to find in those ads.

Carla was guarded at first, but when Mary told her that she herself was a transplant from east of the mountains in Moses Lake, Carla began to open up. Mary had a knack for picking the right staff, a trait that made her a good people manager as well as an efficient retail baker. The business was in its growth stage and needed another staff position to handle the demand. This was an entry-level apprentice role, but if one applied oneself, one would certainly learn the trade. She had a good feeling about this girl from the mountains of Idaho and offered Carla the yet-to-be posted job. Carla carried with her an edge that had been honed razor-sharp by the trials of her former home life and the challenges of growing up small-town gay in the late 1970s. She was a pretty girl, slight in stature but big in personality, "a bright light with a devil's tongue," Mary would come to say.

Carla's grin was infectious and her mouth intrepid, given that she would draft off a "fuck you very much" without batting her aqua eyes and called everyone Hon who walked in the door. This bit of "Eastern red," as Mary jokingly called it, would have to be tamed if Carla were to be successful anywhere but a shit-kicker truck stop out on I-90 east, much less survive the yuppie clientele of the Surrogate.

Baking was a craft in itself at the restaurant and was to be revered. It required dedication and a passion for the work, or one wouldn't make it through an apprenticeship. Mary never needed question either of these attributes in

Carla, and it soon became apparent to everyone else that Carla was indeed an excellent worker. She would take any shift and perform every task in an exacting manner, effectively using her work hours to study the art of baking and developing the commitment required to run a successful business as a restaurateur. For Carla, this was college on her terms, and she devoted herself to mastering her studies. Working ten-hour days, six days a week during an apprenticeship that lasted eighteen months, Carla only backed off at Mary's insistence after she found Carla asleep on a pallet of flour sacks next to the rhythmic wump-wump-wump of the giant Hobart mixer. When awarded her baker status, Carla was given charge over all baking inventory as well as a nice pay increase. In less than two years she had managed to hew out a place for herself in Seattle's exclusive Capitol Hill neighborhood and finally started to live a life of her own.

Mary and her husband, Arthur, owned a house a few blocks away on 16th Avenue between Prospect and Highland, offering a place of calm for this rogue of a small-town girl. Arthur had worked at Boeing since graduating from the University of Washington and was remarkably wet in his humor for an engineer. He enjoyed Carla's demeanor and a special banter that presented itself from the moment Mary brought her home for dinner her first week at the Surrogate. Arthur was the one person who could get away with saying, "She's more of a man than I am" and receive a return volley, something like "I've been telling Mary that f-o-r-e-v-e-r, dearest Artie," with a big grin. Arthur fell ill in mid-1980, and it was Carla who kept his spirits up with their brand of humor, along with a bottle of Balvenie that they would pass back and forth when he was up to it. She pulled many double shifts at the Surrogate during that season so that Mary could spend more time at home and not worry about the bakery.

When Arthur tragically passed away at thirty-five, leaving Mary a thirty-three-year-old widow, it was Carla who wrote "FUCK YOU CANCER" in twelve-foot-high oblique letters in the street outside the front gate of Lake View Cemetery. She left the chalk behind for others to add names of their loved ones also ravaged by its uncensored cruelty. The cold tears of a Seattle November washed away the epitaph the next day, but not before garnering the attention of many, including the local paper.

The holiday season was brutal as the graybird Seattle weather magnified the pall cast by Arthur's absence, leaving Mary numb and unmoored. Carla accompanied her to the weekly support group at St. Mark's Cathedral and waited in the quiet of the vast sanctuary until the group dispersed. She would take Mary's hand while they strolled in the Arboretum, where the two walked in silence or reminisced about Arthur's love of the place. Carla stood guard over Mary as she wept in the ivy-covered alcove at the Volunteer Park Conservatory, the exact spot where Arthur had proposed to her only ten years earlier.

Perhaps it's a survival mechanism, but time has a healing process that naturally distances us from the visceral pangs of grief as the days slowly pass. The darkness that had rolled in like thick fog over the top of Capitol Hill and stayed for six months finally began to retreat, and suddenly the Northwest skies of ash gave way to sapphire, as the spring of 1981 arrived. Life had commenced its push through the soil of Mary's flower beds and her heart as she began a transition into the acceptance phase of losing Arthur. On a sunny morning the first week of May, she made the three-block pilgrimage up 15th Avenue East that she had avoided like the plague these many months. Walking through the serenity of Lake View Cemetery toward Arthur's resting place, she noticed a muffled sound distinct from the bird songs that followed her along the route.

Mary walked in the dewy grass, climbing a small rise between the smooth granite obelisks leading to Arthur's monument, where she found Carla sitting on an adjacent stone bench. Her face was buried in her hands as she sobbed so intensely that she shook while rocking back and forth. Mary realized now that Carla had been so preoccupied with caring for her that she hadn't had time herself to grieve Arthur's loss. Mary gently placed her hand on Carla's shoulder, with nearly disastrous results.

Carla bolted straight up and spun around, wielding a bottle of scotch like a club while launching into a barrage of expletives. Her swollen, bloodshot eyes were raccooned with smudged eyeliner and mascara, the raw emotion making her normally even skin tone red and mottled. When she recognized that it was Mary, she wilted into her arms.

Gradually, they began to laugh between the tears. As they sat on the bench, they cracked open the bottle of Balvenie and passed it among the three of them, splashing Arthur's round on his headstone, starting a ritual that would continue on through the years.

The summer after Arthur's passing, Mary decided that it was time to bring life back into the house on 16th Avenue. She knew that Arthur would want her to resume the

Gathering, a dinner group they had started years earlier. Mary and Arthur had hosted the event quarterly for an interchangeable group of thinkers who enjoyed airing their opinions over a great meal and drink. Carla met many new friends through these soirees. The crowd was significantly more restrained and sophisticated than the butch barflies she would encounter at Tugs, the Brass Rail, or the godforsaken Monastery, with its hot tubs full of more than just indiscriminate E-fueled club kids.

The membership of the Gathering was cultivated from people of experience and education. These professionals, both younger and older, weren't the self-tormented artistic types but more practical visionaries who appreciated moderation and a few beautiful things in life, rather than surrounding themselves with mediocrity.

Carla was now a central figure of the group, receiving equal standing with Mary, who graciously overstated Carla's baking prowess and other talents. As an amateur chef under Mary's tutelage, Carla was, according to many in the know along 15th Avenue East, "fast becoming the best-kept secret within the culinary elite of Capitol Hill."

It was at the relaunch of the Gathering that Carla met Audrey.

Audrey Garner was a well-known art dealer with an exquisite gallery on Broadway. A beautiful and confident woman, she dressed the part: Dior pumps, a classic long pencil skirt, a three-quarter-sleeved close-fitting cashmere top, and a long layered haircut that allowed her silver-streaked blond hair to fall naturally around her shoulders. In a time when many exaggerated their faces with bronze Rubiglo blush, bold shadows, smoky eyelids, and lined lips,

Audrey wore her makeup light: a little face powder, soft peach lipstick, and a thin brown pencil line that added just enough to ignite the flame of her hazel eyes. Almost six feet tall and athletically slender, Audrey had the gift of looking as if she had stepped from the pages of a fashion magazine and moved with an ethereal grace that Carla, as an artist, would instantly admire.

She had visited Audrey's gallery once when she first moved to town, but Audrey wasn't there at the time. It was only a brief walk-through, but Carla remembered the mixture of high-end traditional works and local offerings. So, when Audrey approached her, Carla could speak semi-intelligently about her observations.

"You appear to have something more than just a casual regard. Are you a creator as well?" Audrey asked.

Without too much detail, Carla relayed that art had been her first love, but she had struggled to be able to channel that desire into completing her degree and walked away from it. She used that abandonment as a tool to get her out of small-town USA and found another creative dream to pursue. "I haven't opened my portfolio in two years," she said matter-of-factly.

"Well, if your artwork is anything like your culinary creations, I should like to see something from you," Audrey said. "Perhaps you could drop by the gallery this Saturday afternoon—say, four thirty? We can review your portfolio, then grab dinner and drinks—my treat."

Once the arrangements were set, Audrey glanced down at her wristwatch and excused herself, explaining that she had some overseas business that required her attention, but she was looking forward to Saturday. At thirty-two, Audrey was ten years Carla's senior, but that didn't detract from the perceptible gravity between the two of them, and Carla quietly hoped she wasn't just imagining it.

The remaining workweek was hectic. Carla had booked a last-minute corporate catering event for Friday night, and by the time her head hit the pillow, it was two thirty Saturday morning. Rolling out of bed at ten, she plunged her coffee press and was pulling the best of her portfolio together when the phone rang.

"Good morning, darling! You up yet?"

"Hi Mare, yeah . . . just."

"How was the event last night?"

"Smooth—they paid their balance and tipped really well, so I'm pretty sure they're happy."

"I've got some exciting news I wanted to share with you. Can I grab some food and come over?"

"Sure, come on up, I'm just pulling my art stuff together. I have coffee ready."

"OK, great, see you in a few minutes."

Ten minutes later the door buzzed, and up came Mary with a covered tray containing quiche, blueberry scones, and fresh fruit.

"That buzzer is just obnoxious," Mary said. "We should talk to old Joe about it."

"Now, don't rock the boat yet—he gave me the first chance at this place and I love it."

"Yeah, you're right. This is a great upgrade, but I wish you would have moved in with me."

"Well, I adore you for that, but I'm less than two blocks away. I think of it as a long hallway." Carla smiled. "You had some news to share?"

"Oh yeah! Sorry! So last night, well, it went even better than you think. They left a message first thing this morning and want the Surrogate for their upcoming Christmas party! This is huge—it's actually too big for us, and if we are going to take it on, we will have to subcontract staff to pull it off. So here's the deal. If we are successful, you become the catering director and make a substantial bonus from these jobs, starting with this one. What do you think?"

"Of course we will!"

"Great! I thought you might say that. Now, I have to talk with you about something else." Mary took a more serious tone.

"Sure, anything. What is it?"

"All right, so this Audrey thing tonight . . ."

"You mean her reviewing my artwork?" Carla replied with a sly smile and a glint in her eye as she sipped her coffee.

"Very cute, Carla. Look, I've known Audrey for twelve years; maybe I'm being a little overly protective, but I'm going to have my say."

Carla felt a flush come over her. "By all means, Mary, please do."

"Arthur and Audrey grew up on the same block," she began. "They even went to school together for a bit at St. Joe's. He always thought she was harmless, and Arthur being Arthur, he had a soft spot for her. But women have an intuition about other women that men seem to lack, especially when it comes to the more attractive ones. Now, I really do like Audrey, but I want you to be careful. She's extremely savvy, and she doesn't do anything without calculating. That's good and bad. Are you following me?"

"Um, I think so, but she is gay, right?" Carla goaded.

Mary glanced up at the ceiling with a chuckle, then dropped her eyes to meet Carla's as she replied, "Let me sum it up by saying that I believe Audrey has the ability to become whatever suits her purpose in the moment."

"Ouch! Well, what do you think her purpose is with me?"

"That, my dear, is something you will have to ask her yourself. I want you to have fun, but mostly I don't want you to get hurt. Remember this: the *A* in *Audrey* isn't for 'average.' She became a successful entrepreneur by reading people, assessing vulnerabilities, and capitalizing on what she could gain."

"Now Mary, do I detect a jealous bitch sitting across the table from me? If so, I'm flattered."

"Yes. Yes, you do, and I'm OK with that today as long as you get the message."

Carla smiled at Mary's concern.

"By the way, so this is your art? It's really good. Maybe Audrey has something here . . . Why don't I know more about this?"

"Well, that's a long story. Short version: I needed to put it away so I could focus on the art of baking. But recently, I've started dreaming of it again."

"You keep on dreaming, because I need something for the space at the bottom of my stairs," Mary smiled. "Plus, I think we could also use a few things at the Surrogate besides our beautiful menu board." She got up from the table and brought the dishes to the sink to wash them as Carla continued to sort through her artwork.

"All right, dearest, I'll leave you to it." Mary pecked her on the forehead and in her most motherly way said, "Dress warmly—they say we may get snow tonight from that Alaskan clipper."

"Will do."

"Love you, mean it, and you'd better call me tomorrow—I'm serious!"

"Oh, I will! And Mary, thank you for everything. I love you too."

Carla spent the next two hours detailing her portfolio and the two hours afterward detailing herself. While showering, she thought about Mary's words and the truth about Audrey being an actual woman compared with the girls she had entertained on rare occasion in her Seattle experience. Was this a date? Would sex be expected? She felt the thrill of anticipation begin to take hold.

Then, as if on cue, a familiar habit of self-dismantling appeared as Mary's caution thundered back. *What could Audrey possibly want with me? Maybe I'm just a trick for her.* The thought made Carla feel empty and a bit nauseous. Catching this destructive narrative, she countered with *Stop it! You are not a victim! You are in charge of your life and doing a damn fine job at it!* abruptly dismissing the negative presence. Carla had always been her own worst critic; perhaps that was why she fled her artwork in the first place, or maybe it was because she had used it as her best friend and lifeline to escape her unbearably painful adolescence. Either way, she had learned how to tame the undermining voice early before it could ruin her evening. Carla turned the faucet to cold, splashing the water on her face to soothe

the swelling around her eyes brought by the tears of insecurity that had begun to form.

Dressing in black, she put on cashmere tights underneath a short pleated wool skirt, a long-sleeved turtleneck, and a low-slung belt. Black leather knee-high John Fluevog boots with a three-inch-thick lugged sole elevated her to five-foot-eight.

Examining herself in the mirror, Carla at last was seeing the obvious difference between the girl left behind in West Valley and this woman emerging. A metamorphosis had been taking place since she arrived on Capitol Hill, and it finally revealed itself that afternoon in the mirror. Taking a makeup cue from Audrey, she lightly rimmed her eyes with a charcoal pencil, very slightly smudging the lower lid, then using a hint of gray shadow and mascara to accentuate them. Choosing Drakkar Noir, she lightly touched her wrists and behind each ear before donning her heavy wool overcoat and gathering up her portfolio for the twenty-odd-minute stroll to the gallery.

Walking south on Broadway, Carla couldn't help but glance at her passing reflection in the storefront windows as if seeing herself for the first time. She paused to freshen her light pink lipstick and smiled as she felt the sense of release from what she had been carrying far too long. It was her time to embrace the life she had built, discarding the childhood version built on circumstances beyond her control. Carla became conscious of the strength within herself; she had tasted freedom and resolved never to relinquish it.

~

A soft bell tone sounded as I opened the gallery door. When I entered, I spotted Audrey on the phone at her desk in the rear of the space. She glanced up, greeting me with a smile, and silently motioned me over with an exaggerated wave of her hand. Still smiling, she winked and handed me a note that read, "Carla, please flip the front door sign to 'Closed' and twist the lock on the door. Make yourself at home—I'll be off in five minutes."

I smiled and nodded. After fulfilling Audrey's requests, I wandered throughout the space, noting what a woman like Audrey would choose to place in her gallery these days. Venturing into a window-lined second room along Broadway, I sat down on a wide padded leather bench facing three large works. The first was a richly warm-hued oil painting of an English hunting scene, antique and very traditional, mounted in a heavily carved gilded frame. The second was a strong palette-knifed work depicting a city streetscape, definitely Pioneer Square in the rain. A third painting was a simple monochromatic watercolor of a country road during an evening snow. It had a mysterious quality that lured you inside to experience the insulating silence of the heavy snowfall. The snow had begun to pile up on the barbed wire fence posts and the long-since-abandoned barn, now to my right as I continued walking along the empty road inside the scene. So captivated was I that I felt the winter swirl wrapping around me, and just as I anticipated a falling snowflake to land gently on my tongue, I sensed Audrey's presence.

"Enchanting, isn't it?"

"Yes, it's magical. Reminds me of my hometown this time of year. It called out to me from within the frame, and suddenly I was walking down that road." I smiled looking up at her.

"It still does that to me. A local artist named Val Persoon painted it. I've had many generous offers, but it's not for sale. I keep it down here in the winter months so that others might experience it too. That said, don't you look adorable! Let's go over here—I'm excited to see what you have brought me." Audrey led us to a large white laminated table in the rear of the space, where she offered me a glass of white wine and a seat. I opened my portfolio as she rolled up a chair across from me. She turned the book 180 degrees and then handed me a spiral-bound notepad and pen, indicating the noteworthiness of her forthcoming commentary. We touched glasses and began working our way through my portfolio.

Audrey's expertise was evident as she scrutinized and then provided her observations on each piece before moving to the next. Nearing the end of the portfolio, she became transfixed by a particular image. Taking a sip of wine, she resumed her gaze in silence with only the sound of her pencil eraser rhythmically tapping the desk as she scanned the image from top to bottom and side to side.

The large charcoal sketch, measuring 36 by 24, was the piece that I felt most connected to of all my work. As I bashfully took notice of the intensity with which Audrey absorbed each detail of the drawing, I sensed my insecurity rising once again. I struggled to silently exorcise its pervasive voice, and just as I was about to scream for it to "get the fuck out of my head," I caught a glimpse of something that gave me hope. It was revealed by the light reflecting from the glossy white surface of the tabletop that betrayed a welling in Audrey's eyes just before she pushed herself back from the table in her rolling chair. Reaching for a nearby tissue, she gently dabbed under each eye. Her only comment was, "This one, we can discuss later," and then she resumed her analysis of my final two pieces.

Our dinner destination was a brisk walk north on Broadway to a small but lively bistro that Audrey had been to on occasion. She ordered a bottle of Chardonnay, followed by a request that it be served in their actual crystal, not table glassware. "But of course, Ms. Garner," was the reply of the maître d' upon his departure.

"The business of art is not at all unlike the restaurant business," Audrey stated. "Although in the right environment, art is a much more lucrative prospect, with less work. Now, don't misunderstand me, it has its moments. The art world is full of exaggerating swindlers, backstabbing, and outright liars. Those are the good people!" She laughed.

"Which of those best describes you?" I asked with a smile.

"Touché, Carla! I've played each of those roles at one time or another during my career; it's called survival of the fittest," she responded light-heartedly.

The wine steward arrived with the bottle and crystal glasses. After Audrey's approval, he poured our wine and made a swift departure. Our conversation revolved around personal details of our upbringings and current interests. Audrey swirled the pale gold wine in her glass and set the tone by being remarkably transparent in her disclosures. She didn't cast visions of grandeur or paint a clean canvas. Audrey spoke candidly about growing up on Capitol Hill as the only child in a very dysfunctional home, which I could instantly relate to.

"My father was an alcoholic bank executive at Seafirst Bank and a well-known philanderer," she said. "My mother was careerless, chronically depressed, and sadly detached with more medications in her bathroom cabinet than the shelves at Benson's Pharmacy on 19th." She paused for a sip of wine.

"Eventually their personalities collided. The boil-over produced summer front-yard battles that were legendary on our block, often followed by an equally mortifying session of opened-window makeup sex.

"The majority of our neighbors consisted of other Catholic families who had apparently taken the papacy's edict against contraception more seriously than my parents," she continued. "These families, including Arthur's, with their ten to fifteen children, proved to be a godsend for me. I was able to blend into the various tribes, giving me a hint of normalcy. But I always knew this was a temporary reprieve from the uncertainty that landed on me when I returned home each evening."

Audrey's education at the University of Washington was the genesis of her independence. Moving out of her parents' house the July before her first semester, she began to create a life by her own tempo from across the Montlake Cut. Free at last from the daily burden of managing her parents' drama, she devoted herself to her studies in art history and devoured everything fine art along the way. When Audrey finished among the top in her class, graduating summa cum laude, she was given the opportunity to pursue her PhD with a full scholarship but instead made the decision to test herself in the business world. This, she said, was her first entrepreneurial step, and "with a little luck and the foresight to make a few strong acquisitions, I suddenly found myself a gallery owner, which, of course, brought about its own unique set of challenges."

The travel, the showings, the temperamental nature of the high-dollar procurement clients and of the artists themselves, made for a very dynamic environment, one that developed into a 24/7 proposition. The business changed Audrey, and she wasn't happy with what she saw herself becoming over the years. This led her to conclude recently that the gallery now owned her, and it was Audrey's intention to change that.

There were many parallels between the core of Audrey's home life and mine. I told her that I had finally come to terms with my abusively dysfunctional family and how I had spent most of my emotional energy distracting myself from that day-to-day unsettled existence. Even though it was behind me now, I would catch it trying to sabotage my life today, I confessed. As the younger of two daughters, I became the pawn in divorce hearings that tore my life apart. When the judge dropped the gavel, it meant that I would be raised by my father, becoming the spoils for him and a constant reminder of his bitterness. Martin's hatred dominated the house during those early years. His ranting about how my mother was "nothing but a whore" and the cruel proclamation that my beloved sister was in fact just half of that became too much. I heard this theme repeated throughout the rest of the Lister family, and with nowhere else to turn, I was driven into a period of self-destruction to cope with my emotions.

"In my despair, I would rediscover the beauty of life. It was through a love of art and my journey with it that I found salvation. Adolescence had carved a painful rut into my heart, and unfortunately the truth came too late to stop the scarring, but at least the healing had begun. My move to Seattle was an exodus of biblical proportions and the best decision I could have made. It allowed a clean break from what haunted me throughout those years and gave birth to my metamorphosis into whoever this is I'm becoming."

Audrey said, "Carla, you are an intriguing young woman, to say the least."

Snow had begun to fall during our meal, and as we made the trek back toward the gallery, an icy arctic blast from Puget Sound swept up East John and cut across Broadway. We screamed at the top of our lungs like schoolgirls as I looped my arm through the space where Audrey's hand entered her wool trench coat. Bracing against each other, we scurried the remaining block into the driving snowfall.

Audrey's flat was above her gallery, and it soon became clear that she was serious about leaving work life outside of her living space. The back corner of the gallery had a double-locked heavy steel sliding door that led to her private staircase. At the top was another industrial-type steel door with two deadbolts. With the same footprint as the gallery beneath, the large room had a bank of windows facing east over Broadway, plank flooring, brick walls, and exposed steel beams, creating a very chic modern space smelling of sandalwood. It was superbly decorated with a blend of old-world antiques and new designs integrated into a warm, rich space that easily could have been overwhelmed by an industrial motif.

Audrey sat me on a large, comfortable sofa in front of a stone fireplace that looked every bit like it had come from the European castle that it had. She lit the fire and tossed me a cashmere throw that was on a neighboring leather chair.

"Take off those Captain Fantastic boots, Carla, and get comfortable, for God's sake!"

"What? You don't like my boots?"

"That's not it at all. I *love* Fluevog boots—on you. I just can't wear them. Care to join me for some tea with a splash of Campari? I have an English afternoon tea that won't keep you up all night; it's really nice and comforting."

I had no idea what Campari was but thought if Audrey enjoyed it, it must be good. "Yes, that sounds nice, thank you."

"If you don't mind, would you please pull the kettle when it sounds? I'm going to grab a quick shower—I've been in these clothes since five o'clock this morning."

"Sounds like a baker's hours to me," I responded with a chuckle.

"I told you there wasn't much of a difference!" Audrey exclaimed, her voice trailing off as she walked into the rear of the flat.

Sitting alone in the beautiful space, I thought about our dinner conversation and the preconception of her that I had held. The trappings are really just that. We're programmed throughout childhood to accept certain roles foisted upon us by society, parents, or the circumstances of our upbringing. I applauded her for kicking a hole in the system and found inspiration in the unencumbered honesty that we seemed to share.

Audrey reappeared in light-pink flannel pajamas with white snowflakes of various sizes and gray wool slippers. Her hair now down, revealing its expertly cut long layers, and with the warm scent of tobacco flower trailing, she placed an ornate silver tray on the coffee table and took up residence with me on the long sofa. We used the large rolled arms as backrests and sat facing each other, feet to feet, sipping the concoction in front of the fire. There was a brief silence that wasn't at all uncomfortable. The feeling was more of contentment with each other's company, and even though we had really just met, there was a purity present that was rare between people. I casually studied Audrey's makeup-less face, admiring the clear, fine skin that hinted of her Scandinavian heritage.

It was a perfect palette for her hazel eyes, now flickering with the image of the fire in the hearth. I silently told myself that Audrey Garner was perhaps the most beautiful woman I had ever seen in person, reminding me slightly of another girl that I had loved back in the mountains.

Her serene voice finally broke the spell, with a mention of artists in the community.

"I'm not really an artist per se, Audrey, and I'm reminded of that each time I walk around a gallery such as yours."

"Carla, I believe we are all artists of some type; it's just that some have learned to become better listeners of themselves. The interpretation is where the freedom of expression is brought to life. When you learn to listen with all of your senses, then, and only then, will you trust yourself to interpret what you hear. That's where the seat of your true voice resides, and once it's discovered, I think you might surprise yourself with how much of an artist you actually are. For example, the outfit you put together this evening is a fabulous interpretation of various pieces that, when assembled in a certain way, become art."

"That's an interesting way to look at it."

"But it's true. Collectively they evoke a response from the wearer, or creator if you will, and of course the observer."

"I have never really thought of it in those terms."

"It becomes a trap for many of us who have chosen to live out our vocational lives in a creative space. A simple discipline is to practice living the moment. What I mean is to stop periodically throughout your day, take a few minutes to absorb your surroundings, and find the art in them. It might be static, like the geometry of a building, or random, like the changing shape of water spraying from the fountainhead at the Broadway Park reservoir. Today at lunch, I found beauty in the shape created by a mother holding the hand of her child as they prepared to cross the street. Trust me, this practice will open you to new perspectives."

"I promise I'll give that a try."

"I do hope you will. Especially after examining your work this afternoon, as I detect a substantial measure of indwelled talent. Is it something that you can make a career out of? Well, that remains to be seen. However, I believe you have the potential to use your voice in that venue if you so choose."

"That's very kind of you to say, Audrey, but—"

"Stop," interrupted Audrey, holding up her hand. "There are no buts here, Carla, only choices. You have currently chosen a career in the restaurant business; all I'm pointing out is that you clearly have a companion gift, and with its maturation come options. They are yours alone to explore, and if your ambition is to pursue that avenue, I want you to know that I am here to support you in it."

"Thank you once again; that's very gracious," Carla said. "What can I do for you in exchange for such encouragement?"

"Succeed in whatever you decide to do!" Audrey exclaimed with a laugh as she sipped her tea. "Actually . . ." she began, and then rose and went to an antique set of cartographer drawers opposite the seating area, where she withdrew a large leather portfolio. Opening it midway, she dropped a ribbon into place and reclaimed her spot on the sofa with the elegance of a feline leaping over the armrest. Laying the collection on the coffee table, she said, "The work of yours that I said we would discuss later . . ."

"Yes," I replied.

"Your self-portrait . . ."

I felt my face instantly flush with embarrassment but nodded affirmatively with "Ah, yes, that."

"Well, it was marvelously accomplished," Audrey said matter-of-factly as she playfully nudged her own portfolio down the coffee table to me with her foot. "You used a mirror to image yourself?"

"Thank you, and I did—how could you tell?" I responded, feeling slightly vulnerable.

"Simple. Your true anatomical structure is balanced right-side dominant, and your sketch is the opposite. I tend to notice detail. But I am curious about something else that we have in common, especially in light of our dinner conversation."

As I opened Audrey's book to the ribbon-marked page, I was met by the same subject matter as the one she was commenting on. The work was obviously her, nude and expertly rendered in charcoal, ink, and red chalk, but with the face unintelligible.

"I can't seem to get it right," she remarked.

"You must be mad!" I exclaimed. "This is exquisite. I can see right through this sketch into your muscle, bone, tendons, and joints. The art of your structure, its function, and the unity of them all captured within the work. This is absolutely masterful."

She smiled at my reaction. "Thank you Carla, and I might say the same about yours. The formidable question is, why do we disfigure our faces? What is the shame we are holding on to, or, better yet, hiding from? Myself, I've spent thousands of dollars on shrinks who just pumped me full of Valium. I even surrendered myself to powerful men who tried to pump me full of something else," she said with a wink and sad half-laugh. "But in the end, they both left me further detached from myself, with more baggage to carry than I had in the first place. I haven't found the source of the obstruction, beyond the basic analysis that it all goes back to childhood . . . like, no shit! At some point we have to move on, right? This business of art has been my hiding place, my façade. I guess I'm taking a break at last to have an existential moment in my own life and evaluate my future."

"I think I understand," I said. "I'm only beginning to learn about forgiving myself, and that's a lot to accept, especially with shame. But I'm finding, as a result of that single action, I end up forgiving others as well. Just a thought is all."

"Well, it's a great one, Carla. Here's to forgiving ourselves," said Audrey, raising her teacup aloft with a nod. Then, switching topics, she said, "You asked me if there was something you could do for me. I've thought about it and there is. I want to commission a drawing from you."

"What? What kind of drawing?"

"A simple sketch."

"What's the subject?"

"Not what, Carla, but whom. I want you to draw me, face intact."

Almost choking on my sip of tea, "Oh God, no! Way too much pressure, Audrey!"

Audrey laughed, and grabbing my hands, she conveyed the sincerity of her request. "I've never let anyone sketch me, Carla, but I know you are the one. Please consider it, will you?"

I agreed to think about it for a week but didn't refrain from telling her that the proposition made me nervous.

It was approaching midnight, and my baker's hours were creeping up on me. I casually mentioned that I should probably be heading out for home soon.

"I think you might want to look outside before you make that decision."

The snow had not let up since we left the restaurant, and when I walked over to the bank of windows, I found Broadway empty of cars and foot traffic, with six inches of fresh snow on the ground.

"Well shit, I see what you mean."

"I would drive you home, but my car is bad enough in the rain on these Seattle hills. I have some pajamas you can wear, and a drawer full of toiletries from the airlines. You can sleep out here on the sofa or with me. I recommend with me, but only if you don't snore. I do snuggle, but I don't bite," she smiled at me with a wink. "Besides, our dear Mary would murder me if I did anything inappropriate to you."

Audrey's king-sized bed was impressive, with the finest sheets that were rose petal soft, topped with a high-loft down comforter that made the perfect nest for a cold, snowy evening. I gladly accepted her invitation. Audrey had thoughtfully set out a few items in the bathroom for me as she readied for bed. I took a shower, washing my face with some exotic product from Israel, followed by an eye cream and moisturizer that dissolved into my skin on contact. The bright pink toothpaste from Italy had a medicinal taste, but it was pleasant enough, and my mouth felt wonderful and alive. I took the small bottle of crimson-colored mouthwash and poured some into a glass on the counter. Swishing it around, I felt its pleasant cinnamon-based potency, but when I gargled, I began to choke and cough, almost spewing mouthwash all over the bathroom mirror.

"Hey! Be careful—that mouthwash is concentrated!" Audrey laughed from the bedroom.

Recovering enough to respond with watery eyes and a raspy "Thanks for the warning!" I bounded into the bedroom wearing her pajamas with the long legs rolled up, diving under the comforter as Audrey giggled.

The kiss was something of a dream. It was beautifully soft and loving. Like two feathers held aloft on a warm breeze, Audrey's strong and lean frame lightly floated above me, with only our lips and tongues meeting. The tenderness of patiently caressing each other with our mouths was entirely unique for me; I had only been with much more aggressive and unrefined females. Audrey's ever-so-gently brushing my face with the back of her elegant hand and fingers was by far the most sensual experience of my life. The feelings I held of anticipation and restraint changed into a state of enjoying each second of the experience. I began lightly stroking Audrey's arms and shoulders, feeling the tight roundness of her deltoids and the crease of the well-defined triceps, then gently cradled her face as we floated into a timeless unity. We were just two butterflies effortlessly playing together in a meadow of wildflowers without distraction.

We awoke the next morning comfortably intertwined, reminiscent of the amorous marble statues of antiquity, and it was clear that our journey together had begun.

17

LAWE OF ATTRACTION

It was early Saturday morning one week later when she happened into the Surrogate. If I hadn't stepped out of the kitchen to refill my coffee, she would have passed through without notice. At a glance, the girl appeared to be just another jogger waiting in line to order an espresso drink, a frequent sight on Saturday mornings. This one was tall and athletic, with tawny hair pulled back off her face with a wide headband, dressed in running tights and a thick gray sweatshirt with a large orange P stitched on the front of it. But it was the familiar eyes of an angel that instantly made my heart flutter.

"Virginia?" I asked, stunned.

"C-Carla?" she replied, with equal disbelief.

We were both clearly lost for a second. I snapped out of it first and excitedly told her to grab a seat, pointing over the counter to a semiprivate booth that had just opened up in the corner. I told the crew that I was taking a break and quickly brought over a sampler of frittata, a raspberry scone, and a ham and cheese croissant, all of which I had prepared for that morning's rush. A coworker followed close behind with two cappuccinos and waters.

After we sat across the table from each other, I reached out and took her hand.

Virginia started the conversation. "Wow, it's been, what, four years? I had no idea that you were in Seattle! How are you?"

"Yes, four and change . . . I'm great—I've been here over two years now, and I'm learning so much," I said. "This city has an inspiring energy; I really haven't felt more alive."

"Well, it shows—you look absolutely beautiful. Please don't take this wrong, but I wouldn't have recognized you in your natural hair color and without the entire Clinique counter covering your lovely skin."

"Thank you, no offense taken," I responded. "I've had some positive influences here—no need to hide myself behind that garish club kid mask anymore. You must be almost finished at the UW Medical School, right?"

Virginia affirmed, saying that it had been a challenging and all-consuming season but she was now finally over the hump. I detected the evidence of attending a major medical school on Virginia's face. She looked a bit drawn, with faint dark circles under her eyes indicative of the long hours and the toll of its stressors.

"Are you living on campus?" I asked.

"Technically yes, but it seems like I'm always in the library, the lab, or making hospital rounds. It's relentless at times, but it's something that I've always wanted to do, so it's worth the sacrifice, at least for now. I recently decided to look for a place on this side of the Montlake Cut, just to give myself a break from the U District and get some balance back into my life."

Virginia asked if I was keeping up with my artwork. I laughed while throwing my thumb over my right shoulder toward the large, colorful chalkboard menu behind the counter. "Funny you should ask—I've only recently been in an emotional space for that again."

After a very condensed recap of my Seattle experience and career at the Surrogate, I started digging a little deeper. "So what's with the Princeton sweatshirt? I thought Dawgs and Cats didn't get along," I teased, clearly making a reference to the mascots of each institution.

Virginia smiled, showing just enough of her pearls to make me grin too. "Clever girl."

I qualified the statement with, "If I were to ever like boys, that Town Lawe would be a boy that I would like too."

Virginia, caught a little off guard, blushed and then said, "It's funny how small-town news seems to find us wherever we are."

"I'm sorry, I hope I didn't overstep."

"Please, not at all. I was just surprised—you know it's not common to run into folks from Pole Pass over here."

"Yeah, my friend Mary is the only one I've met from east of the Cascades since I arrived. But you are dating Town Lawe, right?"

"Yes, that's true. I'm going to see him in Princeton for Christmas break. Two full weeks, and I'm really looking forward to it," Virginia beamed, sipping her cappuccino.

"Be sure to bring him a Dawgs shirt," I said with a wink.

"Well, and that too." She paused. "Can I ask you something, Carla?"

"As long as it's not a request to sketch you in the nude, though that may make a nice Christmas present for someone special, then yes, by all means, please ask away."

She laughed at the randomness of my stipulation, which made her overture a little easier. "OK, at least not today. It sounds like you are really busy, but I was thinking . . . would it be possible for us to spend a little time together? Just to see how it goes, no pressure. It's been so long, and this is a whole different world over here."

It was clear that she was a little surprised by how fast I responded. "Sure, Virginia. I know we have a lot to talk about. I think I'm ready for this now. In fact, would you be my guest at a little dinner gathering next Wednesday?"

"That's perfect—I'm off rounds on Wednesdays and would be honored. What can I bring, and what's the attire?"

"I know this is so cliché, but just bring yourself—oh, and a bottle of wine; either red or white will do. Dress is semicasual, but no scrubs, OK?" I said with a smile.

"Oh darn, and I just received next season's line, they're all the rage."

I took out one of my business cards and wrote down the Gathering, adding Mary's address with the date and a time of six o'clock, and slid it across the table to her. Virginia placed her fingertips on the card to retrieve it, but I held it firm to the tabletop while looking into her eyes. "I need you to promise me something first."

"Yes, what is it?"

"You can't mention this to anyone back home. I'm thriving here, and I don't want to put that at risk."

"Carla, I promise."

"Not even Town, OK?"

"I swear."

With Virginia's confirmation, I released the card.

As we got up to say our goodbyes, I pulled her in close for a long hug, and on tiptoes I kissed her tenderly on the cheek, telling her for the first time in at least twelve years that I loved her. When I noticed my curious coworkers pretending not to pay attention to us, I proudly introduced them to Dr. Virginia Tecoi, my big sister.

18

RECKONINGS

A light mist was in the air as I made it three blocks north along 15th Avenue East before abruptly terminating my run at Volunteer Park. I sat on a bench across from the Asian Art Museum tear-blind with emotion, trying to collect myself while staring down at the tops of my running shoes until they resembled a Monet viewed from two feet away. The Seattle drizzle became a downpour as I sprinted across the park road, seeking shelter inside the museum. In the women's restroom, I dried off with paper towels and the wall-mounted hand dryer before making my way to the cavernous main gallery of polished granite. I shut my eyes and listened to the soothing low-pitched hypnotic patter of rain on the massive glass skylight above. Deep down, I was ashamed for having run from this chapter of my life, and seeing Carla was one of two recent signs that it was time to deal.

As I allowed the past to surface into the present, I began free-falling through a library of memories stowed neatly away since those days with Carla in West Valley.

The sensation reminded me of the despair I felt the day Lana died. It was a year ago during my third year of medical school, when I served an eight-week sub-internship in oncology. Lana had just celebrated her tenth birthday in the pediatric oncology wing of Children's Hospital, and she appeared by all the medical data to be making progress in her fight against leukemia. I brought the birthday cake adorned with pink bunnies and whimsical butterflies to her party on the ward. Lana beamed as she hugged my neck and we said our goodbyes that afternoon.

A day later, my pager woke me at three thirty in the morning, and upon calling in to the service, I was directed to the head nurse on the oncology ward, who relayed the news professionally: "Dr. Tecoi, I'm so sorry to disturb you, but I thought you would want to know . . ." Helplessness, grief, and heartbreak cycled through my heart like a jackhammer breaking up concrete. I walked around in shock for two days, even seriously contemplating abandoning patient-based medicine and moving into a strictly research-focused modality. Thankfully, I found a therapist with whom I could process this rite of passage for all young physicians and developed tools to properly file emotional encounters, like the death of a patient. By opening the door to my past, I recognized that Lana's death was the trigger that would prepare me for difficult emotional encounters. She was about the same age as Carla when we were separated by the divorce, and in the weeks I monitored Lana, she filled a void left by Carla and our days together in the West Valley farmhouse. I owed it to Carla as well as myself to clean this wound out completely so that it might finally have a chance to heal.

Our mom had tried to secure custody of Carla through the court system, but the deference toward the Lister name by a corrupt judiciary eventually brought her to a legal dead end, and after a year and a half of fighting, she was emotionally spent and close to financial ruin. When I was included in the restraining order, it forced me to contend with the humiliation of small-town whispers and trash talk that no child should endure.

Mom attempted to give me a new start by moving us up the hill to Pole Pass. The relocation provided enough distance, and still allowed us to be close enough if Carla needed her. Since I had been banished from my former life down mountain, I immersed myself in studies and athletics, burying memories that made me sick in the pit of my stomach. I claimed a sense of control in my new surroundings, and the rewards of gaining top grades and competitive victories in sport became my companions. Constructive for a time, this also unlocked a subconscious back door that I used to escape the emotional pain that was pulling me down into a vortex of depression. The practice left me a high achiever but detached from my emotional self.

Before this saga began, it was just Mom and me. She was a single mother with a two-year old daughter and wasn't looking for a husband or provider. Mom was an educated woman who held a midlevel management position at Simplot, one of the largest food and agriculture businesses in the world. Although lonely from time to time, we were a happy, self-sustaining household. She knew Martin from the Simplot Farmer Cooperative events. He owned the largest farm equipment dealership in West Valley, and after they served on a co-op committee together, he began pursuing her. As a single woman, Mom grew weary of the corporate culture of the day and, as she later told me, was tired of fighting against impenetrable glass ceilings and unsolicited advances from her bosses. It was the fleeting glimpse of a "normal life" that temporarily blinded her to the realities of being involved with a founding family such as the Listers.

The hypnotic tempo of the rain continued as I recalled the uneasiness I felt around Martin from the beginning. Carla was born during their first year of marriage, which should have been a happy time, but there was always something amiss in the house. I tried to suppress my intuition because of the dread that accompanied it. Mom chose not to accept its presence, but I knew she had to feel it too. Children sense when they aren't wanted, and it became plain to me that Martin did not want Carla and me to be close. After a rocky start, the household settled into a tolerable dysfunction and maintained that status into my middle-school years. The turning point was one summer afternoon when I was thirteen years old.

I found it resting next to an oil spot on the gravel driveway where Martin always parked his truck. Housed in a worn suede drawstring pouch that had become shiny over the years was a gold medallion about three inches in diameter. I began to remove it from the pouch and immediately became nauseous; it scared me enough to drop the pouch and medallion on the front stoop. About that time, Mom opened the screen door, calling me to join her and Carla for lunch in the backyard garden. I pointed to the object and told her I had found it in the driveway. She dismissed it as something from Martin's lodge ceremonies, but her countenance betrayed her; I knew there was more to it.

Martin arrived home earlier than normal from the dealership that afternoon. Clearly agitated, he was obviously looking for something as he retraced his usual steps from where he had parked his truck all the way through the house, eyes scanning the floor and surfaces. After he checked his coat pockets in the closet and started flipping over the sofa cushions, I asked him if he was searching for "that thing." He stopped and stared through me from the opposite end of the room.

"Yes. Where is it?"

"I think my mom put it somewhere—it's probably in your room."

"Where's your mother and Carla now?"

When I said they were at the grocery store, I realized that it was just the two of us in the house, which sent a chill up my spine. He said flatly, "Show me where she put it," and began walking toward me. By the time he took his first step, I had bolted out the front door, sprinting halfway down the driveway and disappearing into the corncrib. Martin left shortly thereafter, but I didn't go back to the house until Mom and Carla returned from shopping. When I told her about the incident, it seemed to sink in. At dinner, she mentioned to Martin that he was lucky that I had found his trinket before it had been crushed in the driveway. He agreed and said that he had just wanted to thank me for finding it but I ran out the door before he could. I swore to myself that I would never be in the house alone with him again.

Over the next month, there was no peace in the farmhouse, and the constant tension finally came to a head in an intense confrontation. Mom took Carla and me with her to an old friend's place over in East Valley. Divorce papers were soon served, and the nastiest of custody battles commenced. When the judge made his decision to split up the children and award Mom no alimony or child support, she returned to work at Simplot, but in a reduced capacity and for about half the pay of her previous job, thanks to the Listers. The total cost of those years was the last remaining reserves of her life.

At least she had good insurance policies in place when the sickness came. I knew that in her final days she found some level of peace knowing that I would have a guaranteed opportunity to continue my education and become a strong, independent woman—attributes that she readily admitted to having forsaken.

The rain began to fall heavily, filling the museum with a rumble as I dropped my face into my hands and did something that I had never done before: I wept for my mother. Through the tears, I spoke as if she sat next to me. I told her that I missed her, and more—that I forgave her. This was a conversation that felt long overdue, but it was right on schedule.

~

When I returned to the back office and the small desk where I had been working on the restaurant inventory before encountering Virginia, the din of the cash register and front-of-house conversations disappeared. I stared down at the order form trying to regain my focus and not miss something we needed. My emotional tide was rising as Mary came into the backroom to retrieve the scheduling book she had forgotten the previous evening. She had to greet me twice before I acknowledged her presence with an "Oh, oh, good morning."

"Are you OK? You look like you've seen a ghost," she said, placing the back of her hand on my forehead.

"Well, I kind of have . . ."

"Do you want to talk about it?"

"Yes, I really do, but not now. I need a moment; do you think it would be OK if I went home early, like right now? I just finished the inventory order."

"Of course. Angela can handle the shift, and if there's a problem, I'll have her call me. I can always run up here if she needs help. You sure you are OK? It's just that I've never seen you like this."

"No, no, I mean, yes, I'm good. Just a little shocked, I guess. It's a laugh-cry thing, and I definitely don't want to be doing that here."

"OK, if you change your mind, I'll come over to your place and we can chat about it. I can even bring some chicken soup—it's good for everything, you know." Mary gave a concerned smile.

"So I've heard. Thanks for understanding. I promise I'll tell you all about it tomorrow."

When I slipped out the back door into the gray downpour, I didn't bother opening the umbrella and let the rain soak me to the skin like a cold shower as I ran the two and a half blocks to my apartment building. Once inside, I stripped off the wet clothes and put on my robe. I lit some candles and cranked the squeaky faucet handles on the cast iron tub, letting the rust clear before placing the rubber stopper in the drain. As the tub was filling, I warmed some milk, adding in a couple of shots of Frangelico and a dash of nutmeg. The comforting warmth of the bath and the soothing concoction was a welcome embrace, and I closed my eyes, ready to relive the event of an hour prior. As I granted my emotions the permission to appear, it wasn't long before the tears began to flow.

I was elated to see Virginia. We had spoken only once in twelve years, four of which had passed since our last encounter. I was a brooding, small-town antisocial artist who created distance from everyone with destructive habits and behaviors out of sheer boredom, or so I rationalized. Since the move to Seattle, I had come to recognize that this boredom was only an excuse for my self-destructive behavior. The truth of it was that hurt, anger, and insecurity were my real puppet masters.

The last time Virginia and I saw each other, I was extremely cruel, slashing wildly at her with accusations so hateful that recalling them now made me wince. Our mom had recently passed away, I had just turned eighteen, and Virginia was now trying to reconnect with me after eight years apart. She thought it was important that I know some of the things that Mom told her as she lay dying in a Spokane hospital bed. Things like the fact that she never gave up on being reunited with me, and there wasn't a birthday or holiday that she didn't send a card, even though Martin always sent them back and threatened to file a motion of contempt and haul her into court.

But it was the last truth I heard that day that pushed me over the edge: the revelation that I was in fact Virginia's full-blooded sister. That piece of information was too much for me to handle at the time, and I flew into a rage. I vividly recall the hurt deep within her eyes after being told in no uncertain terms that she, too, was now dead to me. Saying nothing further, as tears started down her cheeks, I coldly watched Virginia walk back to her car and then drive off to return to school in northern Idaho. The irony of it was that the only father I knew would be dead within a week of my outburst, leaving me completely alone in the world. Today, I more than just welcomed this reconnection; I desperately needed it.

19

THE GATHERING

When I arrived at the bottom of Mary Burke's front steps with a chilled bottle of Blue Nun, I had no time to be nervous. Mary caught sight of me walking up and came out on the porch to welcome me with a warm smile and a hug.

"Come inside, Virginia, it's so nice to meet you." She took my coat and handed me a completed nametag, explaining that anytime she had guests, they all wore them. I complimented Mary on her beautiful home and the smell that hit me as I walked in.

"Thank you—I'll take credit for the house, but the smell, well, tonight, that's your sister's doing. Speaking of, let's go see if she needs a hand, shall we?"

Entering a kitchen that was more commercial than residential, we found Carla prepping two large beef tenderloins for the chateaubriand that would be the star of this evening's culinary adventure. Upon seeing me, Carla shoved the large roasting pans aside and excitedly flew around the stainless steel island. Enveloping me with a hug and a kiss on the cheek, she offered me a glass of wine from the private bottle she liked to nurse on cook nights.

The doorbell rang, and Mary excused herself to greet the seven members arriving for cocktails and hors d'oeuvres. Tonight's mix included a couple of longtime Hillers, and Mary quickly made the introductions: Marcel Denny, a retired judge who served on both the state and federal benches. Carmen Petersen, a beautiful young beat reporter for the *Seattle Post-Intelligencer* who had lived her entire life on the Hill; Carmen actively promoted its most recent growth spurt through her upbeat reporting on the neighborhood. David Darrow, a prince of a man who led the Youth Division at the Downtown Seattle YMCA. The adventurous Opal Lee Stansberry, whose dreams of becoming an author were sidelined when she came down with a case of "the pregnant"; the single parenthood that followed kept her chained to a switchboard at Pacific Northwest Bell. Esther Watanabe, a fourth-year archaeology student at the UW who had just returned from a monthlong dig in southeastern Washington. Everyone's hairdresser, Roberto Montalvo, who had recently left the notable salon of Mary & Roy Shampoo in Pioneer Square and opened his namesake studio in the Fremont District. Last but not least, Audrey Garner, who flitted in behind the others.

Carla popped out of the kitchen with her wineglass, greeting all with a hug and a peck. Everything had been staged for a quick ten-minute finish, giving her time to socialize and announce the evening's courses before Mary reviewed the boundaries of the evening.

There were only two rules about dinner discussions at the Gathering: (1) Members were to remain civil. (2) The content and bearers remained private to the group. Each member had signed an agreement, drafted by the judge, committing to adherence to these tenets. All topics were open, no matter how controversial or taboo. Indeed, the more charged, the better.

This portion of the evening officially began at six thirty, when dinner was served, with a hard stop at eight thirty. A roll of five dice determined the order of presenters. Each topic was alive for fifteen minutes, at which time a continuance would be issued if a majority of hands indicated a desire to do so. Rarely would the group get past two or three topics during the evening.

As an initial pledge, I was invited to roll first, and when I dumped the dice from the leather cup, five sixes tumbled across the table. Esther yelled "Yahtzee!" as the room erupted into a chant of "Fix-fix-fix" while laughing. The next-highest totals were from Carmen, followed by the judge. I was on the spot for a topic and tossed out a relatively soft pitch about the rising costs of medicine. That drew some perfectly acceptable jeers, in a light-hearted way.

"Virginia, honey, don't worry, most of us here have been booed at our first attempt. Might I suggest something with a little more, shall we say, sting to it?" offered Roberto. Receiving his hint, I took a mulligan and introduced the subject of patriarchal hierarchies in professional fields. This was met by cheers, table slaps, and wineglasses aloft from all. The topic extended into four rounds, consuming the first hour of the event, an impressive feat for any newcomer.

Carmen went next, her topic just as volatile, as it addressed the increased homeless population, spurred on by out-of-state loafers. They had flocked to the area from other parts of the country because of recent legislation allowing benefits without an established state residency. This imported brand of vagrant, she argued, was not to be confused with the older and harmless winos or hobos who had quietly and unobtrusively roamed the 1st Avenue area for decades. Those poor souls, abandoned by society long ago, were now being displaced from their meager haunts by this much younger and far more aggressive form of bum. The new breed pissed and shat in doorways and alleys, leaving their garbage and nauseating aroma behind for the taxpayers and tourists to enjoy. They brazenly harassed commuters going to and from work in downtown Seattle, Broadway, and the U District, and at this rate it wouldn't be long until they polluted 15th Avenue and Volunteer Park with their disgusting habits. Enabling this behavior was an issue that Seattle was going to have to contend with now, or accept the long-term consequences of their failure to do so.

The final topic of the evening, delivered by the judge, was former Governor Dixy Lee Ray. A nonpolitician with a lighting rod for a personality, she carried many impressive academic accomplishments and was known for conducting state business in her eclectic ensemble of white tube socks, a skirt, and a blazer. Despite her unorthodoxy, she managed to change the landscape and seascape of the Pacific Northwest for all. Environmentalists loathed her for allowing access to the emerald waters of Puget Sound by supertankers and endorsing nuclear power plants, having no problem with the disposal of their waste into the sea. The heavily funded energy and oil industries loved her because of these same positions.

The bell sounded at eight thirty, and commentary on the topic was immediately ended. A customary toast was given in honor of Arthur, Mary, Carla, and the Gathering itself. Afterward, the group helped clear the table and then began to slip out, exchanging Christmas wishes on their way.

Roberto gave me a hug and leaned into my ear, whispering that I must come see him soon, handing me a crisp new Montalvo and Company card. Audrey, Esther, and I stayed to assist with the remaining cleanup and to have another glass of wine. A conversation ensued when Esther heard that Carla and I were both from the Pole Pass community. Esther told us about her recent UW partner dig with WSU and the frustration of its being suddenly shut down and commandeered by the federal government.

The controversy arose when the team reported what they believed to be human remains discovered a couple of miles from their state-approved dig site. After a brief tussle over jurisdiction, their team was barred from further access to either location. There was no chatter anywhere regarding the discovery of remains or other evidence from the second site. Typically, when remains are unearthed, it becomes a headline somewhere, if not in the mainstream press, at least among the local Native populations; and state archaeology departments are aware of the find, with steps taken to resolve the manner legally and consistent with Native customs.

Instead, it appeared that this was just locked down. When questions were posed to the state archaeology department regarding the remains, the schools were told that the remains were missing and assumed to have been removed by superstitious local Natives, likely taken to one of their sacred locations to ceremonially reinter, thereby avoiding some ancestral wrath. This explanation lacked credibility to Esther. According to her contacts in the neighboring tribes, they were alarmed that nothing had been reported to them, and they filed a petition with the federal government to launch an investigation in support of their own.

The site where the remains had been found was so remote that it was unlikely that a tribal member would stumble upon it, much less take the risk of removing any remains in a haphazard manner. The feds' rapid expulsion of the team from the site raised Esther's suspicion that the Smithsonian Institution had procured the discovery under cover of restricting the area. There had long been rumors among archaeologists of this occurring with unusual discoveries, especially in relation to ancient mounds and other indigenous finds. They were viewed as a cult of modern tomb robbers, and if they got hold of a find, it never saw the light of day again.

However, in this case Esther had managed a few photographs before the expulsion. Her intention was to eventually use the photos as part of her dissertation if this panned out. Just before the whole thing erupted, she handed over her film to Karl Rickover, her UW departmental head of the undergrad program. Since the new site was out of the scope of current budgeting, Rickover wanted to review the find before putting his department on the line and making a presentation to the endowment for funding an excavation.

Rickover, himself a UW alumnus, didn't have the best reputation among the hardcore digger community. He had gained minor notoriety penning scholarly articles for publications like *Today's Archaeology*, writing about preservative excavation techniques amid other environmentally friendly methods that were becoming popular platforms of the day. Rickover parlayed his limited fame into a position on the Washington State Board of Archaeology and Historic Preservation, ultimately finding his way to the departmental leadership role at the UW. Along that journey, he had told more than a few enhanced tales of discovery and was known for overplaying his involvement in ethical oversight. Subsequent whisper-talk suggested that he would look the other way if there was something in it for him, and judging by his home, there must have been a lot in it for him. He lived in a large, stately house on 14th and Aloha just a few blocks away from Mary's, furnished with the finest antiques and an art collection that rivaled that of a small museum.

Rickover had been a client of Audrey's on two occasions, the second being the purchase of a very large and expensive painting whose installation he insisted she oversee. As she was leaving the house after the job, Rickover unabashedly asked her for a "fuck," which she politely declined.

"Really? Ewww! He actually said that to you?" we all laughed.

"Yes, Esther, exactly that! It's not that shocking—I'd want to fuck me too!"

We howled at Audrey's delivery. Then, taking a more direct tone, she said, "To Virginia's Gathering topic, my dears, I know of several female shop owners that would have acquiesced to his crudity in hope of increasing their business and customer contacts. Unfortunately, that's been part of the gallery ethos for years. I did appreciate his getting straight to the matter and not wasting any more of my time, though."

"Well, he has nerve, I'll give him that," I said.

"He clearly operates under the philosophy that it never hurts to ask," said Audrey, adding, "One thing that caught my eye during that installation was an obscure sculpture I'm 99 percent sure is in the catalog of unrecovered art and antiquities that were stolen by the Nazis during World War II."

"Did you report that asshole?" Carla asked.

Audrey silently answered by dropping her chin and peering over the top of her eyeglass frames at us.

Esther professed that she knew he wasn't to be trusted but was keenly aware that in her subordinate position it was expedient to employ a strategy of departmental allegiance. That is, if one were to survive with top marks and guaranteed support within a highly competitive program. We all agreed.

Mary passed through the living room just long enough to catch part of the dialogue and drop a bomb of her own. "By the way, Esther, his last name is actually Reichauer. It was changed to Rickover when his family was brought here from Germany, part of some post–World War II scientist grab by the US government. Operation Paperclip . . . according to Arthur."

"Mary?"

"No big mystery, Carla. When Arthur began his career at Boeing, he was in the senior Rickover's department. The guys used to joke around, calling him the Fuehrer behind his back. Brilliant aeronautical engineer, but once a Nazi, always a Nazi, Arthur used to say."

"That explains his Hitler moustache," Esther cracked.

"All right, girls, I hate to break this up," Mary said, "but I've got to be at the bakery by three thirty tomorrow morning, and I need more than four hours of beauty sleep these days."

"Why did you do that to yourself?" Carla asked her.

"I don't know—just to keep me on my toes, I guess."

"Well, if you need me to sub for you, I'll do it."

"Thanks, Carla, but I'll be fine. Just come in for breakfast when you get up."

"OK, fair enough."

Carla and I loaded the remaining glasses into the dishwasher, enjoying a brief moment of smiles, acknowledging that this connection was a good thing; we planned to see each other Friday night at her apartment for dinner and a sleepover. Esther kindly offered me a ride back to campus, and along the way we made a coffee date for Friday morning on the Ave.

The Gathering had been unexpected and refreshing, totally in keeping with the things I'd been experiencing of late. Escaping my med school bubble for entree into this diverse community was fun . . . an ingredient hidden away on a shelf somewhere behind my fear of failure. As I drifted off to sleep, I marveled at the encounter at the Surrogate, unable to comprehend the coincidence regarding the confluence of our waters. How, in less than a week, had I not only gained a sister, but found several friends and another community I never knew existed? My next step would be to call Roberto first thing in the morning for a hair appointment.

20

ROBERTO

Arriving in the heart of Fremont by bus, I walked north through the small village under gentrification until I found Montalvo and Company, on the west side of the street. Though booked solid, Roberto had excitedly scheduled me for an after-hours appointment. Greeting me with a hug and a cheek-to-cheek kiss, he hung my coat, then sat me at his station and excused himself before disappearing into a backroom. The smooth jazz sounds of Grover Washington Jr. washed over me, as Roberto reemerged shortly with an ice bucket, two glasses, and a chilled bottle of Chardonnay that another client had given him earlier. "Cheers to us," he said with a big smile as we clinked the stemware.

Roberto confidently took his position behind the chair and released the simple three-strand braid, letting my heavy hair drape over the back of the chair.

"Now, what are we going to do with this ton of hair tonight?" he asked, pulling his lean tint-stained fingers through my tresses.

"I don't even know where to start, Roberto. I haven't done anything with it in a long time. Do you have any ideas?"

"Oh honey . . . I have ideas, trust me," he said in a mischievous way that made us both laugh.

"Go for it! I'm in your hands," I replied, feeling completely secure with his abilities.

"I was hoping you'd say that. Let's get to it, then!"

The next three hours were filled with conversation yielding much laughter, a few tears, and a level of understanding that would create a lifelong bond between the two of us.

Roberto, himself a transplant from Mary's hometown of Moses Lake, had an acute awareness of an east-of-the-Cascades upbringing. He possessed a unique ability to disarm anyone, or any subject for that matter; this made him a brilliant conversationalist and an ideal fit for the Gathering's diverse membership and often-precarious topics. We spoke a little about Carla and how he simply adored "that one," as he often referred to her.

He recounted his own Eastern Washington upbringing: the confusion, isolation, and despair that he had felt until he was able to escape to Seattle and begin to make his own way in life.

Once he graduated from Sabina's Beauty School in Moses Lake and passed the state boards, he was "wheels up" and over Snoqualmie Pass, leaving only painful memories and a few family members in his wake. After a brief salon apprenticeship, he was on his way to establishing himself as one of the premier hairdressers in Seattle.

Listening to Roberto's story helped me comprehend a little of what it must have been like for Carla during our years apart.

The abandonment by those she loved and depended on; the devastation she must have felt, and feeling like a misfit. I knew she must be an amazingly strong and resilient individual not only to have survived the emotional toll of that period but also to pull up stakes and create a better life, just as Roberto did. I never harbored ill feelings over the things that Carla said that day in Pole Pass, but now I had a greater understanding of why they were said, and was grateful that she was even speaking to me.

"Survivor's guilt," stated Roberto resolutely. "Virginia dear, life is to be lived in the now, not in the past, which we can do nothing about, or in the future, which until we reach it is mere fantasy."

"I like that."

"Thanks—I find that doing my best today, whatever that may be, is sufficient. Life is more manageable that way."

Amazed by our reconnection, Roberto, in his most spiritual way, said that the love bond between Carla and me must be very powerful to bring this relationship back into orbit. In his view, it was destiny and not just happenstance. I agreed.

"So what's this I hear about a boyfriend?" Roberto asked while applying the high lift tint.

"Yes, Town Lawe . . . the most intimate person I have ever met."

Roberto stopped mid–foil packet with jaw dropped. "Wait a minute, his name is Town Lawe? Oh my God, I love that name!"

I told him about the first time we met on the pool deck and the magic I felt for a millisecond when our fingertips touched. "It was like an electric current, but without that pop of a static."

"Oh, you were turned on! That's a great sign," Roberto said slyly.

"True, but it was something beyond that."

"Uh-huh . . . got a photo?"

Roberto set the timer for my color, refilled our glasses, and took a seat across from me as I produced a picture taken the past September. Town was still tan, his hair lightened by the sun and piled up like a white mop on top of his head. He was sparsely dressed in crew attire consisting of a Princeton Crew sleeveless T-shirt and a square-cut orange-and-black Speedo. The photo was taken as he and the team were hoisting a racing shell above their heads in front of the boathouse on Lake Carnegie.

"Good God! Hello body! Don't bring him in here, or it might get ugly!" Roberto blurted out, covering his mouth with the back of his hand before taking another sip of wine.

"I'm going to schedule him with you the next time he comes to visit."

"Oh please do, and you tell him if he wears that outfit, I'll do his hair for free!"

"I'll pass that on when I see him next week!"

"You do that!" he laughed.

"I haven't worn my hair down in ages," I told Roberto as he had me flip my head down to dry the underneath layers with a diffuser.

"Good, because it's time for a change."

When Roberto was finished with the dryer, he lifted my head back up and gently raked his fingers through the long layered haircut before spinning me back around in the chair so I could see his handiwork.

"I knew you were a beauty, Virginia, but God bless, girl," he said, looking at me in the reflection of his floor-to-ceiling mirror and using the remaining Tenax on his fingers to piece out my fringe, just so.

I immediately burst into tears. "Roberto, this looks so great, I love it! Thank you, thank you, so much!"

"Oh, sweetheart, it's been my pleasure," he responded, giving me a hug and handing me a box of tissue. "The highlights came out perfect even for winter, and they'll make this mane of yours much easier to style rather than you always having to pull it back."

As we said our goodbyes, I scheduled my next appointment for the first week of February 1982 and asked what I owed him. "Nothing but a smile; Carla took care of the rest, honey."

~

After my early rounds Friday morning, Esther and I met in front of Café Allegro on the Ave.

"Wow! Roberto's work?" she said as we walked inside.

"Yeah."

"It looks great. I won't let anyone else cut my hair again, trust me—I learned that lesson the hard way."

We sat down with our espressos and pastries at a table next to the large window, where we watched the street activity while chatting. Esther, a native Seattleite raised in the Wallingford district, became fascinated with archaeology after attending the Tutankhamun exhibition at the

Pacific Science Center in 1972. She hadn't been to Egypt as of yet, but sites in Japan, Mexico, and the Americas had succumbed to her early studies. As brilliant as she was, Esther wouldn't dare bask in the light of her intellectual performance or other earned accolades. Instead, the opposing voices of doubt on one shoulder and assurance on the other produced a cacophony of bickering back and forth that would drain away any reserves of confidence. I could instantly relate, furthering her description by citing the self-imposed pressure that took residence between our ears. The pervasiveness was guaranteed to wake you up in the middle of the night a couple of times a week. At least at our current stations we could identify the nuisance for what it was and laugh about the self-inflicted torment we experienced.

"So, what was it like growing up in Pole Pass?" she asked.

"You know, it was a nice small town. I think it's a good place to grow up, then get out, and maybe even return to someday."

"I hear you have a boyfriend at Princeton?"

"Yeah, he's a special guy."

"I'm sure he is; what's he studying?"

"Molecular bio, but he has always had a passion for archaeology."

"Oh shit, he's lucky and he's smart." Esther's compliment was accompanied by a smile.

"What about you?"

"I just haven't found the one," she said. "Until I do, I'm not wasting my time with dating around."

"That's a great philosophy. I have another friend who lives that way."

"It works for me—the other way is just too distracting."

"I've always thought that too."

My pager began its annoying flash and vibrating dance across our table. "Crap. Sorry, Esther, would you please excuse me for a minute while I call in?"

"Of course, no apology necessary."

I returned a few minutes later from the pay phone at the rear of the shop. "Esther, I'm really sorry, but I need to get back over to the hospital. Being on call is part of my tuition," I said, rolling my eyes.

"No problem, I totally get it. Let's connect when you get back from Princeton, OK?"

"Yes, of course. Dinner on me, and I'll leave my pager at home."

"Great, I'd love to!"

"Hey, I just thought of something," I said. "Town's dad is a lawyer connected to federal land trusts, and he's in Pole Pass. Do you want me to ask him about your situation?"

"Oh, that would be amazing!" she exclaimed. "You don't think he'd mind?"

"I doubt it, he's really wonderful."

"Wow, thank you for thinking of that—it's really kind."

"No big . . . I'm happy to help."

21

THE KINDLING

I was catnapping as the No. 10 Capitol Hill crept up Pine Street from the waterfront of downtown Seattle. The tranquilizing low-pitched whir coupled with the ebb-and-flow motion of the old-style trolleybus lulled many tired commuters to sleep during their return journeys. I stirred when the bus made a hard left onto 15th Avenue East and the driver began calling out the upcoming stops. Returning the medical book I had dozed off with to my backpack, I snapped into full consciousness, a technique I had mastered during med school. Looking through the bus window into the darkness, I saw the pink neon teakettle sign of the Teapot Chinese restaurant drawing closer as the driver yelled, "Group Health . . . next stop, Harrison." I pulled the cord a minute later, making my way to the front of the coach as he belted out, "Reee-pub-li-caan" in the theatrical manner of a baseball umpire calling a pitch. The bus lurched to the curb, followed by the *shhh* of air pressure releasing, as the accordion doors folded open.

"Merry Christmas, miss, have a nice evening."

"Thank you, sir, and Merry Christmas to you," I replied, stepping out into the cold December night.

I walked past the Surrogate, recalling the previous Saturday morning when I had ventured inside for a shot of espresso. It was not the first time I had done the exact same thing, but last week was set aside just for us; and like the tumblers of some cosmic combination lock aligning, our lives were now opened to each other. I had no idea what tonight would bring, but whatever it did, I knew that Carla and I would face it together.

Arriving at her building, I scanned the resident panel looking for apartment 420 and the label reading Jake Oph. I pressed the button and was greeted by the static-laced crackle of an aged intercom: "Yes?" said the voice of teenage boy.

"I'm sorry, is Carla available?"

"Yay! C'mon up, fourth floor, take a right off the elevator." A loud buzzer released the lock on the outside door.

"Isn't that buzzer a bitch?" Carla laughed and hugged me, kissing my cold cheek as she welcomed me into her apartment. "Sorry for the voice—can't be too careful these days. Wow, look at you! I love your hair! Roberto is the best, isn't he?"

"Yes, he is, and thank you so much! But you didn't have to—"

"You're welcome, and I wanted to, so shut up!" Carla replied, taking my coat.

"Your place is so nice," I said, gazing around the room. "I love the high ceilings and wood floors."

"Thanks—I upgraded buildings last month, and I love the extra space with front-facing windows. My former digs around the corner were pretty dreary, so when this apartment became available, I jumped on it. Want a tour?"

"By all means."

"So my favorite is the big front room with the bay window looking out over 16th—it gives great light even on the grayest Seattle days."

"It's huge. I love your Christmas tree too, and those velvet chairs are spectacular!"

"Thanks, I've never done white lights before; they do give a nice soft glow. I just got the chairs—they're perfect to curl up in with a cup of coffee and a book. A friend of Audrey's owns a vintage store off Broadway and made me a great deal on them. If you ever need something, I'd love to introduce you. He has a wonderful eye for furnishings, and because he's *family* he gives a fair deal."

"Well, when I figure out where my new place is, I'll take you up on that!"

"The dining room, you can see, is pulling double duty as a makeshift studio."

We walked into the kitchen just as the oven timer sounded. "Perfect. Let me get dinner out of the oven real quick; we don't want it to dry out."

"Oh, that's where that smell is coming from," I said, eyeing the large cast-iron Dutch oven that Carla relocated to the stove top.

"Beef barley stew tonight. I thought it would be an ultimate foil to the cold, wet weather that rolled in."

"Yum!"

"I get the soup bones and beef from an organic farmer that delivers to us from Duval. You *are* hungry, right?"

"Bordering on starvation."

"Excellent! Would you mind grabbing the charcuterie tray from the fridge? I'll toss a baguette in the oven and fetch a bottle of wine from the cellar. We can sit in the living room and have a glass and snack a bit before dinner."

Carla reached into one of the lower kitchen cabinets that she had fitted with cross bracing to retrieve a bottle of wine, and we moved to the living room sofa.

"Cheers!" I said as we clinked glasses.

"Ahhh . . . relaxed at last. It feels good to sit down. So, how was your day?"

"Good, thanks," I replied. "Early hospital rounds, then a short break; met up with Esther for coffee on the Ave at seven this morning."

"Seven? Geez, what time were your rounds?"

"They began at four."

"Well, if you ever decide to leave medicine, I know a bakery that would love to have you! How was Esther? I really like that girl; she's smart, with a great wit."

"Yeah, she's a really neat girl. School is a grind no matter what your studies are. I think we are both just fighting to get through the oversight of professional academia. What time did you start today?"

"I went in at five just to take care of some catering inventory and lend a hand for the morning rush."

"Oh, that's right; don't you have a big event coming up?"

"Yes, a corporate Christmas party on Tuesday night—it's going to be the largest one we've done since opening the catering arm of the business. It's for a new company on the East side called Microsoft. We just catered a press event for them last month, and it went well. Nice people—they were left hanging when the catering company they used had double-booked with Boeing and apologetically ditched them. In this business, when opportunity knocks . . ."

"Congratulations, sounds exciting!"

"I know we have the team to pull it off, and that helps."

"Are you sure you can spare a night with me?" I asked.

"This is my calm before the storm. Tomorrow through Monday I will be balls to the wall, please pardon my vulgar."

"That's funny. Pardoned."

Beep-beep-beep sounded the oven timer.

"They're playing our song again—dinner's ready!"

"How can I help?"

"I got it—you just sit your butt at the table and get ready to eat!"

Carla brought in the hot baguette swaddled in a cotton towel, setting it on the dining table next to the Dutch oven.

"Don't touch this pot; it will leave a mark on you," she said as she ladled generous portions of the rich dark stew for us. "Around here we just pull off hunks of bread and smear them with that fresh butter, all casual and efficient like."

"Oh my, Carla," I said between spoonfuls.

"You like?"

"No, I love it. Is this your recipe?"

"You certainly know how to get to a girl's heart, don't you? Yes, it's mine; I'll share it with you, but I really need to teach you how to make it. It's all about technique with this dish. Mary's taught me so much, always a stickler for things. She would make me redo the most menial tasks during my apprenticeship. It drove me crazy at times, but now I know why, and it makes sense."

"She's been a huge influence in your life, hasn't she?"

"She really has. She and Arthur—rest in peace—pretty much adopted me when I arrived in Seattle. Mary has been a mentor, a guardian, a mother, a sis . . ." Carla stopped herself.

"No, no, no, a sister," I asserted. "You should say that—it's true! I could see it at the Gathering."

Carla began to get teary but held it back and carried on. "Thank you . . . she's a 'lifer,' as I like to say."

"What about Audrey? Have you been dating long?"

"OK, so this is like I'm coming out to my family." Carla regained her smile with a little sniffle.

"I'm happy for you!"

Carla smiled. "Only a couple of weeks . . . and I have to say that beyond the infatuation there is something much deeper between us that I don't have the words for. It's a connection that I know will always be between us. I guess it's a love thing?"

"I think I know the feeling. I hope I can spend more time with all of you."

"Well, speaking of: I have the privilege of extending the offer of full membership in the Gathering—the vote was unanimous."

"Oh, wow, thank you! I'm honored, and of course I accept."

"Congratulations! I think you will enjoy the mix; we are up to about twenty people now, and that's a good number for the rotations. But enough about me for the moment—catch me up on you, and then I want to know everything about Mr. Town Lawe. No skipping the juicy stuff, either," Carla said slyly.

"All right. Let's see . . . school is a grinder, some of the dogma absolute bullshit, but to survive, it's like anything else: you suck it up and power through."

Telling Carla about the loss of Lana and how it almost broke me, I could see that she felt the pain as I recounted the event. "It was the catalyst that put me into therapy. Today I know the breadth of Lana's gift."

"It's amazing how trauma drags us along until we confront it. At least that's what happened with me after Mom and Martin split up."

I offered Carla my perspective on the era following the divorce and our relocation up mountain to Pole Pass, revealing in the process that I had discovered I was depressed.

"I dreaded that first summer, terrified at the prospect of no schoolwork or sports to occupy my mind. The walls were closing in, and all I could do was pray. The last few days of school came, and everyone received their yearbooks—everyone, it seemed, except me. Mom was trying to rebuild, we were barely making ends meet at the time, and ordering one just got lost.

"My track teammate saw that I didn't have one, and she marched into the office insisting that as a varsity athlete and honors student, I receive one immediately. She even paid for it. I was speechless. Before handing it to me, Carol opened it to our track team page and wrote the first paragraph of my new life. I was so touched that I broke down and sobbed, like a full-on ugly cry! She gave me the sweetest hug, saying she was proud to be my friend, and invited me to her house for a swim. That was the day I met Town; I can't explain it but I swear to you it was love at first sight. The song 'Close to You' still reminds me of that moment."

"Virginia, that's a beautiful story."

"I'm so lucky. By the way, this is the best stew I have ever eaten."

"Thank you, I'm glad you like it. Dessert, on the other hand . . . I have some lemon tarts, but they won't do with this red wine, that's for sure."

"Oh, I have something to contribute," I said, and then retrieved an item from my backpack that resembled half of a brick wrapped tightly in aluminum foil.

"Is that hash?"

We both laughed.

"Got a cutting board and cleaver?"

"Ha-ha, what do you think?" Carla said, as she produced both on the dining room table within seconds.

I slapped the foil package on the cutting board with a thud and unwrapped what we both believed to be the darkest hunk of chocolate in Seattle.

"Whoa, Nellie! That's major cacao! Where did you get it?"

"Not just cacao, but Criollo cacao, 92 percent pure. I helped a beautiful little Peruvian lady, and she brought a two-pound block of it back for me the last time she visited. You think this will go with red?"

"Shit! We just might eat that whole thing tonight and be up for a week!"

After finishing our stew, we migrated to the living room, where we began whittling away at the block while experiencing the interplay between the chocolate and the dark character of the fine Cabernet that Carla had selected.

"Virginia, this is about as close to a perfect pairing as it gets."

"I agree. To red wine and cacao!" We raised our glasses in toast.

"So, let me begin this long-overdue conversation with my apology," I said.

"You don't have to . . ."

"No, please." I held up my hand. "I'm completely aware that this will sound selfish, like some grand confessional of the I's, but I want you to hear it from me at least one time in this life. Afterward, I won't bring it up again—promise."

"OK, fair enough, but I get to go after you."

Not once did I break eye contact with Carla during the moment that followed.

"I want you to know that I am so sorry that I didn't try harder. I'm sorry that you were abandoned and caught in the net of a marriage that probably should never have been. I can't know the pain that you went through during those years, nor can I heal it. I'm just so proud of you, and amazed by the lovely person I see today. I want you to know that I accept the responsibility for contributing to your pain. All I can say is that I love you and that I never forgot about you. I wouldn't expect you to trust me with the life you have created for yourself, but I want you to know that I won't betray it if you do."

My words were given and met with overflowing eyes from each of us. Carla blotted hers with a sleeve in silence as she gathered herself to respond to my tidal surge of contrition. She got up and gently sat her petite frame down on my lap, wrapping her arms around my neck like she did as a little girl in our living room before innocence was lost. We sat like that for several minutes. Then she refilled our glasses and pulled me over to the sofa, where we occupied each end and let our legs stretch out over each other's.

She tossed a blanket over our legs and began to speak. "Thanks for saying all of that. I realize it wasn't your fault. I want you to know I understand that now. I owe you an apology for the vile things that I said to you in the park. You never deserved such hatred from me. I was lost, and angry at the entire universe, something that haunted me for years. I missed you both desperately. You never knew it, but I saw you run at a West Valley versus Pole Pass track meet one time. You got disqualified for tripping that girl." Carla snort-laughed through her tears.

"Wait—you were there? That was Alice Ibelsof, my main track rival. She used to elbow me during the cross-country events and say nasty things about Mom, always trying to psych me out. Carol kicked her feet together once, and she bit it hard. That was the last of her taunts. I think she's related to the Listers."

"Yeah, she might be part Lister, like Martin was. Some friends and I went down to the field when we were in ninth grade," Carla continued. "I saw this girl from the other side of the track and thought she was beautiful; then they announced your name over the loudspeaker. I was in shock, and too ashamed to tell my friends or even approach you."

"I'm really sorry."

"It was a strange time, but as a kid you adapt to circumstances, or you don't survive without being miserable. I ran the gamut of misery and eventually found my way out. The things Martin said back then, the things the Lister family talked about, they were all just lies. I guess I knew it deep down, but it was easier to not fight against it. They always painted Martin as a good father. He met the outward needs . . . I never went without food, clothing, school supplies, etc., but Martin didn't love me. I was just another possession, not much different from one of his tractors or lodge trinkets. Living as a Founder relation brings a lot of strange minions around, but the Listers were the creepiest of the bunch. They always seemed to be scheming. Do you remember Jig Lister?"

"Oh yeah—he hung around in Pole Pass sometimes," I recalled. "I was in the post office once and could smell him from across the room. Poor hygiene, that fellow."

"That's totally him!" Carla said with a laugh. "He always smelled like sour dishrag and vomit. One time the bastard tried to peek at me through the open bathroom window, thinking I was taking a shower. Thing is, I had the shower running but was sitting on the toilet sneaking a smoke, and when he stuck his jug-head in the window, I smashed the cigarette out on his face. I got him just under his left eyeball, the dirty prick. He yelped bloody murder and fell off the milk crates he was standing on, running for the hills, holding his eye. He didn't come around me after that.

"I told Martin what that stinky pervert did and what he got for it. All Martin said was, 'Just let it be, and if you are going to smoke, don't smoke mine—get your own goddamned cigarettes.' After that, I started sleeping with a big butcher knife, its handle sticking out between the mattress and box spring so I could grab it quick if needed. That was around the time I became aware of not wanting anything to do with guys. I was sixteen."

"I'm so sorry you had to go through that alone," I said.

"Hey, look, you have got to stop apologizing. Didn't your therapist tell you that?" Carla laughed.

I nodded, took a sip of wine, and smiled.

"I felt the anger building up inside of me. I was my own version of Mount St. Helens about to blow. There was a period of about a year and a half when I would lock myself away in my bedroom for days on end, just drawing and painting. It was the only thing that took my mind off the butcher knife stashed under the mattress and its invitation to put an end to the life I was trapped in. The morning after we met in the park, I began working on a sketch, and with each touch of the charcoal to the paper, it was as if I was slowly releasing a beautiful bird from its cage. The morning after I completed it, Martin was dead."

"I remember Town called me with the news. He went off West Canyon Road at the hairpin, driving home from drinking at the Mineshaft?"

"Yeah, that was the official report. He had driven that stretch a thousand times drunk as a skunk, including a few days earlier. He staggered into the house that night and told me that the Listers weren't to be trusted. 'No good, low-down, dangerous,' he muttered as I took his boots off and put a blanket over him on the couch. The last thing he said before he passed out was, 'If something happens to me, you check my boots,' and he started snoring. At the time, I just chalked it up to Founder family feuding that was ongoing in those circles. But there was more to it. In the depths of myself, I believe they murdered him."

"Really? The Listers? But he was part of that clan."

"Yeah, he had Lister blood in him, but he wasn't a full-share Lister. That's why my name didn't reflect the Lister branding, thank God. The best he could do for himself was the hyphenation. Things had gotten intense around the house over the last few months. I don't think it was about money; he was always bragging about how well the dealership was doing. It was when anything to do with the lodge came up. He would become really ill-tempered, agitated with the smallest things. I remember seeing him wringing his hands, pacing around downstairs of the farmhouse about a month before his death. I asked him what was going on, and he looked over at me with an expression that I can only describe as distressed, and said, 'You should really get away from here, Carla.' You know, in retrospect I think it was the closest thing to 'I love you' that he ever said. It was certainly the best advice he ever offered me. Heartbreaking, really."

"Wow."

"Yeah, so when the Pass County sheriff came knocking at about six o'clock that morning, I had a cold chill run through me before I opened the door. He said, 'Sorry, Miss Carla, I hate to tell you this, but there was an accident, and your dad is dead.'

"Through the barrage of confused feelings, I asked what happened. 'It was a single-car accident off West Canyon Road. We believe it occurred between two thirty and three this morning. We don't know if he fell asleep at the wheel or if he swerved to miss wildlife, but he went through the guardrail at the hairpin and flipped down into the bottom of the canyon. I know that this is a shock to you. I don't mind taking you to the morgue to make the identification, but if you can, have another family member verify the identity, Carla—I would.'

"Sam Waterson is such a nice man," she said. "He has a daughter my age, and I could tell he was looking out for me.

I thanked him for delivering the news and said I needed some time alone to think. When I closed the door and met the silence head-on, I felt the sadness hit me. It was a mixture, but Martin was the only father, or provider, or whatever, that I had known. I mean, I lived with him for eighteen years. I guess I thought that was what love was, but I didn't enjoy the feeling. I spoke aloud to him, said that I was sorry he died, and for not being the daughter he wanted, but I wished him to rest in peace. In that moment of goodbye, it was as if he had brought his last drunken ramble back to my mind. I immediately went into his bedroom closet and starting going through his cowboy boots. In the most beat-up pair of ropers I found a key for a safe-deposit box at First Bank in East Valley.

"It wasn't two minutes later that I heard cars heading up the gravel driveway—it was those damned Listers and some of Martin's lodge pals. 'Oh Carla, honey, we are so sorry. We can't believe any of this. It's just horrible, horrible it is,' blathered Eunice, as she scanned the inside of the house. I played the grieving daughter, manufactured some additional tears for them, and said that I would have to lean on them for wisdom, blah, blah, blah.

"'We are your family now, Carla, don't you fret about anything.' That's what that old sow had the nerve to say while smothering me between her torpedoes and squeezing the life out of me with her clammy sausage arms. I know that sounds harsh, but remember, these are the same people who told me my whole life that my mother was nothing but a whore and that she and my bastard sister left me behind, so they could go mix with others. Whatever the fuck that means! After the recent turn of events and the interactions with Martin and his drunken mumblings, I was much more wary of them than in the past, and that's saying something. So, I just soaked up the attention during their visit, never breaking from character.

"They insisted that I shouldn't be alone during my time of grief; perhaps I should move into the big old Lister house up in the Pass until the funeral. They could 'love on me, cook for me, and help me navigate any of the paperwork.' I told them that I just couldn't leave the house, not now, but I would certainly welcome Eunice to stay with me just until we got things sorted out if she could. I knew that would throw her. 'Well, well, uh, uh . . . I'll have cousin Mavis come stay with you. She will be perfect—you know, she lost her father when she was younger too.'

"I acted as if I was disappointed and asked Eunice if she would go to the morgue and make the identification, and she did it. I figured this way I wouldn't have to look at Martin's burned-up corpse and have that image stuck in my mind, only to come out in my artwork for who knows how long.

"True to Lister appearances, they wasted no time in conducting a high-profile memorial service. It seemed like all the farmers from the area were packed into Adams Memorial Chapel, where a parade of family and lodge members eulogized and shared their remembrances of Martin. The reading of the will immediately followed the burial, and that was when the shit really hit the fan!"

"Don't stop now!" I said, refilling our wineglasses.

"Everyone gathered in Stanley Lister's office, tissues in hand, still carrying on with their solemn performances. Stanley was the executor of Martin's estate and wore his smug look of arrogance as he sat down at his desk. Just as he was about to begin the proceedings, there was a firm rap-rap-rap on the heavy mahogany door. Without waiting for a response, in walked a stately man in an Armani suit who moved quickly to the front of the large office. The room was silent as the man clicked open the latches of his briefcase and produced a file folder."

"Whoa. Who was it?"

Carla paused for a theatrical second. "Daniel Lawe!"

"Shit! Town's dad? C'mon, really?" I was flabbergasted.

"Yeah, really! You should have seen their faces—almost like yours!" Carla laughed. "I swear Stanley turned green and looked like he was about to barf on his desk, and Eunice was livid. I thought her eyes were going to squirt blood at any second. The first words Mr. Lawe spoke were, 'Good afternoon, folks, I'm sorry we are convening under such unpleasant circumstances.'

"'N-n-now, see here, Daniel, what's this all about?' Stanley bristled.

"'Hello, Stanley. Am I correct in understanding that this is the reading of the last will and testament of Martin P. Nelson-Lister?'

"'You are, but what has that to do with you?'

"'Well, I must inform you, Stanley, that you have been replaced as the executor of the deceased's estate, by me. I have a copy here of the independently verified will that I am prepared to execute immediately. It is the document that Mr. Nelson-Lister contracted me to draft and file for him twenty-one days ago. It supersedes all preceding documents of this nature, and as you may guess, Stanley, it is ironclad.'

"'You wait just a g-g-g-goddamned minute, Danny Lawe!' Eunice yelled, as she jumped up out of her chair.

"'Madam?'

"'You shouldn't monkey around in other people's family affairs—I would have thought you had learned that lesson by n-n-now!' she stuttered while shaking that ham hock she calls a hand at him.

"Mr. Lawe raised his voice: 'Sam, would you mind stepping in here, please?' A second later, Sheriff Sam Waterson walked into Lister's office from the waiting room, and Mr. Lawe continued: 'Sorry, folks, I thought we might be able to conduct this in a courteous and civil manner. I understand that grief makes people say and do many things that they normally might not. Stanley, would you mind if we conduct the reading here?'

"'Well, I don't know about that . . .'

"'All I can say is that everyone named in the document is present. My only obligation today is to execute the legal and final will of Martin P. Nelson-Lister. Now that everyone in this room has been notified of its existence, as witnessed by the Pass County Sheriff's Office, the time and place of its execution are immaterial to me. Either I read it here, right now, or on the steps of the courthouse across the street in the time it takes us to walk over there.'

"All eyes shifted back to Stanley. 'OK, go ahead on and read it, then,' he said as he sank down in his chair, resigned to whatever was about to unfold.

"'Thank you, Stanley.'

"So, after reading through the official legalese, Mr. Lawe got into the dispensations: 'To my beloved Fraternal Order of Farmers Lodge Brethren—I leave our Lodge with my regalia consisting of: 2 robes, 1 sash, 1 Lodge ring, 1 pen and pencil set, 1 Lodge pocket watch and fob, and 16 Lodge service pins. All of these items reside in my locker on the Lodge premises. Do with them what you will, and keep up the good work.'

"Mr. Lawe prefaced the next line with, 'I have no idea who it's intended for, but this is exactly how the deceased wanted it read: "Repent."'

"I noticed a few curious glances between Stanley, Jig, and Eunice, with Reginald Harrison raising an eyebrow too. Then Mr. Lawe called my name, 'Carla Nelson,' and I could feel the heat rise into my face as everyone in the room turned their attention toward me. '"To Carla: For what it's worth, the only thing that I can leave you with is the farmhouse, the surrounding property, outbuildings, and everything in them with the exception of the International Harvester combine, which belongs to the tractor dealership. Make a life for yourself."'

"That announcement brought a sizable grumble, with looks shooting everywhere. Stanley stayed silent, refusing any eye contact with Eunice. I glanced discreetly over at her to see that she was staring at Stanley with fists balled up so tightly that they were white.

"'Next we have Eunice Lister.'

"Eunice interrupted, muttering, 'Well, there ain't nothing goddamned left, is there now?'

"Mr. Lawe ignored her but looked up from the paper just long enough for me to catch a smirk on his face before he carried on. '"Eunice, you were great at treating me like an inconvenient family member. I didn't hate you for it, but then you stole my tractor dealership. You knew it was my pride and joy, and you managed to swindle me out of it and hold me hostage. For that, I hated you. Your inheritance is the sweat off my balls."'

"This was followed by a gasp and a muffled Tourette's-style stuttering outburst from Eunice, with Jig rubbing her back to calm her down. Stanley, Jig, and Charlie Lister all received the same as Eunice."

"Oh my God. I don't believe it!" I exclaimed.

"Believe it. I swear every bit is true. But Eunice wasn't done yet. Stanley said, 'If that's all there is, we would like you to leave now.'

"'That's it, Stanley, as far as the will goes. However, Martin did have a private burial insurance policy. If you care to submit the charges for the beautiful service you organized, I'll make sure that you are reimbursed accordingly.'

"'Y-y-you get the hell out of here r-r-right now!' Eunice seethed.

"'Mother!' Stanley said. 'That's not helping anything.'

"Eunice was so bent out of shape that she could barely get her words out, telling Stanley to 'sh-sh-shuut up, d-d-d-dummy!' I swear, her stuttering and bugged eyes made me snort-laugh. I tried to cover it up with a look of shock and dismay, but I don't think I was successful. I stayed behind as Mr. Lawe had advised me to do, and went around to everyone apologizing, saying I was as shocked as they were.

"Eunice said, 'That no-good s-s-son-of-a-b-b-bitch half-blood. I told you to watch him and not trust him too much.'

"'Mother, please!' Stanley urged. 'You need to calm down—your blood pressure.'

"Then Eunice got down to business. 'Look here, Stanley, Carla's a smart girl. She knows full well that Martin was a tad bit shady. Don't you, Carla? I bet she even suspects he probably wasn't even her real daddy. Now, Carla, we need to talk about a few things. Maybe we could have lunch tomorrow?'

"'Yes, ma'am, of course,' I said.

"'Why don't you come to the big house at noon and we can discuss the opportunities.'

"So I had lunch with Eunice and Stanley, but I changed the venue from her house to Andy's Café, because I was in the mood for their French toast, and . . . I was a little scared of being in that big Lister house alone with them. Over lunch, Eunice apologized for her outburst at the reading, saying she shouldn't have allowed that son of a bitch Injun attorney to rile her up so goddamn much.

"Then Stanley got to the point of our meeting. 'Carla, that farmhouse and property is a lot of responsibility for a young person to be saddled with. The maintenance in itself on a small farm is a full-time job. Martin was a pack rat, and those outbuildings need to be cleaned up, probably full of rats, and a real firetrap. I can send Jig and the boys over to help go through all that junk and haul it off.'

"Playing coy, I agreed with the responsibility part and asked them if I should just put it up for sale. They knew the property would sell quickly if I put on the market, and the way they swarmed after Martin's death, they were looking for something else besides just real estate.

"'Carla, it seems to be in the best interests of us both if we could come to an agreement. One where you wouldn't have to deal with all of this and could make a fresh start in life, just like Martin's last wish for you.'

"'Do you mean sell the property to you?' I asked.

"'Sell is such an unfriendly term between family members . . . but yes, I'm sure we could arrange a transfer that is fair to all.'

"'Don't you own that old Pole Pass Dry Goods building on Main?'

"'Yes, that's been in the family for over a hundred years now.'

"'Glad to hear it. I want that building in exchange for my property, straight across.'

"'Now Carla, what on earth would you want with that old building?' Stanley said, as Eunice remained quiet.

"'I want to put my art gallery there.'

"'Well, I don't know . . . That's a very nice historic building in the heart of Pole Pass. Like I said, it's been in the family a long, long time.'

"'Sitting empty a long, long time is more like it. With the amount of work it needs to bring it to current codes, you know it's a fair deal, and I can close by Friday.'

"'Oh, I'm not sure . . . We will have to think about that one. After all, Listers aren't in the habit of divesting ourselves of family property.'

"'Didn't you not two minutes ago intimate that we are family? Since that's the case, the property is still in the family, then, isn't it?'

"'Well, well . . . ,' Stanley said, flummoxed.

"'She's got you there, genius,' Eunice finally piped up with a rare chuckle.

"'Well, regardless, we still have to think about it, Carla.'

"'Please don't think too long, because I'm meeting with an agent from East Valley after I leave here, and I intend to sign their listing contract. They claim to have a guaranteed buyer at top asking price.'

"Stanley and Eunice immediately exchanged looks, both realizing that they had underestimated me. Eunice thought she was paying me a compliment by saying, 'You just may have some Lister blood in your veins after all, Carla.'

"'OK, I guess we have a deal, then. I'll draw up the papers and see you Friday at NPL&T for closing,' Stanley said.

"That was it. I moved my stuff into the Twin Village apartments in West Valley and said goodbye to the old farmhouse once and for all. I couldn't have done any of it without Mr. Lawe."

"Yeah, that's him for sure. But how did all of this come about?"

"When I opened the safe-deposit box at the bank, there was a bundle of fifty one-hundred dollar bills, the farmhouse deed, an envelope containing a little book, and his updated will. There was a note clipped to the will that read: 'Take this to the legal office of Daniel Lawe in Pole Pass.' Mr. Lawe sat with me for hours listening to my life story and fragmented dreams that I couldn't assemble into anything intelligible by myself. He helped me see things clearly, and then he took the time to create a plan with me, just like I was his own daughter. I have never felt more cared for by a man than by him. He advised me how to respond at the reading of the will, and also, because of my ambitions, he's the one who prompted me to trade for that property on Main Street. He knew they would be expecting to inherit the farm property at the reading of the will—I guess Martin must have told him as much. The Pole Pass Dry Goods building sat unchanged in value for two years, and in the past six months it's more than doubled!"

"Congratulations. And please forgive me . . . I'm slightly stunned over this whole thing. It's a little weird, right?"

"More than a little! Incidentally, he did ask if I wanted you to know, but after what I said to you in the park that day and all that was happening in the moment, I told him that I wasn't ready to talk. I was still ashamed, and pretty confused. He tried to assure me that it would be OK if I sought you out, but I just wasn't there yet, and I trusted him to keep this confidential."

"Your trust wasn't misplaced. But why didn't you start your gallery?"

"Yeah, well, the Lister weirdness didn't stop after the property closing. I had been in my apartment for about a year, working on and off at the building, when I got a call from Charlie Lister. He wanted to meet with me all the way over in East Valley for lunch to show me a property he said was a goldmine. I didn't want to deal with the Listers anymore, but I also needed to keep a cordial relationship, so I met with him. We ate across from the new outlet mall still under construction at the time, and he talked about how this type of development was the big new thing. It would bring the region into the mainstream, retail-wise. Lacoste had already signed on, and Mountain Golf, IZOD, and Brittania contracts were on the way. He said he had a spot across the street that would make a great artisan gallery, with busloads of tourist traffic. I could trade the Listers my Pole Pass property and they would even build out the space to my liking. I told him that I'd think it over and call him back, even though I knew my answer was 'Hell, no.' I got back to my apartment and found it had been broken into and ransacked. Top to bottom it was a disaster."

"What did they take?"

"One thing was missing," Carla said, taking a sip of wine.

"Well?"

"They took my vibrator!" She half-snorted wine out of her nose and began to laugh. "It must have rolled out when whoever flipped my bed over."

"You're kidding me! They took your vibrator?"

"No, I'm not kidding! It pissed me off; I had just changed the batteries, too!"

"Sorry to laugh, but that's just gross, and really creepy!"

"Well, that's why I figured it was a Lister. This may sound paranoid, but a few months after the break-in, I began to notice I was being followed around town. That did it—I was done. School turned out to be a bust, and the gallery would have to come later. This was part of the plan I made with Mr. Lawe.

"I dropped the final rent check with my notice to vacate my apartment in the mailbox right before I made the early-morning exodus westward. I just disappeared, leaving everything behind, or so I hoped. Mr. Lawe was the only one who knew how to get hold of me, and I gave him power of attorney for the property just in case the Listers attempted any shenanigans in my absence. He advised me to get a post office box in Seattle instead of having the mail delivered to my doorstep. I leased one on Broadway, and he and I speak every month."

"Do you have any idea what they were looking for when they broke in?"

"What? You don't think they were after my Vibrocator 2000?" she laughed.

"Ha-ha. Probably not!"

"I'm pretty sure I know what they were after."

"Yes?"

"The safe-deposit box at the bank in East Valley contained the deed to the farmhouse property, Martin's updated will with the note to contact Mr. Lawe, and a small black book."

"Oh yeah. What was in the book?"

"It was written in some gibberish; I couldn't understand it, so I took it to Mr. Lawe."

"What did he say?"

"He couldn't make sense of it either—said it appeared to be encoded and needed a cipher. He urged me not to say anything about it until we could determine its content. It's in the safe at his office."

"Sounds like a good idea."

"Well, everything was fine until about a month ago when I was on the way to pick up my mail. As you know, Broadway is a pretty eclectic scene by any standard, but I can spot an east-of-the-mountains fashion statement a mile away. The guy's polyester leisure suit and hillbilly hairstyle gave him away like a flashing sign, but the clincher was that he looked familiar. I couldn't place from where, but it wasn't Seattle. I don't think anyone from Pole Pass would recognize me by my face or hair these days, but my stature is a bit harder to disguise.

"I bypassed the post office and cut through Seattle Central College in case I was being followed. I saw him again two days later farther north on Broadway, hanging out by a coffee cart looking at everyone who walked by. So, either he's a professional people watcher or he's looking for someone in particular. That's really why I asked you not to say anything about me if you spoke with someone back home—also why I have a fake apartment label and answer the intercom in disguise."

"No, I'd probably do the same. I'm glad Martin's book isn't here, but the Listers don't know that. I'm sure you considered giving it to them, and just be done with it?"

"Yeah, I thought about that for a minute after they trashed my place, and then I questioned why Martin had hidden it away in that safe-deposit box all the way over in East Valley. He obviously had accessed that box a few weeks earlier, to deposit the new will along with instructions for me, so there is a reason why he put that stuff away. I'm curious that there's more to it."

"Well, you know what they say about curiosity and the cat . . ."

"Yeah, but satisfaction brought him back, with eight more lives to go!"

I laughed. "Good one. Do you mind if I tell Town about this when I see him next week? I know he'll keep your secret."

"Not at all. I'd be interested in his opinion."

"I'm sure he'll have one."

"Virginia, new subject. Did she . . . uh . . . did Mom ever tell you anything about our bio dad?"

"I know this is disappointing, but she never mentioned anything, other than that we have the same one, and it damn sure wasn't Martin."

"That's a bummer—I was hoping for something more, I guess."

"I know you were, Carla; so was I. There's been suspicion that he may have been Native—I even took a blood test this fall, and the results were inconclusive. Town told me that they can't really get that level of detail yet, but not to be discouraged."

"What led you to think that he might be Native?"

"I hesitate to tell you, because I don't want you to think I'm crazy."

"Really? Me think you're crazy? Ha! You should hear some of the dreams I have."

"Dreams? What kind of dreams?"

"I have a repeating dream of soaring around in the mountains like a bird. It's always the same route. I've had it since I was thirteen; in fact, I've had it three times this week, which is a little unusual. OK, now your turn."

I told Carla the truth of all I had encountered the past summer on tribal land. Her eyes intensified as she absorbed my words, not at all dismissive.

"I believe there's so much more than what we see every day," she replied. "We just have to be open minded about it."

"Did you know that during the divorce trial, Stanley Lister threatened Mom that if she didn't withdraw her custody request for you and other claims, they would present a complaint alleging that she was involved in witchcraft and already instructing me in Wiccan practices, and also that she had planned to begin your apprenticeship very soon?"

"What? That's insane!" Carla exclaimed.

"Well, I know it wasn't true. There was so much corruption already involved in the trial; Mom was scared to death that I might be removed from her as well. She couldn't take the risk, and I know it tormented her until the day she died. When their divorce became final, Martin's last words to her were that you would disappear permanently if she ever revealed any of what she knew. To my knowledge, that was their last personal contact."

"What the hell was he into, and did she think he was serious?"

"I don't know other than something to do with the lodge, and she believed it was serious enough for her to stay away from her youngest child."

"Honestly, I'm glad I didn't know any of that."

"For sure."

"You know, as odd as Martin could be, I did see him change over that last year. I think he came to realize that he was just another stooge for the Listers."

"I'm glad he began to see them for what they are, but I have horrible memories of him, and it's hard to feel any sympathy after what that man put us all through."

"Yeah, I understand," Carla said.

"At least he did you right in the end, and that counts for something."

"Virginia, I think I would have settled for an 'I love you.'"

BOOK THREE

THE ARCHIVE

22

PRINCETON

I greeted Virginia with a smile as she stepped onto the snow-dusted tarmac at Trenton-Mercer Airport on Tuesday, December 21. As the line of passengers hurried toward the terminal to escape the cold New Jersey air, she broke ranks and rushed into my arms, pressing her head into my chest.

"It's so great to see you! I've missed that face! How was the flight?"

"Too long, but seeing that smile as I walked off the plane makes up for it! Don't you look dashing—what's the occasion?" she asked, gesturing toward my traditional Ivy League winter outfit.

"Well, thanks, and the occasion would be you," I replied.

She kissed me playfully while squeezing tightly.

"Arghhh," I let out.

Virginia detected an involuntary twitch that accompanied the groan.

"Did you hurt your intercostals on the rower again?"

"Nah, it's my shoulder. I'll be OK, just a little tender. I'll tell you about it later."

"Well, why don't you come by my office and let Dr. Virginia give you a complete examination?"

"Trust me, doctor, I had planned on it, but first things first. I've just come from an interesting meeting that I'll have to tell you about over dinner."

"Sounds intriguing—any chance I can freshen up first?"

"You bet! I do have a little surprise for you, though," I said, as we approached the Mercedes-Benz station wagon in the airport parking lot.

"Oooh, Mr. Fancy . . ."

"Not mine; it came with the job."

"The job?" she asked. Then she noticed a very large dark figure sitting in the passenger seat.

"Who is that?"

When I opened the passenger door, out jumped a huge long-haired German shepherd.

"Meet Harry," I announced. "He came with the job too!"

After a quick examination and approval of Virginia, Harry provided a big wet kiss across her face as she bent down to formally introduce herself.

"We're house sitting for a department chair and his wife while they are in Europe for two and a half weeks. So, unfortunately, no Nassau Club for us this visit, but you'll like this as much, if not more. There's a great library, and I've been told that the house has a few resident spooks."

"Oh really? Sounds exciting!"

"I haven't seen any so far, but it's only been three nights."

"Maybe they're a bit shy."

"Possibly."

It was a twenty-minute drive to Nassau Street, where after a quick lap through the heart of Princeton we made a right turn down a beautiful tree-lined lane near the Graduate College. The cobblestone driveway led to a tall wooden fence surrounding the back of the three-quarter-acre property. The original house, a 1700s colonial, had been expanded and updated over the years and displayed beautiful grounds, as far as Virginia could tell in the fading purple-tinged light.

"Wow, I didn't realize that academia paid so well."

"It may help that Professor Chesterling's wife is a pharmaceutical executive."

"Yes, that might have something to do with it."

"Come on in, and let's get you settled."

I picked up her bags and lugged them inside with Harry close on my heels.

"Please do follow me, miss," I said, leading her upstairs to a nice-sized bedroom with a private bath and large fireplace. From the overstuffed chair parked in front of the hearth and the respectable stack of books on the floor, it was evident where I had been spending my evenings. After placing her bags on the floor next to the closet, I asked if thirty minutes was enough time.

"That's perfect. I'll be quick, but I want to take a look at your shoulder. Right now, OK?"

"It's nothing, really. I promise you can give me a thorough examination when we get back. Plus, if I start taking stuff off, then you will start taking stuff off, and we might never get out of here for dinner."

She had to agree with my hesitation.

"All right, but as soon as we get back here, then."

"Yes, yes, I'll play good patient, and you can play naughty doctor."

"That's only half funny, smartass."

I smiled at her. "It's about a fifteen-minute walk across campus; the reservation is at five forty-five."

"I'll be ready."

Harry bopped me with his snout as we walked down a rear staircase leading directly into the kitchen. "I know, boy, I know. Come on, let's get your dinner." He had been fed and let out to do his business by the time Virginia descended the stairs at promptly thirty minutes, wearing indigo jeans and a gray cashmere turtleneck. I detected a kiss of Polo as I wrapped her neck with my Princeton scarf.

"Allow me to help you into your coat, miss."

"Why, thank you, kind sir."

"Hood up or cap?"

"Neither. Thank you."

"Hey, your haircut is super-sexy, but it's cold out there, and I don't want you to get a chill."

She smiled and produced a pair of fashionable earmuffs from the pocket of her duffle coat, and we stepped out into the cold night air.

"I noticed the big stack of books in our room—how is school going?" she asked.

"It's busy . . . there is a lot happening in the research department at the moment. That CDC report published in June ramped up immunology research a hundred percent, and now we're part of this new task force on Kaposi's Sarcoma and Opportunistic Infections. People are really concerned," I noted, taking her hand as we shuffled through an icy patch of unsalted sidewalk.

"Yeah, same at the U-Dub," Virginia said. "Most of those cases have been in the Bay Area. I have friends in research labs that are working around the clock attempting to isolate something viral attacking immunity."

"So far, the target seems to be gay males, and we can only guess the extent of transmission beyond the exchange of body fluids or needle sharing. At this point, we can't be sure that mosquitoes aren't able to act as hosts and spread it to other populations, or if it could become airborne and weaponized."

"One tech referred to it as a 'gay plague,' which I thought was pretty shortsighted. If this gets any further into the press, it's only a few rumors away from a catastrophic mass hysteria. It's a scary time," Virginia added as we crossed the street and stepped onto campus.

"There is definitely a quiet fear brewing and a lot of questions regarding the origination point of the infection," I said. "I've heard lab back-chatter that this might be connected to the CIA or another agency, and perhaps it got out of hand. Who knows, but after the Tuskegee experiments, and their Bluebird and MKUltra mind-control programs, and God knows what else they have done, I wouldn't put it past them."

"Town, that's almost too horrifying to think about."

"Maybe that's exactly what they are counting on."

"Stop, you're freaking me out!"

"OK, fair enough—I have plenty of time to do that," I said, grinning at her. Then I continued, "On to that pile of books you mentioned: you know the school's library and its available resources are second to none in many respects, but that's not where I found what I needed."

"Meaning?"

"Today I confirmed that there is more to the literary inventory in Princeton than what occupies the general stacks of the university library."

As we exited the campus through the FitzRandolph Gate and walked across Nassau Street, the splendor of Princeton at Christmastime was displayed in full array: every lamppost trimmed, storefronts nostalgically decorated, the sound of carolers making merry, and the bustling crowds doing their Christmas shopping. We agreed that the traditional feel was very reminiscent of Main Street in Pole Pass at Christmas. We strolled down Witherspoon before ducking into the small, unassuming restaurant, instantly engulfed by clouds of saffron, lemon, and the scents of authentic tagine cooking.

"Ah, Mr. Townsend, sir! Very glad to see you!" exclaimed Anil, the owner. "Who is it that you have brought to us this evening? Wait a minute—is this the reincarnation of Helen of Troy? My heavens, what a beauty! May Allah strike me down if I'm lying," he pledged, holding one hand toward heaven while putting the other over his heart.

"Hi, Anil, no—Helen was last week, remember? This beauty is Virginia of Pole Pass," I said with an exaggerated sweep of my hand as she laughed with the exchange.

Anil shouted toward the kitchen, "Hey, Mother, come look who Mr. Town has brought with him tonight!"

Before I could make the formal introductions, Anil continued, "Miss Virginia, I am your humble servant

Anil, and this is my wife, Khadija. We are the owners of this establishment. Our son, Geoffrey, is a student at the university as well. He is in the engineering department, and he brought Town to us. Town is like our own son now."

"I'm very pleased to meet you both," she said warmly.

"You like the Moroccan food, Miss Virginia?"

"I don't believe I have had it, but it smells wonderful."

"Then you are in for a treat, my dear. Khadija makes the best tagine I have ever eaten, and you can tell from my figure that I know good food!" Anil laughed while patting his well-rounded midsection. "She has chicken and lamb tonight; I will bring you both to enjoy. Now come, please sit and warm yourselves while I make some hot tea and honey. Town, you like the special tea for you both, eh?"

"Yes, thank you, Anil, that would be perfect," I replied.

We settled into the cozy booth, and soon Anil arrived with the tea and a small crock of honey. He gave us a wink, discreetly touching his lips with the blade of his finger, and departed to greet new arrivals.

This tea had kick. Anil's special version included a shot of cask-strength whiskey from a bottle that he thought he was hiding from Khadija in the kitchen.

"Wow, that warms a person right up," Virginia coughed out, rapidly waving her hand in front of her watering eyes.

I chuckled but said nothing, taking in the fact that she was actually here with me for Christmas.

"What?" she said with a big smile.

"Nothing, I'm just enjoying a second with my thoughts, and you," I replied, not at all distracted by the commotion of several diners arriving.

A moment later, Anil arrived with our dinner. "Please enjoy, and if you need anything, you let me know. Oh, I just spoke with Geoffrey—he is very sorry that he is still out of the country, because he wanted to verify that Miss Virginia was as beautiful as you described her and the photograph you showed him wasn't from a magazine. Don't you worry, I told him she was more breathtaking than Nefertiti and that he should take you with him when he wants to find a bride," Anil said with a big smile and wink at a blushing Virginia.

"Thanks, Anil, you blabbermouth," I responded, and he departed the table with a laugh, singing something in Arabic to the tune of what sounded like "Jingle Bells."

"OK, so I might brag just a little bit," I admitted to her.

"Oh, don't worry, 'Mr. Town,' I think you're very sweet," she said with an alluring smile as she nudged me under the table with her foot. "So, you were going to tell me about the meeting you had today?"

"Oh yeah! OK, so it all started when I pulled out my mom's archaeology notebook. As you know, it's pretty much been tucked away in my drawer for the last three years because of school, but this past quarter I needed to break up the textbook monotony and I dug it out. I began casually reading some before bedtime and found myself captivated by her thoughts and conclusions.

"There is a familiarity to her writings and logic that's as eerie as it is comforting. I came across the passage that Dad referenced regarding the last expedition team she led, and notations that some of that funding came from right here at Princeton. Naturally intrigued, I sought out the records by visiting the endowment office, which was a dead end. Then I began exploring campus libraries and research centers looking for any references to the actual expedition, and nothing. I was deflated and about to give up when a seasoned librarian assisting me at my last stop told me of an alternate resource, and directed me to the Archive."

"The Archive? Now that sounds mysterious."

"Just wait: the librarian was careful to point out that since the Archive is a private institution, its board of directors reviews each request and grants or denies access based upon their assessment. There is no appeal process if you are declined, end of story. I immediately walked over to the off-campus building and logged a request to view the form. Two weeks passed and then I was contacted, and my interview was set for this afternoon at one thirty.

"Great timing!"

"Yeah, so I arrived a few minutes early and was brought into a large boardroom to await my interview. I walked around checking out the portraits of the past chairmen mounted in order of their tenure, getting as far as Milton Franklin Rhodes, whose leadership term was during the mid-1800s."

"Milton Franklin Rhodes . . . sounds familiar."

"Yeah, he was big banker and politician."

"Go on," Virginia said, taking a drink of the potent tea.

"The artist who painted the portrait captured a self-assured man with steel-colored eyes searching outwardly as if ready to face any challenge that dared come his way. Probably my imagination, but I swear I detected something else in them, like a secret."

"Ooh, mysterious, I love it!"

"Maybe. I was studying the myriad of Masonic-type regalia attached to his red ceremonial sash when my eye caught the top edge of a medallion peeking out from behind the sash. 'That's weird—what's he hiding back there?' I said to myself as the squeak of the heavy paneled door announced the entrance of my host, a tall, slender fellow in his thirties, if I had to guess, with slicked-back hair and dressed in a fabulous suit that I wish I had in my closet.

"'Greetings, Mr. Lawe, I see you are becoming acquainted with our historic leadership,' he said.

"'Yes, sir,' I replied. 'Very impressive indeed.'

"Shaking my hand firmly, with direct eye contact, he introduced himself. 'My name is Aaron Van Kaiser. Welcome to the Archive.'

"Yes, Mr. Van Kaiser, thank you for taking time from your day this Christmas season to address my request.' I matched his formality. We took our seats across from one another, and Van Kaiser began the interview.

"'One of our charges as curators for this branch of the Archive is to secure historical documents that might otherwise be lost or go missing in an open-sourced institution,' he said.

"'I understand.'

"'We keep stringent records of every transaction within the unit itself. It is quite laborious, but in doing so, we track the number of requests, by whom, and whether the request was granted or declined. We also require a brief summary of the researcher's findings within fourteen days of completion. In short, the process provides a type of information our membership uses to make certain predictions, financial and otherwise.'

"'I find that fascinating,' I interjected.

"'Our consortium's charge maintains governance over the private Archival unit of the entire Ivy League of institutions.'

"'That must be millions of assets.'

"'Yes, the majority of which have never been requested for view,' he replied. 'Your inquiry falls into that category. Which is of particular interest to a few of our members.'

"'I see.'

"He opened a file folder and continued. 'You have a legacy of Ivy in the family. Great-great-great-grandfather, William and Mary; Dad, Harvard; and sister, Carol, currently at Yale Law, top of her class, according to the latest transcripts. Your grandfather didn't finish school in the traditional way. He abruptly took leave of his studies at William and Mary prior to his last year and returned home to care for his mother. He did eventually finish at the University of Idaho College of Law. Honorable. Then we have your mother, who provided a contract-based service that we are familiar with, and the main thrust of your research. That leaves you, Mr. Lawe . . . a bit of a black sheep in not pursuing the vocation of your namesake, perhaps?'

"'Well, my sister will certainly keep the lineage intact,' I responded, 'and I'm confident that her temperament is much better suited for legal matters than my own.'

"'You seem to have found a home among researchers and other lab rats at the University . . . also present on the faculty watch list of candidates for postdoctoral research associate.'

"'I'm certainly flattered by your assessment, but that's a few years and many study hours away. Thank you for the vote of confidence just the same.'

"'I'm only the messenger, Mr. Lawe. You might be surprised at how far in advance these decisions are made. Now, let us get to the matter at hand. After the review of your application, and satisfying our internal questions, we are comfortable granting your request in full. There is a standard agreement that I have for you to read and sign. It's fairly strict about care of documents and what is and is not permissible. Also, a written summary of your findings and conclusions is expected within fourteen days of the term of your research. Incidentally, we've taken the liberty of adding a companion document, which, though not within the scope of your current subject matter, may prove beneficial in your overall research.' I thanked him.

"After I signed the agreement, he told me that my eligibility for admission begins tomorrow morning, with access through the first week of January. We wished each other a Merry Christmas and Happy New Year, and as we were walking out together, he said, 'Funny thing about researchers—the successful ones have a certain trait, an overwhelming inquisitiveness bordering on obsession. A positive attribute for the field, I suppose. You know there's an old saying, "All roads lead to the doghouse." Are you familiar with it, Mr. Lawe?'

"'Yes, sir, I am.'

"'Well, I'm certain that you will have a few questions after your research; I return to Princeton on January 5 and will be available for a chat.' He said it as a statement, not an offer."

"So what does that mean?" Virginia asked, leaning in and intrigued.

"I'm not sure . . . the whole meeting was rather strange. He was very conversational regarding their function as a body. Don't know if that's the norm, but what I took from our parting discussion was to expect the unexpected. So, the dilemma is that the Archive closes at noon on Christmas Eve until Tuesday, January 4. Because of the short timeline, I'll have to spend a day or two in research while you're here."

"'I' nothing!" she exclaimed. "'We' is more like it! You know I'm a crack researcher."

"I thought you'd say something like that, so I requested permission to bring the best researcher I know along with me. You just have to sign some paperwork when we get there tomorrow morning."

Anil approached the table and asked if we would like more tea and perhaps dessert. "No thank you, Anil," we both answered.

"You like Khadija's food, Miss Virginia?"

"Anil, I love Khadija's food!"

"Ah, very nice—I will tell her you are a convert. You please come back for more, OK?"

"Yes, we will definitely return for Khadija's superb cuisine, and of course your special tea," she replied. "Now we need to walk it off, with a stroll through town."

"Ah yes, very nice here right now. Cold, but very nice, and happy time."

We headed out into the Princeton chill, walking up to Nassau Street, and turned left toward the University store. Virginia chose an assortment of Princeton sweats, tossing them in the small cart. "You can never have too many of those, I guess," I said, my offhand way of telling her that I had already procured certain items for her.

"Thanks, but these are gifts for others. I'll tell you about that when we get back to the house. Believe me, we have lots to catch up on. But right now, I want to get a look at you."

"What, here?"

Virginia hauled me over to the dressing mirror on the sales floor. "Look in the mirror. You're leaning left like the Tower of Pisa, and I know it's not from that spiked tea at dinner."

"Yeah, I guess I am favoring that side a bit."

"Let's get you home. We have plenty of time to play together in downtown Princeton."

Back at the house, Virginia helped me strip down to my boxers. "Hey . . . easy now, big boy, let me have a look at you," she ordered. She peeled my undershirt slowly over my torso, and it became obvious what was bothering me.

"Town, what the hell happened here? Seriously, and don't bullshit me either! This needs an x-ray at the very least," she said, rotating me slowly as if on a stool in a clinic. The nasty bruise encompassing a good part of my shoulder looked like someone had hit me with a baseball bat.

"I already had one. No breaks, just sore for a few days. The doctor gave me an ice wrap and a sling to get me through. He said I was lucky."

"This looks like it happened today."

"Yes, early this morning as I was heading across the campus toward the engineering quad, I got hit by a truck."

"Thank God you're OK," she said with feeling.

"I almost wasn't. A truck ran up on the curb at the Washington Road and Prospect crosswalk. If the jogger next to me hadn't pulled me back, I would have had my head taken off by the huge passenger-side mirror, rather than it just tagging my shoulder."

"What about the driver? Drunk or medical issue?"

"Probably drunk; it was a hit-and-run."

"Anyone get the license plate or anything?"

"No, and the jogger must have been in a hurry because he didn't stick around for me to thank him. So there I sat on the cold sidewalk, surrounded by pieces of broken mirror at around 6:15."

"That's awful."

"Yeah, and rare drama for here at Princeton. So, doctor lady, now that we have that all sorted, how about prescribing me some nice PT?"

"Well, I don't know . . . you sure you feel up to it?"

"Only one way to find out. But no rough stuff this time," I laughed.

"All right, I'll try to restrain myself."

After our proper reunion upstairs, I lit the fire in the living room and Virginia joined me, wearing faded Princeton sweats, with her new best pal, Harry, following behind.

"Hey, those look great on you."

"Thank you; they make great winter pajamas."

"I poured you a glass of bourbon from the bottle that Dad sent last birthday," I told her.

"Splendid," she said, practically sitting on top of me as she dropped herself on the sofa.

"Careful—shoulder, shoulder," I reminded her.

"Oh, sorry," she said with a giggle. "After that little romp, I think you are going to make a complete recovery."

Harry walked around the coffee table as if to check on me and then found a spot about three feet from the large stone hearth. "I really want to hear what's been happening with you, and here I dominated the whole dinner conversation with my doings."

"That's sweet to say, but our dinner and the conversation were perfect. I'm just glad to finally share this in person rather than over a telephone line!"

"OK already—I can't take the suspense!"

I sat quietly amazed, sipping my bourbon, as she summarized the sequence of events from her first encounter with Carla through her evening at the Gathering.

"The Carla in Seattle thing—that's a wrinkle in your reality, isn't it?"

"Yeah, I know! I can't believe that she's the same girl. It's like a light has been turned on inside of her."

"That's great! I'm excited for you. So, she's . . . umm . . ."

"Yes, she's gay, if that's what you were hinting at."

"Well, good for her, but I was going to ask if she was still doing art."

"Ha-ha, sure you were. If you saw her girlfriend, I think you might say great for her."

"Oh really?" I laughed in response.

"She's working on art again, time permitting. I've seen some of her stuff and it's very good. I'd pay for it, and that goes for her cooking too. She's a talented girl."

"No doubt—it runs in the family."

Virginia smiled and then continued, "I met several interesting people at the Gathering, including my new hairdresser, Roberto—he's wonderful. He enjoyed the picture of you in your crew attire."

"What? You're showing that photo around, are you?"

"Well, he loved your name, and after he saw the photo, he said he would do your hair for free if you wore that outfit."

"Oh perfect! I can't wait."

"Esther is a senior at the UW, in archaeology."

"Now you're talking."

"I knew you'd like that. She'd just returned from a fresh dig site about sixty miles northwest of Pole Pass."

"What were they digging up over there?"

"She thought they'd discovered an ancient site. There were unusual markings and at least one set of remains."

"Ugh . . . you know I don't like the unearthing of ancestral burial sites; it's always bad juju. What prompted the digging around there in the first place—isn't it kind of in the middle of nowhere?"

"It was completely accidental," Virginia replied. "A group of alums were on a fishing trip in the backcountry and reported their discovery of potsherds and other items to the University's archaeology department. There were days of heavy rain a few weeks prior that drove the river over its banks. It must have washed the artifacts out."

"I bet WSU wasn't happy about the UW digging in their backyard."

"Exactly, so the two departments joined in the project. They tracked what they believed was the original settlement about a half mile upriver on the Washington State side and secured light excavation permission. The remote site was a tough five-mile hike, and once there, they worked for a week at a time. Their focus changed when Esther's team returned to the site after a week off. She was leading the group as the trail made its final turn west, which afforded a nice view downriver. That was when she caught a glint of something in the distance. It was just a quick flash that she estimated to be about two miles southeast of the current site. Around noon the next day, she and a team member headed downriver, scouting for artifacts along the way.

"It took them a couple of hours, and when they arrived, they found evidence of a massive landslide, likely caused by the earlier deluge. Their target turned out to be a large quartz flake peeking out of the fresh cliff face. Esther scaled the loose earth and began wiping away the perimeter of the quartz to discover that the flake was actually the top third of a granite triangle."

"Wow, that's pretty cool."

"Just wait! While her teammate searched the lower debris field, Esther continued to remove the mud from the face of the rock, and that's when she hit the 'mother lode,' as she called it: a geometrical impression in the middle of the granite triangle."

I took a sip of bourbon and asked, "What did it look like? I mean, did she describe it?"

"Not really, just that it was very intricate and must have been old."

"I'd like to know more about that. What happened next?"

"They hurried back to the original site before nightfall and brought the rest of the team down the next morning. When doing the rough prep of the site, they also found what appeared to be some human remains. It was a femur mixed in with the cascade of earth."

I interrupted, "Of course they stopped immediately, right?"

"Yep."

"I think I'm going to like this Esther of yours!"

"Well, it gets more complicated. This location turned out to be just over the Washington State line and into Oregon. So, it had to be reported to Oregon officials immediately."

"Sure, I bet they hated that. But who needs a scandal when your academic future is on the line."

"Yeah, and there's more. They discovered that this swath was barely into the watershed that extends north of Hell's Canyon."

"Oh, they're all screwed, then. The feds took over at that point, right?"

"Yep, the programs of Washington, Oregon, and even Idaho schools have all been shut out from further examination of the area until the Bureau of Land Management decides what to do with the site. Would you ask your dad if he knows anything about it?"

"Sure, I can ask him, but I'll bet you get a better response. He's definitely concerned about my becoming distracted. I probably shouldn't have told him that I started going through Mom's notes."

"Good idea; I have something else to thank him for anyway."

"Oh? What's that?"

"We can discuss that in tomorrow morning's installment—I'm beat."

~

Harry crawled out of the overstuffed chair at five thirty the next morning and began gently pressing his nose against my face.

"OK . . . OK, I'll take you for a walk, but be quiet."

I took note of the pain in my shoulder as I grabbed my clothes and brought Harry into the bathroom, trying not to disturb Virginia. I quickly dressed, and as we were slipping out of the room to go downstairs, Virginia, half asleep, mumbled, "Where are you going?"

"Taking Harry for his morning walk. Go back to dreamland—it's 2:40 a.m. UW time."

"Not without me you don't," she said, getting out of bed and putting on her jeans.

Knowing her stubbornness, I didn't argue. "OK, we'll meet you downstairs."

A couple of minutes later she appeared in the kitchen, ready to go. "Do I smell coffee?"

"Yes, courtesy of Mr. Coffee himself. Here's a mug for the stroll. Just looked at the thermometer and it's a balmy 18 degrees out there. You sure you don't want to stay here all warm and toasty and enjoy your coffee?"

"I'm quite sure. How's that shoulder?"

"Definitely sore, but I'll make it.

We walked into the crisp air of the back garden through the kitchen door, out the side yard gate, and onto Battle Road West, where we resumed the previous night's discussion.

"So, I had dinner and a sleepover at Carla's place last Friday night," Virginia said.

"It sure sounds like you two have had a chance to get some clarity."

"To say the least," she affirmed.

We turned left onto Springdale Road, continuing our conversation.

"That's exciting," I said.

"We just shared the story of our lives, and I bet you will be as surprised as I was."

Making a right through the pillars, we continued around the Graduate College as Virginia recited the events culminating in the reading of the will.

"Come on! Really?"

"Told you! I had the same reaction."

"Holy smokes, I bet Lister and Harrison shit in their pants when Dad walked into that room!" I exclaimed.

"It was tense for sure. Your dad, true to his nature, really helped Carla. That's what I wanted to thank him for."

"He's so good that way."

"Based on advice he gave her, she now owns the building that used to be Pole Pass Dry Goods."

"Across from his office?"

"Yes."

"I've always thought that was a great property!" I said. "You have two large storefronts beneath two units above, all just waiting to be rehabbed. It wouldn't take but forty or fifty grand to redo the whole thing and make it magazine-worthy."

"That's a lot of money."

"Mark my words, it will be worth it someday. With all the construction going on in the valleys, those downtown Pole Pass properties are going to jump."

"You might be right; Carla said her property's value has doubled in the last six months."

"That's great, whatever she decides to do with it."

"She really wanted to open an art gallery there, but things got weird with the Listers, so she left."

Upon hearing about the break-in, I responded, "That's sick! Sounds like something a Lister would do. It was probably the peeper Jig—he's a real scumbag, very shallow end of the gene pool. What the hell were they searching for, anyway?"

"Carla thinks it's a small book that was in the safe-deposit box with the will."

"That must be some book. What's in it?"

"She couldn't tell; it was written in some 'gibberish,' as she put it. It's in your dad's safe."

"Dad is skilled with a lot of things, but not codes," I said, shaking my head.

"He said it needed a cipher."

"Yeah, that's a whole lot of trouble there."

Making a right at Cleveland Tower, we completed our loop and headed toward home. When we entered the side gate, Harry made a dash around the corner and through the wide-open kitchen door.

"Damn, I keep forgetting to pull that door until it clicks. I did the same thing yesterday, and Harry was searching the whole house for squirrels. I can't blame them—it's freezing out here!" I laughed. "How about I feed Harry and make you an espresso?"

"Espresso? Make it a doppio!" Virginia ordered.

Excusing herself to retrieve a recent photo of Carla, she returned a few moments later slightly puzzled.

"What's up? Forget to pack it?"

"No, I found it; it's just that I was sure I closed my suitcase after I grabbed my sweater this morning. Probably because I was still half asleep when we left."

"Or, a ghost!" I teased. "Why don't we take a quick shower and head over to PJ's for some pancakes, and then it's a quick walk to the Archive from there."

"Pancakes! Yum! Definitely a buddy shower to conserve water. I'll scrub your back and take another look at that shoulder."

"You're the doctor."

Tabletop sketch, December 1981.

PJ's had achieved landmark status in Princeton, widely known for its tables covered with various inscriptions ranging from the sentimental standard of "Scott ♥ Judy 78" to advanced mathematical equations that summed up human existence on a tabletop. The restaurant played host to many a hungry Tiger looking for a pre-class start to their day or a miraculous cure for a night of what could have been better decision making. There was a line out front even when school was on break, and this early Wednesday morning was no exception. After a brief wait, we were seated at a table next to the front window, where we could enjoy the snow now falling.

"Coffee?" offered the waiter.

"Yes, two please," I requested, as Virginia made her return from the restroom.

"With all this caffeine, I'm certainly awake for our adventure this morning. Do you think it might be helpful if I knew what we are searching for?"

"Clues."

"Oh, you have such a flair for discretion. C'mon, I need a little more than that."

After the waiter took our order of blueberry pancakes, bacon, and eggs, I reached into the breast pocket of my peacoat and pulled out my mother's notebook along with a paper outlining the day's goals and put them on the table.

"She was involved in an excavation close to the ancient city of Edrei, Syria," I began. "I use the Hebrew biblical name of Edrei because she was contracted to excavate to that specific period of the city's history. Ancient sites undergo name changes with each conquest, and it's been called Daraa since the twentieth century. She was commissioned to oversee the reactivation of a previously abandoned dig site.

"New data was available, and the Syrian government believed there was a likelihood of finding what her parents were looking for when they lost their lives fifteen years earlier. Her assignment was to uncover anything related to the battle of Bashan, in which, according to biblical accounts, Moses routed its Amorite king and his army. By the description, this king was a sizable fellow—anywhere from nine to twelve feet tall—and went by one of the more avant-garde names of the day: Og."

"Og? Nine to twelve feet tall? What, like Goliath?"

"Not really. The oldest accounts of Goliath have him at about six-foot-nine, and he was associated with the Philistines, although some believe he may have been an Amalekite. Og is reputed to be the last of the Rephaim, a legitimate clan of giants. That trail leads down a rabbit hole of the Anak, then to the Nephilim, all worthy of our attention, just not today."

"That might be fun."

I smiled and continued. "So according to records I found in the University library, archaeologists have unearthed and cataloged several artifacts determined to be from that particular battle, but there are no references to the items my mother listed in her notebook. That leads me to believe they weren't reported and must be in a private collection somewhere, possibly connected to the sponsor of the dig.

"Now I'm going to go down a path that may sound a mite strange, but hang in here with me, OK?"

"I can't wait!"

"On April 19, 1954, Mom wrote in her notebook that while excavating, the workmen uncovered a field of debris containing toppled columns and a large stone obelisk about 4.5 meters long by 1.5 meters wide by 1.5 meters deep. It was in strata determined to be pre-Edreian, likely even pre-Atharaa, which dates back to 1490 BC. The obelisk was badly damaged, showing evidence of charring—probably from a sacking, she thought initially, according to her notes. There was a series of vertical symbols that had been partially defaced, and neither she nor her two companion archaeologists could determine its message, though they believed it to be an offshoot of a Canaanite language. That evening she had a dream of being lost in a maze of time. She wrote that it seemed she was *sliding through history, being one with the ether.* The next morning, she woke up with an undeniable feeling that she had been there before."

"Like déjà vu?"

"Not quite . . . It could be intuition, clairvoyance, or maybe it has to do with the story Dad told me about the Glider."

"Wow! OK, more please!"

"Here's what she wrote over the next week or so:

> *20 April 1954. This morning I awoke with the disturbing foreknowledge of something buried beyond the toppled obelisk of yesterday. I instructed Martha and James to conduct today's dig two grids east of the obelisk. When the workers hit the period of the obelisk, they discovered fulgurites of scorched desert sand, the result of immense heat; I suspect a catastrophic annihilation. I did not share in their enthusiasm of the discovery. I was confused. Over the next week, our team carefully excavated a four-grid area, rewarded for the effort with nothing but desolation, until we found a large ripple blending into the glassy*

sand. The diameter of the area was approximately 15 meters, and irregular in its border. As the team cautiously scraped a small area of the material encasement away, we determined it to be a field of molten bronze, one meter in thickness. The team believes it to be an effigy of the great Og. I allowed them their moment of triumph, but in my silence, I knew differently.

Whatever this represented had been wiped from the face of the earth with a destructive force equal to the fire-and-brimstone account of Sodom and Gomorrah. However, we found no evidence of brimstone in the layers of earth, just an intense focused heat that had encompassed this temple complex.

"That's all I have. After she reported the find to the government, her contract was paid along with a handsome bonus, and her entire team was withdrawn from the site. I'm hoping that the Archive might have notes or at least an artifact declaration, since this was funded through some affiliated endowment. So we'll see what we dig up today, pun intended."

"Order up!" the waiter announced as he arrived with our breakfast.

23

THE ARCHIVE

Virginia and I walked across Nassau Street through the gentle snowfall and took a shortcut through the all-but-empty Princeton campus. Crossing Chancellor Green onto Chapel Drive, we exited the campus onto University Place and entered the classic, austere three-story building that was home to the Archive. The receptionist completed our check-in and welcomed us to the institution. We had just exchanged our identifications for access credentials when an attractive woman appearing to be in her forties walked confidently across the foyer toward us, arriving with the scent of fine literature. Her porcelain skin and deep auburn hair were striking, and she wore an impeccably tailored skirt suit that matched the emerald green of her eyes. She extended her hand in greeting to us both and spoke formally.

"Welcome to the Archive, Mr. Lawe and Ms. Tecoi. My name is Esmeralda, and I will be your personal facilitator for the duration of your research project."

As Esmeralda led us across the foyer, I discreetly directed Virginia's attention to the finely toned calves sheathed in Esmeralda's 1940s-era seamed stockings. A quick elbow to my ribs and shake of her head prompted a grin. We entered an elevator, and Esmeralda placed her hand against a dark glass wall, revealing a touch-sensitive panel in which she input a long series of symbols reminiscent of hieroglyphs. She glanced over at us with a smile and said, "Security protocols," as the elevator began its descent. When the doors opened, we were in a very large library three floors below ground. Esmeralda reviewed the policies while pointing out the restrooms and the dining room where we would take our lunch. A walk through a maze of bookcases brought us to the examination suite that would be our home for the term of our access.

The rectangular room contained a large oak library table with four oak chairs, a box of cotton gloves, two spiral-bound notebooks with ballpoint pens, and a list of lunch choices.

Opposite the entry wall of floor-to-ceiling tinted windows were a light table, a microfilm viewer, and an A/V station.

"It appears that you have all the research tools covered, Esmeralda," I said.

"We pride ourselves on the accommodation of our guests, Mr. Lawe."

Esmeralda rolled in a standard library cart with the authorized study materials, verbally acknowledging each item as she placed it on the table: "One leather-bound ledger, one accordion file folder, and the supplemental item which Mr. Van Kaiser added to your profile, consisting of one manila pouch with string and button clasp, contents private. Please review your lunch choices—I'll be back promptly at eleven thirty to collect them. In the meantime, I will be at the desk across from the elevators if you require assistance."

"Thank you, Esmeralda."

"Certainly, Ms. Tecoi."

After Esmeralda left us, we sat down at the table and got settled. Virginia turned to me and asked, "OK, so where do you want to start?"

"Let's be systematic and begin with the ledger, since it should be a line-listing of supplies and expenditures, and hopefully an itemized accounting of the artifacts uncovered and by whom they were received."

"Sounds good to me."

The burgundy-colored leather-bound volume contained the date "1954" precisely written in gold across the spine. Opening the ledger, I found it surreal to see my mother's handwriting in a book that had been locked away less than a half mile from where I had been living for almost four years. How many times had I walked past this piece of her? My pause didn't escape Virginia's critical eye.

"Are you OK?" she asked, laying her hand on mine.

"Yeah, it's just a little real . . ."

"I bet."

The ledger began with initial expedition purchases and fees, followed by ancillary expenses, a catalog of discovered artifacts, their location at the time of entry, twenty-three line items with a short description to the right of each number, and four pages of additional costs . . . more provisions, extra labor, and the typical escalations due to constant haggling with locals.

After spending an hour on the initial overview, we began a line-by-line examination of the reported artifacts and the detailed descriptions accompanying each item.

"What do you make of this?" Virginia asked, referring to the lack of any corroborating evidence to support what Mom had written in her own notebook.

"I'm not sure."

No mention of an obelisk, no molten bronze, no desert glass, no anything of consequence other than spear tips, several swords, a decayed battle shield, some pottery, a few skulls, and a stratum of what the team concluded was "bone ash" likely due to a plague burn.

Slightly dejected, I said, "Let's get into that accordion file."

Virginia released the cord and flap closure and removed the contents of each of the four pockets, placing them in batches across the table. "I suggest we review each pile in order, one page at a time."

Tedious as that would be, I concurred.

The first pile was an overview of the expedition. It was a typed fifty-six-page brief featuring the excavation goals, the coordinates of the dig, the grid layout, the schedule of excavation, and the start and finish dates of the dig.

We had just finished reviewing the first pile when Esmeralda lightly tapped on the door and then entered the room. "I am sorry to disturb your studies, but it is time to collect your lunch selections."

"Oh, yes, Esmeralda, here you are, and thank you," responded Virginia, handing her the menu with our choices marked.

"You are most welcome, Ms. Tecoi. Robert will be expecting you in the dining room at precisely twelve noon."

"Thank you, Esmeralda, we won't disappoint."

"My pleasure, Mr. Lawe."

After Esmeralda left the room, Virginia looked over at me and said, "'My pleasure, Mr. Lawe' . . . don't you get any ideas."

"Well, it's obvious that I have a thing for studious older women."

"I'm glad you see my point."

"In all seriousness, it's strange, but she carries an atmosphere of comfort with her."

"I think you are confusing comfort with charisma—Esmeralda definitely has that in spades."

With only about twenty-five minutes until lunch, we decided to summarize what we had discovered thus far—which wasn't much, but enough to give us a sense of our afternoon direction.

Our lunch was served in a formal dining room that was in keeping with the finest Ivy League manor houses I had visited during my tenure at Princeton. Large, heavy-framed oil paintings of picturesque landscapes, sailing ships, and portraits of dignitaries adorned the walls of a room grounded firmly by a twelve-foot dining table fashioned from an ancient slab of elm. A well-dressed man, introducing himself as Robert, promptly fitted me with a jacket as he welcomed us. Robert pulled out Virginia's chair and then replaced it deftly as she took her seat at the table. I remained standing until Virginia had been properly seated and then sat down, indicating that despite my jacket faux pas, I understood the etiquette of such a venue.

"May I suggest a glass of Mourvedre from the Bandol region to accompany your tea-smoked duck salads this afternoon?"

"Yes, Robert, thank you."

"Gladly, sir."

As we finished our main course, Robert arrived with the tea tray and an assortment of digestives.

"Earl Grey and biscuits baked this morning, sir."

"Thank you, Robert."

"Will there be anything else, sir?"

"No, thank you, all has been magnificent."

"It has been my pleasure, sir. Please enjoy your research at the Archive."

We returned to our room and resumed the investigation, starting with the accordion file's second stack. This was a collection of engineered diagrams from the dig site, divided into a network of numbered search grids paired with aerial photographs of the terrain. The only thing noteworthy in the stack was a single page that showed additional grids east of the original excavation chart. This appeared to correlate exactly with my mother's account.

"Clue?"

"Yes, I'd say this qualifies."

Piles number three and four consisted entirely of eight-by-ten photos from the excavation. There appeared to be over three hundred in total, each one dated and numbered on the back. Unfortunately, they were not filed in numerical order but randomly shuffled—or, as Virginia noted, "carelessly jumbled together."

"This is going to take a couple of hours to sort through and organize," she said with frustration.

"For sure. Well, it will have to wait until tomorrow—we need to get back to the house and take care of our charge, Harry."

"Oh, dear sweet Harry, I almost forgot about him. I'll set the room up for the morning; you find Esmeralda to let us out of here."

I found her seated at an ornate desk across from the elevator, intensely studying a codex authored in what appeared to be an extinct hand.

"Sorry to interrupt your concentration, Esmeralda . . . is that a Coptic language?"

She was caught slightly off guard. "Oh, Mr. Lawe, I apologize. I was so involved that I didn't see you there. Yes, this is of the Sahidic dialect. It is the Archive's copy of 'The Gospel of Thomas,'" she responded, setting down the magnifying glass and removing her white gloves.

"I see the illuminative texts interest you?"

"It all interests me, Mr. Lawe; it always has."

Virginia joined us and we walked to the elevator. Esmeralda placed her hand on a blank stainless steel pad. The doors opened, and after she repeated her security protocol, we began the ascent. Upon retrieving our identifications from the receptionist, Esmeralda asked what time she might expect us the next day.

"Is the same time OK?" I asked.

"Yes, of course, we will look forward to hosting you at eight thirty tomorrow morning. Please enjoy your evening."

"Thank you, Esmeralda, and you as well," Virginia replied.

We left the Archive and walked into the blinding white of the fresh snow that had fallen continually since breakfast that morning. With virtually no motor traffic on the roadway, we opted to take Alexander Street past the Princeton Theological Seminary to College Road West and the Graduate College, rather than hike through the drifting snow.

Harry provided an exuberant welcome home, and Virginia accompanied him to the garden, where he conducted his business. The fresh snow made him frolic around in the drifts like a wild dog, and I couldn't resist joining them in the garden to give chase around and over the boxwood hedges and other plantings that now resembled marshmallows of various sizes. Twenty minutes later, even Harry was ready for a break. While he went straight for his bowl, we shed our soaking-wet clothing in the laundry room and raced upstairs to the shower. The warm water had just begun to sink into my shoulder when Harry's bark alerted us to the insistent ringing of the doorbell.

"Oh, man, this was just getting good. Keep it warm for me—I'll be back in a second," I told Virginia.

I quickly donned a heavy robe and ran downstairs to see what the emergency was.

"It's OK, Harry, sit!" I commanded, and then opened the front door to an older gentleman standing on the doorstep.

"Hello, you must be the boy who's looking after the place for the Chesterlings while they're away," he stated rather tersely.

"Why, yes, sir. My name is Town Lawe and I'm one of the prof—"

"I'm Jamison from next door," he interrupted, "and you should know that I saw a man snooping around here earlier today. I ran him off and notified the police. They came by and walked around the house, looking for signs of a break-in. They didn't find anything but footprints. We don't want any goddamned snoops or burglars around here, understand me?" Jamison rattled off without pausing for a breath.

"Yes, Mr. Jamison. Loud and clear. Would you happen to have a description of the individual?"

"White, green ski jacket, blue jeans, and a brown stocking cap. Nothing but a goddamned, no-good shithead, if you ask me."

"Thank you, sir. I'll keep an eye out for him and promptly report anything amiss to the proper authorities."

"You do that, but if he comes into my yard, I'll hack him to death with my machete—no questions asked." With a wink and a chuckle, Jamison turned heel and headed down the walkway toward the street.

"That sounds completely reasonable to me, Mr. Jamison. Merry Christmas and Happy New Year to you, sir, and please feel free to contact me if you need help disposing of the corpse!" I shouted after him.

Without turning around, Jamison raised his hand into the air, acknowledging my gesture.

I closed the door and hurried back upstairs to finish my shower, hoping that Virginia was still in there.

"Who was that?" she asked.

"The next-door neighbor—he's a character."

"A social visit?"

"In a way. I'll tell you about it after you help me work the ache out of my shoulder."

Virginia kneaded my upper back and neck as the warm water penetrated the stiffness that was settling into my injured shoulder.

"I will give you about four hours to stop that."

"Only four hours? I must be slipping."

"Actually, the opposite."

"Well, you know the right words and how to put them in the correct order, don't you?" she said, sliding her hands down around the front of my waist.

The gray daylight had just about been absorbed by the December darkness when we emerged from a tangle of bedding to head back to the shower.

"Starving?" I asked her.

"Famished; we need to refuel."

"OK. We have a stocked fridge, so let's eat in tonight, if it's OK with you."

"That's what I was hoping you would say. Let me cook for us—I've been inspired by Carla. Plus, I could go for a snowy night with my two boys in front of the fire, in our PJs."

After our roasted game hens and root vegetables, we retired to the fireplace of the living room, where Harry was stretched out on his spot enjoying the warm hearth. I handed Virginia a glass of bourbon and took a seat beside her on the couch. "To a quiet and peaceful Christmas with you. Cheers."

We clinked glasses, and then after a moment she said, "Tell me about the neighbor who came over."

"Oh, yeah. The quirky, gruff Mr. Jamison with a machete."

"What? A machete?"

"Not really. He just said that he had witnessed a suspicious character walking around the property today while we were out. He ran him off and called the police; they came out and found footprints but no evidence of a break-in."

"That's alarming! I wouldn't think that kind of thing happened in this area."

"It's Christmastime, and sometimes prowlers get wind of people being out of town. It will be a good idea for us to leave the car out of the garage tomorrow and turn on the TV, just in case. Now, Mr. Jamison did say that he would hack whomever to death with his machete, no questions asked, if they were to show up on his property. I can respect that," I said with a laugh.

"Good God, I hope it doesn't come to that!"

"I would think that Harry might have dissuaded anyone with burgling intentions. I bet he's moved on by now. Mr. Jamison gave the police a description of the person: a white guy, green ski jacket, blue jeans, and a brown stocking hat."

"What if he comes back?"

"Well, I could always borrow Jamison's machete," I chuckled.

"Town, I'm serious."

"Yeah, I get it, but with being chased off once already, I really think they've moved on to an easier target."

"I suppose so."

Next morning at the Archive, the elevator doors opened at eight thirty sharp, and Esmeralda greeted us in the foyer. Today she wore a form-fitting crimson skirt suit over a cream blouse, her signature seamed stockings disappearing into matching bow pumps.

"Good morning, Mr. Lawe and Ms. Tecoi. I trust you both enjoyed a pleasant snowy evening."

"Good morning and thank you, Esmeralda. It was nice and quiet. How were your studies?"

"Marvelous, Mr. Lawe. Thank you for asking."

"I think your dad should meet Esmeralda," Virginia said after Esmeralda departed the room.

"Dad believes he's still married—I mean, he wears his ring, and it's been almost twenty years. She's probably married anyway."

"Trust me, Esmeralda is as single as she is ready to mingle."

"Like I said yesterday, there is something about her; I just can't put my finger on it."

"Well, how about putting your finger on one of those last two piles and handing it to me."

"Sure, I'll take one too."

After three hours, we hadn't finished organizing the photos into their numerical sequence. Esmeralda's tap on the door signaled a welcome intermission from the eyestrain of viewing the time-faded labels. I handed Esmeralda our lunch selections and mentioned what had become obvious now that the sequence was nearly completed.

"Esmeralda, I have a question."

"Yes, Mr. Lawe, how may I be of assistance?"

"Virginia and I just spent the last three hours placing these 269 photographs into an ascending order that chronicles the expedition we are researching. My question is in two parts: Would there be a reason they were completely out of order? Also, it's clear that several photographs are missing within the string, twenty-five total is our current estimation. Does this seem odd to you?"

"That does appear to be unusual," she replied. "Allow me to submit your lunch requests and I will delve into this further, and have an answer for you this afternoon."

"Thank you, Esmeralda, that would be greatly appreciated."

Over lunch, Virginia and I continued to discuss the gap in the photos. The highest numbers in a string were numbered 302 to 312. It would be fair to conclude that photo 312 was the extent of the photo catalog. The highest number before an interruption in sequence was photo 269. Some gaps were sporadic, with one, two, or three photos missing.

But the entire 18-photo string from 283 through 301 was absent, confirming the earlier tally of photographs unaccounted for to be 25.

Robert reentered the room and approached us with a silver water pitcher that I'd wager was sterling. "How was your winter squash soup, sir?" he inquired, topping off our glasses.

"Fabulous, Robert. Thank you."

"And your Cobb salad, Ms. Tecoi?"

"It was absolutely amazing, Robert, thank you."

"You are most welcome."

We continued our conversation over tea and digestives, concluding that there was little progress to be made until Esmeralda reported her findings. When we got back to the room, we cleared the table and attempted to avert the discouragement from a trail that had temporarily gone cold.

"Why don't we get into that supplemental?"
prompted Virginia.

"Sure, why not."

Suddenly, the lull was interrupted by Esmeralda's familiar door tap and entry into the room. "Please excuse the intrusion; I have information pertinent to your inquiry."

"That's great news, Esmeralda."

Esmeralda crossed the room to the microfilm station, loaded the roll into the reader, and turned the machine on.

"I pulled our inventory ledgers, which are cataloged and stored in a more secure area of the Archive. These include a brief description along with the item's location number and other internal markers. I have managed to locate the microfilm for this particular sector of photos, and fortunately, when these items were originally logged, the number of photographs was recorded as well. In addition, the images themselves were preserved. In other words, the missing images should be included on this spool of film. However, there is not a description that accompanies each individual photograph, only the total number."

She spun the hand crank until the first quad of photos filled the screen.

"Esmeralda, you are a genius! Thank you so much!"

"My pleasure, Ms. Tecoi. Also, to answer your original questions more thoroughly, Mr. Lawe: Those photographs should not have been out of order, and based upon evidence from the microfilm inventory verification, all 312 images should have been present in that file."

"Interesting."

"More than interesting, Mr. Lawe—it's criminal. The Archive takes these rare situations very seriously; an investigation is already underway. Would you and Ms. Tecoi please provide me with any information regarding the missing photos and anything else you may suspect?"

"We would be glad to. Can you give us an hour just to double-check our audit against some of the earlier data we reviewed?"

"Yes, of course, Mr. Lawe. I will return in one hour, and thank you."

This meant that our temptation to review the microfilm would have to be resisted for at least the next hour.

"Hand me the expedition ledger, will you?" Virginia said.

"Sure, got something?"

"Just a hunch." She opened the book about three-quarters of the way through and began slowly turning the pages. "Bingo! Come and look at this."

Her excitement was evident, and I practically jumped over the table.

"Remember these twenty-three lines and descriptions at the bottom of this page?" Virginia said as she swept her finger down the lower third of the ledger's verso side.

"Yeah, what about . . . Oh, wait a minute. I'll grab the photos!"

Just as Virginia suspected: Photographs 1 through 23 corresponded with the numbers and descriptions listed on the page. I picked up the ledger from the table and with great care opened it until the spine creaked in protest. This was enough to confirm that someone had meticulously removed several pages from the non-paginated book—most likely using an X-Acto knife.

"I'll get Esmeralda," Virginia said as she hurried out of the room.

24

CAPITOL CONFRONTATION

I was recovering from the seventy-two hours of work necessary to pull off the catering job as Audrey brought the café au lait into the bedroom.

"How did you sleep?" she whispered, gently stroking my face with the back of her hand.

"That depends . . . What day is it?"

"It is Thursday, the 23rd of December, in the year of our Lord 1981. The time is eleven o'clock in the morning, Pacific."

I bolted up in the bed. "Eleven o'clock? I'm late!"

"Easy, girl," Audrey said, placing her palm against my chest as she softly pushed me back down onto a stack of pillows. "Mary has it all taken care of. I called her last night and told her that you jumped into bed at three in the afternoon and hadn't budged. She gave me strict orders to keep you here as long as possible and said she'd see us at her house on Christmas Eve."

I relaxed and reached out for the coffee that Audrey was still holding. "Thanks . . . I feel like I could lie here all day."

"You've been working nonstop, and also covered a lot of emotional terrain. You really need to rest or you're bound to get sick. Sit tight while I get the oatmeal and fruit that I made for your breakfast."

"Yes, Miss Audrey," I said, with sarcastic resignation.

I leaned back with my coffee and looked out the bank of windows in time to catch a red-breasted robin on the birch, returning my gaze. Audrey came in with a bed tray of oatmeal, warm maple syrup, raspberries, and a side of cream.

"Yes, I can cook, among other things," she said in response to the astonished look on my face.

I smiled without saying a word.

"I've got to get back downstairs and help out. By the way, we're staying open until eight tonight to accommodate those last-minute Christmas shoppers." She bent down and kissed my cheek. "Now eat up, and rest. I want you healthy for our first Christmas together!"

I managed to drift off for another hour, but that was it. I lay there until I couldn't, and jumped in the shower. Once dressed, I told Audrey that I was going to run up to my apartment and gather a few items for Mary's present that we were working on.

"Look, Mary will hate me if you show up at the Surrogate."

"No, she won't—she's well aware of my stubborn ways. But I'm going straight home and then right back here anyway, if that makes you feel better."

Walking north on Broadway, I navigated the melee of Christmas shoppers like a ship's captain charting a treacherous channel. Following the right turn onto Mercer Street, I began the eastern hill climb toward 15th Avenue. I topped the hill across from 13th Avenue and then almost jumped out of my skin. The man I feared had been looking for me walked down the steps of one apartment building and immediately approached the next. He paused briefly and appeared to record something on a small notepad. Fortunately, he hadn't noticed me, but this confirmed my suspicion that this character was systematically canvassing the Hill. I became incensed by the invasion and for an instant even entertained facing off with this creep. Sensibility overpowered the urge, and I quickened my pace, heading straight for the Surrogate. I arrived a few minutes later, slightly out of breath.

"Carla, what on earth are you doing here, and why are you out of breath?" asked Mary when she saw me.

"It's nice to see you too, Mary," I replied, still huffing.

"Come with me into the backroom; I have some business to settle up with you."

"Uh-oh, that doesn't sound good."

"It's not good," Mary said, handing me a business envelope.

I opened the envelope to find a check for one thousand dollars.

"Whoa! I thought you said—"

"It's not good. It's great!" Mary smiled. "That is your override from the Microsoft catering job."

"Wow, this is amazing! Thank you so much!"

"You earned every penny of it, and you have already been requested for their Spring Fling event, so there's more where that came from."

I was automatically reaching for an apron when Mary said, "Just what in the hell do you think you're doing?"

"I was going pitch in around here and prep some things for tomorrow morning."

"It's already been done—remember, tomorrow is only a half day, and you aren't working."

"Oh geez, you're right. I feel like I've lost a day. OK then, I need to grab some things at my place and head back down to Audrey's. We'll see you tomorrow afternoon, I guess?"

"Yes, around four will be great, and regarding that check, you know these start-ups . . . You'd better get over to Rainier Bank on Harrison and get the cash. Like right now."

"Oh, OK, gotcha! I'll run straight over there before I go home."

I hugged Mary, mashing my face into her cheek and emphatically kissing it several times before snatching a fresh gingerbread man off the cooling rack.

"Hey! Don't burn your mouth!"

"I won't! Gotta fly. See you tomorrow! Love you, mean it!" I rattled off, as I made a mad dash out the front door and smack into the chest of none other than . . .

The unexpected impact sent him reeling backward onto the sidewalk, and we both froze as our eyes met.

"Carla, is that you?" the man asked as he began to push himself up from the cold pavement.

A thousand thoughts went through my mind in that millisecond, but running wasn't among them. This was my neighborhood, and I was ready to fight a horde of demons at the gates of hell if they threatened the life that I had built here. Out of my own depths I conjured a presence that was as menacing as any nightmare and began to speak in a smoldering tone to the stalker sprawled out on the concrete in front of me.

"I don't know who you are or what you want, but you have two seconds to answer those questions before I stomp the fucking eyeballs out of your head!" And to show him I was serious, I kicked him in the ribs with the instep of my John Fluevogs, sending him back to the sidewalk, this time facedown.

"No, no, no, you misunderstand!" the man coughed out while holding up one hand in surrender as he attempted to prop himself up off of the frozen pavement with the other.

By this time, a few locals had begun to assemble. "You OK, Carla?" asked the burly lumberjack in a flannel shirt.

"Yes, I'm fine, Ned, I've got this, but thanks for checking in."

I turned to the man on the pavement. "Well, Mr. East of the Mountains?"

"Carla, I've been looking for you here for about a month now."

"Yeah, I gathered. Why?"

"My name is Lars Svensen. I was a friend of your mother's—Eve Tecoi."

"Oh sweet Jesus! Why didn't you say so?" I reached down to help him to his feet, noticing that the heavy overcoat he wore covered a frame of skin and bones. "Here, come inside with me, please."

We entered the Surrogate, and I sat him down in a corner booth, catching Mary coming out of the kitchen in confused wonder.

"Everything OK here?"

"Yes, ma'am," I answered. Then, "Lars, please let me get you something to eat, perhaps some soup and a sandwich?"

"Thank you, Carla."

"Coming up!"

"Thanks, Mary—I'll grab the coffee."

"Oh, none for me; just some water, please."

Suddenly the reason Lars looked familiar hit me like a Mack truck. It was his house that Mom brought Virginia and me to the night she left Martin. "Oh my God, I do remember you, Lars!" I exclaimed.

A thankful and teary smile appeared across his gaunt face. Lars had worked with Mom at Simplot and was one of the friends Martin insisted that she dump once they married. A confirmed bachelor, he was a highly regarded member of the LDS community in Pole Pass. He drank the water in one tip of the glass and in between coughs asked Mary if he might trouble her for another.

"Lars, why have you been looking for me?"

"Your mother was a best friend to me, Carla," he replied. "Unfortunately, I never had a chance to say goodbye or thank her for being the dear that she was. I was out of the country on a mission trip when she fell ill. It wasn't until my return that I found out she had passed away. I was sick that I hadn't been there for her. After the divorce, we rarely saw each other. Simplot transferred me up to Coeur d'Alene during the divorce hearings, and after the threats I received from the Listers, I was just thankful to be out of the area. The last time I saw her was right before I left on the mission. She made me swear that if anything happened to her, there was something I needed to deliver to you, and only you, in person."

"What is it?"

"A letter." Lars produced the decade-old envelope from the inside pocket of his overcoat.

Mary arrived with some chicken soup and a grilled cheese sandwich. "Still OK here?" she asked.

"Yes, thanks. Mary, this is Lars—he was a friend of my mother's back in Pole Pass. Lars, this is my best friend, Mary."

"Pleased to meet you, Lars."

"Likewise, Miss Mary."

"Let me know if you want more soup, Lars—I have plenty."

"Thank you for the hospitality."

Lars handed me the yellowed but still sealed envelope and began sipping the hot soup in an effort to shake off the chill that had penetrated his thin frame. Instead of excitedly tearing into the letter, I calmly put the envelope in my coat pocket for a more personal review and asked Lars to share what he remembered about Mom.

"Your mother was like a breath of fresh air in the stale smoke-filled boardroom of the corporate environment. The office was dominated by ladder-climbing, martini-lunch-club alpha males, who felt entitled to throw around their self-importance. Eve wouldn't stand for it. She was more competent than many of them; she had to be. Pregnant and unmarried in 1957, she had no inhibitions about confronting loose talk around the office, and in those days there was plenty of it to go around. It was after she got together with Martin that I saw her change. She appeared to lose her sturdiness. Maybe it was just that she was tired of dealing with corporate America and saw a chance to simplify her life, you know . . . have a traditional family.

"Once the Listers insisted she cut ties with 'outsiders,' I saw her only occasionally, and she was definitely different, a shadow of the bright-eyed live wire that I remembered. You know, you resemble her quite a bit, Carla—and you have the same aqua eyes. Here, let me show you a photo of her from the company Christmas party; this was taken just before she became pregnant with Virginia."

Lars opened his wallet and removed a worn picture from the plastic sleeve. The resemblance was remarkable.

"Wow, I see what you mean. Lars, did you ever, umm, date her?"

"Oh no, no, Carla. Ours was a completely platonic friendship. Please don't misunderstand me, I adored her, but you see I had other interests. She was really the only person I could trust in that regard."

"Oh, oh, I see. I'm sorry, that must have been difficult."

"Those were just the times we lived in."

"Did she ever mention who my father was?"

Lars looked surprised at the question. "I see that you already know it wasn't Martin. Well, from what she told me, I was the only other person who knew that she was carrying you when she got married. The—I mean, your natural father, didn't even know. She never said who he was, even after the divorce. So, I'm sorry, I don't have an answer for you. Perhaps the letter?"

"Where are you staying?" I asked him.

"I rented a studio apartment for the month at the Morris down on Summit Avenue."

"Oh, I know the place—the big dark brown brick building on the corner. A friend of mine lived there for a bit, until the roaches ran him out.

"That's the place. Now that I've honored your mother's wish, I'm leaving this afternoon and heading back to Spokane to spend Christmas with my roommate and his family. A month of canvassing Capitol Hill is tougher than any missions I've done over the years."

"Speaking of your search, how did you know where to find me in the first place?"

"Well, when I returned to the Pass and couldn't locate you, I asked around through some circles. A friend at the DMV found your vehicle title transfer, and from another acquaintance who worked for the post office I learned that a C. Nelson had rented a PO box on Broadway around the same time. So, I just began checking every apartment building, working my way up from Summit, and then you literally ran right into me. You were a needle in the haystack."

"That's a little scary—if you found me that easily, someone else could too."

"Well, it wasn't easy . . . but I suppose a private detective with the right contacts and some luck would be able to."

"No, of course, Lars. I'm sorry, that was selfish of me. How will we find you if Virginia and I want to chat further? I mean, if you are OK with it."

"Here's my address and phone number in Spokane. Please call if you are passing through. Jim and I would love to have you over for dinner."

"Thank you, Lars. Thank you for everything, including being such a good friend to Mom."

"Carla, your mother was a gift to me; she was a beautifully special person. Thank you for the lunch, and also for not beating me senseless in the street. Now, I really must be going if I want to get out of town before rush hour. I'd like to at least make Ellensburg tonight."

"Let me send you off with more soup and another sandwich for your journey."

"Thank you, Carla, you're very kind."

Lars departed the Surrogate, and I sat down with Mary in the back office, telling her about the man I had suspected was searching for me over the past month.

"Look here, Carla," she said sternly, "you promise me right now that if anything like that happens again, you won't hide it from me! Clear?"

"Yes, I'm sorry, I didn't want to worry you; you've been through so much already."

"That's true, but losing you is something that would do me in. So, pinky-swear, no secrets when it comes to safety."

"Yes, I swear."

"OK, so, what about the letter?"

"I don't know, Mary. Maybe I should wait until Virginia gets back and we can read it together."

"You could, but because your mother wanted it delivered personally to you, maybe the contents are just for your eyes?"

"I didn't think of that."

"I mean, you can always tell Virginia what it says."

"You're right, I guess I could."

"Well, trust yourself, and whatever you decide will be the right thing."

"Thanks, Mare. I love you."

"I love you too—now get your butt to the bank and cash that damn check!"

I deliberated over my options walking the three blocks south on 15th Avenue East to Rainier Bank. Surprisingly, I wasn't in a rush to read the letter. Part of my hesitation was a fear of the unknown. I had lived this long without whatever information the envelope contained. The life that I had manifested from the wreckage of my West Valley days was full of not only contentment but also happiness. The career, the friends, the love, and now the return of Virginia—this was indeed my true family. It dawned on me that this envelope might be a virtual Pandora's box, containing revelations that could put it all at risk. I would be considering my actions carefully.

25

THAT'S CLOSE ENOUGH

Esmeralda entered the room, notepad in hand, prepared to record our observations. A master in the fading art of shorthand, she assured Virginia and me that her writing would be on pace with our dictation. After showing Esmeralda the evidence of the ledger having been tampered with, we switched on the microfilm reader and were all set to begin providing descriptions of each photo when I noticed the time.

"I'm sorry, Esmeralda, it's 3:45, and I need to get home to let Harry out."

"Harry . . . Mr. Lawe?"

"Sorry—Harry is the dog we are caring for. Virginia, can you go through the microfilm and help Esmeralda with this part?"

"I can, but you will be much better, and faster. Why don't I go home and take care of Harry? You can meet me there and take me out for a nice dinner."

"Are you sure? I'll be quick—shouldn't be more than an hour, and I'll catch you up over a nice dinner at a little place I know across from the big Christmas tree in Palmer Square."

"I promise not to keep him from you too long, Ms. Tecoi," Esmeralda said. She escorted Virginia to the exit, and I began reviewing the recovered photographs, pairing them with descriptions from my mother's journal.

~

After the confines of the Archive, poring over documents with me for two days, Virginia welcomed the bracing Princeton air as she walked along the salted sidewalk toward home. Taking a more scenic route back to the house, she cut across the graduate campus and entered the walled sanctuary of Wyman Garden through a little-known gate tucked discreetly between the trees. She paused for a moment beneath the snow-covered portico of arched

Wyman in winter, December 1981.

wisteria canes, inhaling the quiet of the garden's winter dormancy.

As her distractions retreated, Virginia drifted. Somewhere between Carla, Eve, and Town she felt a surfacing . . . something urgent . . . then it was gone. She returned to the bench from her meander, and then, "Oh, crap! Poor Harry." Fortunately, only ten minutes had passed; it could have easily been hours. She hurried the last few blocks home, deciding that he would get a stroll around the neighborhood to stretch his legs after a long day inside.

Virginia unlocked the front door to a very agitated Harry, who darted past her and around one side of the house to the large hollies in front of the eight-foot cedar fence that surrounded the rear of the property. After a quick sniff he ran to the other side, with Virginia trailing him to the garden gate. Propping his front paws up on the fence, he began sniffing the air as if he had treed one of Princeton's legendary black squirrels. The hair on the back of Virginia's neck stood up, and then a neighborhood cat scampered along the top of the fence like a tightrope walker heading toward the back of the property. "OK, Harry, good boy, thank you for keeping the cats away. Let's go for a walk, OK, good boy?" Harry cocked his head and gave her kiss on the face, and they headed back around front when suddenly Harry's pace lagged and his nose went skyward again, clearly catching another scent before turning back toward the garden gate.

Virginia walked into the house a few steps ahead to get the leash, when the ambient light in the foyer was suddenly extinguished by the slamming of the heavy front door behind her. There was no chance to turn around; the intruder grabbed a fistful of her hair and brought a large knife blade against her throat. The viciousness of Harry's barks and cries at the front door faded into the background as the intruder yelled out his instructions.

"You have one chance to give me what I want, or else I carve up that pretty face!"

Tightening his grip on the ball of hair, he marched Virginia down the hallway and into the library. There he violently pinned her face to the side of the bookcase, where she couldn't see anything except the opposite side of the room.

"I want that book! Where is it?" he demanded, grinding her face harder into the bookcase.

Virginia screamed, "Stop it! You're hurting me! What book? I don't even live here—I swear I don't know what you're talking about!"

"Did you think I was kidding when I told you one chance? Maybe I start by slicing off your ear, since you don't use it! Now, I want that book, you stupid whore—"

He never finished the sentence. A large hardcover volume flew from the shelf across the room, striking him in the right ear with such force that it knocked him to the floor, where he lay in agony clutching his head. Virginia fled down the hallway, out the front door, and almost right through me, on the walkup. Harry sprinted into the house just in time to see the attacker staggering toward the kitchen door and latched onto the inside of his crotch from behind. The man broke free and made a panicked escape into the garden.

Virginia, pumped full of adrenaline, screamed "MAN!" and pointed to the house.

I barreled up the walkway, followed closely by Mr. Jamison, the next-door neighbor, with his machete, as he announced that he had seen the guy come out of the bushes and immediately called the police. They were on the way.

We entered the house just in time to see Harry standing at the closed kitchen door with a mouthful of blood-soaked denim.

"I'll take the back—you go around front in case he runs out the gate!" I told Mr. Jamison before bolting through the kitchen door and into the garden with Harry.

Harry made a mad dash following the blood trail until he reached the eight-foot fence at the back of the property. Seconds later I scaled it and gave chase through the neighboring yards.

The attacker glanced over his shoulder just long enough to see me closing in hot pursuit and dove full speed through the final hedge. Unable to regain his balance after breaking through the snow-covered wall of laurel, he stumbled onto Springdale Road directly in front of a delivery van just moments from its last drop of the season. The gruesome scene left behind ten yards of bloody roadway and a lump of whatever remained of the attacker, piled up underneath the vehicle now sideways across the road. Jamison rounded the corner of Battle and Springdale as the event unfolded and ditched his machete in a bush as he approached the site. A Princeton police cruiser dispatched to the original disturbance arrived seconds later, siren blaring, and drove onto the sidewalk to pass what they believed was a vehicle breakdown blocking the street. Jamison ran toward the squad car, waving his hands.

"I'm the one who called! That's the perp, right there!" he shouted as he pointed under the van. "He broke into the house and attacked a young woman, we chased him, and he ran right in front of their van—not their fault, they couldn't have stopped."

The officers exited their vehicle at the same time as the distraught van driver, and Mr. Jamison turned his attention to me.

"You OK, son?"

"Yeah, I think so. That smell . . . it just triggered something," I replied, sickened by the horror of the sight in front of us.

"Well, that's about a gallon and a half of blood there," he said, unfazed.

"Geez, Mr. J, the guy's dead, for crying out loud."

"Better him than her, I say."

"Yes, of course."

More sirens approached as the officers told the parties to stay put until our statements were recorded. I explained that Virginia was the one attacked and I needed to get back to the house and check on her. Mr. Jamison agreed to stay on the scene, and the officers released me to return home, where another unit would arrive shortly. I found Virginia and Harry next door with Mrs. Jamison in front of the fire, Virginia wrapped in a blanket, holding an icepack to the left side of her face and a shot of brown liquor in her right hand. I rushed over to her.

"Are you all right?"

"Yeah, I'm just still full of adrenaline."

"I can see . . . you're still trembling. I'm so sorry! I should never have let you come home alone, especially after signs of a prowler."

"Did you catch him?"

"God did."

Mrs. J made the sign of the cross. "Dear God, what happened?"

"You or Mr. J didn't . . . ?" Virginia asked cautiously.

"Not that I wouldn't have liked to have caught him first, but no," I replied. "He was struck down on Springdale Road by a van. Mr. J stayed behind to give a statement so that I could get back to you. The police will be here in a couple of minutes to go over everything. Do you feel up to telling me what happened before you give an official statement?"

Virginia recalled the event up to the point that she encountered me on the walkup to the house.

"You must have been terrified!"

"Yes, but it was surreal . . . I was focused on survival, like when heavy trauma comes into the ER. I guess that's a good tool to have."

"Yeah, I can see that. Look, I know this won't come off as delicate, but we don't have much time. I have one suggestion."

"The library book?" Virginia said, as she looked at me.

"Exactly."

"James Townsend Lawe, I swear that it happened just like I said it did! You of all people shouldn't be surprised!"

"Surprised? Of course I'm surprised! But that doesn't mean I don't believe you!" My own adrenaline rush fueled the animated delivery.

Mrs. Jamison intervened as she refilled Virginia's shot glass: "If I may. I believe you too, Virginia. That house has a couple of ghosts to be sure, and the library is particularly active. Mr. J and I have lived here for three cycles of neighbors in the past thirty-something years. Each of them has had experiences in the house, always benevolent or humorous, but my advice is to leave that part of the story out of your report to the police."

"Mrs. Jamison is right, Virginia," I said. "If that ever got back to a medical board or to the UW, you might get bounced, or placed under some type of scrutiny that you don't need."

"Indeed," added Mrs. J.

"Yeah, I get it."

"Just tell them that you managed to break free. Trust me, they will be using dental records to identify this guy."

Minutes later, Mr. Jamison walked in the front door with two uniformed officers and a detective. After an hour of questions, and retracing the steps of the event, Detective Omicinski said, "I know this goes without saying, Dr. Tecoi, but you were very fortunate. We're sorry you went through this ordeal here in Princeton, but if you can think of anything else, don't hesitate to contact us. Please try to enjoy the rest of your visit, and a Merry Christmas and Happy New Year to you."

Virginia and Harry remained with Mrs. Jamison while Mr. J and I went next door to assess the damage and clean things up. Mr. J hooked up a hose in the laundry room and began washing down the bloody trail in the snow leading from the house through the garden. I grabbed the bleach and quickly cleaned up the kitchen where Harry had managed to tear into the intruder before he escaped out the door. I ventured into the library and saw the tome lying open on the floor just inside the doorway, where the investigators had left it. After placing the book on a nearby console table, I offered a heartfelt thank you to the friendly specter that had saved Virginia that afternoon. I half-expected a response, but my other half was taken aback when a small table lamp across the room came on, illuminating a stack of four leather-bound antique books.

When I tapped the bulb without result, I followed the lamp cord down the wall in search of a timer that the lamp would be plugged into, but there wasn't one to be found. Turning my attention to the books stacked neatly on the table, I discovered that they were actually an artful deception. Opening the cover of the top book revealed a beautifully crafted Tantalus set nestled within the hollowed-out volumes. "Ahhh, I think I understand," I said to myself, just before Mr. Jamison reentered the house.

"All done!"

"Thank you, Mr. J, I'm here in the library."

He made his way down the central hallway to the room.

"Join me in a drink before we head back next door?"

"Don't mind if I do."

I poured the liquor from the decanter into three shot glasses, releasing the fragrance of distilled apple into the room. I passed Mr. J his glass, leaving the other next to the Tantalus.

"Nothing like a traditional New Jersey applejack to knock the chill off," he said.

"Cheers," I offered, holding the glass aloft with a nod to Mr. J and discreetly to our unseen host.

As we left the room, I whispered over my shoulder, "Thanks again."

"What's that?" Mr. J said.

"Nothing, just mumbling to myself."

"You know, there are ghosts in this house—I'm not bullshitting."

"So I've heard," I replied as we cut across the snowy lawn on our way next door.

"Dinner, you two?" Mrs. Jamison asked as we walked in the front door.

Virginia had set the table for Mrs. Jamison's famous Battle Road West pot roast.

"Smells delicious! Are you sure you have enough for four?"

"I have enough for six," she replied, "and we don't have room for leftovers with Christmas dinner on the horizon."

During the meal, Virginia and I discovered that the Jamisons were both Princeton alumni who had met while in school. Albert took such a ribbing that as a history major, he learned how to write out the equation of his namesake's most famous theory, even though, according to Sophie, Albert was terrible at mathematics.

Sophie Jamison had a PhD in psychology and was a retired clinical director for the Princeton counseling center. She now served in an adjunct role for students at the Graduate College.

"Which period of history did you focus your studies on, Mr. J?" I asked.

"Please call me Albert . . . Hellenic was my era of choice, but it never stops there. One always manages to bookend the studies—history is like pulling a loose piece of yarn on a wool sweater," he chuckled.

"Well, I'd say that ancient and classical Greek culture is about as fascinating as it comes."

"The birth of democracy, the great philosophers, strides in the arts and sciences, the life of Alexander the Great . . . the rise and fall of Alexandria. Yes, there's enough to indulge the curious mind for a while," Albert affirmed.

"Virginia and I are conducting some historical research on a Syrian site around the ancient city of Edrei," I said.

"Oh—for some reason I thought your pursuits were more biological in nature, based on John Chesterling's departmental oversight."

"Yes, scholastically they are; I'm in molecular bio, but anthropology and archaeology have always been of joint interest to me. My late mother was an archaeologist for the British government at one time; the Edrei dig is one she led back in the 1950s and referenced in her field journal, which I inherited. She mentioned Princeton as a source of funding for the endeavor; that proved irresistible to me."

"Well, that's quite a coincidence. Has your quest been successful?"

"It's certainly been interesting. Are either of you familiar with an institution known as the Archive?"

Sophie dropped her knife, which hit the side of her plate with a clink. She and Albert exchanged a quick glance, and both took a drink from their wineglasses.

"I guess that's a yes?" Virginia cut through the awkward pause.

"That's an interesting lot over there. You've been utilizing their resources?" said Albert.

"Yes, they appear to be the sole curators of what we were looking for. Do I detect a note of reservation?" I asked.

Albert and Sophie exchanged glances again.

"If you don't tell them, Albert, I will," Sophie asserted.

Mr. J. knew better than to trifle with his wife, and he opened up. "The two comments I'll make are, the Archive owns, or has first-person access to, the largest knowledge cache on the planet. They are the modern-day equivalent of the revered library in Alexandria. The breadth of their holding is almost incomprehensible. Whether you realize it or not, when you access their resources, you are in a handshake deal with the devil."

"How so?" I asked, taken aback.

"At its elementary level, their pursuits are to hoard knowledge and use that knowledge for profit beyond just financial. It's about absolute power for a select few. The leadership of the Archive is made up of the most powerful families in the world. Their immediate and ongoing concern is power, as they already possess the majority of wealth on the planet. The rank-and-file members are just climbers, very wealthy individuals who fund the day-to-day operation through personal endowments and membership fees collected as house commissions from their investments. It's a status thing among this set, and a delusional few families believe they will find their way into the elite ranks. I say delusional, because every person at the highest level in the Archive was born into that position; it's a monarchy."

"I figured it was exclusive, but that's more than I imagined. In my initial meeting with one of their representatives, I was made privy to their daily operation and investment strategies."

"That's very interesting. They must believe there is a payoff of some sort down the line regarding your research."

"I'm not sure how . . . but then again, I guess we really won't know until we are able to consolidate the information."

"May I ask how you know so much about the Archive?" Virginia queried.

"I used the facility many years ago for my own studies."

"Aaand . . ." Sophie chimed in.

"I became obsessed."

"More like possessed, aaand . . ." Sophie pressed.

"I lost my kid sister to the Archive. Brilliant girl, with an IQ in the high 140s. The allure of almost limitless information contained within that system was too much. Excuse the reference, but the Archive was her Hotel California—she went in one day and hasn't come out. I'll never forgive myself for introducing Esmeralda to its charms."

The look on our faces easily betrayed the acquaintance.

"I see that you've met her."

"She's our facilitator," I said.

"It might be best if you didn't mention this conversation, at least until your project is completed. The Archive is a bit cultlike, you see," Albert advised.

"Oh, balderdash, Albert!" Sophie exclaimed. "Please tell Esmeralda that we love her; she's always welcome here with us. To stay, if she wants," she added.

Back next door, we took our nightly chat and nightcap into the library to keep our unseen host company.

"Well, that was quite a day."

"And aren't you the king of understatement!"

"I . . . I can't believe this happened—it's surreal."

"I've already compartmentalized it."

"You're going to have to teach me that trick someday."

"Not sure how healthy it is, but yeah. I wonder what book that guy was looking for, anyway."

"There is a roomful of them here—maybe a rare collectible? Apparently our resident spirit librarian didn't appreciate his methods."

"I do owe whoever it is a thank you," Virginia said.

"I won't tell the professor about this until they get back. I'd hate to ruin their holiday."

"Hey, I just had a really frightening notion. What if it's not the Chesterlings?"

"What?"

"No, think about it . . . you said the back door to the house was wide open when you returned from your walk with Harry, and then, an hour later, you almost get flattened by a truck! The next morning, the damned door is open again when we get back from our walk, and I know I closed my suitcase. That means someone looked through our stuff when we were out. What if this person was searching for your mom's notebook?"

"But how would someone even know about that?"

A cold chill ran up our spines as we said it in tandem.

"The Archive!"

26

MERRY PRINCETON EVE

We opened our eyes to the brightness of a Christmas Eve snowfall blanketing Princeton. After an abbreviated walk and romp around the backyard with Harry, we sat down for breakfast before making the trek to the Archive.

"Town, why didn't you tell me about this bruise on the side my face?" she asked, touching it gingerly.

"It's hardly noticeable—does it hurt?"

"Not too bad, but Esmeralda is going to wonder about it."

"Well, we could always tell her the truth. I mean, there is a police report filed. Princeton might as well be Pole Pass, the way news travels around here."

"I guess we could, but based on our suspicions, I think we need to play it by ear."

We finished breakfast while drafting the timeline of our findings to date and summarized what I had discovered in the photos the previous afternoon.

"So everything my mother recorded in the notebook appears to be identified in those images," I said. "We may never know what the actual text of the stolen pages says, but it's safe to assume that it's close to her own observations."

"Where do we start today?"

"I think we should try to figure out why on earth someone would want to steal that information."

"And why they would want your mother's notebook, and how they knew about it in the first place."

"Well, they had access to my application. I disclosed the book as source material on the 'Request to View' form."

"OK, so all we need is the why."

Having given ourselves a little extra time to trudge through the fresh snow, we arrived at the Archive a few minutes early. Esmeralda was already in the foyer, speaking with the receptionist and another facilitator, who promptly exited the scene upon our approach.

"Good morning, Esmeralda, I'm sorry we're a bit early—we didn't want to take a chance on being late."

"Good morning, Mr. Lawe and Ms. Tecoi." Esmeralda's distraction was evident as she greeted us. Then she instructed the receptionist to pass along any developments immediately.

"Yes, Esmeralda, the instant I know something."

"Thank you, Edna." Turning to us, she said, "It's eight thirty; please allow me to escort you downstairs before our few hours together slip away."

As we descended to sub-three, I couldn't help but mention her evident distraction.

"We have a junior facilitator that seems to be unaccounted for this morning," she said.

"Oh, perhaps it's just a snow delay—it is pretty slick out there," I said, masking my suspicion.

"Unlikely, Mr. Lawe. You see, he lives a mile away and walks to work. Our day at the Archive begins promptly at four a.m."

As we entered our study room, Esmeralda closed the door behind her and thanked us for the assistance regarding the missing assets, now officially cataloged as stolen.

"Yesterday, when I mentioned that the Archive takes these matters very seriously, I was not waxing dramatic. Would you two consider making a determination as to why this information would be profitable to someone?"

"Yes, of course, Esmeralda, we're happy to help," Virginia replied for us both.

"Thank you. The Archive will not forget your contribution."

On her way out of the room, she reminded us that in light of the half-day schedule, only a Christmas tea would be served.

"Well, I guess that lines up with what we were thinking anyway," I commented to Virginia.

"While you get started, I'm going to run to the ladies' room," she said. "I won't be but a minute."

While she was out of the room, I started working the problem backwards, beginning with the twenty-five photographs on the microfilm. Even with the low resolution of the projector, it was evident that this was a unique discovery, just as described in my mother's notebook. However unusual the find was, if financial gain had been the motivation for the theft of the images and their original descriptions from the ledger, it eluded me.

When Virginia returned, she told that she had passed within earshot of Esmeralda's desk and overheard half of a conversation: "'Oh dear . . . That does explain his absence . . . Say again? . . . Yes, they are here with me now. . . . I understand. Thank you for the update; please carry on.'

"I'd say the cat's out of the bag, Town."

"Apparently so. Let's see if she provides us with an update," I replied, and then an idea occurred to me. "Hold on a second—what if we approach the motive from an angle of what they might lose if the information were brought forward?"

"That makes sense, and then who is this information to be shielded from, us or the Archive?"

"Exactly! We're still missing something."

"You know, we haven't looked at the supplemental yet," Virginia said.

"You're right! With all the activity, I completely forgot."

I opened the pouch and removed a softbound leather book held closed by a tarnished brass buckle and a wide leather strap stitched into the spine. Laying the book on the table, I released the strap from the buckle, which revealed a set of embossed letters that ran across the center of the cover. Virginia and I paused for a several seconds, as if we were having trouble deciphering them.

She read them aloud: "'Townsend Jacob Lawe, Esq.' Whoa, Town, I didn't see this coming."

"Yeah, me neither! It's my great-great-great-grandfather Jake. I don't know a lot about him. We do share a birthday and my middle name. His signature appears on the official document involving the sale of land to Northern Passage Land & Title—the same land that became the Title Mine. What in the world is this doing here?"

"I guess we're about to find out."

Suddenly Van Kaiser's curious parting comments came back to me. "Remember what Van Kaiser said? *All roads lead to the doghouse.*"

Esmeralda's fingers tapped lightly on the door before she entered the room.

"Esmeralda, I'm at a loss regarding this supplemental."

"How so, Mr. Lawe?"

"Well, for one, why does the Archive have my great-great-great-grandfather's journal?"

"I will inform Mr. Van Kaiser that you would like to understand more about its provenance."

"Thank you."

"Certainly. Now, would you have an update for me as to your progress?"

"Yes, we do, but it's only a working hypothesis based upon the presumption that this theft is not driven by increased gain, but motivated by the preservation of something else. Perhaps information that may expose certain actions or persons."

"Thank you, Mr. Lawe and Ms. Tecoi."

"Esmeralda, do you think the unaccounted-for facilitator might be involved in this?" Virginia couldn't resist asking.

"I am sorry, Ms. Tecoi, I'm not at liberty to comment on that issue." Esmeralda's nuanced delivery confirmed that this was the Archive's inclination. "Thank you again for your thoughts regarding this issue. I'll leave you to your final hour before the Archive closes for the Christmas holiday."

"Wow, that was an interesting exchange," Virginia said after the door closed behind Esmeralda.

"Yeah, I guess our strategy for now is to read as much of this journal as we can in less than an hour."

"I'm a way better crammer—I've got this," Virginia declared, reaching for the journal.

She was right, and I went back to the microfilm station, searching the photos for anything I might have missed the day before.

The time evaporated, and Esmeralda was soon tapping on the door. "I trust the hour was productive?"

"Indeed, Esmeralda. Thank you once again for being an excellent facilitator."

"It has been my pleasure. I did have a chance to ask Mr. Van Kaiser about your inquiry."

"What was his reply?"

"*All roads lead to the doghouse.* He said you would understand."

"Thank you—I guess I was hoping for a little more."

As Esmeralda escorted us toward the exit, I mentioned our chance encounter with Albert and Sophie.

She smiled. "Oh, Albert, always the smart one . . . he conducted his research and got out before it was too late. Sophie was the best thing for him. I hope they are well and happy."

"They both were clear in their affection for you, Esmeralda; they specifically wanted you to know that their home is your home, always," Virginia said.

"They are very kind souls. Regretfully, I made some concessions in my youth that still require my attention. Perhaps one day. Please do give them my kindest regards and wish them a Merry Christmas, will you?"

"It would be our honor," Virginia said.

"Thank you," she said with a smile. "Merry Christmas to you both, and Happy New Year!"

"Merry Christmas and Happy New Year to you, Esmeralda," I said, helping Virginia into her coat.

When we were almost out of sight, I looked over my shoulder and saw Esmeralda still in the doorway, observing our departure.

~

Back at the Chesterlings', we relocated their faux Christmas tree into the library and settled in. I started a fire and poured two shots of applejack, and then took a seat next to Virginia on the sofa.

"Merry Christmas Eve to you, Ms. Tecoi; to Harry; and of course to our most benevolent host."

"Hear! Hear!" Virginia seconded. "By the way, his name is Charles."

"Now how do you know that?"

"Simple deduction. Look at the book on the table."

The book, titled *Homes of the Revolution*, lay open to the same page where it had fallen after striking Virginia's attacker. If I had paid closer attention, I might have noticed that the inset photo was of the house that we were in. Charles Margerum was the home's original owner, and according to this book, this residence played host to covert rebel meetings until George Washington and the Continental Army beat back the British and Hessian troops. The critical local battles at Princeton and Trenton were responsible for repelling British forces out of southern New Jersey once and for all.

"Nice work! Thank you, Charles, and for your hospitality as well!"

"Cheers, Charles," Virginia added.

"Ah . . . I feel like we can finally relax and enjoy the rest of our time together, just the four of us."

"Forget relaxing, we still have work to do!" Virginia said as she finished her shot.

"What are you talking about?"

"I found some interesting stuff and I need your help."

"Can't it wait for just a couple of days?"

"No way. I'll forget something."

"But my shoulder is sore," I said with a smirk.

"Too bad, bucko, you got me into this. Butch it up, and I'll give you some Christmas Eve PT later."

"You win."

Virginia recited her thoughts from reading the journal and began to recall more detail as we talked. "All right, here's how Jake Lawe connects to the Archive."

"I'm all ears."

"So, from what I read, Jake Lawe was an observer."

"What?"

"He had been delivering information about the West to unnamed persons in Philadelphia and DC. The other thing is that he was also passing information to someone here in Princeton identified as MFR."

"MFR . . ." I thought for a few seconds. "Milton . . . Franklin . . . Rhodes! That's the portrait I was standing in front of in the Archive's boardroom when Van Kaiser came in. The timeline fits."

"There's more. Jake advised MFR regarding the tribal land and the subsequent private purchase of a parcel sold by the federal government to Northern Passage Land & Title. That's what became the Title Mine."

"Oh man, I think that's kind of what my dad was afraid of."

"No, he negotiated this deal in order to keep the peace. He made the parties so gold-crazed that they couldn't wait to get the deal done. The Archive financed the project, and they initially owned the mine along with the saloon, brothel, and boardinghouse, and some of the town of Pole Pass."

"I think I need another applejack! Charles, how about you?" I chuckled as I refilled the glass.

"I'll be Charles's proxy," Virginia said.

"What about the Listers, Adamses, Harrisons, and Butterfields?"

"They were credited as Founders, but they were just pawns used by the financiers. By the time the mine 'pinched,' they were left with some land holdings and somehow ownership of the worthless mine site."

"So, Jake arranged the financing for the town Founders through his contacts at the Archive, and the investors used the Founders as front people."

"Exactly. He more or less brokered it. But listen, in his last entry, dated May 1875, he wrote, 'Something is wrong here. I have advised MFR.'"

"The mine was closed by then . . . that entry had to be right before he died. How did you get through his journal so quickly?"

"I didn't—I started at the back of the book!"

"Genius! I wouldn't have thought of doing that. I can't wait to ask Van Kaiser about all of this when I meet with him on January 5."

"Yeah, and I can't wait to hear all about it right after that meeting!"

"Absolutely! I promise to call you as soon as I can get to a phone."

"Now, Mr. Lawe, how about a little dessert before your Christmas Eve dinner?"

27

MARY CHRISTMAS

The cold drizzle stopped just long enough for Audrey and me to unload the tightly packed sports coupe parked on 16th Avenue. This time last year, Mary was consumed with grief over Arthur's passing; we knew from her shift into a somber tone around Thanksgiving that this Christmas would be another painful notch in her memory belt. Mary met us at the door with a poor attempt at masking the sadness, and with no tree in the house, she and Audrey laid the presents next to the fireplace while I brought the other provisions into the kitchen.

"I'm going to make up some of Audrey's spiked eggnog before I get started on dinner!" I shouted from the kitchen.

Minutes later when they joined me, Mary mustered a laugh. "That's a lot of food and booze for three people!"

Before Audrey or I could reply, the doorbell rang.

"I wonder who that could be?" Mary said, in a way that suggested she'd rather ignore it.

"Oh go on, it's probably a special delivery or something," Audrey countered.

Mary opened the door to a porch of twelve friends singing Christmas carols and bearing gifts. The revelers barged past the stunned widow, kissing her on the cheek and shouting "Merry Christmas!" on the way into her house, carrying gifts and other items. Suddenly, Mary had a fresh tree standing in her living room, and the smell of Christmas past and present arrived. Audrey had spearheaded this endeavor, inviting members from the Gathering to crash Mary's Christmas Eve with a massive slumber party. Someone thoughtfully turned the stereo to an FM station committed to the season with a twenty-four-hour Christmas format, followed by cheers of "That's more like it!" One by one, guests cycled into the kitchen, delivering various items that I had requested for the meal and getting a cup of hot bourbon-infused eggnog. Everyone held their cups until all were served and I could take the floor.

"Mary . . ." I tried to keep it together but of course struggled. "None of us can know the loss you feel, but what we do know is the love we have for you and those memories that we each hold of Arthur. Merry Christmas, our dearest Mary, we love you!"

There wasn't a dry eye in the house on 16th Avenue East as everyone toasted Mary, and Arthur, wherever his soul had led him. It was a breaking point for Mary as she wept a little bit more of the emptiness away and allowed the loving embrace of this chosen family to engulf her. Audrey, Esther, and Roberto decorated the tree while Mary and I prepared the main course of prime beef tenderloin encrusted with rosemary, salt, and horseradish, and Carmen cooked up her mother's favorite collard and cornbread recipes. The desserts brought in from the Surrogate helped make this a legendary Christmas Eve feast.

By eleven, everyone was in pajamas and scattered throughout the downstairs in sleeping bags, one by one falling asleep in the warm glow of the Christmas tree and the crackle of the fire.

Blueberry pancakes started coming off the griddle at seven, as Audrey dished up eggs and bacon. Mary turned the stereo on to Vince Guaraldi's *A Charlie Brown Christmas*, rousing the house with a big smile and a hearty "Merry Christmas!" The pajama brigade marched through the chow line filling their plates, with Mary handing out mimosas as they passed her.

While we enjoyed our breakfast, Mary began opening the gifts that had appeared as magically as the tree they lay under. There were several classic books, all collectors' editions in beautiful leather bindings; wonderful wines; and a spectacular clear quartz crystal to help "amplify Mary's intentions during the coming year," Roberto instructed. Then Audrey handed Mary a festively wrapped gift, saying, "This is a token of everyone here."

Mary unwrapped the package and was deeply moved by its contents. Audrey and I had pooled our talents to create a 26-by-24 sketch of the Gathering. It was imprecisely drawn, but one could easily identify group members by their nuanced shapes and at least one telling feature. That is, with the exception of Arthur. He was featured perched atop the large antique French buffet in the dining room, legs draped over the front edge, hands bracing against the marble top as he leaned out toward the group in mid-comment.

"Just a little something for the spot at the bottom of the stairs," I said.

Audrey and I remained with Mary as our friends departed for their respective Christmas destinations. I insisted on handling the cleanup duties while Mary and Audrey relaxed in front of the living room fireplace with a cup of nog on this cold and rainy Seattle Christmas morning.

"Thank you, Audrey. Merry Christmas to you." Mary tapped Audrey's mug with hers.

"Merry Christmas to you, Mary, and you are so welcome."

"You know, Arthur was very fond of you," Mary told her.

"Arthur was a chivalrous man. He was like that as a boy too. I knew he had found the right person when he married you."

Mary laid her hand in Audrey's as the two friends enjoyed the fire, experiencing an unspoken knowing in their relationship.

28

VAN KAISER

Virginia and I enjoyed the remainder of our Princeton holiday together, and as usual the goodbye left a vacuum for us, and especially me, as I missed her companionship, her hand in mine, and the warmth of her smooth body next to me in bed. We often discussed how it was harder for the one who didn't travel and was left with a silence of sorts. This time I leaned on the thoughts of my upcoming meeting with Aaron Van Kaiser to get over the blues that followed our parting. When I entered the Archive on January 5, 1982, Esmeralda Jamison stood in the foyer wearing the same stunning ensemble of emerald green that she had worn when we first met her.

"Welcome, Mr. Lawe. I trust you and Ms. Tecoi enjoyed a wonderful Christmas and New Year's celebration?"

"Indeed we did, Esmeralda, thank you, and how was yours?"

"It was fabulous—I found a marvelous hermetic alchemy text to study. Amazing. Thank you for asking."

"I see . . . a little 'as above, so below' personal enlightenment for the New Year?"

"Bravo, Mr. Lawe. You are obviously familiar with the concepts," she smiled.

"Only on an elementary level."

"We all have to start somewhere. Mr. Van Kaiser is awaiting you in the boardroom, if you would please follow me."

"Always a pleasure, Esmeralda."

"Rogue," she said, with a soft wink and a closed-mouth smile.

After we exchanged pleasantries, Van Kaiser anticipated my first line of inquiry. "Townsend Jacob Lawe was an informant. He shared certain information with federal sources and kept our local associate body abreast of the opportunities for profit."

"Was he a member of the Archive?"

"I am not at liberty to discuss the membership status of Townsend Jacob Lawe. But I will disclose that services rendered in pursuit of Archive goals are always rewarded, even posthumously."

"Well, if a chairman of the board was his principal contact here, then I can draw my own conclusions."

"You very well may, Mr. Lawe. However, as a researcher you know that partial facts can be more deceptive than no facts at all." Van Kaiser easily parried my amateurish stab at extracting more information, and I nodded in agreement before trying another approach.

"Is there anything that you can tell me about the missing facilitator, the stolen photos, and the missing ledger pages?"

"The facilitator is no longer missing, and I understand Ms. Tecoi was unharmed, other than a scare and a bruise."

I took the confirmation in for a second. "Have you recovered what was taken?"

"Not yet. However, we are hopeful that our investigation into the matter will conclude shortly."

"To be candid, Mr. Van Kaiser, if I am to assist the Archive in the fullest capacity, you might provide me with as much detail as possible."

"I understand your frustration, Mr. Lawe; rest assured that I will support you with every resource that I am authorized to enlist. But you must appreciate that both of our interests are at stake here."

"Very well. What can you tell me?"

"After the Oregon Treaty was signed in the late 1840s, settlement of the Hidden Pass area increased and stories of gold in the area began to surface," Van Kaiser began. "Lawe discovered that a group of new settlers to the region—Lister, Adams, Harrison, and Butterfield—had devised a plan to stage a false-flag assault on the Hidden Pass Trading Post. They were intent on the wholesale slaughter of the proprietors, resident trappers, and even a few settlers. Their goal was to spark outrage and catalyze a brutal reprisal against the local Native population. The inevitable consequence would have been the annihilation of local tribes and the subsequent seizure of all Native lands in the region. As the lone survivors of the supposed massacre, the four families would file their official land claims and divide the region among themselves.

"Lawe presented the conspirators with three fist-sized nuggets of gold and advised them that if they approached this using another method, they could have all that they wanted and more, without risk. He introduced them to a fellow financier from our institution, and the necessary political and fiscal arrangements were made. The Archive's investors were pleased with their gains while they lasted, and Lawe proved himself valuable again when he advised our group to divest themselves of the Title Mine holdings, months prior to the mine pinching. The so-called Founders were left with Northern Passage Land & Title as well as the deed to the now-worthless land."

"Thank you for the history lesson," I said. "Please forgive me if I'm missing something here, but how does this connect to my original quest?"

"My suspicion is much more than I am able to disclose at this moment, Mr. Lawe. However, if you choose to continue your search, I'm confident that you will find your answers . . . and others."

Van Kaiser's remarks were puzzling to say the least. I didn't want to leave the meeting with my frustration evident and managed a smile with an equally enigmatic parting statement of my own.

"Thank you for your time and resources. I'll be in touch."

29

GRADUATION

The skies over Puget Sound were beautifully clear as the pilot announced our final approach to Seattle-Tacoma Airport. I had whiled away the flight hours reliving my past four years at Princeton, culminating with the previous week's graduation. Having Carol, Dad, and Virginia in attendance made a memory I would always hold dear. The addition of Albert and Sophie, as well as Anil and Khadija, made it all the more special. My only regret was that it was a whirlwind affair, and we weren't able to properly celebrate Carol's announcement of officially accepting a job at a prestigious Seattle law firm specializing in tribal advocacy. "This is your day, Town, not mine," she said, as we toasted her over dinner anyway. The trio returned westward the morning after the ceremony, while I remained at Princeton to put my things in storage until fall and say goodbye to friends who would not be returning next year.

Virginia had completed her finals but was scheduled for rounds at Children's Hospital today and couldn't pick me up at the airport, but Carla readily volunteered. Upon entering the terminal, I caught sight of the girl I had seen in person only once before. She playfully peeked out from behind a column in the gate area. Her jet-black hair was cut short, but soft and feminine, the familiar aqua eyes now bright and friendly. A much better picture than what I remembered seeing from Barber Jimmy's chair.

"Hi—Carla?" I said, as she approached me with a bashful smile. I stretched out my hand, which she gently brushed aside, instead giving me a big welcoming hug. I instantly recognized the smell of Hermès Eau d'Orange Verte as she pressed herself into me before speaking.

"Hi Town, welcome to Seattle."

"Thank you for picking me up."

"Glad to do it! Good flight?"

"Yes, thanks. No screaming babies." I laughed.

"I was thinking that you might be hungry."

"Always."

"Great, let's get you up to the restaurant, and I'll take care of that for you."

"I don't want to put you out."

"Really?" She looked at me like I had three heads, and at least one of them should know better.

"OK, you don't have to tell me twice." I chuckled as we walked arm in arm down the concourse toward baggage claim.

I wasn't sure if it was because she was Virginia's sister or that Carla and I wore the same fragrance, but she instantly felt like an old friend.

"So, let's get right to it—you love my sister?"

"Yes, I do."

"That's a great answer, because she loves you too."

"So she says." We laughed.

"You're going to ask her to marry you?"

"Why? Are you in a hurry to bake a couple of cakes?" I fired right back at her with a grin.

"OK, you don't have to answer that one."

As we drove north toward Capitol Hill, Carla opened up about Virginia. "Yeah, Virginia . . . she came at the right time for me. I feel somewhat overwhelmed."

"Well, I know that she needed you back in her life. I'm really happy that it worked out the way it has."

"It's crazy how life changes so drastically—or I guess it's more that our circumstances in life change."

"Or it's just that we finally see that particular set of circumstances."

"Yeah, like they've been there all along, and when we're prepared, we finally experience it."

"I think it's something like that. My godmother Chilok taught me to look at it like chewing your food enough before you swallow, so you don't choke. It's a universal principle."

"I'd like to hear more about this ancient wisdom stuff while you're here."

"Sure, I'd be glad to discuss anything you want."

Carla found a spot on 15th Avenue East directly in front of the Surrogate and neatly parked Audrey's Porsche. "You must be my good luck charm—I never get a spot out front! Come on inside and we'll top off that tummy."

After seating me in a booth, Carla presented the menu: "I have a ham and sharp cheddar croissant, or a ham and Swiss version."

"Yes, please," I said, indicating that I would eat both.

"Hmmm. I like a hungry boy," she beamed. "Yellow curried rice on the side?"

"Deal."

"Drink?"

"Water, please, and a shot of espresso."

"Done. Don't go away—I'll be back in a minute."

Upon her return with only one plate of food, Carla slid in across from me.

"Aren't you eating?" I asked.

"You kidding me? The last time I ate here, I got ptomaine."

"Toe . . . what?"

"Ptomaine. Never mind, it's often mistaken for food poisoning. You're a regular joke killer."

"Ha-ha, that's comforting . . . sorry, that was clever. This is delicious, by the way," I said as I swallowed another bite. "Well worth the coming onslaught of gastrointestinal woes."

I confessed to her my Main Street encounter with the haunting girl on the opposite side of the glass, and she recalled it.

"I remember that day, Town . . . so, so, long ago."

"Sorry to bring it up. It's just that you have . . . I mean . . ."

"Survived, grown, transformed . . . yeah."

"Yes, all. So, have you ever thought about going back to the mountains?"

"You know, Mary and Audrey have both said they want to make the trip to Pole Pass this summer."

"You should! You could all stay with us at the house. There's plenty of room, a great pool, the river, and I know Dad would love having a house full of women!"

"Thanks for the offer; I'll ask them if they were serious."

"You probably want to take a look at your building too. By the way, that was a genius move, getting it."

"Oh, thanks! Virginia told me what you said about the rehab of it. Definitely something I want to do when the time is right. I think the Listers have figured out they aren't getting it back."

"I'm glad you are considering it. That would make a great mixed-use property."

"I think it will make a great gallery one day."

"What about the other side? You have two full storefronts."

"Not sure; I haven't really considered that."

"Bakery? Coffeehouse?" I smiled.

"Town Lawe, you're a sneaky devil, aren't you."

"Well, stranger things have happened."

"It would have to be an awfully stranger thing to uproot me from here."

"Well, good, at least you'll know if it's the right thing."

"True. I like your thinking," Carla said, as I caught her eyes drifting as though she was actually entertaining the idea.

"And thanks again for letting us crash at your place these next few days."

"I couldn't have you sleeping in a hotel—you might get bedbugs! Besides, Audrey doesn't mind. I think she actually gets a little lonely when I'm not around."

"That's nice—I'm happy you found someone special."

"Oh, I've been fortified with wonderful friends here."

"So Virginia tells me."

"You'll get to meet some of them tomorrow at Virginia's pre-graduation dinner."

"I'm looking forward it."

Mary walked into the restaurant and over to the table as I took my last bite of lunch.

"Town Lawe, this is Mary Burke, my best friend, my mentor, and my boss."

"It's my pleasure, Mary Burke. I have heard so much about you," I said as I stood and held out my hand to greet her.

"Thank you, Town, and I you. All good things of course," she smiled, taking my hand in hers. "How was your lunch?"

"It was great, thank you. I'm so full I need a nap."

"That's funny—my dear dead husband, Arthur, used to say that very same thing."

"Oh, I'm so sorry."

"Thank you, but it's OK, he's still around," Mary said with a smile.

Carla turned to Mary. "I thought I might take Town over to my place and let him unwind; then I'm headed down to Audrey's. Is there anything I can do for you before we leave?"

"No, honey, you go on. I'm not staying long myself. Town, it was nice to finally meet you. I'll see you tomorrow."

"Thank you, Mary, and likewise. Have a great afternoon."

We hopped into the car, and a few minutes later we arrived at Carla's place.

"What a cool apartment, Carla. I love the natural light."

"Oh thanks, I've really enjoyed it. Audrey says it's a little like taking a vacation when she stays here for a couple of nights, so much quieter than Broadway."

"I bet."

"It will be fun to see your dad—I still speak with him once a month."

"He's not billing you, is he? I'm sure he's lonely and more than happy to chat with you."

"Now that you mention it, I have never received a bill from him."

"Good," I said with a laugh.

Carla showed me around the apartment and poured us both a glass of wine, and we sat in the living room.

"So, Town, I have some questions for you."

"You mean like how I plan to provide for Virginia, babies, etcetera?"

"No, no . . . but those are good. I was thinking more on the Native side of things."

"Oh, sure. How can I help?"

"Virginia told me about her experiences, and also about you, and the time you were attacked."

"Ah, yes."

"This is about a recurring dream that has started up again, increasing in frequency."

"I'm not very good at dream interpretation, but I can try. That might be best left to someone who studies that type of psychology."

"No, it's not like that. This is more like what Virginia has experienced."

"You mean the possibility of it connecting to some other type of encounter?"

"Maybe. The dream is that I'm a large bird. I think an eagle because of my feathers and my huge yellow feet. I'm soaring over the wilderness in a figure-eight pattern; I get the feeling that I'm patrolling the area."

"Do you recognize the terrain? I mean, is it familiar to you when you're awake?"

"No, just that it's the same place every time."

"Do you have any idea what you're looking for?"

"None whatsoever. I only know that I'm supposed to be diligent about it."

"Can you shut your eyes now and describe what you see?"

Carla closed her eyes and relaxed a few seconds before attempting to recall the landscape.

"The first loop I make is over a dense forest, and then, at the crossover point of the eight, I'm over a mountain range, then a valley and more forest before returning to my starting point for another pass."

"OK, that was great. Now, while it's still fresh in your mind, I want you to draw what you saw for me."

While I remained seated in the living room sipping my wine, Carla went over to the dining room table and began to draw. We both jumped at the sudden ringing of the telephone.

"Would you get that for me?" Carla asked, as the phone was within my reach.

"Hello, Carla's place," I answered. "Her personal assistant Townsend speaking. . . . Yes, Ms. Garner, it's my pleasure. . . . I see. . . . She's right here." I walked into the dining room and handed Carla the receiver. "Ms. Garner on line one, madam."

Carla took the phone with a grin and spoke into it: "Yeah, he's a hoot. I'm just about ready to leave. . . . Red or white? . . . OK, see you in a few. Love you, bye." After hanging up, she turned to me. "Audrey says that perhaps she needs a manservant too."

"I can assure you it's standard equipment for professional women back East."

Carla laughed and gave me a big smile. "You're funny, Town, quick-witted as well!"

"Yeah, I'm a laugh a minute," I responded.

Then she rose and looked at me regretfully. "Hey, I'm sorry to rush off—I could stay here and chat for hours." As she went to get her purse, she said, "If you get bored and want to stretch your legs, Volunteer Park is north on 15th, or you can walk south past the Surrogate and you'll find City People's Mercantile as well as QFC if you want other food."

"No problem; thanks again for everything."

"Oh, and you can get an espresso at six from the restaurant if you like."

Carla hugged me goodbye and was walking out the door when I stopped her. "Forgive me, madam, I do believe you have forgotten Ms. Garner's wine," I said, handing her the bottle.

"Dear Townsend, whatever would I do without you?" Carla smiled.

I had a few hours to kill before Virginia arrived, and after that big lunch and a glass of wine, I took off my shoes and stretched out on the sofa for a power nap. The next thing I knew, I was waking up to Virginia's smile and soft voice. "Hi stranger. Wow, you were out like a light—good thing I have a key."

"Hi there, I thought I had died and a beautiful angel was bringing me back to life. I was half right—you look stunning!"

"Awww, still your sweet self, I see. How was the flight?"

"Uneventful. Carla picking me up, on the other hand . . ."

"Isn't she just great?"

"She's spectacular."

"Told you! How was your nap?"

"I can't remember the last time I slept that well. What time is it, anyway?"

"Just after five. I'm a little fried. I really feel like pizza, beer, and a foot massage."

"I saw a pizza place around the corner—I'll make the arrangements. Why don't you have a nice soak in the tub while I take care of this?"

"You win. Canadian bacon, pineapple, mushrooms, and extra cheese, please."

I ran out to get the pizza and managed to make it back to the apartment in time to hand Virginia a towel as she exited the tub.

"I definitely needed that. The pizza smells wonderful," she said as her stomach growled.

"Didn't you eat today?"

"Something out of a machine. I can't do the cafeteria anymore."

"Have a seat and I'll grab a couple of Red Hooks. You want a glass?"

"Just the one it comes in, thanks," she smiled.

As I reached into the fridge for our beers, Virginia asked about the drawing that Carla had left on the table.

•

"What's this sketch of Pole Pass doing here?"

"What are you talking about?"

"Look, this is part of the area that you took me to. We camped right at the foot of this ridgeline, and I bet the plateau and spring are under these trees . . . here," Virginia said as she tapped her finger on the spot.

"How did you do that? I think you're right."

"It's pretty obvious to me. Yum, great pizza." She laughed with her mouth full.

I recounted Carla's dream to Virginia.

"She mentioned it to me back in December," she said. "I guess I didn't realize this was ongoing."

"Yeah, interesting. Maybe if they come for a visit, she can meet with Myra, or you could both meet with White Feather."

"Come to Pole Pass this summer?"

"Yeah, Carla told me that she, Mary, and Audrey might come for a visit. I invited them to stay at the house."

"Wow, that would be great, wouldn't it!"

"I think so."

"Let's see if we can get them to commit before we head back over the mountains."

"Indeed, we can work on that during tomorrow's dinner," I said strategically.

"Sounds great. My schedule tomorrow is I've got to be in at five in the morning for a few hours, and then I am officially done! Probably back here by ten thirty or so."

"Congratulations! Carol and Dad will be here around two with plenty of time to get situated before your pregrad dinner."

"It's really sweet of Mary to host them at her house."

“Yeah, it sure is.”

“Mary will make them feel right at home; she’s got that gift. How was your time with Carla?”

“Carla has her own magic, you know.”

“She has. Just wait until you meet Audrey.”

“We already spoke on the phone.”

“You work a room pretty quickly, don’t you?”

“I met Mary at the restaurant, too!” I laughed.

“Anything else I should know before bed?”

“I’m really looking forward to a good night’s snuggling with the windows open and fresh, cool Northwest air.”

I found Volunteer Park remarkably serene at six fifteen in the morning. The sun was just rising as I walked north along the main concourse toward Isamu Noguchi’s *Black Sun* sculpture with a café Americano. The large, dark granite work resembled an artful tractor tire, or, to some, a doughnut with a slightly off-center hole. Carla suggested an alternative viewpoint after taking in the whole of the piece: that I draw close enough that the peripheral scenic distractions were obscured, and then the space in the middle of the sculpture would become a west-facing window overlooking the city below, with the Olympic Mountains across Puget Sound in the distance.

I set my coffee down and placed my hands on the massive smooth stone while I peered through its opening. Absorbing the unique perspective for a moment, I was suddenly rewarded with the rising sun igniting the distant snow-covered peaks of the Olympic range. I migrated to a nearby bench with my espresso, and other than a single jogger and a group of speed walkers circling the reservoir below, I was alone.

Sitting in the quiet park, I took note of a lily pond on the terrace beneath me—a simple yet perfect circular design partially covered with dark green lily pads and brilliant pink water lilies floating on the surface. I walked down to the lower level, curious to see if koi also called the water home, but found it difficult to see below the glassy green surface. Instead, my eyes remained locked on the reflection of the sky and surrounding trees that seemed to reach far deeper than the physical bottom of the pond, as if into another realm.

Then it came to me: "As above, so, below." The instant I spoke the phrase aloud, I was overcome by a searing pain in my head. It was so intense that it dropped me to one knee before I threw up onto the gravel pathway. The pain and nausea passed just as quickly as they had arrived, and after regaining a standing position, I made my way to a bench next to the pond.

"Goddamned drunkard," whined a passing speedwalker as his body began lurching from his own gag reflex. The comedic spectacle of this man, as he continued walking with his now-mistimed rhythmic swish and hand cupping his mouth, made me laugh out loud. I rinsed my mouth with the remaining espresso and thought about this epiphany. A surfacing of knowledge locked away deep in the recesses of my mind had fought its way back into my consciousness, like a free diver frantically ascending from the depths for a gasp of air. I quickly pulled out a small notepad and began feverishly recording my thoughts.

I was so excited to share this with Virginia when she returned to the apartment that I didn't consider what her immediate concern would be.

"What? Do you know if you lost consciousness? Has this happened before? Did you feel dizzy prior to this?" She was relentless in her battery of questions.

"Look, I'm OK, honest!" I said, trying unsuccessfully to assuage her fears by explaining the revelation I had had.

"I don't want to hear anything about it, Town, not until we get a scan. Do you understand me? Not one more word!" she said in a strident tone that I was unfamiliar with.

Virginia was able to schedule my appointment for one that afternoon with a diagnostic radiologist who was well known for his ability to wet-read the brain, meaning that he could immediately tell if there was an abnormality. Thankfully the scan was clean—so clean that the doctor wasn't remotely concerned about his final report, available in a week. Virginia broke down at the news.

"I'm sorry, I was really scared that this was something else. But please tell me if this ever happens again. Promise me that, OK?" she whispered.

"Yes, of course, and for the record, thank you. I'm so sorry it gave you such a scare."

"It's OK, I'm fine. I'm just glad you are all right."

We hurried back across the Montlake Cut to Carla's place with barely enough time to change clothes before walking the two blocks to Mary's house.

"I'm a little nervous."

"You should be! These women are going to sift you like cake flour." Virginia laughed enthusiastically.

"Well, at least I'll have Roberto to help me."

"Don't count on it—he'll be even more scrutinizing than the girls!"

"I think you are having fun at my expense."

"Let's hope so, for your sake."

"No, I'm serious! It's like meeting your family for the first time!"

"Oh, just be yourself—they will love you, trust me."

"Into the belly of the beast I go."

"Yeah, the gallows pole awaits you. God, you're dramatic sometimes."

We arrived at Mary's just shy of five o'clock. Virginia began to make the formal introductions to Audrey, Esther, and Roberto, who were in the foyer with wineglasses already in hand. I was struck by the serenity in Audrey's hazel eyes; clear and full of confidence, they also held a power in them.

Esther was bubbly and transparent. I instantly knew she was studying me. It wasn't uncomfortable, but it gave me a glimpse of how I imagined my mother might have been when meeting someone for the first time. Roberto's broad smile, and the bright red shock against his blue-black hair, immediately compelled me to greet him with a hug instead of a run-of-the-mill handshake. Dad and Carol emerged from the kitchen with Mary and Carla as they brought the last of the silverware to the table.

"Hey! It's nice to see you guys too!" I said, as they virtually ignored us.

"Oh, sorry, Town," said Carol. She and Dad stepped around the table to greet us both with a hug and congratulations on Virginia's accomplishment.

After handing Virginia and me glasses of wine, Carla took the floor and set the tone for the evening.

"Tonight we are celebrating Virginia's well-deserved graduation from the University of Washington School of

Medicine. It's one of the toughest programs in the country, and she conquered it. Congratulations, big sister!"

A chorus of clinking glasses followed, and then Carla announced the evening's menu. "OK, for dinner we have prepared a classic Pacific Northwest cuisine of fresh alder-wood-fired Alaskan halibut, sautéed spinach with lemon zest, roasted carrots, and cornbread served with local honey."

Mary's dining room table had become accustomed to vigorous discussions taking place over its rich wood surface. If one happened into the room from off the street, they would conclude that this assembly was an informal and somewhat rowdy family dinner. There was a lot of laughter and raised voices trying to reach the opposite ends of the table with commentary. During a rare lull in the conversation, I caught Esther congratulating Carol on landing her job in the heart of downtown Seattle and thanking Dad for his insider information on the site from which she and her teammates had been excluded.

"I'm sorry I didn't have better news for you, Esther," he said.

"Yes, but thank you for the clarity; that meant a lot to me. At least I'm able to move on."

I excused myself momentarily to retrieve something from my jacket pocket and migrated to the opposite end of the table.

"Hi Esther, sorry to interrupt, but have you seen this image before?" I asked, producing my notebook and the sketch I had made of the Pole Pass glyph and vessel.

"No problem, Town. Not exactly, but something similar. It was a circle containing a square and three vertical triangles in a stepped succession diagonally. Each had one small circle, but in a different location. I can draw it for you if you want."

"Yes, please, that would be really helpful, but not right now. I just overheard you talking about the site and didn't want to forget."

"I'd better do it now—can I use your notebook?"

"Absolutely. Thanks."

By the time Virginia and I departed Mary's, it was almost midnight, and the group was still carrying on.

"Dad seemed to be really enjoying Mary's company, don't you think?" Virginia said.

I had to agree with her. No doubt his solitary life was a lonely one at times.

"Yeah, seems like they made fast friends."

"Carol appears to like her too."

"What are you doing, playing matchmaker?"

"No, I just want him to be happy—whatever that looks like for him."

"Who knows . . . maybe he's in a different space now."

"Mary's an attractive woman, and she's from Moses Lake, you know."

"Yeah, I know. Can we not talk about it? It's a little odd for me."

"Sure, I'm sorry, I didn't mean anything by it. What did you find out from Esther?"

"Oh! She drew the Hell's Canyon glyph for me. I can't wait to study it against the Pole Pass one."

"It wouldn't surprise me if they were related. The sites are pretty close geographically."

"True. I have a few ideas but need Dad's maps to confirm them."

The next morning was a mad rush as we packed up before Virginia's ceremony and enjoyed a parting brunch with the Seattle contingent at Ivar's Salmon House. It was three o'clock when we piled into Dad's Jeep Super Chief for our ten-hour drive home over the mountains.

"Well, at least we'll have some visitors this summer," I said.

"July, right?" Dad reaffirmed.

"Yep, it will be a great time. I'm looking forward to it," Virginia said.

"It will be fun to see Carla's reaction to the changes since she left," I added.

"Carol, how does it feel?" Virginia asked.

"I'm looking forward to Roberto cutting my hair," she replied with a smile.

"That's one more bonus for you taking the job in Seattle," Virginia confirmed.

"I already have a built-in network," Carol said.

"Mary was sweet to invite you to stay with her while you figure out where you want to live," said Dad.

"I know. Really, really nice people."

"You guys have it made," I said.

"How so?"

"Great neighborhood, great friends, and great digs."

"Hey, Princeton is pretty great too, Town. Steps away from New York and the whole world," Virginia reminded me.

"Yeah, I guess so."

"You could always transfer. I bet you would get into the UW program by next spring," Carol offered.

"Town, you do whatever you need to do," Virginia said, releasing me from the mental gymnastics that I was already performing.

BOOK FOUR

REVELATION

30

POLE PASS SLIGHT RETURN

It took a few days to settle into the casual rhythm of the Pass, but once there, it felt great to be home. Virginia was assisting Dr. Dale in the Tribal Clinic three days a week for the summer; Dad was excited about preparing Carol for her job in Seattle, which started in early September; and I volunteered at the Cultural Center three days a week as a break from working ahead on my thesis. The first morning I arrived at the Center, I noticed a night watchman leaving the grounds and asked Aunt Myra about it.

"Yeah, Town, can you believe we've had two break-ins over the past six months?"

"Dad said something about that—hard to imagine."

"Somebody went through the offices, apparently looking for cash or valuables; they managed to open my wall safe. Sheriff believed that a professional had to have done it. Fortunately, all they got away with was three hundred dollars from petty cash. Afterward, we added the CCTV cameras and hired the night watchman—no problems since."

"I guess crime is just the by-product of growth."

"Maybe. In twenty years, it's the only trouble we've had."

I updated Aunt Myra on Esther's discovery and my own suspicions regarding the site in relation to our own glyph.

"If I'm right, this is big, Auntie. Maybe it's our time to know."

I saw her light up: "This reminds me of the days working with your mother and Chilok."

After work, I stopped by Dad's office and found Bernice pounding away. "I swear some things never change!" I said as I walked in.

"Town! Congratulations!" Bernice leapt up from behind her desk and squeezed me. "Carol is in there with him, studying a few cases that she will be working on in Seattle."

"I don't want to disturb them. Does he still lock up the land maps in his office?"

"I'm afraid so, but I bet they won't mind."

With that, my dad's office door opened, and Carol walked out into the hallway, muttering and shaking her head.

"Hey, you OK?"

"Hey, Town. Yeah, there's just a lot of legal wrangling to keep straight, and it's frustrating that so many cases that should be litigated in federal courts will probably never see the light of justice. It's unbelievable how these damned politicians have dyed their clothes with tribal blood."

"Wow, that's really heavy. I'm sorry," I said, as I made my way past her, entering Dad's office.

"Hi Dad."

"Hi son. How's Myra?"

"She's good; the Center is really coming along. She seems a little lonely, though. Chilok's office is still just like she left it. I guess Myra goes down there to eat her lunch almost every day. Must be her way of keeping Chilok close."

"You know, she has a budget to hire someone to help in an executive capacity," Dad said. "I wish she would consider using it. Maybe you could mention it to her; she thinks the world of you."

"I can try next time in, but you know she's pretty stubborn. That reminds me, I'm actually here to see if I might have a look at a few government survey maps of the region."

"Sure, what are you looking for?"

"Western Idaho, Eastern Oregon, and Eastern Washington. Any enlargements of the area around Hell's Canyon and Pole Pass, including both valleys and Native lands."

"No, I meant, what do you hope to discover?" he said, knowing full well that I had sidestepped his question.

"I'll know it when I find it. Do you have the time to show me the sites that Esther was involved with? I need that as a reference."

"Yeah, sure." He opened one of the maps and pointed out the locations.

"Thanks a lot, Dad, I really appreciate it. Can I use the copier?"

"Of course, just ask Bernice to help you. These maps don't copy well on the standard settings, but she's got it down."

When I got back to the house, Virginia was on the front porch with a book.

"Hey, what are you reading?"

"Hey—a real thriller, *The Guide to Rainforest-Based Pharmacology*. How was the Center?"

"It's good. I stopped by Dad's office and picked up some maps. What about a swim? Then I'd love to bounce some ideas off of you regarding all this stuff."

"Sure, I could use a break."

After our swim, I spread the maps across a poolside table and then produced the drawings that Esther, Carla, and I had made.

"What are we working on?" Virginia asked, knocking some remaining water out of her ear.

"I've got a theory."

"I'm sure."

"I think it's obvious that the two glyphs are not just related but in conjunction with one another."

"OK, show me."

"Let's take this enlarged aerial map of Esther's dig sites. Now butt that up against the map of our location . . . and voilà! We have a straight line between the Hell's Canyon site and the glyph here."

"Yes, but you always have a straight line between two points . . ."

"Just wait, I'm not finished. Let's superimpose Carla's sketch of her recurring dream flight onto our maps here. OK, now follow that line . . . it continues over the mountain and straight through the moss-covered plateau where you and I camped. Not only that, but look where the plateau lies in relation to the shape created by Carla's flight pattern!"

I handed Virginia the drawing I had made after superimposing the two maps so she could have a better look at what I was describing.

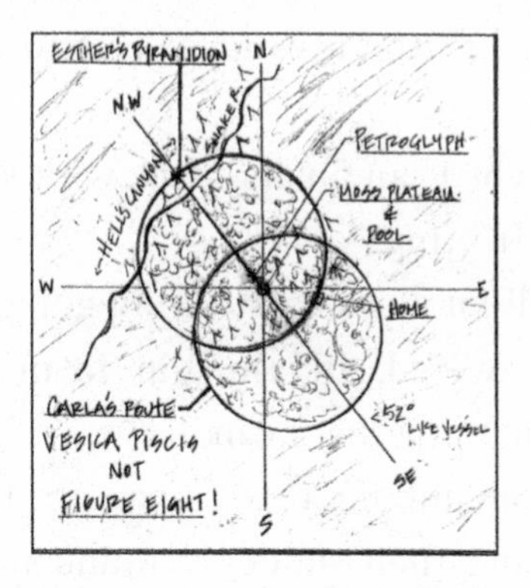

"Wow, a vesica piscis—and the plateau, it's directly in the center, like a pupil in a giant eyeball."

"That's right! This is the shape created by Carla's dreamed flight path. It's well known in both sacred and Euclidean geometries. Also, notice the line is just shy of 52 degrees. It's exactly the same as the bevel on the vessel that came from the Renault expedition, and I bet if we could measure the actual angle of Esther's triangle glyph, it would be the exact same!"

"What's this mean?"

"I'm almost afraid to voice my guess, but I'm going to find out."

"Not without me you aren't!"

"Not without you is right, and I'm thinking not without Carla too. She's the one whose been dreaming of this exact region. I mean, notice how her route boundary is where Esther found the glyph—this is all connected to something."

"So, we have to wait for another couple of weeks until they come to visit."

"I'm afraid so. In the meantime, I'll talk with Myra and see what she says. This is definitely White Feather territory, but don't breathe a word of this to anyone, except Dad and Carol."

"Got it. Maybe I can finally speak with White Feather if he's not globe-trotting?"

"Yeah, we'll know tomorrow. I'm going to show Myra what we've uncovered, first thing in the morning."

"Is there anything that I can do?"

"Yes. You can jump in that sauna after I toss you in the pool," I said, and then suddenly found myself airborne. Virginia had shoved me in the chest with both hands, sending me into the water before I was able to make good on my threat.

"You were saying?" she taunted, prowling the pool deck just before jumping in herself, swamping me with a cannonball.

"All right already, you win."

"That's more like it," she said, giving me a splash for good measure.

At dinner, Carol was still fired up about the cases she had reviewed that afternoon.

"Carol, you have to learn to let it go when you leave the office, at least emotionally," Dad advised. "Otherwise, it will chew you up inside."

"Yeah, well . . ."

"Well nothing. That needs to be a module that's taught in advocacy law. Get a hobby, Carol."

"Hey, why don't we go for a run in the morning?" Virginia proposed. "I need to get myself back in a rhythm."

"OK, yeah, I probably need it. I've been way too sedentary since graduation."

"I'll give you both a full minute head start," I chimed in.

"In your dreams, Town—you'll never catch us," Carol smiled.

I noticed Dad's grin as he saw Carol shake off the heaviness brought on by her concern over the selective justice system.

The next morning, I chased the girls around our former training route, and true to Carol's word, they kept me behind them just like in the earlier years. Over breakfast, the girls made sure that I knew my place when it came to trail runs.

Dad overheard the ribbing and came to my defense. "I bet if you had to run that four-mile loop twice, Town would win."

"That wasn't the challenge, Dad, so MYOB please," Carol said.

"Thanks anyway, Dad," I said.

"Tough room," he laughed, as he walked across the kitchen to refill his coffee cup.

"Sorry, the pot's empty and we're out of coffee," I said.

"Well, I guess you're going shopping today. After all, you did lose the race," Dad replied.

"Oh great, thanks a lot! Make the list and I'll do it on my way home from the Center," I said as they laughed, and Carol began writing.

~

I spread the evidence across the large table in Aunt Myra's office and walked her step-by-step through what Virginia and I had discovered.

"Town, many years ago when I took over the tribal research from Chilok, she told me that our tribe shared this land with another, and it wasn't the Paiutes or the other regional peoples. They inhabited what we have traditionally called the ancestral lands, a very ancient culture far predating us. Chilok, your mother, and I believed that the glyph and the vessel belonged to these people."

"What happened to them?"

"We don't know. They were discreet and they vanished—it's just like Renault said in his journal."

"People don't just disappear—they must have migrated somewhere, or died off?"

"In school we studied many theories of Native migrations; none of them, even the most exotic, involved migrations away from our region, only toward it. We should ask White Feather about all of this anyway."

"Is he around?"

"Yes, he visited John Red Horse last week."

"Virginia really needs his counsel."

"I'll call the chief and see if he can track him down. You can bring Virginia too."

"That's great news. I know she'll be excited. She's assisting Dr. Dale at the clinic this summer."

"I'm sure he appreciates the help. Has she had any more experiences or recall?"

"I don't think so."

"This sister of hers, perhaps she should come too. We might as well take advantage of White Feather while we have him."

"Great, I'll find out when Carla will be here and call you tomorrow."

"OK, by then I should know something."

"If you don't mind, I'm going to leave at two o'clock today. I was roped into doing the grocery shopping at Safeway."

"Hey, can I give you my list too?" Myra laughed.

"Sure, why not?"

~

The incessant rattle of the grocery cart was laughable, and after shrugging my shoulders more than once at parking lot onlookers, I caught my name being shouted over the clanging of metal in the ailing buggy. I turned around, and to my surprise, there was my old classmate Reggie.

The last time I saw Reggie was at our high school commencement. Reginald Bertrand Harrison IV was bound for Washington State University in pursuit of an MBA, with eyes set on returning to Pole Pass as the eventual successor to the family business at the Northern Passage Land & Title.

"Reggie?" I said. After four years, I wasn't sure.

"Good God, it's great to see you!" he said, reaching out to shake my hand.

I didn't quite know what to expect. We weren't really what I would call friends, but I accommodated his gesture.

"Wow, nice to see you too, Reggie. How have you been?"

"I've been great, thank you. I'm graduating this winter, finally. What about you—how's school back East?"

Throughout my short update, I couldn't shake an uneasy feeling, as though Reggie was about to invite me to church or to an Amway presentation.

"That sounds great! Good for you!" he replied, with overenthusiasm.

Maybe it was nerves, but his voice got louder and his speech became more exaggerated with tension as the conversation continued.

"I'm working all summer at NPL&T for those extra-credit hours," Reggie declared. "I'd be honored if you would stop by the office and let me tell you a little about our vision for the future of the area. You know, the entire region is booming—we could always use smart young investors like yourself, folks that are the future leaders of our community. I won't lie, there are high yields for those who jump in early."

It was clear that he was just out prospecting and needed someone on whom to hone his sales pitch. I let my guard down. "Sure, Reggie, I'd be interested in hearing about the opportunities you see on the horizon."

"Well, that's super! Here's my information," he said, handing me his card. "Would you have any time tomorrow? I promise I won't take much."

The pleading look in his eyes persuaded me to accept the invitation, and we set our appointment for eleven o'clock with lunch following. He gave me a vigorous parting handshake, and leaning in closer, he whispered, "We have much to talk about."

I considered the delivery of Reggie's parting comment while I emptied the contents of my grocery cart into the Bronco. Returning the clanging cart to a nearby corral, I caught a whiff of cigarette smoke invading the clean mountain air and traced the source to a Cadillac parked two spaces away. I locked eyes with the occupant as she flicked her cigarette butt out of the driver's-side window, carelessly bouncing it off a neighboring car. Eunice Lister had been glaring at us the entire time.

The lack of anonymity in Pole Pass was one thing I had not missed during my years away at school. The beauty of the mountains and the freshness of the natural surroundings could be tarnished by concerns over busybodies or those who carried family grudges forward through the generations. Someone was always within earshot of a conversation, and I anticipated that a new game of telephone was about to begin.

Since I'd left for Princeton, any thought of founding families was relegated to my adventures at the Archive. Clearly, Reggie's uneasiness during our chat was due to his sudden awareness that Eunice was parked well within eavesdropping distance. It was anyone's guess as to the current state of relationship between the Harrisons and the Listers; founding-family rifts changed about as quickly as the mountain weather. The Adamses were the founding family in the middle that just went along with whoever seemed to have the upper hand. The Butterfields had only daughters, and because of that, behind closed doors they were the weakest of the group. I would have to be off my rocker to trust Reggie Harrison as far as I could throw him, but with recent revelations from Van Kaiser and the Archive, I was intrigued as to just what exactly he and NPL&T were up to.

I arrived at Northern Passage Land & Title promptly at eleven for my appointment with Reggie. The offices had definitely seen better days. The late-sixties dark brown paneling and orange shag carpet, with its darkened traffic patterns, failed the grand old town exterior of the building, which sat on the opposite side of the town square from Dad's office.

From my seat in the lobby, I could hear the muffled voices of what I believed were Reggie and his dad having a heated discussion on the floor above me. I glanced over at the receptionist—a Butterfield daughter—who gave me a sideways smirk, indicating that this was a daily occurrence. The commotion ended, and Reggie came down the stairs to greet me.

"Town! Thanks for coming in. Sorry I'm a little late. I was stuck on a call with a group of developers regarding one of the projects I alluded to yesterday."

"Hi Reggie, thank you, no apology necessary."

"Come on back to the conference room—I've got some coffee and cold drinks if you care for one."

At one end of the room was an impressive eight-by-six-foot aerial map of Pole Pass, including the East and West Valleys. Using a grease pencil, Reggie outlined a grid on the West Valley portion of the map where a new shopping mall complex would be constructed. I asked him what data he was sourcing to conclude that the area could support another shopping mall, when the one in East Valley was only a few years old.

"Ah, very astute of you, young man," came a voice from over my shoulder, as Reggie's dad, Reginald Harrison III, entered the room. Much to Reggie's chagrin, his father needlessly took over the presentation.

"You see, this complex is a covered venue—it will be a year-round destination for upscale shoppers. No outlet stores, which tend to draw the cheapskates, like in the East Valley."

Reggie attempted to regain control of his presentation: "We have had promising discussions with some of the largest Northwest retailers—Nordstrom, Frederick & Nelson, Jay Jacobs, and others."

"Yes, that's true, Reggie, but I'm sure that Mr. Lawe would like to know about construction timelines, projected opening date, and what kind of return he might expect based upon his level of interest in the project," Reggie's father interjected. "Why don't I take you both to lunch, and we can discuss it further?" Reggie's reddened face had a helpless look, but he remained silent. The receptionist rapped lightly on the door, breaking the spell.

"There's a call on line one, sir. It's them again." Reginald's huckster persona evaporated instantly as he pushed his way past her and tromped upstairs without saying a word.

"Sorry about that, Town—let's get out of here before he finishes that call."

Reggie and I grabbed burgers at the Triple, and then we headed over to a picnic table at City Park to chat.

"OK, look. The investment is viable," he began. "I know this will be a profitable venture; otherwise, I wouldn't be soliciting it. We are on the brink of a real estate boom here;

did you know that downtown commercial properties have doubled in the last year alone?"

"Yeah, I've heard that from Carla," I replied, to gauge his response.

"That was a savvy move on her part. The Listers are still pissed off about it. Ha-ha!"

"Do you have the supporting data for the valley?"

"Indeed! Bottom-line projected growth in the West Valley has resulted in the approved construction of new elementary, middle, and high schools over the next two years."

"That's promising. What's the timeline for the opening of the mall?"

"The land is cleared, the plumbing and electrical service is on site; we just need to begin pouring. If we get started soon, our construction teams believe they can have the roof on by November. That way, they can work throughout the winter to complete the interior spaces and aim for a grand opening early next summer. The return on your investment would kick in each quarter thereafter. You could take the dividends out or let them roll into other projects with even more returns as we build out the area."

"What is the buy-in?"

"We are asking for a minimum of $10,000."

"That sounds reasonable enough," I said. "Let me think this through a little bit; I'm still just a struggling student, you know."

"I understand. It's a big commitment, but think of it as building your future here, for the day you might return."

I didn't want to tip my hand regarding the Archive or its involvement with NPL&T, but I asked who the major funder of the project was and if there was a bond just in case construction wasn't completed.

"You need to sign an NDA for that information, but I can tell you that we are 90 percent funded by our investment partners back East. Upon receiving your signed contract and principal, I can disclose who our partners are. They are very well known for this type of investing, and it's the same group we worked with for the East Valley Outlet Mall."

During casual conversation, Reggie confirmed that the founding families remained obsessed with the legend of a treasure cache so valuable that it would put the Title Mine to shame. However, Reggie wasn't caught up in that—he focused on the true wealth in plain sight, the future development of the region. That was where he wanted to steer NPL&T if he could just abolish the company's antiquated practices.

"It's time for modern nimble thinking, Town," he said. "If NPL&T keeps dragging their feet, then another firm will come in here and take this market over, and that won't be good for any of us. Either way, I plan to be a partner in the success."

I had no reason to doubt Reggie's candor about his strategy after witnessing his father belittling him when he crashed our meeting and hijacked the presentation. Hucksters like him have a certain aroma, and it wafted off of Reginald like a used car salesman at year-end.

But then our conversation took an unexpected turn.

"So, Town, the other thing I wanted to talk with you about was the old mine site. Last month at WSU, I heard that there are federal funds that provide money for toxic waste cleanup. I began thinking that if we could secure that funding and have the site remediated, NPL&T could return it to the tribe, or Pole Pass. It could become a historical park or something . . . and it would make a great headline story with NPL&T smack in the middle of it."

"Reggie, that's a brilliant public relations strategy for rebranding the company."

"Thanks—I know it's a little calculating, but we all win. Would you talk with your dad about it? Maybe he could help with the process."

"Yes, totally."

"There's something else that may speed up the process."

"Oh yeah?"

"So I hadn't been up there in forever, but figured I should at least walk the site before talking with anyone about this idea. At the far north end of the property, I found some marks etched into rock fragments. They're pretty faded, and I'm almost sure that they aren't miner markings. They are probably Native; you'd know better than I."

"I'm interested—could you draw them for me on this napkin?"

"Gosh, not well. I still have the key to the gate. It's a ten-minute drive; I'll take you there right now."

"Yeah . . . I'm not a big fan of that site—in tribal lore it's a bad place," I said. "Nothing personal, Reggie, but I'll definitely tell Dad."

"No offense taken, I understand. But it might speed this up, and with greater care as well."

"That's a strong point. OK, I'll go and check them out with you, but we need to be quick about it. I can't go rummaging around up there."

"No problem! We'll drive up, you can check them out, and I'll bring you right back."

On the way up to the mine, I had a queasy feeling. I was violating Aunt Myra's wishes, and although that was many years ago, Myra Three Moons was still my tribal elder, and I was going to hear about it. When we arrived at the gate, Reggie fidgeted with the key in the oversized rusted padlock until it begrudgingly opened. We drove through the middle of the old ghost town, passing the saloon, hotel, general store, and what was purported to be a house of ill repute at the very north end. Reggie parked the car, and we walked through the tall yellow grass and rocks for at least three hundred yards.

"It's just up here, Town, right at the base of this cliff."

Sure enough, very faint markings on the side of a large rock that must have broken free from the cliff face above during the spring thaw. These were definitely not the refined carved images of the ancestral glyph, but they appeared old, possibly part of a picture alphabet. I copied what I could onto a napkin, and we strained to search the rock face above to see if we could determine the location from which this piece had fallen. The sun had already passed overhead, making it impossible to discern anything else. Someone would have to investigate this earlier in the day.

"What do you think, Town, is it Native?"

"I think it's a safe bet, Reggie," I replied, not hiding my excitement.

"Hot damn! You will tell your dad about all of this, right?"

"Hot damn right I will!" We both laughed after I mimicked him.

"What do you think it means?" he asked, as we made our way back to the car.

"I honestly have no idea; it could be anything. Just look at the location. It's not easily accessible—someone would have to rappel from the mesa above."

"Yeah, that would take some balls!"

"Indeed!"

Halfway back down the gravel road to the main highway, we met an oncoming car. It was Stanley Lister, and he waved at Reggie, expecting him to stop. When the dust cleared, they each rolled down their window.

"Hi, Reggie, what were you doing up there?" Stanley said, ignoring me.

"Hello, Uncle Stanley. I was just showing a client around."

"You shouldn't be wandering around in there; it's unsafe. You never know when the ground will give way and you can fall several hundred feet."

"Yes, sir. I'll remember that."

Then Stanley rolled up his window without another word and continued on his way up the old mine road.

"He and Eunice are going to be the tough ones when it comes to letting this property go," Reggie said. "Listers are known for jumping over a pile of hundred-dollar bills to grab an errant nickel rolling across the floor."

"That's a good one . . . I hope I didn't cause you a problem just now."

"Nah, it will be all right. After all, you are a potential client of the firm. Anyway, my dad thinks he's a dick.

Around our house, he says Stanley's one ball away from being called 'Sister Lister,'" Reggie chuckled.

"Ouch!" I joined in the laugh, wondering if Reggie knew that Stanley Lister's absent testicle, and his own father's crooked nose, were the product of tangling with my dad forty-odd years earlier.

"I think he resents the hell out of me," Reggie said. "You know, his son would have been a senior at Pole Pass High this year."

"Oh, man, you're right. That was so long ago, I completely forgot . . . what a tragedy."

It wasn't ever discussed, but Stanley Lister's only son, Arnie, was a victim of the mine site. He had wandered off during the Founder's Day picnic and had apparently fallen into one of the flooded shafts. It took two weeks for his body to surface, and I remember overhearing Dad and Sheriff Sam taking about the grisly state of his remains when the rescue workers fished the six-year-old's body out.

"Just one more reason to get that land cleaned up and made safe again."

"They need to place some charges down in those shafts and cave it all in," I said.

"First the shafts have to be pumped out and dredged of mining sludge until they hit clean dirt or bedrock," Reggie countered. "That may take a while."

"I guess. Well, hopefully no one else ever goes through that ordeal."

"That's one of our goals here, isn't it?"

Reggie dropped me off back in town across from Dad's office, and I promised to keep him updated on the conversation.

"Hey, and don't forget about the investment, either," he said, as he waved and drove off.

~

Instead of popping in on Dad and Carol, I got in the car and drove down Main Street to the Cultural Center.

"Town, where did you find this?" Myra asked.

"Is it important?"

"Yes, I've only seen this style once before. It's an extinct Native pictogram."

"Can you read what it says?"

"Some, but this is incomplete. Is there more?"

"It was up high on a cliff face; I guess the expansion from the spring thaw broke it free and it tumbled down. The sun was in my eyes, so I couldn't tell if there was more above, but it's likely."

"Are you going to tell me where?" she asked again, this time making eye contact.

I knew this was Myra Three Moons, my tribal elder.

"Yes, Auntie . . . hey, I was thinking the other day that you've been working so much."

"Town, let's have it!" she demanded.

"The old mine site."

I had never seen Aunt Myra angry until now. Her eyes grew narrow and her voice resolute.

"James Townsend Lawe, member of this tribe. I swore an oath to Chilok to protect you, as she had sworn the same oath to your mother. That mine is not a place for you to be poking around. You don't move from this spot until I get back. Can you at least follow that instruction?"

"Yes ma'am," I replied.

Myra got up from her chair and left the office, returning minutes later with a smudge of white sage and cedar. She lit the smudge and blew the smoke over me while reciting a cleansing prayer before advancing throughout her office, uttering the same invocation. There was so much smoke produced that it set off the smoke alarm, sending several staff members rushing into the room to see what was going on. She told them to walk throughout the Center and grounds and do the same.

"Don't do that again. It's dangerous, and not just for you. Do you understand?"

"I understand because you are telling me, not because I understand the reasoning behind your words."

"Right now, my words as your elder will have to be good enough. OK, nephew?" She gave me hug.

"I guess so, but I'm not happy about it."

"This isn't about your happiness. Now, go home and think about that."

Funny that as a twenty-two-year-old college graduate, I felt like the kid who got caught with his hand in the cookie jar. The trend continued over dinner as I reviewed the Reggie encounter and our visit to the mine. The latter drew a gulp from Carol and a glare from Dad across the table.

"Don't worry, Dad, Myra smudged the heck out me already, and my Bronco got it too, even though we took Reggie's car up there!"

"So you told her?"

"Yes, sir, of course I did. I thought I was doing a good thing; she said herself that those are extinct markings."

"I understand, but let someone else deal with that site," Dad said sternly.

"Don't worry, I won't go up there again unless I have tribal permission. What should I tell Reggie about the property?"

"I'll make a call to the EPA tomorrow and see if I can get some traction with CERCLA—that's what the Superfund is officially called. But realize that if I initiate the request, the federal government might very well insist that the NPL&T foot the bill for the cleanup, which would total in the millions of dollars."

"I say let the chips fall where they may. At least you tried."

"Well, the reality is that they are the ones who profited from poisoning the land, not the taxpayers," Dad said.

I walked through the kitchen door at six o'clock sharp the next morning, and Carol was already studying her legal notes over a bowl of cereal and freshly made coffee. She looked up just long enough to notice my wet hair and the newspaper that I held.

"River sauna?" she observed, as I tossed the paper on the counter.

"Yep, great way to start the day," I answered, teeth still chattering a little from the dunk in the cold mountain water. I filled my coffee cup and was about to ask her how she was doing when the phone rang. I reached for it quickly, catching it on the second ring.

Carla was on the other end of the line, and after our good mornings, she asked if Esther might join the crew for their visit with us in a few days. She also told me that she had had the dream again last night.

"So, Carla, when did the dreams first start up again?"

"Umm . . . it was last November."

"Ok, so about the same time Esther made the Hell's Canyon discovery."

"Yeah, that's right! Do you think there's a connection?"

"I do. Hopefully, I'll have more than just a theory before you arrive next week."

"Wow, I can't wait to hear what you've cooked up!"

"Pun intentional, Carla?"

"Nice catch, Town! See you next week!" I hung up the phone and went back to my coffee and paper.

"Everything all right over there?" Carol asked between bites with eyes glued to her notes as if they were a cereal box.

"Yeah, she said that she had her flying dream again last night and wanted to check in on us. Also, she was wondering if Esther could make the trip over with them next week—I said yes, of course."

"Oh, that will be great," Carol said as Virginia walked into the kitchen in her pajamas and fuzzy slippers, with a severe case of bedhead.

"What's all this about, Carla?"

"Good morning. I see you found the light socket!" Carol laughed at her presentation.

"Thanks a lot—some of us aren't perpetually beautiful like you," Virginia replied.

"Carla was just checking to see if Esther could come with them," I told her. "Also, she had her dream again last night."

"Oh great, we'll have almost the whole crew! I wish Roberto would join."

"Evidently," I smiled, subtly making a crack about the current state of her hair.

"Smartass. I need my coffee IV, please. Hospital rounds with Dr. Dale today at Pass County. I can't wait to see how our little mountain hospital stacks up against Seattle's best."

"It's a nice facility, at least from what I can remember. Cream?"

"Yes, please. The private institutions tend to fare better because of additional oversight pressures that force them to be current. It makes a difference," Virginia said as I handed her the cup and patted her on the behind.

"You do realize that you guys can actually sleep together in the same room? Dad isn't going to care," Carol said.

"What am I not caring about today, Carol?" Dad said as he walked down the hallway from his bedroom.

I gave Carol the biggest eyes that I could. "You won't care if Esther joins the Seattle crew here next week, right?"

"Absolutely not—the more the merrier," he said, sitting down at the table and pouring himself a cup of coffee.

Carol flashed a grin at Virginia and me.

"Thanks for the coffee—I'd better get showered and over to the hospital. Good morning, Dad," Virginia said, pecking him on the cheek as she headed for the stairs.

"Good morning, doctor. Nice hair."

"I'm taking care of it now, geez!" she said, doubling the stairs on her way up to the shower.

Dad turned to me and said, "Town, regarding last night's conversation about the Title Mine, it might be better for all concerned if you laid out the scenario for Reggie. We've had a relatively peaceful several years, and if this goes sideways, there is nothing I can do to stop it. I just want everyone to know what is at stake if I stir this pot."

"OK, Dad, I'll call him this morning and let him know."

"I think that would be wise."

"I'm going to shower and head off to the Cultural Center. I have some things to do for Aunt Myra, and then I have some studying of my own."

"You know, if you and Virginia would shower together, it might save water."

"Really, Carol? I somehow missed that you were representing the Tribal Water Authority these days," I countered, perturbed by her sellout.

"She's right, you know, and thanks for the paper—it reminds me of the good old days," Dad said with a smile, as he sipped his coffee and walked toward his study.

31

BIRDS OF A FEATHER

Upon arriving at the Cultural Center, I was told that Myra wanted me to come upstairs right away. As I walked down the hallway toward her open office door, I could see that she was paging through books spread across her table, muttering something to herself. She looked up just long enough to catch sight of me.

"Oh Town, good, you're here. Come in. Please shut the door behind you."

I entered the office, and when I turned to close the door, I was face-to-face with a visitor sitting on the sofa, just out of view from the doorway.

"Town, I believe you know White Feather."

"Yes, I do. It's an honor, sir."

"The honor today would be mine, young Tumlok," he replied, as he stood to shake my hand.

Even though White Feather was the one who had approved my Weyekin at thirteen, the only other time I had seen him in person was when he led Chilok's burial procession deep into the ancestral forest. He was an imposing presence, standing not less than six-foot-five, clad in a fringed buckskin jacket, blue jeans, and motorcycle boots. He must have been near my dad's age, but his deep, smooth complexion made it difficult to be sure. His two distinctive features were his pale blue eyes and the platinum streak that ran through his otherwise pitch-black shoulder-length hair. It certainly made sense why he was called White Feather.

"May I ask you a question, sir?"

"Yes, and please, no need to call me sir."

"Thank you. Can you please define 'Tumlok' for me? Chilok once called me that, and I honestly don't know what it means."

He released a short laugh and glanced over at Myra, who shrugged her shoulders with a smile.

"*Tumlok* is a holy word used among some medicine people to describe a very rare occurrence. Earth's most accurate interpretation of this term would be *Bridger*."

"Is this why I have heard voices and seen things that perhaps others don't?"

"Yes, I would suspect so, at least in part. As I said, this is a highly unusual phenomenon. According to ancient texts throughout the world, this may occur when a Glider chooses an eternal mate and has offspring."

"My mother, right? I remember the story my dad told me about the cleansing ritual you performed for him."

"Yes, that's correct. Ancient texts reveal that Gliders are souls that are born and reborn throughout history by their own free will. They do this to assist and preserve humankind. While among us, they have no knowledge of their origins, past incarnations, or deeds. They have no authority over natural or societal laws, and therefore are subject to both. That's the code of the Glider."

"What about Carol—is she a Tumlok?"

"Oh yes, the watchdog." He smiled. "No, she has another duty."

"I don't understand."

"She's your protector. Surely you've noticed her guardian nature?"

"I was attacked when I was ten years old out on—"

"Yes, I remember the event too, and her intervention. It is doubtful that she is even aware of it, and probably won't be for a while. I hear you are fairly serious about a young woman?"

"That's true."

"Carol will soon be released from her obligation."

"I see . . . this is a lot for me to take in."

"Of course it is, but this is your time to know these things. I am hoping that you can help us understand more of what you are experiencing."

"I have recorded notes over the years," I said, "including visitations from my mother. I wrote the thoughts down exactly as I heard them; therefore, they are more streams of consciousness than formally structured."

"Would you be willing to share those with me? It may prove invaluable if I were permitted to transcribe them."

"I guess, but what would you do with the transcriptions?"

"The content would be added to preserved collections that reside across many cultures. This is a great service to mankind."

"Yes, then absolutely, it would be my privilege."

"We would need to begin as soon as possible; there is something unsettling the land."

Myra jumped into the conversation. "Town, would you explain your theory to White Feather and show him your drawings as well?"

"Of course! I can run home and grab everything and be back here by ten thirty."

"Thank you, that would be very helpful."

"Oh, another question, White Feather, if I may?"

"Yes?"

"Did you make anything out of the pictogram from the mine site?"

White Feather smiled. "It's a fragment of a binding incantation, one of four that I placed at the main compass points to keep what is inside that property from getting out."

"That doesn't sound so good . . ."

"These things are temporary at best, Town. This is why it is imperative for us to catalog your experiences."

Before I left the Center, I made the call to Reggie alerting him to the possible consequences of filing a request for federal assets, and his quick response took me by surprise: "Thanks for thinking of that—please ask him to go ahead with the request."

Returning to the house, I quickly filled a rucksack with the items I needed, and on the thirty-minute return to the Cultural Center, I recalled some of the visitations. Most of what I collected during the preteen years was personal in nature and innocuous. But while at Princeton, I did receive some communications that were rather foreboding; one in particular leapt to mind:

There are entities that come from other places. It is not for me to say from where. They poison and devour worlds without conscience. They possess what they do not own, causing only misery, death, and destruction wherever they travel. They have always been, and will always be active wherever life is present in the multiverse. On Earth, they thrive on man's inhumanity to man, and its desolation of natural resources. Only the power of love is enough to overcome these types of energies. They groan when slaves are free; and when humankind chooses to pick up the sword of Life, they shrink away like a plague that has run its course, because they cannot survive in the fullest light of humanity.

White Feather and I convened in Chilok's former office, and I walked him through my early theory surrounding the glyphs and the vessel. He examined the drawings intently but didn't have much to say. I was sure he knew the ancestral forest like the back of his hand and held many of its secrets as well.

"What do you make of this?" I finally asked.

"I believe that you are correct."

"But correct how?"

"The Hell's Canyon symbol is a landmark pointing to the glyph here in the Pass. I know of two others. One is on Vancouver Island, and one is in Utah. The Vancouver mark points southeast, and the Utah points northwest; it makes sense now. That moss-covered plateau you've been visiting is an ancient ceremonial site, and the pool below is to clean oneself before participating in whatever ritual. This geometry that you show explains why the energy in this area is so powerful at times that even I can't withstand the vibration it creates."

"Any idea what ceremonies were performed there?"

"I'm not sure what customs were observed, but I would like to speak with this young lady who has dreams of flying over this area."

"She will be here on Sunday, and we can arrange that."

"Good. Now, tell me what you experienced in these visitations from your mother. And please start at the beginning."

"Yes, but before we begin, you said you wanted to add the information to catalogs of knowledge across many cultures. Could you tell me anything about these locations?"

"Sure. There are vast sacred texts compiled throughout many places with ancient histories. They are found in Tibet, India, Peru, Central America, and elsewhere. Access is reserved for a trusted few initiates, so as to preserve wisdom without corruption."

"Is the Archive such a place?"

White Feather's eyes immediately burned with intensity. "No! That institution is a den of vipers. You must never reveal yourself to them. They lust after knowledge for their own wicked devices, and that increases suffering across this planet. They have no interest in benevolence toward humankind."

"Yes, I've been warned by some good friends in Princeton about their practices. I just wanted to confirm that with you."

We walked page by page through the contents of my notebook. White Feather patiently read aloud everything he transcribed in the document, occasionally sharing knowledge that connected with what he was reading. Not surprisingly, this tedious and exhausting process took the entire afternoon, but we got it done.

When White Feather closed his notebook, indicating that we were finished at least for now, I thanked him for what he had shared with me in the process and headed for home. Virginia pulled in behind me, and we walked in together just as Dad and Carol were about to put dinner on the table.

"Perfect timing," Carol said. "Red or white?"

"White, please. It smells great! Thanks for cooking, you two. I'm just going to get out of these scrubs and wash my hands—please start without me," said Virginia as she hurried down the hallway to her room.

"We'll wait," Dad said. I washed up and helped bring the side dishes to the table. As Virginia rejoined us, Dad asked about her day.

"So, did you find our quaint hospital up to Seattle standards?"

"In many ways, I much prefer it."

"How so?"

"Well, first, the facility is just as modern, but way more serene. The familiarity between staff and patients here really creates a high demand for accountability of care by the practitioners."

"I guess if you have to be in a hospital, Pass County isn't so bad, then?"

"True. I saw several patients I knew, or whose relatives I knew. That reminds me: Town, guess who I ran into in the hallway."

"Who?"

"Eleanor Higgins!"

Surprised, I said, "I thought she was in Spokane."

"Pass County offered her a head nursing position, and she couldn't refuse the money. She said she's glad to be back in the mountains."

"I guess that her blackballing didn't stick."

"I didn't get into that with her, but hospitals tend to have short memories when they need qualified personnel in key positions. Besides, with Lautermilk gone from the area, I'm sure it's a way better environment for nurses."

"How often will you be making rounds with Dr. Dale at the hospital?" Dad asked.

"Hard to say, but I think one day a week. He has four pediatric patients admitted, and the Tribal Clinic stays pretty busy. I'm hoping that he will gain enough confidence in me that I can make those hospital visits solo. Even though he's in family medicine, he's more of an internal medicine practitioner than a pediatrician."

She turned to Carol. "How was your day? You seem a little quiet."

"Ah, OK, I guess," she responded in an uncharacteristically melancholy tone.

I looked across at Dad, and I could tell he knew what was bugging her. "Hey, what's up—did the judge overrule you?" I gibed, trying to bring some levity into the conversation.

"Not funny, Town," Carol said. She got up from the table and scraped the contents of her barely touched plate into a Tupperware container and then headed downstairs to the basement.

Neither Dad nor Virginia uttered a word, so I wolfed down another three bites of food and pushed myself back from the table to go down to the basement and see what was actually bothering her.

"You might want to let her be, son, just for a little bit," Dad advised.

"Thanks, Dad, but after the day I've had, I'm going to check up on her," I said, already starting down the steps.

When at home, Dad was most often found in his study, and Mom had owned the basement. The space still housed much of her library, as well as a drafting table, world maps, tools, and a sitting area where she enjoyed her private time of quiet meditation.

"Hey, I'm sorry I upset you," I told Carol. "Do you want to talk about what's the matter?"

"Thanks, but it's not you, Town."

"What is it, then? Can I help?"

"I just realized that next week is the anniversary of when we lost Mom."

Carol's words hung in the air a second or two before I was able to gather myself. I was barely five years old when Mom came home one day with something called "Stage 4." She wanted to be down here in her special place, so Dad set up a hospital bed for her and slept most every night on this sofa. I recalled the moment of her passing. Chilok and Aunt Myra had taken me down to the river for a picnic. As we sat by the river, Chilok had just released a handful of sand into the water as an example that everything in creation has its place when suddenly she grabbed her chest and shouted, "Louisa!" Myra jumped up without saying a word and took off on a sprint toward the house. When Chilok and I arrived several minutes later, my mother's vacant body had already been loaded into the tribal ambulance. I never got to say a proper goodbye to her, or a last "I love you."

"I can't believe I forgot," I said, as I took a seat beside Carol on the sofa that had been a silent witness to the event.

"I guess that's what being away for so many years does—it forces us to move on," Carol replied.

"I suppose." As with Dad, Carol and I rarely discussed Mom.

"I was only eight. It seems like forever ago, Town."

"Seventeen years . . . was she comfortable?"

"I guess. Mom asked me to hand her a glass of water, and after taking a drink, she smiled, called me her angel, and told me that she always knew she could count on me to take care of you and Dad. Her last words were 'Tell Dad and Town that I love them.' Then she was gone. I screamed for Dad so loud that the porcelain lamp across the room shattered."

"I remember that lamp, but I don't remember hearing any of this."

"I think that knowing how close you were to her, Dad believed he was sparing you by not talking about it. That, and his own pain of suddenly losing her."

"That would be almost unbearable."

Carol and I sat there pondering the moment that had altered our lives forever. I thought about the time at the breakfast table years earlier when I told her and Dad about the visitation I had received, now understanding that it had reopened this painful memory. It also reminded me of how emotionally strong Dad was to keep it together during the aftermath, and to raise us as well as he did.

The door to the upstairs opened, interrupting the moment. "Need anything?" Dad asked from the top of the stairs.

"No thanks, coming right up," I said. "You good?" I asked Carol.

"Yeah, I'll be up in a few minutes," she smiled. "Thanks for coming down—you're the best brother, Town."

"Sure, and thanks for always watching out for me." I squeezed her hand softly as I got up. Then the thought hit me, and I said, "Oh crap, I have to tell Virginia that I saw White Feather today."

"Wow, that's a rare sighting."

"It's definitely worth recounting, so I'll tell you later," I said, as I doubled up the steps.

I caught Dad's concerned glance when I entered the kitchen. "I'll clean up, you guys. Thanks for making dinner, Dad."

"Scoot over and I'll help out. How's Carol?" Virginia asked, as she nudged me over with her hip at the sink.

"She's taking a moment . . ."

"Yeah, Dad filled me in. How about you?"

"It's weird. I guess I'm more saddened by how it fades with time."

"We all cope with loss differently."

"Yeah . . . Hey, before all of this, I meant to tell you that I spent the afternoon with White Feather!"

"Come on!" Virginia said in disbelief.

"True! We went through my notebook together, and he likes the theory regarding the glyphs. But the bigger news is that he wants to see Carla when she gets here next week to ask about her dreams. I think you should join her, and maybe get some answers."

"Finally! That's great news!"

"Hey, Town!" I heard Dad call out from his study.

"Coming," I replied. I dried my hands and headed down the hall. "Yes, Dad?"

"I wanted to let you know that I have already heard back from the people conducting the CERCLA site work. They will arrive here the week after next at the latest, to review the Title Mine property."

"That was quick!"

"Yes. Apparently, the Northwest is the first region in the nation to be evaluated. They currently have a crew examining sites in eastern Washington and Oregon."

"Way to go, Dad! I guess you still have some pull in DC after all," I smiled.

"Hardly, but I'm glad they're going to review this site earlier in the program than later. At least we'll know what we are dealing with as a community."

"Perhaps a glass of bourbon would be in order?" I asked.

"Sure, why not? Come on in and have seat. Virginia!" he yelled out.

"Yes, sir," she said, hurrying down the hall.

"Join the boys for a drink?"

"Don't mind if I do."

"Carol still downstairs?" Dad asked.

"Yes, I think I heard music playing."

"Al Green, I bet. He was her mother's favorite. She'll be down there a while."

"Did you happen to get an ETA on Carla and the gang?" Dad asked.

"Sunday afternoon. They are spending tomorrow night in Mary's hometown of Moses Lake," Virginia jumped in.

"Speaking of Mary . . . Dad, you seemed to get along with her pretty well," I said.

"Yes, she's a sweetheart, a nice girl, widowed far too young."

"Well?"

"Well what? I'm still married to your mother. 'For better and for worse' is what I recall committing to, and the way I see it, I'm still on the 'better' side of things anyway." He smiled and sipped his bourbon.

"Aww," Virginia said, acknowledging the sentiment that Dad held fast to.

"Town, when Carla arrives, we should ask her if she would approve of you examining the book in my safe," Dad said. "Who knows, maybe you will be able to make sense of it."

"Sure, I'd love to at least try, but I am a much better sleuth with my partner here," I said, inclining my head toward Virginia, who reached over and clinked my glass with a wink and a smile. "So, we heard about your little theatrics at the reading of the will."

"Oh, that." Dad took a sip of his bourbon. "I love this place, but there are some absolute knuckle-draggers roaming around here, and every once in a while I get to stretch my legs enough to give them a kick in the ass. I'm not going to lie and say that I didn't enjoy that particular opportunity."

"Well, you certainly gained another daughter in the process," Virginia smiled.

"My pleasure," Dad said with a big smile.

"What do you think the chances are that NPL&T would have to pick up the tab for the Title Mine cleanup?" I asked.

"No idea, but the way those families have mistreated people here over the years, it would be justice proven if they were stuck with the entire amount. Only a few weeks ago, there were fresh reports of people digging on tribal lands again."

"You think it's the Order of the Mine?"

"All the earmarks of it. The Tribal Council is fed up with them, and I'm in the process of drafting a petition to elevate the penalties to a federal standard to be levied following payment of any tribal judgment."

"Will that help?"

"Probably not until someone gets caught and has to pay several thousand dollars in restitution and enjoy a little jail time. But we're in the right direction, and without a shoot-on-sight edict."

"I could ask Reggie—he has been very helpful."

"Yes, that's a little peculiar to me."

"I think he's trying to cash in on this regional expansion and prove that he has the instincts to recalibrate the family business."

"Proceed cautiously. If this mine evaluation goes against NPL&T, the shit is going to hit the fan around here."

"I'm just glad to be home for the summer to watch it!" I smiled.

"I heard you say that you met with White Feather today."

"Yes, he talked me through an extensive amount of history. There was much of that 'It is your time to know' information. I also shared the contents of my notebook with him. All stuff we can talk about splitting logs."

"Chilok and he were very close. He was an orphan, and she practically raised him until his Weyekin. Afterward, she told him, 'You know more than me,' and he began his travels to other tribes."

"Well, he's the one responsible for those pictograms at the mine cliff. It's some sort of invocation to keep the bad juju inside the gate."

"I tried to tell you that place is no good."

"And as usual, you were right."

~

Carol and Virginia met the car full of girls at the town square and led them the last thirty minutes to our house. There was no need to keep watch, as their arrival brought college-girl-type screams that carried all the way down to the river sauna, where Dad and I had just finished splitting the last of the firewood for the coming winter. We high-fived each other before jumping into the river to wash off, and then we made our way up the hill to the house, where the crew was enjoying a poolside beer.

"How was the drive, Mary?" Dad asked.

"It was so easy, Dan. I had forgotten how beautiful it can be east of the mountains, and this place you have here—wow!"

"Yes, we're grateful for it, that's for sure. I want you all to please make yourselves at home while you're here."

Carla bounded over and practically tackled me into the pool with a big hug. "Were you guys swimming?"

"Nah, just a quick dunk in the river."

"Hi Mr. Lawe," she said, greeting Dad.

"Hi Carla. You excited to be back in the Pass?"

"Yes, sir, can't wait to show everyone around town."

"Great, and please, no calling me Mr. Lawe or sir—it's far too formal."

"OK," she said with a shy smile.

"Maybe after dinner I'll take everyone on a walk around the property," I announced. "Sound good?"

The girls raised their bottles in agreement, and I brought Dad one from across the pool deck.

"Everyone OK with wood-fired steak tonight?" I asked. "Dad's a genius on the grill."

"Sounds perfect to me," confirmed Mary, and the others agreed.

After everyone settled into their quarters, Dad fired up the grill to ensure that the coals were glowing red by the time he laid the filets on the grate under the watchful eyes of Carla and Mary.

We took dinner at the poolside table, where our guests updated us on the local happenings of Capitol Hill and Seattle life in general. Carol's job began in a month, and she asked a lot of questions.

"Carol, you will be just fine," Audrey assured her. "Carla and I will get you acclimated; you're going to love it over there."

"I'll take you to the museums," Esther offered, adding that she would secure special-access passes and tours from students who worked at the Burke-Gilman Museum and other locations around Seattle.

"Count me in!" Virginia piped up.

"Drinks afterward at Harry's off Broadway on Lower Queen Anne!" said Carla.

"I'll have dinner waiting at my place to soak up those Electric Iced Teas when you get home," Mary added.

"Oh, no . . . Mary, the way you handled those zombies at the Hallmark Inn in Moses Lake last night . . . You're the driver," chimed in Audrey, and the women all laughed.

"Carol, from Mary's house you are only a twenty-minute trolley ride to your office building downtown. It's about twice that time on foot. I would do that in a heart-beat on summer mornings and take the bus home after work," Carla said.

"It all sounds great!" Carol exclaimed. "Mary, thank you again for allowing me to stay with you until I get settled. I promise to keep a very low profile and find a place of my own within a month."

"Nonsense, it's my pleasure, and you stay as long as you want. I'm actually looking forward to having a roommate. It might cut down on the talking to myself, or Arthur in absentia."

"That's very kind, Mary," Dad said. "I understand the talking-to-yourself thing all too well."

"Esther, are you ready for the coming year?" I asked.

"I'm so ready to be in the new department, I can't get there quick enough."

"Did you ever find out anything more about the Hell's Canyon site?"

"Nothing. Complete blackout. Also, my former department head, Professor Rickover, told our team that the federal government confiscated all field notes and my film. They were supposed to return them but haven't as of yet."

This immediately captured Dad's attention. "That's very interesting, Esther—it doesn't sound quite right. Would you mind if I ask around? I'll be discreet."

"I don't mind at all," she replied. "There is probably not much that I can do about it, but I would like to know for the future, just in case something were to reemerge."

Soon we were leaning back in our chairs, staring at empty plates with satisfaction from a great meal. With about an hour of daylight remaining, I asked:

"Who's up for a tour?"

"Me," said Carla, dramatically raising her hand.

"I definitely need a walk after that steak," Audrey joined in.

"Me too!" Esther said.

"I'm on cleanup here with Dad," said Carol.

"I'll help you," Virginia volunteered.

"I'll clean too," offered Mary.

"No, Mary, this is easy. It's such a beautiful evening for a walk; you go on with the rest of the gang," Dad said.

"All right, then, if you're sure. But Dan, does it get better? The talking to ourselves or . . ."

"Yes, it does. But it's not overnight, and you have to give yourself that room. I still talk to Louisa all the time, and I will say that it hurts less now when she doesn't answer,"

Dad replied, placing his hand on Mary's shoulder and giving her a warm smile.

I led the group around the perimeter of the property, finishing the tour at the river sauna as dusk fell. We sat on the porch and I gave a short tribal history lesson, including how we came to be the stewards of this land.

"Can I answer any questions?" I said following my monologue.

Carla was the first to speak up. "What's over there?" She pointed across the river.

"We call it the ancestral forest, and it's a very special place."

"What is it like?" Carla pressed.

"A forest so dense and full of mystery that even tribal members know to enter the arms of its canopy only with the permission of an elder, or higher. Now, if you want a nice walk in the morning, you can follow this river trail a mile and a half downstream to Eagle Falls. But if you want a really special start to the day, fire up the sauna stove before you head down there. By the time you get back, you will have a toasty cedar room, and of course the water is always cold!"

"That sounds like my cup of tea," Audrey said.

"Great, come on inside and I'll show everyone how to light it."

As we made our way back toward the house in the dark, Carla noticed something up on the northern ridgeline.

"Hey, Town, what is that on the ridge, over there to the right?"

"Well, eagle eyes . . . definitely a light of some sort. We'll have to get a better look from the house with the binoculars."

By the time we got back to the house and I grabbed the binoculars, the light was gone. I mentioned it to Dad, and he chalked it up to other tribal members hiking but said he'd tell Sheriff Max Running Bear about it, if only because of recent trespassers.

After an hour or so of conversation and a nightcap, we turned in early, as Virginia, Carla, and I wanted to be fresh for our much-anticipated meeting with White Feather at the Cultural Center in the morning.

"How'd everybody sleep?" Carol asked, as the crew trickled into the kitchen for coffee and breakfast.

"So much better than at the Hallmark Inn in Moses Lake," said Audrey.

"No river sauna this morning, Audrey?"

"No, Esther, I slept so soundly that I just didn't want to get up."

"Where's Carla?" Mary asked.

"Out for a walk with Virginia; they're right behind me," I said, as I walked into the kitchen from the pool house, where I had slept.

When the two of them came through the kitchen door, I offered a collective good morning and kissed Virginia's cheek, catching a grin they shared that was best described as a cat with a bird in its mouth.

"What's that look about?" I laughed, as she hugged me and whispered in my ear that I was about to find out.

"It's going to be a magnificent day in the mountains," I announced. "Is there anything in particular you all would like to do?"

"I think we will run in to Pole Pass this morning when you three go for your meeting," Audrey said. "We can take the tour and all grab lunch together. Maybe even do a little shopping?"

"Sure, we'll have plenty to chat about after the meeting," Carla replied. "I can't wait to show you the building. Mr. Lawe has the keys."

"Perfect—swing by the office and get them," Carol said, walking into the kitchen already dressed, coffee cup in hand. "Dad left a little early this morning to make sure he finished a project. Also, Carla, stop calling him Mr. Lawe and just call him Dad, OK? See you guys down there. I'm headed in," she said, finishing the last gulp and setting the cup in the sink.

Virginia prompted, "Everybody tell Carol they love her—it's a household tradition when someone leaves."

"Love you, Carol, mean it!" they sang in unison, infused with girlish giggles.

Carol paused for a smile and to blow a kiss to the group before picking up a stack of folders and walking out the kitchen door.

"Town, Carla and I are going to take quick showers and drive together to the meeting with White Feather," Virginia said. "Would you mind chauffeuring the crew and just meeting us there?"

"Are you joking? It would be my pleasure to escort these delicate flowers around our little hamlet. I'd love to start some rumors about my womanizing ways."

"Yeah, you're a real philanderer, all right," Virginia said wryly, shaking her head. "We'll see you there, and trust me, there will be lots to catch up on."

32

EVE'S LETTER

March 16, 1972

Dear Carla,

The one person I could trust to deliver this letter is my true friend, Lars Svensen. I pray that he found you happy and in the best of health. There is so much I want to say to you in this moment, but words fail me, and I won't minimize our sacrifice using the few I have left.

I was bound by an oath for the protection of my two girls, and one other.

That you are reading this means my time here has passed and the oath is honored.

You and Virginia must now take this letter to your father, White Feather.

Please forgive me, my baby bird, and may your wings always carry you home.

With everlasting love,

Mom

Eve Gray Hawk Tecoi

The two young women sat across the table from their father, separated only by the letter that he just read.

"I'm not sure why you're smiling," Virginia said matter-of-factly.

"Yeah, I've heard some deadbeat dad stories before, but this bullshit here takes the cake!" Carla followed.

Curiously, White Feather's grin grew even wider, and when both girls were about to pounce on him from across the table, he spoke.

"Welcome home. Come, we have much to do and not a lot of time."

"Slow down there, big man—I think it's fair to say that neither of us is going anywhere with you, absent an extraordinary explanation!" Virginia said, leaning in.

"Forgive me, daughters. I have many things to discuss with you, but that will come afterward. At this moment, we have matters that are more pressing than the poor parenting on my part." White Feather's words were warm and penetrating, as if he had reached into their chests and held their hearts in his powerful hands.

Departing the Cultural Center, they drove deep into the Native lands, and two hours later they broke through a thicket of bushes and into the same alpine meadow that Chilok, Louisa, and Myra Three Moons had traveled to many years before.

"What is this place?" Carla asked as they continued driving toward the base of the ridge above them.

"Think of the view from the air."

"Of course . . . I know what this is," Virginia said. "This is the Valley of the Ancients."

"Yes, it is," White Feather replied.

They came to a stop at the row of thimbleberry bushes and unloaded various items from the truck. White Feather gave Carla and Virginia each a small backpack to carry while he took the larger one; and then, before setting out, he strategically placed rocks around the vehicle, uttering something as he completed the pattern.

"Ready?" he said.

"Up there?" Carla asked.

"Yes, young eagle. Don't tell me you are suddenly afraid of heights."

33

TOO MANY CROOKS

When the girls and I arrived at the Cultural Center, the information kiosk attendant waved me over. "Hi, Town—they left about thirty minutes ago," he said, handing me an envelope containing a copy of Eve's letter and a note from Virginia, which read, "Town, we are OK, going with White Feather to Native land." That was it. As casually as I could, I invited Mary, Audrey, and Esther to have a seat, assuring them that I would return in a few minutes. Then I sprinted up the stairs to Myra's office.

"I know!"

"Are they OK?"

"They seemed to be. White Feather was in a hurry to get them out of here."

"But to where, why?" I was a little disjointed in my processing.

"Initiation, I suppose."

"What?"

"Town, they are his daughters. Just like you, those girls hold keys to a very unique lineage. Slow down and chew . . .

think about it for a minute. Virginia carries the soul of a very powerful medicine woman, but neither she nor Carla will know their places without the initiation."

"What should we do? I have a group of friends downstairs at the moment."

"We wait. That's all we can do. Why don't I come down and lead the tour? How about that?"

"Thanks, Auntie, thanks so much."

Aunt Myra led our group through the exhibits, providing commentary that included tribal history and tidbits about the founding of the Cultural Center itself. When the tour ended, we sat in the atrium with an espresso from the recently installed cart while Myra fielded several questions from Esther.

Suddenly Audrey nudged Esther, shifting her eyes across the atrium to the man looking through a brochure at the information kiosk.

"Isn't that—"

"Rickover! I don't believe it!" Esther responded in a hushed tone of disgust.

Mary cranked her head around and confirmed the sighting with a "Well, I'll be damned if it isn't."

Myra looked across the space, then turned back with a curious look.

"I'm sorry, Ms. Three Moons," Esther said, "that man over there is Karl Rickover, my undergrad department chair at the UW."

"Should we invite him over?"

"God, no! The man is a nuisance and a fraud," Audrey jumped in.

"True!" Mary backed her assessment.

"I wonder what he's doing here. That's just weird," Esther said.

"It's our high traffic season," Myra said. "Want me to do a little snooping?"

"I am curious."

"I'll be right back, and please call me Myra."

We watched intently as Aunt Myra made her way across the atrium toward the exhibition entrance. After she introduced herself, we witnessed Rickover in action, as he attempted to kiss her hand.

"Thank you, but that won't be necessary, Professor," Aunt Myra responded loudly enough for us to hear as she withdrew her hand before Rickover's lips could make contact.

As a courtesy, she granted him exhibition access at no charge and returned to us.

"You still have the stones in your rings . . . he's known for sucking them out of their settings," Audrey quipped.

"Yeah, that was gross, and what's with the Hitler haircut and moustache?" I said.

"His real name is Reichauer—no joke. What did he say?" Esther asked.

"Only that he was making a tour before the fall semester began, and was interested in the tribal history of this area. He asked me if we ever inhabited the Hell's Canyon region."

"That dirty son of a b—" Esther said, barely able to keep her voice down.

"I bet he's looking for more than cultural history," I suggested.

"Yes, Town, I figured as much," Myra said. "I'll keep an eye on him and check to see if he has any more questions before he leaves."

"OK, great, keep me posted. We need to get over to Dad's office for lunch with him and Carol."

"All right, send my love, and I'll let you know if I hear anything else from White Feather. Great to meet everyone, and I hope to see you again before you head back to Seattle."

We talked about the Rickover encounter all the way up Main Street, until we found ourselves standing on the corner across the street from Dad's building. "And here on our left is the building once occupied by Pole Pass Dry Goods," I stated. "One of the oldest buildings in town, it was erected 130 years ago."

"Wow, I love this building. Why is it empty? Someone should do something with it," Audrey said.

"Tell that to Carla—it's hers."

"Oh, this is different than I pictured. I thought it would be one of those old clapboard ones," Mary said.

"I've spoken my piece about it: two storefronts down, two loft apartments up," I said. "Gut and rehab, $50,000 tops, and it would be worthy of a feature in *Architectural Digest*!"

"I agree 100 percent, Town," said Audrey.

"Ditto. Location, location, location."

"We can check out the inside after lunch," she said.

"Are Carla and Virginia joining us?" asked Esther.

"They . . . they have some business to take care of first; I'll update everybody in a minute. I think it will prove interesting."

We crossed the side street that separated Dad's building from Carla's and entered his law office. He rarely had visitors and couldn't wait to show us around the two-and-a-half-story structure. The upstairs apartment overlooked Main, with a bank of windows that wrapped around to the side street facing Carla's building, a large skylight flooding the front of the unit with daylight. Dad sometimes stayed there if he was working late, but it was evident from the dust that he hadn't done so in quite awhile.

"What a great space," commented Audrey.

"Thank you. It needs a little updating, but there was a time when all four of us lived in this apartment," Dad recalled.

"I remember when Town was brought home from the hospital," Carol added.

"Oh yes . . . things suddenly got crowded around here." Dad laughed. "There's a space half this size above us that I was going to renovate into a master suite, but we moved onto tribal land instead."

"Where does everyone want to go for lunch?" I asked.

"Choices?" Carol offered.

"Great call. It's a meat and three, our mountain take on the Southern staple," I explained.

"We'd better get over there if we're going to sit together," Dad advised. "By the way, where are Virginia and Carla?"

"OK, I need to update everyone before we head over to the restaurant," I said.

The silence that immediately followed the reading of Eve's letter and Virginia's note didn't last long as Mary, Audrey, and Esther all started talking at once.

"Look, I know, I know," I replied, holding my hands up in an attempt to herd the gut responses. Dad and Carol remained quiet. I knew they were considering every angle before voicing any thoughts on the matter.

"That's a pretty rotten thing to do," said Mary.

"I mean, really. I'm not sure what's worse, never knowing, or finding out," Audrey said.

"I get it . . . but let's temper our judgment until we hear directly from Virginia and Carla. I mean, you have to trust me, there is way more to this than we know."

"Town's right," Carol spoke up in my support.

"Yes, of course, but man I can't wait to hear this story," replied Mary.

After lunch, we toured Carla's property, where the crew confirmed my assessment. The bones of the place were so perfect that despite the need for complete renovation, the potential was clear. Mary and Audrey agreed while making suggestions as we walked through the interior of the space. I noticed Esther lagging behind, and with her quietness over lunch, I thought she was simmering over the sighting at the Center.

"Hey, still thinking about Rickover?" I asked, as we fell farther behind the group.

"That obvious, huh?"

"Don't let it too far under your skin; people like him eventually have their day."

"Yeah, I suppose. Thanks, Town."

~

The following day, we still had not heard anything from the girls or White Feather, and while we all hung around the pool, Dad phoned his DC contact to follow up on Rickover's original submission. Beyond his filing a basic report advising of land use to alert game wardens and rangers of the students' backcountry presence, there were no other assets submitted from the UW, WSU, or Rickover. Rickover had plainly lied. An intriguing piece of information was that shortly after Esther reported her findings to Rickover, a moratorium of public access was placed for a 10-mile radius around the site. Dad's contact was unable to verify which agency had frozen the area, just that it was now lifted.

Concern mounted by the third morning with no word from the girls. I explained the Weyekin process, but that didn't help matters much.

"Look, everyone, it's another beautiful day in the mountains," Carol said. "Why don't I take you into East Valley for a change of scenery? We can do some shopping."

"Great idea, Carol. I'd love to tag along too," Dad said.

"That sounds like a plan . . . anything to keep me from looking out the window," Mary said.

"Excellent! I'll take you to my favorite haunts, and we'll have a nice lunch on the river."

"You all enjoy yourselves," I said. "I'm going to stay behind in case they show up, and I have a project to work on anyway."

34

THE ORDER

What little I knew about the Order of the Mine pointed to a small group of Founders who had contrived this not-so-secret secret society during the early mining years. These glorified treasure hunters had no compunction about trespassing on or damaging private property in their search for a fabled treasure worth untold fortunes. Those robed characters that the high school couple witnessed at the old mine site had to be these goons, and the subsequent conversation I overheard between Dad and the sheriff verified as much.

During my third year at Princeton, I received invitations to visit a couple of off-campus fraternal orders, and it was obvious how much they revered their trappings and traditions. Based on those experiences and their local activities, I viewed the Order of the Mine as nothing more than an annoying club of treasure-hunting vandals, bored with their own lives.

Dad's theory that it was these knuckleheads who were the likely culprits trespassing on Native lands got my ire up, and the recent uptick in reports on this side of the Pass was concerning. If they had grown brazen enough to trespass onto the lands we stewarded, eventually the group would intrude on the ancestral forest, and we couldn't allow that to happen.

I smiled briefly from the satisfaction of knowing that the toxic waste evaluation crew from CERCLA was due to arrive at the Pass within the week, and despite my current amicable interactions with Reggie Harrison, I hoped that those responsible for creating this mess in the first place would be held liable for the cost of correcting it. The financial liability would surely strip the founding families of much of their wealth and change the balance of civic power in the Pass as well.

I returned my attention to Carla's little black book and focused on deciphering its code of symbols and numbers. Dad was right; if this format was a fabrication of the author, then it was virtually unbreakable without the cipher. Still, I continued my study until I was interrupted by the phone ringing.

"Town Lawe?" I could barely make out the words through the static of the cordless phone.

"Yes, this is he. Please hold on for a second while I get a better signal." I raised the antenna fully and exited the cloister of the pool deck. "OK, I'm sorry for the delay."

"Town, it's Jamison here, back in Princeton."

"Oh, hi, Albert! Everything OK out there? How's Sophie?"

"Everyone's fine, son. But listen to me. I should have seen this when we were talking about the Edrei site in Syria. Your mother's dig had nothing to do with King Og, and this local group that you have been calling the Order of the Mine is more than just a bunch of goddamned shit-heads looking for treasure."

"What then?"

"Hold on a second, I have someone here who wants to speak with you," Albert said, as he passed the phone to a familiar voice.

"Hello, Mr. Lawe, this is Esmeralda."

"Hello, Esmeralda, to what do I owe the pleasure?"

"Well, unfortunately, Mr. Lawe, this particular conversation is one of necessity rather than of personal satisfaction."

"Oh, I see. How may I help?"

"What my brother says is true. Throughout its history the Archive has periodically fought to uncover a certain sect's infiltration into the institution. Over one hundred years ago, during the chairmanship of Milton Franklin Rhodes, our fellowship was assured of the absolute eradication of this cult from within the body. This guarantee, however, was a ruse. Our recent internal investigations have uncovered that Rhodes himself was a high priest in this distasteful clan. We have also traced an uninterrupted line within the membership, all the way to the present day. You were correct; the ledger pages were removed to prevent divulgence of the true purpose behind the Archive's funding of the Syrian excavation—that being the deeper strata at Edrei, which revealed an ancient Canaanite temple complex. A large sample of the molten bronze from the site was shipped to the Archive in Princeton."

"Oh right, the fulgurites and molten bronze, possible Og effigy?"

"Indeed. According to documents now in our possession, the obliteration of the site suggests a retribution dispensed from beyond natural means of the age."

"Do you mean a Sodom and Gomorrah type of cataclysm?" I asked.

"The term *apocalyptic*—be it comet, meteor, or another scourge in the toolbox of Divine judgment—does come to mind."

"What happened to the material sent to Princeton?"

"It was recast into exact replicas of an ancient medallion that had been passed down through the sect's leadership here at the Archive. These replicas were then distributed to various members, who were to wear them during prosperity rituals under the full moon. One of these medallions was delivered to Pole Pass."

"Would that medallion of Og have been sent in care of the Order of the Mine?"

"In part, Mr. Lawe. It was hand-delivered on October 12, 1957, to a woman named Eunice Lister."

"OK . . ."

"Mr. Lawe, the effigy wasn't of Og. This particular group holds fast to the belief that sacrifice ensures a collective profitability throughout the ranks of their membership. This Order of the Mine is in fact the Order of Moloch."

"Moloch? Sacrifice, as in human sacrifice?" I replied, astounded.

"Historically yes, and mostly children. Today, Moloch appears to be satisfied with devouring the souls of its converts and amassing tithes from their holdings."

"Holy Jesus," I whispered aloud. "How could the Listers or any of these people here get involved in this type of thing?"

"Mr. Van Kaiser believes they were initially evangelized into service following the failure of the mine. There are rumors of abundant wealth yet to be discovered in your region, correct?"

"Esmeralda, those stories have been circulating before the area was first settled in the 1840s. They are only unfounded ruminations of people who will stop at nothing if it means gold."

"Mr. Lawe, to preserve accuracy, I said 'abundant wealth'; I did not specify that to be limited to gold," she countered.

"Yes, of course, please forgive my slovenly interpretation."

"The Lister and Harrison families have carried a balance with the Archive forward since 1874. The funds provided them with enough resources to survive the transition from mining to agriculture."

"Why wouldn't they pay off the debt? They've made a lot of money over the years."

"They attempted to settle the account with cash; it was refused."

"Why?"

"The original contract was to secure this 'abundant wealth' that was the promise, the basis on which the monies were dispersed. The investor alliance at the Archive is not a traditional bank, Mr. Lawe."

"I understand. Thank you, Esmeralda."

"Mr. Van Kaiser suggested I inform you of another recent development, which raised substantial interest among the group regarding the original agreement."

"Yes?"

"A legacy membership by the name of Reichauer reportedly made a discovery that lends credence to the original 'abundant wealth' claims proliferated by this Lister and Harrison duo. Mr. Reichauer recently reported that he was very close to 'finding the key'—his words."

The hairs on the back of my neck stood up as the weight of Esmeralda's words settled in on my already strained shoulders.

"Well, it's evident that I am underinformed."

"This member's family has been very beneficial to the Archive over the last century and, in keeping, has the support of many investors who have little conscience when it comes to interfering with their profits."

I chose my next words carefully. "Thank you for your concern, Esmeralda. I really hope this Mr. Reichauer finds what he is in search of, but I'm doubtful that this is anything but regional lore or a dubious claim by desperate settlers at most."

"Thank you for your insight, Mr. Lawe. There is something else. Reichauer has been positively identified as a follower of Moloch. Please convey my best to Ms. Tecoi, and stop by the Archive for a visit when you return to Princeton in September. Be well, and bye for now." Esmeralda passed the phone back to Albert Jamison before I could reply.

"Hey, you watch out, OK? Get a good machete, one that feels right in your hand, and swing it like you mean it," Mr. Jamison said with a chuckle.

"Thanks, Albert—give Sophie our best. I'll be in touch."

"The Order of Moloch? What the hell?" I muttered as I shook my head. Unfortunately, I could only guess as to the breadth and identities of the local membership except one, and with Eunice Lister being connected to Reichauer . . . I considered waiting for Dad to return from East Valley, but no way could I sit on my hands while my mind ran amok. Esmeralda was hinting at something. Her insistence of my understanding the term "abundant wealth" over gold was of obvious importance. The information that Reichauer—or Rickover—was closing in on "the key" was subtle, but present nonetheless. I had to assume that he knew of the Vancouver Island glyph and that he might even know about the Utah location. If that were the case, then it would not take him long to plot the general vicinity of our site. Esmeralda's caution about bloodthirsty investors, and their support for whatever means Rickover wanted to employ, concerned me for anyone who might cross his path in the wilderness. I needed to find White Feather and the girls before such an encounter might occur.

35

AS ABOVE, SO BELOW

My goal was to arrive at the plateau before nightfall, and the fact that I had to stop by the Cultural Center didn't help matters. I used the drive to rehearse what I was going to say to Aunt Myra in order to get what I needed. There had been an idea stirring inside me since that early-morning epiphany in front of the lily pond on Capitol Hill, and now was the time to put it to the test.

"What are you talking about?"

"Auntie, please, we don't have time for this!"

"Town, do you know what you're asking? This is something that should go in front of the Tribal Council."

"Then just open the safe and turn your back for a second."

"I'm sorry, Town, no way."

"I'm asking you as my aunt, not my tribal elder." I was resolute in my request.

"And why should I do this, nephew?"

"Because I am a Tumlok." Even though I spoke the five words softly, I felt a wave of power well up inside me when I said them aloud.

Aunt Myra's eyes blinked wide when she felt the concussive force of the words hit her. "All right, then, but I'm going with you and the artifact."

"It might be dangerous, and it's a six-hour hike. We'll be lucky if we make it by nightfall," I said, attempting to discourage her.

"No. I go where the artifact goes. Besides, I'm driving, and I know a shortcut."

~

"Hey, isn't that White Feather's truck?" I asked Myra as we topped the knoll of the meadow.

"Yep!"

I estimated from the pollen on his windshield that the vehicle had been there since the trio left the Cultural Center three days earlier.

"You sure that you're up to this, Auntie? There's no shame in reconsidering."

"Shit, if you think because I've added some extra weight that I can't handle myself in the outdoors, you are about to learn a valuable lesson," she shot back.

Myra's duties over the past several years had had her deskbound much of the time, and her devotion to the Center over herself resulted in twenty additional pounds to her five-foot-eight, medium-size frame.

"We have about a three-and-a-half-hour climb over the ridge, and a few hours of light to spare when we reach the plateau."

"OK, you lead the way."

It took us about forty minutes to reach the site of the glyph. I had made the hike down to this site from the opposite side of the ridge before, but being here now with Aunt Myra at a place where she, my mother, and Chilok once stood together in amazement held a profound satisfaction.

"This looks like ash." I picked up the substance from the rock below the glyph and rubbed it between my thumb and fingers before smelling it.

"White sage?" Myra asked.

"Yep, and something else."

"Look here." Myra pointed to the three smudges of ash, forming a triangle around the glyph.

"They held a ceremony," I said, noting that the top smudge of the triangle pointed in the direction of our destination.

"All right, let's get moving then," Myra said, pointing up the rocky incline that lay ahead.

It was just after two when we reached the ridge, and I saw the line between the sites as I had predicted.

"Without question," Myra confirmed, as I pointed out the bearing and referenced my latest drawing made from Carla's description and Dad's maps.

We had about three hours of daylight remaining when we arrived at the ledge where Virginia and I had camped. There was no evidence of recent habitation, and we continued down the trail to the plateau site.

"See the moss-covered rocks creating the outline of the circle? I'm going to dig it out, OK?" I checked with Aunt Myra out of respect.

"Are you sure this isn't a burial site?"

"Relatively. White Feather didn't say that it was."

"OK, I guess that's good enough for me," she approved.

I pulled out my folding shovel and sank the blade into the soft moss just inside the twenty-foot stone perimeter; it contacted rock about four inches down and stopped abruptly with a clank. We worked quickly to clear the interior under the fading daylight, tossing the chunks of soft earth and moss to the outside of the circle, and by the time I reached the center, I was standing approximately one foot down slope of the perimeter at a small depression in the stone floor. Myra and I used our canteens to rinse off the dirt, revealing a tightly joined granite floor and sides covered with symbols.

"Wow! And look at the size of those flakes!" I said.

"Yeah, they're as big as my palm, and cover the entire design," Myra said. "This is amazing! It reminds me of a reflecting pool."

"Yeah, it does . . . and I think I know why."

"What is this place, Town?"

"I'm not sure, but let's clear this center, and maybe we'll find our answer."

"I wonder who built this? It looks really—"

"Ancient?" I offered.

"Yes, yes. Totally ancient!"

"One thing we know for sure—whoever constructed this site is responsible for the glyphs and the vessel, or key."

"Key?"

"Yeah, come here . . . and look at the center," I said, after rinsing some debris from the depression.

"It matches the glyph and the bottom of the artifact!"

"Not only that, it's beveled and the design is etched; it's not in relief. The artifact is designed to fit into it, male to female. Watch this." I moved to set the vessel into position.

"I wouldn't do that just yet if I were you!" a voice commanded from the trail above. Professor Karl Rickover emerged about twenty yards away, waving a pistol at Aunt Myra and me.

"Who do you think you are, trespassing on sacred Native lands, Professor?" Myra shouted at him.

"Slow down, Auntie, it's going to be OK. Isn't it, Mr. Reichauer?" I said, dangling the artifact over the rocks surrounding the pool below.

"Well, that depends . . . you must be the Tumlok."

"Yeah, that depends on you, T-Tum—Town Lawe!" a second voice joined in from a flanked position.

Reichauer sneered at Jig Lister with irritation, as Jig had unnecessarily revealed his supporting presence. The two men now stepped out of the woods and stood on the periphery of the plateau that we had just excavated.

"Jig, keep an eye out for whoever was in the other truck, and don't hesitate to shoot on sight," Reichauer said, which meant they had followed Myra and me from town.

"Professor Reichauer, how did you come to know this word? Was it from your studies in the Archive?"

"Maybe. Then again, maybe I learned it from the dying breath of a medicine man."

"You're a murderer, then."

"Judge not, lest you be judged . . . now give me the key."

"I can't, and you know it."

"Last chance—I have no patience for nonsense. If you don't hand it over, I shoot the lady in the head, then you, and I end up with it anyway." He drew back the hammer on his revolver.

"OK, if it means that much to you. But let Myra leave unharmed; she has nothing you need."

"Sure, why not? I have no problem with that." He laughed.

"How did you even get here? You know, you shouldn't be on this land," I tried stalling.

"Enough bullshit. I gave you my assurance that ma squaw here can leave—now hand it over!"

"OK, OK, we'll do it your way. Myra, I want you to leave."

"I'm not going anywhere! He's going to kill you, and then he's going to hunt me down," she said.

"Please, don't argue, just go."

"You better listen to him. The quicker you get moving, the larger your head start, and you look like you'll need it," Reichauer said, motioning back and forth between us with the pistol.

"Look, Professor, I may have something far more valuable than this trinket, and perhaps we should discuss it."

"I highly doubt that."

"It's a book of codes."

The development immediately caught Jig's attention. "W-w-what book?"

"The one your cousin Martin had. I'm sure your mother has been looking for it."

"What's this about?" Reichauer demanded.

"Founder family business, Mr. Reichauer." Jig tried his best to sound authoritative.

"If we die here, the book and cipher will find its way to someone very interested in its contents," I said. "It really wasn't that hard to crack, once I knew what I was looking for. Your Moloch worship will be found out, and that can't be something either of your superiors would be pleased with. I noticed some interesting eternal penalties for those who lack discretion."

I had managed to stall long enough for the remaining daylight to retreat entirely, leaving the four of us now bathed in the light of a full moon.

"What the hell is he talking about, Lister?"

"I'm sorry, Mr. Reichauer, but we need that b-b-book," Jig insisted.

"Jig, I'll make you a deal," Reichauer said. "We finish what we came here for, and then I promise we'll recover this book, even if we have to tear this town apart to find it."

"Jig, do you think your mother or Stanley would trust him?" I said. "He's a Nazi, you know. He'll sell you out first chance."

"Sh-sh-shut your d-d-damn mouth, Lawe!" Jig said, deliberating his options.

"Myra, you have to leave now—trust me," I told her.

"You sure?"

"Positive, but now."

She disappeared down the trail into the forest as a shot rang past; then I heard a scream and a crash of brush from below.

"You Nazi piece of shit! We had a deal!!" I lost my temper but knew I had to regain my composure quickly.

"Ha-ha, I did give her a head start—she should have taken it!" Reichauer laughed.

"Lister, go check on the squaw and finish her off if needed."

"Don't do it, Jig, it's not worth it!" I tried to reason with him.

"Sh-sh-shut up, you're next, Lawe," was his reply as he raised his sawed-off shotgun to my face before running off the plateau to look for Myra.

"Can you at least tell me what you're hoping to achieve by stealing this, and killing innocent people?" I asked.

"It's simple math, you dim bulb," Reichauer said contemptuously. "Knowledge equals power, power equals profits, profits equal more power, and more power equals more knowledge, etc."

"I see, but where does your Moloch worship fit into all of this?" I could tell by the shifting of his posture that I was annoying him.

"Shut up, no more talk. Hand it over." Reichauer stepped to the edge of the circle, his revolver now pointed at my chest.

"I found some blood, so she's wounded for sure—she's gotta be 'round here somewhere!" Jig shouted from the moonlit forest below.

"Hurry up, then, and take care of it. Christ, this place is full of you potato-heads, isn't it?" Reichauer said with a tone of superiority.

"Here lady lady, here lady lady . . ." We could hear Jig coaxing while he crept around in the moonlight looking for a wounded Aunt Myra.

Suddenly, everything went quiet, and there was a palpable tension as the forest seemed to inhale and hold its breath.

"Lister! . . . Lister? Everything OK down there?" Reichauer called out, not taking his eyes or weapon away from me.

"What the f-f-f-uuu—! Oh g-g-gawd! No! No! No!" Jig screamed out. A blast from his shotgun followed, along with a commotion laden with horrible cries that were soon muffled, as if someone had jammed a rag down his throat.

"You shouldn't have come here, Mr. Reichauer," I warned him. "Remember you brought this on yourself."

"Lister! Lister! You out there? Answer me, goddammit!"

"He can't answer you from where he is, Professor," Myra's familiar voice announced from below, causing Reichauer to whip his head around in her direction.

Taking advantage of his distraction, I lofted the artifact directly at his head, end over end, yelling, "Catch!" He froze for an instant, raising his hands awkwardly to field the spinning object, and I closed the distance in two strides and a dive. The ensuing collision put me on top when we hit the forest floor outside of the circle, and I struggled to gain control of the gun in his right hand. Reichauer was not a small man, and he landed a left punch on the side of my head that felt like a large stick hitting me. But I was determined not to let go of his right arm, and we continued rolling around until the revolver was pinned between my back and the ground. I felt an intense burn across my back as Reichauer fired four quick shots. Still controlling his right arm, I brought my forehead up hard to the bridge of his nose, following this with a left elbow to his ear, knocking him off of me. He recovered the revolver, but it was too late—blood from the wound in my back had reached the ancient soil, and a tribe of Shadow Warriors surrounded us.

Reichauer frantically tried to crawl away, firing his last two shots through the closest warrior with no effect. A massive arm came up from the ground and grabbed his leg, snapping it like a dry twig as the warrior began to pull him down into the earth. Among the cacophony of cracking and popping emanating from his hips and vertebrae were Reichauer's dissipating screams of agony as the dirt filled his mouth and lungs, until Professor Karl Reichauer was no more. The only evidence of his presence was the medallion of Moloch that lay on the ground.

My eyes caught the silhouettes of three silent figures standing atop a large rock up the trail. Virginia and Carla rushed to my side to assess the wound in my back.

"It's not real bad, but this needs to be cleaned and patched," Virginia said.

"Daughter, there is ground alder tincture in that backpack," White Feather called to Virginia.

"It's great to see you!" I said with relief. "I'm OK, but please check on Aunt Myra; she's bleeding."

"Be right back." Virginia kissed me and headed toward Myra, while Carla widened the hole in my shirt and drenched the back of my shoulder with the alder tincture.

"Ow! Ow! Really, Carla?" I yelped, as she grinned.

"Can't have you getting an infection, can we? Let this dry—it should help keep the wound clean."

Virginia found Myra crouched next to the brook below. "Where are you injured, Myra?"

"It's my arm. Reichauer was a shitty shot. I used my knife to cut myself and wiped the blood on several leaves. Then I hid in the underbrush waiting for one of them to try to finish the job. It's an old-timer's trick," she said, her smile visible in the moonlight.

"Let me clean and dress this with a few butterfly strips until we can stitch it properly."

While Virginia tended to Myra, White Feather approached me with instruction for the task I was to perform. "Town, as a Tumlok, you are the only one allowed to open the gate, but you need to begin the process just prior to the zenith of the full moon."

"Yes, White Feather, you tell me when."

"I won't need to. It will feel like you are being pulled apart at the seams."

"I guess now would be the time, then," I said, as I felt the moon's energy surging through me like never before. Virginia and Aunt Myra rejoined us from below, and I stepped into the circle.

After I seated the artifact firmly into the center depression, water began to seep up from the ground.

"OK, hurry out of there," White Feather instructed.

We watched in silence as the underground spring that fed the ceremonial pool below was diverted upward, quickly filling the basin of the plateau. The surface became as still as glass and reflected the moonlight, like a giant mirror that lit up the surrounding forest.

“Where’s White Feather?” I asked, noticing his absence from the group.

“Here he comes,” Virginia said, as White Feather climbed back up to the plateau from the ceremonial pool, wrapped only in his buckskin shirt.

A pulse of blue energy emanated from the center of the basin and rippled across the water, accompanied by a very low hum.

“The time is close. Virginia, Carla, remember what I have taught you,” White Feather said with a quiet smile.

“We will, Father, but do you have to go?” Carla already knew the answer when she asked.

At that moment, another energy pulse occurred, only now the blue ripple remained as a corona around the perimeter, as did a low-cycle hum and the smell of ozone.

“I’m afraid so, daughters. This is the fulfillment of my obligation on this plane. It’s time to be reunited with my fellow travelers.”

With that, the crackling sound of high voltage swirled around us, and the basin suddenly began pulsing a translucent blue wave across the surface.

"Where does this lead?" I asked him.

"This doorway leads to the current location of those you call the Ancients."

"And you are going in there?" Myra asked, as if second-guessing the decision.

"Yes, dear Three Moons, it is my proper place," he smiled. "You see, I am the remnant. My soul made the choice to remain behind so that our tribe could continue along their journey. It was my responsibility to close the portal and guard the key until a Tumlok joined me on the same timeline."

"But you traded the key away to Renault," I said.

"It was for everyone's protection. I knew that when it was my time, it would return to me. It came back through your mother. Pay attention, Town Lawe: that's how creation works."

"Are you a Glider?" I asked him.

"No, Town, Gliders like Louisa repeatedly sacrifice themselves throughout the multiverse protecting the goodness of life. We are a mere contingent of travelers who try to leave worlds in better condition than how we found them."

The forest again fell quiet as the portal opened, meeting us with endless geometric patterns that danced around us like diamonds sparkling. There were energies in human form that smiled at us from within the depths, while welcoming White Feather's reunion with his companions.

"Time to say goodbye . . . for now," White Feather announced. Then he raised his hands toward us to bestow a parting benediction.

"My daughters, Virgines White Wolf and Lmoxitine White Eagle, you have blessed me abundantly in our days together. Remember your purpose, and pursue the path while feeding others in the ways of the Ancients. Town Lawe, Tumlok, son of a Glider, you will see much that many will not understand until they cross into the morphic field. Dispense those visions with care for the benefit of humankind, and much will follow within the timeline. Myra Three Moons, Daughter of the Tides, remain vigilant and continue to share our abundant history; it portends the future. But remember this: all work and no play is not what you are here for."

"Will we see each other again?" Carla asked.

"We are each other, my baby White Eagle."

And with those last words, White Feather vanished into the portal. A brilliant blue ripple collapsed into the center and immediately began to pulse with a rainbow of color. The power and pull was increasing, and the forest trembled from the energy present. "Town, it's time to close the portal," called a voice from the forest behind me. I turned and was shocked to see a shimmering image of my mother standing on the periphery.

"Mom?" I replied falteringly, as my heart skipped and I felt tears in my eyes.

"Yes, honey, it's me. As a Tumlok, you alone can walk onto the passage without shifting dimensions, but don't stay too long, son," she said, smiling proudly.

When I stepped onto the water's surface, I entered a sphere of pure energy. The frequency touched every atom of me, a connection each of us has to everything else in all of creation, and I understood White Feather's parting words to Carla. Answers to questions I had pondered, and many more, instantly became part of my personal lexicon. Then as I began to lose myself in awe, "Town, it's time to go," my mother said, as her presence appeared beside me in eternity. Heeding her words, I carefully removed the key from its base. She smiled as her presence began to fade. "I love you, son . . ." The energy bubble dissipated into the earth with the water, returning the plateau to its familiar state and me along with it, standing in the center, holding the key.

After a moment, Virginia broke the silence. "Town, are you OK?"

"I—I think so. I mean, what the hell just happened?"

"Once you stepped onto the portal, you disappeared. Where did you go?"

"I didn't go anywhere. I was . . . I'm not sure."

"We can figure that out later, but we should get you and Myra to the clinic."

"Did you see her?" I asked, as the tears suspended in wonder began to fall.

"Yes, we saw her standing in the forest," all three confirmed, with Myra making the positive ID. "Town, it was her, I know it was her. I felt her."

"Me too, for the first time since I was five," I said, and for once without the feeling of loss.

"How's your back?" Virginia asked me.

"I think I'm OK. My whole body is still tingling a bit."

"I suspect it's the alder and remaining adrenaline rush; let's get moving," Virginia said firmly.

36

EVIDENCE

When we reached the ridge crest, the moonlight revealed a blanket of fog covering the Valley of the Ancients below, with the sound of drums and song, rising to meet us as if a celestial celebration were in progress. We descended the rocky terrain, and the fog and the sounds of powwow seemed to retreat farther into the distance like a mirage. We stepped onto the meadow as dawn peeked over the eastern ridge at our backs, and the reality of our experiences took hold.

"What are we going to do about Reichauer and Jig?" I said.

"I think we begin with the tribal sheriff," Myra advised.

Virginia and Carla agreed that it was our best approach. Sheriff Max Running Bear was an elder and a supporter of our traditional customs. He would be the place to start.

"Yes, but I think we need to go back to the house and discuss this with Dad, and Carol too."

"That's fine, but the immediate need is to get Myra over to the clinic and address that cut—we can't risk an infection," Virginia insisted.

"Hey! Where in the hell is my truck!" Myra shouted, noticing that the only vehicle parked among the thimbleberry bushes was White Feather's.

"Didn't you place a protective—oh, never mind," said Carla.

"What?"

"You needed a new truck anyway, Three Moons, and I'm sure White Feather would want you to have his," Virginia said, showing Myra the keys to the almost-new vehicle.

"You up to driving us out of here?" I asked Virginia.

"Uh, yeah," she replied, with a shake of her head.

We arrived at the Tribal Clinic, where Dr. Dale was already in his office catching up on paperwork.

"Dedication, that's what I like to see in a new practitioner," he said, upon seeing Virginia as she led us through the private rear door.

"Good morning, Dr. Dale, feel like suturing up Myra?" Virginia asked, as I headed to the nearest phone.

"Sure, if you prep for me. Myra, you get in a knife fight again?" Dr. Dale said with a laugh as he examined the wound.

"Well, it's a story your Aunt Chilok would be proud of, I'll say that much!" Myra replied without revealing more.

As Dr. Dale irrigated and stitched Myra's arm, the sound of car keys tapping on glass pierced the silence of the closed clinic.

"We were just about to head back to the house!" I said, unlocking the front door and holding my hands up to the chatter as Dad rushed into the clinic with Mary, Esther, and Audrey in tow.

"Town, are you all OK?" Dad asked.

"Yes," I replied. "You didn't have to make the drive—we're a few minutes from heading your way."

"You try telling this crew to sit tight for one more hour after Carla and Virginia have disappeared for three nights."

"I guess that was ambitious."

"Well, the call I received from the sheriff after we spoke didn't help, at least on my end," Dad said, in a much-lowered voice.

My stomach lurched.

"Sam phoned right after you, saying he was investigating two bodies that were found at the Title Mine."

"What? Who are they?"

"Esther's friend, the professor, and Jig Lister, I'm afraid."

"Come again?"

"The CERCLA crew found them inside the property first thing this morning. Looks like they were slide victims."

"A slide?"

"Yes. Both bodies were caked in mud, compound fractures—even their eyes, mouths, and ears were packed full of dirt and rock. I haven't told the girls yet." He saw my disbelief. "Do you know something about this? Where's White Feather, anyway?"

"It's a long story, Dad, but we weren't anywhere near the mine. I'll tell you about it back at the house, with a bourbon chaser."

"OK. I'm looking forward to it."

Virginia entered the waiting room. "Hi Dad!"

"Hi kid, you seem none the worse for wear, after three nights in the forest."

"Yes, sir, I'm fine, thank you."

"Carla?"

"She's well. This one, on the other hand . . ." she added, grabbing me by the arm.

"What?" I replied curiously.

"Back in the exam room, pronto. I want to see you under the lights."

"What's wrong with him?" Dad asked.

"It's just a scrape," I answered.

I sat shirtless as Virginia extended the magnifying lamp from its mount on the wall.

"Are you sure you don't need my pants off as well?"

"You are incorrigible at times," she said, flicking the back of my ear with her fingernail.

"Ouch! Isn't there something about doing no harm?"

"OK, so, there is nothing else here besides the tincture stain."

"What? Let me see."

"Town, I can't explain it . . . the portal maybe? What exactly happened in there?"

"All I can say is I had the answers . . . now I can't remember anything other than my mom."

"What answers?"

"Everything, Virginia."

"Some things aren't for us here, according to White Feather," she said.

"Yeah, to have the road map of creation while confined to this decaying body pretty much sums up an image of hell to me."

"Good point. The futility of marking time." Virginia handed me a mirror, and I angled myself in front of another at the exam room sink.

"Wow."

There was a quick rap on the door. "Sorry to barge in, but look at this! It's already happening." Carla parted her hair, revealing a shock of white roots about two inches long.

"OK, no Western medical explanation for that either," Virginia laughed.

"Hey, you have the same thing." I pulled on a section of Virginia's mane.

"So I do."

There was another rap on the door. "I'm done," Myra said, showing us her bandaged forearm.

"Quick, come in. Close the door," I said.

"What's up?"

"Dad told me the bodies of the professor and Jig were found at the old mine site."

"What?"

"Shhh, keep it down—the others don't know yet. We'll get the details back at the house."

~

As Carla and Mary made breakfast, Dad broke the news of Professor Reichauer and Jig Lister's demise.

"Sorry for not telling you earlier," he said.

"It's completely understandable," Audrey nodded.

"I didn't like him, but I never wished him dead," responded Esther.

The house phone rang, and Carol answered. "Oh yes, he's here—just a second, please. Dad, the sheriff's office is on the phone."

"Thanks, Carol, I'll take it in the study."

"Dan, please hold for Sam," said the operator patching through the sheriff's call.

"Dan, these federal folks of yours are getting a little antsy. We can't have them disturbing the site until we conclude our investigation."

"I understand. How long?"

"Not sure; we'll go as fast as we can . . . but it's a strange one up here."

"Why don't I come up and chat with those folks."

"That would be great. I'll send word that you are on the way."

"I'll be there in about forty minutes."

"You driving the truck?"

"Yes, why?"

"I'll make sure you don't get pulled over. Just slow down on Main Street."

As Dad explained his need to meet the sheriff, he included me in the trip. "Town, why don't you come with and give me that update along the way. We'll do that bourbon chaser when we get back."

"Aunt Myra?" I looked at her, still remembering my promise.

"White Wolf, this is your territory now," Aunt Myra directed to Virginia.

In response, Virginia opened her pack and produced two fresh white sage and cedar smudges that she and Carla had created while they were with White Feather. "Take a smudge, both of you, and don't stay longer than you absolutely have to. Cover yourselves before and after," she instructed, adding, "and the truck too!"

"I wish I had that bourbon chaser now," Dad said as I gave him the details along the way. "Look, we aren't going to talk about any of this up there with Sam; let's see what the evidence reveals."

"Yes, sir. I'm just observing." I replied.

When Dad and I reached the mine, there was a contingent of restless engineers milling about outside the gate. He jumped out of the truck and took the lead. "Hi folks, sorry about the delay. My name is Dan Lawe. Would someone be kind enough to point out Mr. Perry?"

"Hi, I'm John Perry," said a voice from behind him.

"Hi John, it's a pleasure," Dad said, shaking his hand. "This is my son, Town."

"Pleased to meet you both," John Perry nodded.

"Has the sheriff updated you on what's going on?" Dad asked.

"He's been tight-lipped since taking our statements. The coroner's van left about a half hour ago."

"I guess your team discovered the bodies?"

"Yes, like I told the sheriff, it was when we were conducting our initial topside survey. We had only been here thirty minutes or so. The poor kid who found them—it shook him up pretty good."

"The sheriff assures me that they are working as fast as possible," Dad said. "We're going on up to meet with him now. Is there anything you can do in the meantime?"

"Yep. I'll have my guys walk off the outside fence perimeter, take some soil samples . . . should take them an hour or so."

"OK, we'll meet you back here in an hour and go from there."

We found Sam sitting in his Jeep at the base of the same cliff where Reggie had shown me White Feather's markings.

"Hey, Sam, how's it going?"

"Howdy, Dan, Town, thanks for coming out. The deputies have combed the entire site and can't find a slide other than that pile of rocks over there. I have no explanation for the condition of the bodies or for where they were discovered."

"Where were they?" asked.

"Over there." Sam pointed to a spot approximately thirty feet away from his Jeep.

"Have you checked the mine shafts for any sign of a cave-in?"

"The deputies are down there now, but even if they find something, those two bodies didn't walk up here and drop dead—not in their mangled condition, that's for damned sure."

"So there's an accomplice?"

"No tracks, not even from the victims, nothing! It's like they were dropped from an airplane."

"Have you checked the mesa on top of the cliff there? Could they have fallen from above?"

"Checked up there. Nothing but a few painted symbols on the face—seem to be part of that fallen rock over here. Looks Native to me."

"Yes, Reggie Harrison brought Town up here a couple of weeks ago to get his take on them. It was when Reggie presented the idea of donating this land back to the tribe."

"I see. Was there any particular meaning?"

"White Feather said he placed them a long time ago, a spell or something to keep whatever from leaving this site."

Sam shook his head. "Well, I'm fresh out of logical explanations."

A crackle came over the radio.

"Go for Sheriff."

"10-4, Shug, copy."

"Definitely some recent activity past the far shaft," Shug said. "I just came out topside and on the way to explain now, over."

"10-4, copy that."

"Sam, you say the CERCLA team found the remains," Dad said. "Who unlocked the gate for them this morning?"

"John Perry said it was Reggie Harrison. He arrived seconds after they did."

"Have you interviewed Reggie?"

"He was just located in West Valley at the construction site for the new mall and is coming in for questioning."

"How did Eunice and Stanley take the news?"

"Deputy Ron delivered it about the time I called you. As you might imagine, it was a tough visit."

"Yeah."

"You know, that's another thing—Eunice and Stanley both claim they had no idea about this federal agency showing up here. They seemed more distraught over that than Jig's death. We had to ask them to refrain from coming up here."

Dad and I exchanged a quick private glance.

Deputy Shug crested a small hill and approached the sheriff's Jeep. "Sheriff . . . Dan, Town," the deputy greeted us.

"What do we have, Shug?" Sam said as the men leaned over a map that was spread out on a folding card table and weighed down at the corners with rocks.

"Well, there's been recent activity below for sure. There's a large cave beyond shaft six. Deputy Jack walked a narrow edge and found a fire pit with quite a few sets of footprints. We didn't explore further, in order to preserve the evidence."

Shug quickly located the area of shaft six on the map. "Look, here's the shaft, and this is where the cave is. Well, I'll be . . . it's practically directly underneath us."

"So it is. Nice work, Shug," Sam said. "I'll get the photographer and lab folks back up here, and I want you to escort them."

"Yes, sir."

"I want close-ups and casts of those footprints."

"I'll handle it, Sheriff."

"Sounds like we are getting more questions than answers," Sam said.

"The Order?" Dad asked.

"They have to be involved in at least one of these two scenarios."

"I guess the site is going to be closed for a while."

"Yeah, I'm afraid so, Dan. Sorry."

"Well, I'd better head down to the gate and speak with the CERCLA folks."

"I'll keep you posted—thanks for coming up here, you two."

As Dad and I returned to the gate, we found Eunice and Stanley shouting at the CERCLA foreman. "We didn't call you! You have no right to be here; now get off our property before I call Senator McClure and Governor Evans!" Eunice yelled.

"Town, you let me handle this, OK?"

"Whatever you say, Dad."

John Perry was professional and kind in his response to them both. "I'm very sorry for your loss, ma'am. I promise you that we will conduct our research as quickly and as delicately as possible."

"Not good enough! Y-y-y-you get the f-f-f-hell out of here now!" Eunice screamed and drew closer as if she were going to physically attack the man.

"Mr. Perry," Dad interceded as he hurried over, accompanied by a sheriff's deputy.

"Yes, sir," he replied, relieved at the intervention.

"D-d-d-damn you all to hell, D-D-D-Danny Lawe! This is your d-d-doing! And you!" Eunice pointed at me with such malice that it made my skin crawl.

"Pardon me, Eunice, you're mistaken. The request came from the Harrisons." Dad remained calm and instantly moved between Eunice and me as if blocking her hatred.

Stanley Lister stepped forward, and I saw Dad's fists close and his posture shift just slightly.

"Daniel, I—I don't want any trouble," Stanley said, putting a hand up, understanding exactly what was coming his way if he was misinterpreted. "You see, the Harrisons hold only a minor stake in this land; they haven't been on the deed for years. As far as the law is concerned, this is Lister property. The Harrisons had no right to speak on its behalf."

"I see," Dad responded, relaxing only slightly. "Well, since these folks are here, wouldn't you want to know if there is any contamination? The federal government has set aside funds to assist in the cleanup where they deem appropriate. This could be a great opportunity for you."

"No! We don't want that, and if you do this against our will, we're going to sue for criminal trespass and emotional distress. Mother just lost a son and I a brother, for crying out loud!" Stanley said firmly.

Just then the deputy's radio cracked. "Go for Deputy Sims."

"Sims here, Sheriff."

"Is Dan Lawe still on-site?"

"Yes, Sheriff, I'm standing next to him."

"Dan, do those federal guys have the ability to do some dredging?"

"Yes, we do," John Perry quickly volunteered, easily overhearing the query.

"Great. Mr. Perry, you are now officially part of this investigation and can come on up here with your equipment."

Stanley's face drained of blood instantly.

"Oh, n-n-no you don't!" Eunice gobbled, pressing forward again and shaking her balled-up fists.

"Stanley, you know the law. Please take her away before she gets an obstruction charge and ends up in jail," Dad advised.

"Mother, he's right. There's nothing more to do here."

"You'll get yours, Lawe! You, and yours, just you wait!" was Eunice's final threat as Stanley escorted her back to the car.

The gates opened, and the CERCLA crew drove their machinery up through the old town to meet with the sheriff. An accommodation was made, and both parties were able to retrieve the information they needed.

~

We left the site soon after Eunice and Stanley, stopping as soon as we were off mine property and smudging ourselves as well as the truck. By the time we got back to the house, Myra, Virginia, and Carla had provided a tribally sanitized view of our encounter in the ancestral forest. This story was about the initiation of White Feather's two daughters and a passing of tradition that was a long-lived tribal passage to be held at a sacred site. I then provided everyone with the interpretation of Esther's glyph and why it had been important to someone like Professor Reichauer.

"It's a map. You see the stepped triangles indicate the direction—in this case, southeast. The circles within the triangles represent days on foot. This was three full days."

"How did you come up with that?" Esther asked.

"It's a three-sided figure, and a circle is the symbol of completion in any culture. I reasoned that three circles top to bottom meant that if you left at sunrise the first day, you would arrive by sunset the third, depending on the time of year, naturally."

"Wow, Town, really well done," Carol applauded.

"Thanks, sis, but you also have to understand the cosmology to maintain a proper heading. You know the skies have changed over the centuries. If you used the current star charts for summer, you would end up at the Cultural Center."

"Whoa. That's amazing!" Esther exclaimed.

"And that explains why Reichauer showed up there," Audrey said.

"In part. He failed to understand this piece of the puzzle, but it isn't over yet. They are going to find more answers at the mine. Otherwise, Reichauer and Jig Lister would not have been found there."

"I wish we were going to be here for that news. I hate that we head back tomorrow morning—nothing like a good mystery," Mary smiled.

"We'll give you regular updates, Mary," Dad replied.

The next morning, I was shocked to have Dad join me in the kitchen to cook breakfast for our departing guests.

"What are you doing up at four a.m.?" I asked.

"Someone has to meet Eddie Night Raven and get the paper," he replied, more bright-eyed than me.

"I see, you've picked up the slack in my absence."

"Only Sundays," he smiled. "Besides, I wouldn't saddle you with cook—"

"Cooking breakfast for eight," Mary said, finishing Dad's sentence as she put on an apron."

"Mary, you're a guest! Go back to bed—we'll handle it."

"Sorry, Dan, where I come from, guests earn their keep. Now you two move aside, and how about some coffee?" she laughed.

"Yes, ma'am, right away."

"Dad, I'll go down and grab the paper for old times' sake. You hang out just in case Mary needs a hand."

We sent the crew of Mary, Audrey, Carla, and Esther off after a huge farmhouse breakfast, and as we said our goodbyes, I wasn't the only teary-eyed one. They would be missed by us all.

~

In three weeks, a toxicity profile identifying contaminants and their respective levels was furnished to the CERCLA committee in Washington, DC. Following their review, a determination of funding eligibility would be made. The sheriff filed his report for the deaths of Jig Lister and Karl Rickover as accidental, the result of falling two hundred feet as the two men were exploring the Native pictogram on the cliff face above. The coroner didn't argue, and the case was closed, adding two more tragic accidents to the site's history.

Pole Pass fell eerily quiet that first week of August 1982, only to be shattered the following Monday when shocking news arrived from the lab in Boise. The report detailed the compounds discovered in each of the shafts that the CERCLA team had dredged. The first six contained the expected mining toxins of heavy metals, ammonium nitrate, and cyanide, among others. But an unmapped shaft just beyond the cave area that was discovered during the photography and footprint casting revealed evidence of organic compounds associated with human remains.

The sheriff's department re-secured the site and contracted a full-scale dredging of the shaft while interviewing everyone still living who was remotely associated with the site. The challenge from a forensics position was one of dating. The water temperature in the shafts hadn't been constant, making it impossible to create an evidentiary timeline with current science. Human bone fragments no larger than a quarter were recovered, some charred, but their origins were indeterminable. Attempts to question people about the mine were equally frustrating. If anyone knew anything, they weren't talking . . . with the exception of Reggie Harrison.

His information led to a discreet search for two autopsy reports, a quest that proved to be in vain. They had been misfiled or destroyed, or never existed.

"Oh, they exist!" insisted Nurse Eleanor Higgins, responding to Virginia's disclosure of the investigation.

"Any ideas?"

"The Pole Pass morgue was originally in the subbasement of the old County Hospital. When the hospital expanded, the morgue was relocated to the northwest corner of the new basement. It's a beautiful facility—I mean, for a morgue," she told Virginia over coffee in the hospital cafeteria.

"I see."

"The problem was, they didn't plan their record storage well, and during the move they transferred the records to hospital inventory. I know, because I had to pull an autopsy for a wrongful death of a farmer friend. The morgue files were a mess, and the girls in records were too busy filing their nails to file the records properly. I finally barged in there myself and found what I was looking for under 'Miscellaneous' in the general admission files. I'm not kidding you, Dr. Tecoi, Miscellaneous!"

"Please call me Virginia. Do you think these two files could be there? We would need to make copies—covertly."

"We can look; the records people nowadays wouldn't let us just march in there and rummage, but I do know someone who may help on the Q.T."

Eleanor's niece was a summer intern in records, and with her help, Eleanor found the two files—as suspected, in Miscellaneous. Upon review of the autopsy files, Virginia discovered that Arnie Lister's abdomen had been punctured; the culprit, according to the coroner, was rebar. A corresponding photo of the wound, however, revealed that it wasn't round like a rod of rebar; the perforation exhibited a diamond shape, an exact match including location with the previous victim, seven-year-old Terrance Barnhill, who was found in the mine shortly after he went missing back in 1957.

Virginia delivered her observations to the sheriff, who with Reggie's statement went directly to the state prosecutor's office in Boise. Warrants were granted and served simultaneously for the original autopsy files, the Lister residence, and the Fraternal Order of Farmers lodge. Eleanor Higgins accompanied state authorities to where the autopsy files were stored to ensure their recovery in case of further mismanagement. The search of the Lister family home came up nil, but the lodge yielded something unimaginable in Pole Pass. A large stone vault hidden beneath the basement brought investigators to an inner sanctum, containing a shrine to Moloch.

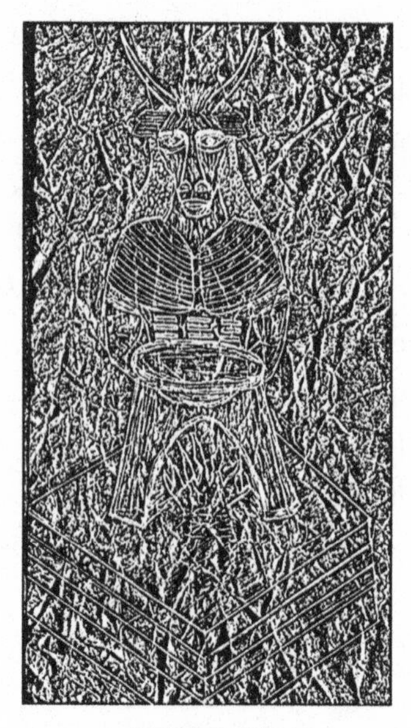

MOLOCH

Under the watchful eye of the ancient effigy was a large altar and bloodstained ballock dagger, Exhibits A and B during the trial.

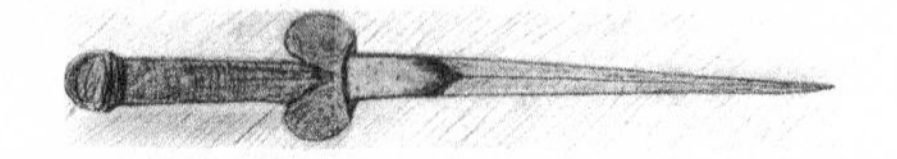

37

FALL SEMESTER 1982

The week following my return to Princeton, I received an invitation to meet with Aaron Van Kaiser at the Archive. He greeted me in the foyer, and we chatted casually on our way to the boardroom, where we had first met nine months earlier.

"Congratulations on the success of your project."

"Well, I really haven't looked at it in those terms, Mr. Van Kaiser."

"I told you last December, *All roads lead to the doghouse*."

"Yes, sir, you did."

"You mentioned a few items?" Van Kaiser asked, as we took our seats in the boardroom, now absent of several portraits.

"Yes, indeed." I handed him a padded envelope containing the medallions of Moloch once in the possession of Karl Reichauer and Eunice Lister.

"The key, Mr. Lawe?"

"Oh, forgive me." I reached into my breast pocket and produced the little black book that Carla had inherited.

"So, this is what Mr. Reichauer was chasing." Van Kaiser smiled as he fanned through its pages. "I wonder what's hidden in here."

"I'm sure someone in the membership will be happy to decipher it for you," I said with a straight face.

After my reply came a rhythmic tap on the door that could only be from the perfectly manicured nails of one person in Princeton.

"Good morning, Mr. Lawe, welcome back to Princeton." Esmeralda Jamison smiled.

"Why, good morning, Esmeralda, and thank you, it's nice to be back."

Van Kaiser inclined his head affirmatively to Esmeralda, who then handed me a familiar manila pouch with a string and button clasp.

"A gift from the Archive, Mr. Lawe."

"Thank you; I'm not quite sure what to say."

"You are welcome. The Archive's tradition is to reward those who contribute to its success," Van Kaiser said, indicating that our meeting was now over.

"Thank you again for the gift, and I hope to see you around Princeton."

"Indeed, Mr. Lawe. You are welcome to conduct your research with us anytime," Van Kaiser offered, as I left the room.

Esmeralda and I didn't speak much on the return to the lobby, but I could feel her magnetism pulling at me. "I have some additional paperwork for you to review and sign. That is, if you wish," she said, handing me the Archive's permanent membership agreement and an ornate pen.

"Please read it over carefully before signing, Mr. Lawe."

"Is there a compromising component to this document?"

Esmeralda laughed in her reply, "The highest of civilizations are constructed upon the foundations of compromise, Mr. Lawe. In regard to this document, you simply agree to abide by the terms of use, and the Archive agrees to be an available resource for your endeavors. I will caution you; the term *permanent* is binding, and not to be taken lightly. There is of course, an annual membership fee."

"Of course." I smiled, pausing for a second before gracefully declining the offer. "You know, Esmeralda, I think I'm going to take a rain check on the permanent membership, at least through this year of study. Notwithstanding I am humbled by the gesture and confidence of the Archive and intend no disrespect."

"Well, I won't deny that I am disappointed, Mr. Lawe. I had hoped to be working more closely with you this fall. My recent studies have led to the most amazing original tantric text; it was once inventoried in the Alexandrian library. The artwork alone, Mr. Lawe . . ." she responded in her most alluring way.

"I'm sure the content is as exquisite as you are, Esmeralda," I replied with sincerity.

"I do hope that Ms. Tecoi understands what she has." Esmeralda smiled, holding me with her hypnotic gaze.

"Well, if she ever forgets, I'll send her to you for a refresher course."

"Indeed, Mr. Lawe, please do."

"Until we meet again, Ms. Jamison."

"Bye for now, and enjoy your semester, Mr. Lawe."

I exited the building into the signature fragrance of a Princeton fall morning without remorse over my feigned ignorance of the key. The Archive had the coded book, two medallions, and who knows what else, from their internal investigation; I possessed the answers I had originally sought, as well as others to questions I hadn't known existed. Another striking discovery was that the Princeton branch of the Archive had been under the leadership of one woman over the past decade. *The Honorable Esmeralda Jamison 1972* at the bottom of the permanent-membership contract confirmed what Albert and Sophie had shared with me over dinner earlier in the week. Esmeralda's tenacious research habits and cunning smarts were recognized by her mentor early in the apprenticeship. Eleven years earlier, her covert sleuthing brought down the chairs of two European Archive branches, and she was rewarded with the title of Madame Chair of Princeton, her special charge. Having now rid the Ivy League institution of the Order, Esmeralda enjoyed a standing Sunday dinner date with a famed pot roast on Battle Road West.

38

JUSTICE SERVED

Interest in the murder trial of Eunice Lister stretched well beyond our region. The proceedings were moved from Pole Pass to the state capital of Boise over concerns of a fair trial, but locals suspected this was as much about having enough space for national press and others fascinated by the macabre details of the case. Dad secured seats and hotel rooms for us—himself, Carol, Virginia, Carla, and me—through the duration of the weeklong trial, which began Monday, January 10, 1983. We convened each evening in the hotel restaurant, where Dad and Carol would summarize their view of the day's proceedings and speculate if there were enough mitigating circumstances to keep Eunice off of death row.

The prosecution effectively used the testimony of forensic experts to show beyond circumstantial certainty that the ballock dagger was used to puncture the abdomens of both Arnie Lister and Terrance Barnhill. The eyewitness testimony of Stanley Lister, who pointed his finger at his own mother from the witness stand, corroborated this.

"She did it! My God . . . my own mother murdered my little boy! She took my son Arnie as a sacrifice to Moloch," Stanley testified between his sobs in the packed courtroom.

"Did you assist her, Stanley?" the district attorney asked.

"Yes, I-I did. I chloroformed him, and after he was dead, I sunk his little body in the shaft. I don't know how I could have been so evil!" Stanley appeared to be reliving the horrors of the event for the first time.

"Stanley, I know this is difficult, but please tell the court the exact sequence of events leading up to the death of Arnie."

"Yes, sir. A senior member of the Order arrived at the West Valley lodge; he was from the Seattle chapter. He oversaw our activities and visited on only two occasions."

"Which two occasions, Stanley?"

"The sacrifices of Terrance Barnhill and Arnie."

"What was this person's name?"

"We only knew him as Mr. Barnabas."

"Can you please describe Mr. Barnabas for the court?"

"Pale complexion, black hair, average build, with hard features . . . he was a cruel man."

Even in the heat of the stuffy courtroom, the description sent a chill up my spine, and we all figured what was coming next.

"Thank you, please proceed."

"Mr. Barnabas and mother—I mean, Eunice Lister—had originally targeted Daniel Lawe's boy, Town."

At this admission, Carol grabbed my left hand and Virginia grabbed my right, while Dad and Carla, who flanked our seats, leaned forward, looking at me.

"Why this child?"

"In retribution for his ancestor Jake Lawe. He betrayed the Order back in the 1800s by revealing Founder family involvement. It was Barnabas that pushed retribution as a duty to the Order.

"So, this was about a century-old grudge?"

"There's more to it. The Order believes that this unsatisfied debt was prohibiting our membership from receiving all the prosperity that was due. The original founding families insisted that they only survived after the mine pinched because of their offerings to Moloch."

"Stanley, are you stating on the record that your Lister ancestors conducted human sacrificial rituals to Moloch?"

"Yes, sir. That's what I was taught, and not just Listers; other founding families participated as well. I've seen references to that practice in the book of family records."

The courtroom gasped at the implications of Stanley's testimony.

"Thank you, Stanley, please proceed."

"The intended target was going to be the Lawes' soon-to-be firstborn; they had just returned to the area when Mr. Barnabas became our director after dispatching the former. But the child was a girl, and the offering in this case had to be a boy. That's why Terrance Barnhill was taken. But this would only grant an extension, according to Mr. Barnabas."

We all looked at each other.

"Go on," the district attorney prompted.

"We had not seen Mr. Barnabas for many years, when he showed up unannounced in October of 1970. I swear to God, I told the group it wasn't a good idea. But Mr. Barnabas wouldn't listen—none of them would. Eddie Night Raven, the newspaper's editor, was overheard telling someone that he would often see Town Lawe at the gate when he delivered the paper before sunrise. Barnabas demanded that we resolve the debt and made me drive him out to the property where the Lawes lived. He stepped out of the car and instructed me to pop the trunk and wait for him, which I did, until daylight. Then I left because I didn't want to be seen out there. We never heard from Barnabas again."

Dad's intense gaze was fixed on Eunice Lister while Carol stared at the floor and nodded in silence, as if finally remembering her role in the event.

"What happened when you returned without young Lawe and Mr. Barnabas?"

"Mother was furious, and also scared of reprisals from the Order, or Moloch. She insisted that it was all my fault, and Arnie had to be taken as a replacement for my stupidity, to make this right."

"Stanley, just one more thing: what happened in 1973?"

"Yes, sir, the LeToure boy."

"This is Kincaid Allen LeToure, the child who went missing for a short time?"

"Yes, sir, that's correct.

A sob came from Barbara LeToure, who sat a few rows away from us.

"Please tell the court what happened."

"My brother Jig was always trying to prove himself to Mother. The boy was a random target; he was taking a leak behind the ARCO filling station out on Crescent Road, in West Valley. Jig managed to sneak up behind him with a chloroform rag—then, like the fool he was, brought him back to the lodge. The boy almost regained consciousness, and Dr. Lautermilk gave him a shot of something to knock him out cold."

"Dr. William Lautermilk? He was a member of the Order?"

"Yes, sir. Lautermilk was involved in this incident because like Jig, he had a predilection for youngsters. Lautermilk is the one who also provided the chloroform for the two other sacrifices."

"Please continue."

"That's when our cousin, Martin Nelson-Lister, unexpectedly walked into the Order's sanctuary and saw Jig and Lautermilk molesting the boy and put a stop to it. He took the kid, who was still unconscious, and his bike out to West Canyon Road to make it look like a bike crash."

"Was Martin Nelson-Lister a member of the Order as well?"

"No. Marty—Martin ran the day-to-day activities for the Fraternal Order of Farmers. He thought the Moloch altar, robes, and other things were just part of being a member of the inner circle."

"So, then, to be clear, Martin had no knowledge of the sacrificial murders of Terrance Barnhill or your son Arnie, or any of the family history of murder—is this correct?"

"Yes, that's the God's truth. Marty had nothing to do with any of it. In fact, if he hadn't walked in on Jig and the Doc, they would have sacrificed the child with the dagger. Marty was devoted to the good work of the Fraternal Order of Farmers. Mother just used him as a prop and for his tractor dealership."

The gravity of the testimony landed on Carla, and she dropped her head, keeping it down for a minute as Virginia put her arm around her.

"Tell us what happened to Martin, if you will."

"The LeToure boy ended up committing suicide, and Marty's conscience couldn't take the guilt. He wanted to go to the child's funeral, and we had to talk him out of it. He began drinking a lot more to deal with it, and Mother knew he would crack and tell someone. He was a risk that had to be dealt with. We invited him to a meeting at the Mineshaft Bar in Pole Pass and spiked his vodka with pure grain alcohol, got him staggering drunk. When he passed out, Jig took his shirt and stuck him behind the wheel of his car with a rock on the gas pedal. He went through the guardrail into the West Canyon, and the car burned. Mother picked up Jig, and they drove to the lodge, where they burned Marty's shirt at the altar of Moloch. That's when Mother noticed her book was missing from the sanctuary."

"What was in this book, Stanley?"

The question removed the smug look from Eunice Lister's face as she sat at the defense table. Her eyes bulged and fists clenched so tightly that they shook.

"Objection, immaterial," her defense attorney demanded.

"Overruled," the judge countered. "You may answer the question, Mr. Lister."

"Well, when Mr. Barnabas left the car to grab the Lawe boy, the book must have fallen out of his pocket. It was full of symbols and shapes and writings that were very strange. We never knew what it meant, but Mother was convinced that it would lead to greater power within the Order, and she was hell bent on figuring it out."

"Was anyone able to 'figure it out,' Stanley?"

"Not that I am aware of, sir."

"Was the book recovered?"

"It was not. We searched everywhere, and ultimately believed it burned along with Marty in his car."

"Stanley, thank you for your testimony. I have no further questions for this witness, Your Honor."

~

Stanley Lister received a plea deal of life in prison for his cooperation in turning state's evidence. Although he escaped lethal injection, he couldn't outrun his own conscience and hung himself with a bed sheet within the first month of his sentence at the state penitentiary.

Dr. Lautermilk, who after leaving Pole Pass had started a part-time practice on the Oregon Coast, died of a heart attack the year before the activities of the Order were uncovered. Tragically, when the testimony from the trial was splashed across the media, several children from Lincoln City, Oregon, came forward with testimony of his exam room fondling and threats about disclosure. His own grandchildren were not exempt.

Eunice Lister stood defiant before the judge and jury as her sentence was read: guilty on two counts of capital murder, and as an accessory to premeditated murder. When the death sentence was read, she smiled for the onlookers before waddling off in irons. Spending her last two years incarcerated at the women's prison in Pocatello, Idaho, she herself was brutally murdered in a ritual killing by unknown perpetrators. Prison authorities believed it to be a reprisal by another cult for Eunice incessantly running her mouth on the Row. The details of her murder were too gruesome for the newspapers, but the official report stated that she was found hanging upside down from the steam pipes in a basement corridor used to shuttle prison laundry. She had been skinned alive, and then someone corkscrewed a two-inch auger bit through one side of her head until it poked out the other. Those responsible used her blood to draw their demonic symbols on the concrete floor and walls, which occult experts agreed grounded her soul to the spot of her death until final judgment.

Sheriff Sam told Dad that ever since her murder, reports of a stench and flies suddenly engulfing those entering the area were commonplace. When word of this spread throughout the facility, inmates on laundry detail refused to push the large carts through the passage alone, and even long-time maintenance staff and guards insisted on pairing up. The warden decided to dispel "this superstitious nonsense" by walking the corridor solo. He reemerged pale as a ghost, and insiders said he'd pissed in his pants. What wasn't in dispute was that he immediately went on vacation and never returned to the prison. Long after, there were reports of "a stuttering woman's voice screaming obscenities, followed by growling laughter."

It soon hit the papers that the current local membership of the Order consisted exclusively of Listers. Eunice, Stanley, and Jig were the only ones proven to be involved in the murders, but evidence was uncovered linking others to the illegal prospecting and desecration of Native lands. Charlie Lister was found to be the ringleader of this operation and was the only one who went to jail. The rest paid hefty fines and left the Northwest after communities voiced their outrage.

Reggie's decision to come forward had been sparked by a conversation he had overheard between his dad and Barley Adams about the crazy cult involving the Listers. He remembered that it was Stanley who insisted that no founding-family member should go to Kincaid's funeral, and his dad had told him long before, "Never be around Jig Lister alone, under any circumstances." When he learned about the Superfund committee, Reggie saw the opportunity to put some heat on the Listers and get NPL&T completely out of their influence. When justice was served, Reggie felt as if he had paid a debt of gratitude to the memory of Kincaid. He told me at my investment closing that the day Kin beat his ass in the fourth grade taught him a valuable life lesson, and he was a better person for it.

The Title Mine property was approved for cleanup, and the Lister family was held responsible for the repayment. Complete bankruptcy followed; their entire holdings were seized and sold at auction. After the invocation of Virginia White Wolf, the land, also clear of toxic waste, is a beautiful Pass County park, overlooking Pole Pass and the West Valley below.

EPILOGUE

March of 1983 found Mary Burke entering a season of change. Arthur had left her well provisioned through his life insurance policy, and she had two King County real estate holdings in a rapidly growing city bordered by mountains and water. She loved Capitol Hill, especially 16th Avenue East, where she and Arthur had made their lives together. Mary had built the Surrogate into the success that it was without regret, but also without ownership. The Hill, and that passage of life, would forever be etched onto her soul, just as Arthur himself was . . . but Mary knew it was time to expand into the next phase of her life.

She considered a place in the San Juan Islands where they had vacationed often, but she quickly recognized that the memories and isolation of full-time island living wasn't what she needed. Then came an idea that surprised her somewhat, but she knew it was right. Later that week around the dinner table with Carla, Audrey, and Carol, she confessed her yearnings, and the idea born of them. Carla and Audrey stopped mid-bite and looked at each other, then swallowed and returned their gaze to Mary.

"There must be something in the water. Audrey and I have been talking about that space at least a few times a week for a month!"

"Bakery and coffee in one side, art gallery in the other," Audrey confirmed.

"Got a name?" Carol asked.

The three women looked at Mary.

She thought a moment and then said, "C&M Bakery and Espresso. I mean, it is simple."

"And the White Eagle Gallery," offered Audrey.

The renovation of the two commercial spaces was completed in time for a grand opening party just before Thanksgiving. Carla and Mary worked round the clock with their staff fulfilling one hundred pie orders for the holiday season. Audrey made the gallery unique, specializing in high-end Native works of North American tribes and reserving space for young artists to showcase their creations as well. One familiar item made the pilgrimage east of the mountains: the beckoning watercolor from Val Persoon—still not for sale, but on display for visitors to experience its mysteries.

It was mid-December when Mary, Carla, and Audrey were able to move into their upstairs loft apartments just in time for a magical and white Pole Pass Christmas. Their open-house party held another reminder of our special connections.

"Merry Christmas, Dan, and thank you so much for allowing the invasion of your home over the past eight months while this was built out!" said Mary, as Carla and Audrey pressed in around him.

"Hardly an invasion—it was more of a reprieve from myself, honestly."

"Well, we have a small token of our affection for you," she said.

"Oh, you really don't need to do that."

"Everyone, if we can have your attention, please," Mary addressed the intimate gathering while tapping her wine-glass. "Thank you. Carla and Audrey have a presentation to make."

All eyes focused on the two women holding the festively wrapped gift.

"Why, I really don't know what to say."

"Don't say anything, Daniel, just open it already!" Mary laughed.

When Dad unwrapped the package, he found a portrait of my mother. She was reclined on the bank overlooking the river where the sauna was later built. The fall sunlight was filtering softly across her face, faceted by the colorful leaves, as if the rays were destined only for her. We had never seen Dad speechless, but Carol and I followed suit as we took in the beauty of the oil painting. Carla and Audrey had painted it using select photos of my mother that were set around the house.

"Mary conceptualized this—all Carla and I did was paint it," Audrey announced, with tears veiling her hazel eyes.

"Well, it's . . . absolutely stunning," said Dad, drawing his kerchief to blot his own eyes.

There was a piece of Carla, Audrey, and Mary within the image; it was as if Mom were an amalgam of these three women, all beautiful in their unique ways.

~

When Mary, Carla, and Audrey left for the Pass, Virginia moved in with Carol, and they lived together at Mary's house, where they kept up the tradition of the Gathering, but with a simplified menu. Both swore they would occasionally encounter Arthur's presence, sitting at the dining room table working on what appeared to be mechanical drafts of some type.

After finishing my master's in one year at Princeton, I made the difficult decision to transfer to the University of Washington for the PhD program. While Princeton would forever hold my academic heart, the UW program was its equal and also possessed a world-class crew facility that always needed volunteers to maintain the shells. But the inescapable truth behind my westward migration was that the dream of chasing the elusive girl through the forest had returned, and with each appearance she became more transparent, as if she were vanishing.

Before departing Princeton, I stopped at the Archive to bid my farewells to the Honorable Esmeralda Jamison and Aaron Van Kaiser. I wasn't completely surprised when Van Kaiser informed me that Esmeralda had taken leave to their French location, where she was in pursuit of the last testament of Mary Magdalene. I smiled and asked him to convey my best regards; I also asked if he would see that she received my thank-you card for the kind words she had spoken to the chair of the PhD committee at the UW. "I'll see that she receives it. Do keep in touch, Mr. Lawe" were his parting words.

When I moved to Seattle, I joined Carol and Virginia at Mary's house on Capitol Hill, where we lived together for the next two years and finished our commitments. During that time, there were revelations that once again reminded me of Chilok's lesson,

To us, this life is a paradox. Our path is straight, yet it is made up of corners. It was designed this way, so the splendor unfolds only in glimpses. This is for our own benefit and for the preservation of all. It's the reason we are given only what we are ready to receive each day. This lesson is about patience. Patience develops virtue. The reward is digesting the fullness of each glimpse before moving on to the next.

The first manifestation came shortly after I arrived, over dinner with Carol and Virginia.

"Carol, you don't have to protect me anymore," I said, referring to what White Feather had told me a few years earlier at the Cultural Center. Carol looked at me a little sideways.

"I mean, you should at least date or something . . . remember what Dad said about a hobby?"

I caught Virginia's sly smile as her eyes went down to her plate, where she began to chase a bite of food around with her fork.

"OK, what?" I asked, awkwardly.

Carol shifted in her chair. "Town . . . look . . . Oh, hell, I should have told you this a while ago."

"Told me what? Spit it out already!"

"I've been seeing Esther."

"Seconds anyone?" Virginia got up from the table and headed quickly toward the kitchen.

"Oh, I see . . . um . . . well, I love Esther! How long have you—you guys been, um, dating?" It was impossible to conceal my surprise.

"Please don't be hurt—we began seeing each other a little after I moved to Seattle."

"So, for over a year now. And I'm the only one without a clue, including Dad?" I couldn't help but laugh.

"Pretty much," Virginia said with a smile, returning to the dining room with a shot glass of bourbon for me.

"Here I thought you were just great friends. I feel a little foolish, but of course I'm happy if you are. I think Esther's terrific."

~

The next occurred while I was reading through my gift from the Archive. The familiar pouch that Esmeralda Jamison had handed me a year earlier contained the original journal of Jake Lawe.

I found myself intrigued by his remarkable journey from London to the foundations of Pole Pass in the mid-1800s. However, what I discovered in those pages far surpassed one man's grit and tenacity. Much like my Weyekin at thirteen years of age, it provided another piece to this cosmic puzzle that we are all trying to put together.

From the journal of Townsend Jacob Lawe:

May 1835
Her carriage was drawn not by a team of horses, but of her own will and determination.

Jake encountered "her" while exploring and charting terrain apart from his colleagues in the area then known as Hidden Pass. He was standing on the edge of a cliff as he sketched the western vista when she silently approached him from behind.

"What-you-do?"

Startled by the presence, he dropped everything and instinctively whipped around with his pistol, only to find a long gun pointed a foot away from his face. He cautiously holstered his weapon and ineloquently used a few de-escalating terms he had learned in various Native dialects, which were answered with silence. He then attempted to communicate in an excruciatingly slow version of spoken English and primitive sign language while taking note of the woman dressed in buckskin, whose wide-brimmed hat shielded her eyes but not the high cheekbones and bronze skin. After he showed her a few of his drawings, the woman continued her expressionless stare until she couldn't help but burst into laughter.

"I sketched better than that when I was five years of age," she said in perfectly proper English.

Initially bewildered, he answered a second later, "Well, miss, I see you have me at a disadvantage in ways more numerous than one," and recognizing the humor of the situation, he began laughing with her. Jake introduced himself along with his vocation and invited her to share the food he had brought along for the day's trek. It was rare to meet anyone in this territory, much less someone of formal education. She accepted, and they enjoyed a snack of deer jerky on the large rock outcrop overlooking what is now part of the West Valley. Through conversation he discovered that she was the product of Native and French stock. Her father had been educated at the Université de Paris before leaving France prior to the Revolution. It was through him that she received a proper education while they lived in York, which was renamed Toronto in the past year. Her mother was originally from the Hidden Pass area, and several years prior, on a return visit, both parents perished from the pox. She had promised to bring them the remainder of the way and lay them to rest, according to her tribal traditions.

"I make the pilgrimage every two years by way of the Hudson Bay Company routes. That is why I am here now."

"I am sorry about your parents. I lost my mother when I was young, and my father shipped me off to America. Do you ever transport small items in and out of the area?"

"Thank you for the condolences. I have done so one time in an urgent situation, but found that task better suited for a courier. Many tribes do not care for the Hudson Bay Company, and it is in my best interest to bear no allegiance to them during my journeys."

"Yes, I understand. How long will you remain here?"

"Until July 1, at the latest. I will miss the worst weather that way. What prompted you to abandon the modernity of the East and embrace the rigors of the Western frontier?"

Jake provided the short version of how he came to migrate west after being inspired by the tales of Lewis and Clark and their Corps of Discovery expedition.

"Oh yes. We have them to thank for the crowds," she said, unenthusiastically.

"You have been here over twelve years now. Your opinion?"

"It is magnificent. The beauty and freedom are worth any hardship that I have endured to date."

About that time, a Native party of six horses rounded the bend into the clearing where they were seated. Jake discreetly placed his hand on his gun in preparation to defend them if needed.

"That won't be necessary. Now slowly and naturally, place your hand in a more neutral position."

The party quickly rode up to them and formed a half circle, leaving nowhere to go except over the cliff at their backs. The leader of the party canted back and forth in a show of strength, but before Jake could speak, the woman stood up and stepped toward the young warrior, taking off the wide-brimmed suede hat shielding her face. The young warrior instantly recognized her and became very conciliatory, even offering an escort for them, and drinking water if they wanted. Raising her outstretched hands toward the party, she appeared to shower them with a blessing. The group tipped their heads out of respect, then pulled their mounts to the right and departed.

When she rejoined me without replacing the hat, the first thing I noticed was the white shock that ran through her raven-black hair. Her skin was a deep tan, like burnished copper, and her vivid green eyes sparkled like the clearest mountain streams that I had witnessed. She was intoxicating to behold.

He continued with their encounter:

"Well, that appeared to go well. Thank you."

"Only scouts making their rounds. They like to bluster about when they discover something."

"Might I inquire as to your current status?"

"You may," she replied.

"Well?"

"I am unmarried," she answered him resolutely.

"Thank you, but that is actually not what I had in mind."

"Oh, it isn't?"

"I can assure you it was not my immediate intention."

"Well, now, I am uncertain if I should be discouraged or relieved. I think it might be the latter after this bit of incivility on your part," she said, standing up and vigorously dusting off the seat of her buckskin pants.

"Wait a minute, will you? I do not even know your name!"

Oblivious to his request and inquiry, she checked the position of the sun and said that she must be going. Walking toward the southern tree line to her awaiting horse, she urged him to return to the trading post.

"Another scout party will come through here soon, and you are beyond the agreed boundary. You have such nice blond hair, it would be a pity for it to become separated from your head."

"Will I see you again, before you depart for Toronto?"

"Perhaps, someday."

"Until then, whatever your name is," he said, regretfully bidding her farewell.

"And to you, Jake Lawe, thank you for the meal."

The only time he saw her again was in a recurrent dream. Jake chased her deep into the forest, but she remained beyond his reach. Then one night she began to fade away, until finally she was gone, and he stood in the forest alone. It haunted him, and Jake made the overland journey to Toronto in search of her. When he reached the Huron people, they told him of a powerful medicine woman who traveled throughout the tribes. She had not been seen in over three years, and they believed she had gone the way of her ancestors.

August 1837
The Huron called her White Wolf. The European settlers knew her by the French name her parents had given her, Virgines.

Since the day we met, I believed that Virginia's and my paths were destined to cross. But even with everything each of us had experienced along our journeys, I swear I reread this story fifty times, trying to fully digest its truth before taking another bite. Good thing—otherwise I might have choked on what followed.

Ten years had passed since that trip to Toronto by the time Jake fell in love with and married the Native woman who would become our great-great-great-grandmother.

July 7, 1847
Lmoxitine White Eagle, the daughter of a tribal elder known as Gray Hawk, has agreed to marry me and become the mother of my children.

"Yes, love, Carla and I know all about this," Virginia replied, as I read the entry to her.

"Really?"

"We had a good laugh about it when White Feather told us the story. He said he was remembering much more the closer he came to his return."

"Maybe you guys could have shared that with me?"

"Aren't you the one always preaching about timing? Plus you're the one who had all the answers."

"Yeah, well, that wore off immediately."

"Look, Jake Lawe was almost sixty and needed an heir, and she stepped in," Virginia laughed.

"But that means we're kind of related to each other."

"Like White Feather said, ultimately, we are each other."

"Yeah, but . . . awkward."

"Trust me, Town, Carla has her own path within this timeline, and she's finally on it with Audrey. All is as it's supposed to be."

"I found something else. There was a suspicious fire that burned their original house down—they almost didn't make it out."

"That's horrible."

"Jake and Lmoxitine escaped with their infant son, who was sleeping in the same room, and of course everyone suspected that the Listers set the fire."

"And with good reason, I bet."

"Within a month there was an accident at the mill. A retaining strap broke, and a pile of logs rolled over Stein Lister and two of his youngest sons. Stein's lower leg was trapped between logs when a kerosene fire started from the lantern he was holding; he had to cut off his lower leg at the knee with an axe and cauterize it with the embers to escape. Couldn't free his kids, though, and watched them burn to death."

"So Moloch got a double sacrifice, I guess," Virginia concluded.

"Apparently the price of failure."

~

When Virginia and I relocated to Pole Pass, Carol and Esther weren't far behind. The town was nearly unrecognizable from the years of our youth; this once-sleepy mountain hamlet was evolving into an exclusive retail and lifestyle haven before our very eyes. C&M Bakery and Espresso as well as the White Eagle Gallery were doing a level of business that one might expect in a resort town like Jackson Hole or Telluride, with elite boutique designers like Chanel and Hermès now clamoring to develop space among the quaint shops on Main Street. The Northwest American Indian Cultural Center was regarded nationally as one of the top must-see attractions for First Nations history in North America.

Carol and Esther moved into the beautifully renovated loft above Dad's law office and the practice that Carol would soon inherit. Esther joined Aunt Myra at the Cultural Center as the executive director, affording her as many Native archaeological exploits as she could handle, and access to mysteries otherwise unavailable to a non-tribal member. Aunt Myra finally had the peace of mind to take time away and focus on her personal life, as White Feather had urged. Happily, not long afterward, she began dating her childhood crush, the tribal sheriff, Max Running Bear. They married within the year and a few months later proudly announced that Myra was expecting. The bakery played host to the Gathering, with a local membership including old-timers like Barber Jimmy seated alongside transplanted residents who had relocated to the area for a life much different than in the cities they had fled. Mary and Carla were approached by a major toy manufacturer about designing a board game version, but they believed there was a sacred nature to the Gathering that would be sullied by commercialism, and they declined the offer. To this day, each Gathering ends with the traditional toast made in honor of Arthur Burke, with shots from the original bottle of Balvenie that never seems to empty.

The natural bond that Mary and Dad shared as widow and widower was soon overtaken by the deep friendship they had developed. A turning point in the relationship came one night when my mother visited Dad in a dream. They stood together inside the traditional longhouse of the cleansing ritual, holding hands and looking out through the roofless structure into the universe.

"Daniel, Mary deserves love and happiness, as do you. I'll be waiting right here, and I know Arthur will be waiting for Mary. Please do us the honor, and love while you are there; it feeds the Earth."

During the next months, Dad appeared to age-regress about twenty years and shortly thereafter turned his legal practice entirely over to Carol.

He now spends most of his time with Mary, even pitching in at the bakery during the seasonal rush and making gallery deliveries for Audrey. Twice a year, they drive to Seattle to check on Mary's properties and visit Arthur's gravesite with that bottle of Balvenie for a chat and a round or two. The return trip always includes a layover in Moses Lake for Broasted chicken at the Ripple Tavern and a zombie in the lounge of the Hallmark Inn.

When Virginia and I first arrived, Dad insisted that we move into the house with him. Everyone knew he could use the help around the land, and also that he would be too stubborn to ask for it. Within the year, Virginia and I were married in a small ceremony by the river. She wore a beautiful hand-beaded buckskin dress crafted by Aunt Myra's cousin, and Roberto pulled back her dark blond hair into a single twist wrapped in pink wildflowers. I vividly remember the aura of light emanating from her as we exchanged our sacred vows. We were given the primary reins of stewardship for the property as Dad embraced his expanding relationship with Mary; they split their time between her loft above the bakery and a cabin we built for them next to the river.

Our dear friend Roberto spent the last months of his life between our pool house and Pass County Hospital. Virginia and Dr. Dale kept him as comfortable as possible until the virus that I still believe to be of dubious origins took him from us.

Although he had a steady stream of visitors, it was on one of his last days that Roberto took Virginia's hand and told her about the little girl who was in the room with them. She had come to see him more frequently in the past week; her big smile and love energy told him that she was waiting at the crossroads. When he delivered a perfect description of Lana, Virginia smiled, remembering the gift that she herself had received from this ministering little angel.

Today, Virginia White Wolf Lawe runs the growing pediatric practice at the Tribal Clinic and continues her training as prescribed by her father. Virginia's method of integrating the truth of our eternal nature with modern and natural medicine is known far beyond the tribal communities of the Pacific Northwest, and Carla's hand-painted sign in the waiting room of the clinic sums it up perfectly: "It's only a matter of matter."

This paradox of life returned Virginia and me to the land we now steward, but our fulfillment arrived one crisp December evening in the splendor of Townsend White Moon Lawe—the joy of all creation Gliding through his eyes of starlight blue.

FIN

ACKNOWLEDGMENTS

Carol Eustaquio—Esther Tang—in memory of Johnny D. Moore—in memory of Robert Miranda—in memory of John Montalvo. Few days pass that I don't think of each of you and the fingerprints left on my life. Thank you for reawakening the boy who grew up on 17th Avenue East.

Danelle Corrick—A godsend from east of the mountains. Thank you for your enduring kindness and friendship.

Donna Renner—This work would not be complete without your loving presence in my life. Thank you for reading a binder of unedited words; your support, and belief, helped push me over the finish line.

In memory of Steve "Shug" Renner—The Princeton chapters are a direct reflection of your generous spirit and kindness. You are always a prince of a man in my book.

Steve, Mimi, and Stosh Omicienski—Thank you for your friendship, your love, and so much Princeton inspiration!

Sandi Newton Rice—*Buy someone dinner, and feed them for a meal; teach them to fish, and you have fed them for a lifetime.* Thank you for teaching me to fish in Charleston, South Carolina, March 2018.

Terry Rice—Thank you for your generous spirit and good nature. I sure miss our Lake Valley Drive poolside table tennis tournaments and the nonstop laughter!

Scott Norton—I am so grateful for your time, wisdom, expert developmental editing guidance, and encouragement as I fumbled through this process. You are an inspiration far beyond these pages. Much love, with gratitude always.

Elissa Rabellino—A patient editor is like the finest record producer who accepts no less than the best from their charge. Thank you for accepting the challenge of working with this cast of characters, including the writer. In this you have helped another author realize a dream, one that I left behind in the fourth grade.

Sunah Cherwin—Much gratitude for your proofing expertise!

Vincent Mason, MD—Thank you for the family wit, humor, common love of gospel music, and being my pediatric consultant!

Doug Mann—Dougie, one of the most creative people I know. Thank you for your unyielding friendship and encouragement throughout the years.

Nataliya Burdeynyuk—I'm so grateful for your excitement, early input, and support. Perhaps a Ukrainian translation is in order!

Monty Powell—My dear friend. Your strength, creative force, and tactical abilities are an alignment of Aquarian proportions. Thank you for your willingness to share those gifts with me and the universe at large.

Anna Wilson—Thank you, Anna, for your amazing drive, point-blank analysis, and fortitude. You are an inspiration and a deep well of creative caring beauty.

Dan Harding—Your abiding friendship is a staple in my life for which I remain grateful.

Zak and Julie Godwin—God-Wins. Can't write that story any better!

Elizabeth Brown—Thank you for your friendship, your hospitality, and reading the early drafts of this manuscript. Your commentary was of course spot-on, and margaritas on the deck are now our tradition!

Mike Vinje—Thank you for your hospitality and positive influence. I will continue to boast that we have the pleasure of owning two of the best shells on the mountain!

Rachel Corum—Thank you for your dogged pursuit of content and sacrificing your eyesight to read the early work on your phone! And yes, you do over-serve your guests.

Kim Fournier—Always the encourager! Thank you!

Jeff and Mia Fleetwood—Thank you for our friendship and keeping my ink cartridges and paper tray full!

Katie Mirian—Thank you for your love, for your belief in this project, and for managing this tangle of curls that some call hair!

Walt Fuller—Thank you for the nudge in finishing this process.

Toni and Allen Hauser—Thank you for your hospitality, support, and belief.

Philip Pirecki, Karen Pirecki, Megan Pirecki—Thank you for the early readings, the support, and our summer family weeks in Franklin, where 219 miraculously triples in size to accommodate our joy when we are together.

Bekah Doran—Hey kid! It's done . . . finally!

Breeon and Duncan Phillips—219 has been a great place to finish this project. Thank you for the gracious gift of our partnership and your role in *Town Lawe*.

Kerry Miller—It does still count as optimism if the glass is half full of good Scotch!

Mike Brown—Thank you, big Mike, for your huge smile and weekly encouragement. I hope you enjoy the read!

Janet Greene—Thank you, Janet, for reading the author.

Kim Stone—My sweet big sister, who has always worn the disguise of a cousin. Thank you.

Jeff Stone—Tops in my book as a man who leads with love. Your kindness and truth is a beacon.

Town, Virginia, Carol, Carla, Daniel, Louisa, Myra, Chilok, Roberto, Mary, Audrey, Esmeralda, and Esther—Thank you for showing up day after day, mostly without complaint or protest. Your willingness to manifest yourselves across these pages still leaves me in awe.

Jennifer Pirecki—Thank you for your tireless readings, red pen, and urgings to press on through the difficult transitions that we have weathered over the last few years. How could I ever repay your belief in this book, much less your belief in me? Onward we travel together through the portal, writing the next chapters of our lives. I adore you and wouldn't have it any other way.

Made in the USA
Monee, IL
03 July 2021